THE FAST DEATH FACTOR

VIRGINIA CROSBY

A BROWN BAG MYSTERY
FROM COUNCIL OAK BOOKS
T U L S A

Council Oak Books
Tulsa, Oklahoma 74120
© 1990 by Virginia Crosby
All rights reserved. Published 1990
Printed in the United States of America
97 96 95 94 93 92 91 90   5 4 3 2 1

Library of Congress Catalog Card Number 90-81817
ISBN 0-933031-30-0

Designed by Carol Haralson

For Christina and David Crosby, and for
Christine Kopitzke, who listened,
advised and encouraged; and
for Leigh Crosby, who would have.

MONDAY, JULY 17

"SORRY, TERRY, IT WON'T WORK. I'VE AL-ready promised a colleague she can sublet my place while I'm in Japan."

As she spoke, the young woman bent toward the sand to pick up an oval stone, then threw it out to sea. She thrust her long blond hair back over her shoulder and stood gazing toward the horizon, eyes narrowed against the glitter of sunlight dancing on the water. The other woman went ahead a few paces, then turned to face her.

"Probably a dumb idea anyway. Like most of my ideas lately. But I've got to get away from that place. It reeks of bad faith; you can smell it. Enough to make anybody puke."

The younger woman tucked her cousin's arm through hers; the two women fell into step.

"Why waste your energy on hating Tipton? You're always too impatient, Terry. Take it easy. You're going to get an offer."

"And you're always a Pollyanna, Ellen — just like Mom." A sudden broad smile transformed her somewhat heavy face, the face of a Roman emperor Ellen called it, into a puckish caricature.

"Look, I know you're going through a rough period. Why didn't you stay in London a while longer? I thought your work was going well."

"Oh, the work was okay. I got all the shots I wanted — and then some." She paused reflectively. "It was the after-hours part that went sour." She kicked up a puff of sand. "I think I'll embrace the celibate life."

Her cousin turned to smile at her. "That will be the day."

Terry disengaged her arm, kicked again at the sand. "Believe me, Ellen, you're well out of it."

"Out of what?"

"The college."

Ellen shrugged. "I enjoyed my two years there."

"Bunch of shitheads."

The younger woman laughed outright. "You're obsessed. What about your secret passion. Surely she doesn't fall into that category."

Terry scowled. "Cut it out. Being family doesn't give you special privileges."

"Well, you did embarrass yourself with the dean that time."

"That's your reading."

"You might give her a few points for ignoring it. After all, Anne did support you in your tenure fight."

"Maybe — in a limp sort of way. And only because she's an administrator with a few shreds of principles left that . . . " Terry broke off, her attention riveted suddenly by someone or something on the rocks at the base of the cliffs that lined the shore.

"My God. Look at that."

"What?"

"That blond kid over there. *Death in Venice.* You know — the flick? The spitting image of that gorgeous androgynous adolescent — what's his name?"

"Tadzio, isn't it? What are you doing?"

Terry was fiddling with the camera slung over her shoulder. "I've got to get him. He's a must for my show if ever there was one."

Ellen squinted in the direction of the rocks. "He doesn't look like one of your marginals to me."

"If he turns out to be Mr. Straight, I'll cook you a crab dinner. That kid's either gay or being kept by a rich Laguna widow. Or both of the above."

"But isn't he too beautiful, Terry? Hardly in the same category as your old bums or decrepit queens."

"Beauty can create outcasts too, cousin mine. He's one of the most decadent-looking creatures I've ever seen. Or will be, when I'm through with him. Wait here."

She plodded across the heavy sand. The young man was leaning back on his elbows now, face tilted upwards to receive the full blast of the late morning sun. He opened soft violet eyes as her shadow fell across his body.

"Hi. My name's Terry Logan."

Some thirty minutes later she came trudging back. Ellen, who had stretched out on the sand, her feet lapped by the dying waves, rose, brushing off her shorts.

"Not quite as gorgeous close up."

"Oh?"

"Great bones, but hard living has taken its toll. Spelled d-o-p-e. Guess what he says his name is? Angelo. His friends call him Angel. God, isn't that perfect? A fallen angel dope head." She turned and waved at the young man as they started on up the beach. "Wave, Ellen."

"Why?"

"He says he knows you. Lives on your street."

Ellen dug out glasses from her shirt pocket, put them on and waved obediently. "Oh, sure. That's the kid who moved into the neighborhood several months ago. Our mutual landlady reports he goes on about becoming an actor, but he hardly ever leaves the place." Terry snorted. "I know; a loser's dream. Just the same, maybe he's not quite what you think."

"Are you kidding? No way. Spaced out — and quite chatty. Wait until you see the prints. 'Divine decadence.'" She laughed. "And there's someone else who is going to be mighty impressed. If that's the word. A closet case at good old Tipton College."

Angel's watch alarm went off, jerking him awake. He got sleepily to his feet, clutching the small towel he used to cover his head for what he called "special moments." He reached down for his beach towel, gave it a shake. A small square of now empty white paper and a short straw fell out. Angel tucked the straw into the top of his swim trunks, flipped sand over the bit of paper with his foot and headed for the steps that led from the beach to the street above. At the top of the stairs, he paused for a moment. The beach was beginning to empty. The woman who had taken his picture had probably left by now. He grinned as he thought of telling Dodie about it. Better not. Later maybe. When it could do him some good. If that woman didn't send him a print as she'd promised, he knew how to get in touch with her.

The figure in the black and orange baseball cap stood at the front window. The ocean was darkening now as the sun eased gently out of sight. A voice called plaintively. "Hey, babe. Hey."
The friend turned but didn't move toward the young man sprawled in the dilapidated wicker chair, no longer touched by the youth's beauty. Ethereal. Angelic. A case of *envoûtement*. That

seemed to best describe the enraptured captivity that had lasted for almost six months. Now the softness of the full lips, the delicate modeling of the face and the heavily lashed violet eyes had lost their mesmerizing appeal. The friend noticed instead the signs of spoilage: the skin going bad, the empty expression. Above all there was the grating, whining voice; a vulgar voice for the vulgar mind that had interfered with a delicately arranged fiction.

"Drink up, Angel. How about the Joy Boy for some Chinese food?"

"Why do we always have take-out," the voice whined. "Why can't we go for once to a fancy restaurant? With flowers and sexy waiters." He giggled.

"Why not?"

"Cool." The young man's head fell forward. After a moment he looked up, finally focusing on the figure by the window.

"And after dinner, do I get my present?"

"That's right, Angel."

"How about a kiss, babe — so I'll know you're not still mad at me."

The friend didn't respond, reflecting on the made-to-order history of pharmaceutical indulgence: the fifteen-odd years of amphetamines and crack; the steady diet of drugs laced with booze . . . not recommended to strengthen physical resistance. The young man barely tasted his drink, seemed about to rise, then flopped back in the chair. He took another sip, looking up at his friend blearily from under a fringe of dark golden lashes. "Ugh. I hate sweet wine. Tastes gross."

"Small wonder, given the junk you live on."

"I'm not doing dope like I used to." He pouted. "Since you stopped being a pal."

The tone was cross, the eyes narrowing in anger as he looked across the room at the figure in the window. Then just as suddenly, he smiled again, spoke in a sing-song voice. "I'm a good little angel. Honest to God, Dodie." He made a sweeping gesture with the glass. "Cut way, way down." He giggled. "Way down upon the Swanee River. Just look in the fridge — nothing but veggies and good stuff. Go ahead, look. You can even look in my secret hidey-hole." He winked conspiratorially.

"I did. When I was cleaning up this swamp."

"I meant to, babe. Honest. I know you like things neat." He brightened. "Hey, I changed the sheets. I remembered to do that."

"All right, Angel, if you say so. But you forgot the stash in the toilet tank."

Angelo grinned. "Oops. Naughty me." He pulled at his drink again, then made a face. "Gork."

"It's a specialty of mine — a Kir Imperial." The friend smiled. "Works as an aphrodisiac for some people."

"Hey. Cool, babe. Then maybe we oughta stay home — like the soap ad says. And you can get out of that dumb suit. Doesn't do a thing for your gorgeous bod. You're not still mad, Dodie?" He wiped his nose with the back of a hand. "You know I've got to look after myself. You'll walk out on me one of these days — just like all the girls." The giggle turned into a belch, followed by a heavy sigh. "I feel guilty, babe. I know you've been good to me." He gestured vaguely toward the wall that held expensive audiovisual equipment, the VCR, racks of video cassettes.

"I'm surprised you haven't pawned the stuff."

The violet eyes puddled. "Oh babe. Those things are gifts. I wouldn't do that with a gift."

The friend made an impatient gesture.

"Besides, how would I have killed time?" He laughed. "Just a prisoner of love. I have been good, Dodie," he whined. "I've done everything — just like you said."

"Right." The tone was indifferent.

"You *are* mad at me. Look. You can make it a little less."

"It's all right, Angel."

"Or," he glanced over his shoulder at a Vuitton bag near the door, "or you could give . . ."

The friend interrupted, impatient. "I said it's all right, Angel. It's over and done with." The friend smiled. "You've been worth it."

"It's a hell of a world for sensitive people. I swear, Dodie, I'll never ask again. And I'll never say anything . . . "

"Forget it, Angel."

"Well hey — come my way." He grinned, slowly ran his tongue over his lips, at the same time stretching out long legs with a graceful and seductive movement.

For a fleeting moment the figure in the baseball cap felt the tug of beauty and remembered pleasure. The boy seemed to doze off, still smiling.

The friend waited, eyes fixed on the clock behind the bar of the kitchen counter. A minute passed. The young man came awake again and began to talk. The friend paid little attention to the ramblings, listening instead to an inner music. Three minutes dragged by. At last Angel tipped up his glass, drained it. Suddenly the smile on the young man's face faded, the legs were drawn in. "Babe. Oh God, Dodie." He began to gasp. "That stuff's dynamite."

"Take it easy, Angel, I know what to do."

The friend checked the wall clock again. Almost 8:15. If Charlie Peese had been right, it should be over in less than two minutes. The boy got to his feet, staggered, then doubled over as he dropped to the floor. He began to shake, struggling for breath. The friend's own breath became labored, as though in empathy, then the melody took over, a fetish tune of the mind that brought assurance, power. Angel's friend moved quickly to kneel beside the boy, stroked his hair, mumbling something about calling the paramedics. Then it was over.

Fifteen minutes later, the lights in the bungalow were out, the front door on the latch. Carrying the Vuitton bag, Angel's friend got in the rented car parked further down the street under eucalyptus trees, slipped the brake and allowed the car to roll silently down the hill to the stop sign at the bottom. Professor Peese's information had been on target. It had been a perfect dry- run for what was still to be done. The timing would be tight, but OK. And if he tucked in at the buffet table first as he was sure to, there would be more leeway between the time he finished the drink and the onset of the attack. Angel's friend began to sing an old-timey Southern tune, jazzing up the rhythm to the lullaby words that Grammy had made up many years ago, the fetish song that made everything come out right. "Grammy's little Dodie is the smartest baby, Grammy's little Dodie is the smartest one . . . "

Turning onto the freeway, the friend let out a breath of relief, then whispered triumphantly, "Dodie, *excelsior!*"

WEDNESDAY, JULY 19

AT A QUARTER TO EIGHT JOELLE LIEBER-
man unlocked the doors to the foyer of Wyndham
Hall and hurried toward the reception desk to dis-
charge her burden of purse, sack lunch, and plastic
food containers — her contribution to this
afternoon's party in honor of a retiring member of
the Department for Development. Joelle stored the
food in the small fridge set into the cupboard behind her desk, locked her purse in the bottom
drawer, fluffed up her blond curls, and arms
akimbo, sat motionless a moment to cool off. It
was already 85 plus outside, and the translucent
blue of the sky was fading fast under the grimy
haze of Southern California smog. As she flipped
over the page of her desk calendar to Wednesday,
July 19, Joelle heard footsteps pounding down the
stairs to her right. A moment later the person
came into view.

"Hi, Professor Logan. I thought you were still in
England."

Terry Logan glanced stonily at Joelle and hurried
out the east door of the building.

"Well fuck you, too," Joelle muttered.

She had a fair idea why Ms. Logan, assistant professor of Psychology, was in such a foul mood; not that it excused her rudeness, for Joelle's code of acceptable behavior was strict. As she did every morning, Joelle had made a quick visual check of the parking lot. President Merton's Volvo was as yet the only car in the area reserved for administrators, and any meeting now between Julian Merton and Professor Logan was sure to strike sparks.

Since Wyndham Hall housed the administrative offices of Tipton College, the secretaries and receptionists were usually better informed about what was happening on campus than the Board of Trustees — or even the faculty. Joelle, who liked to think of her centrally-located desk as the nerve center of the building, was well placed to register changing attitudes and status among Tipton faculty and staff — administrative or clerical; her friends on the grapevine circuit could usually be counted on to fill in any gaps. Her various contacts in the upstairs offices had kept Joelle up to date on what had turned out be the spring semester's *cause célèbre:* a controversial and messy tenure case that had divided the Science division and brought forth a raft of letters and petitions from faculty, students, the women's coalition, and the gay organizations — to no avail. The Hall's rumor mill had pronounced that Ms. Logan, an avowed and outspoken lesbian, was going to sue on the basis of sex discrimination. No immediate action had been taken by Professor Logan, however, and at the close of the semester she had gone off to Europe thumbing her nose at the college, the triumphant recipient of a generous research grant from the McBride Foundation.

Why, Joelle now wondered, had Ms. L. returned so early? For whatever reason, it was obvious from Terry Logan's surly exit that it wasn't kiss and make-up time between her and His Nibs. A check with the second floor was clearly in order. And she would soon have the opportunity. Summer vacations had depleted the support staff, and Joelle had been tabbed to fill in on a part-time basis in various offices. This morning, to her delight, she was scheduled to work a few hours in the Dean of Faculty's office.

Joelle was musing about that; or, more specifically, musing about the dark young man who served as the dean's administrative assistant, when Victor Laszlo, vice president for Development, breezed by with a cheery greeting and a flash of teeth that won him only the shadow of an answering smile. At least he hadn't stopped as he sometimes did to drop a flower on her desk or produce one of his yucky compliments. Still and all, she managed to squeeze out a drop of sympathy for the old boy — scheduled, according to the Hall's grapevine, to be a sacrifice to the new régime — one that, in Joelle's analytical view, was going in for gentrification. "Old

Crotch" as the women staffers secretly called him, from his habit of sitting straddle-legged, Old Crotch definitely didn't qualify. Unlike Turner Van Voorhees for instance. Even without that IVth tacked onto his name you knew he was upper crust, in a different class from Victor with his summer garb of old-fashioned leisure suit and white patent loafers.

From her desk, Joelle could see Turner standing on the steps just outside the door to the Hall, talking to Vince Riley, director of Buildings and Grounds. Tall enough to encourage a slight slouch, his narrow aristocratic face shaded by a panama hat, Turner Van Voorhees was, in Joelle's opinion, one of the sexiest men she had ever seen — a rival to Tom Cruise in her personal pantheon of Hollywood gods. Turner had the arrogant good looks, the elongated physique that stimulated fantasies in Joelle's mind. In this she was not alone. Other women in the college community had experienced a variety of stirrings from motherly to lustful when he had been introduced the year before as Tipton's newly appointed vice president and treasurer, a post that included overseeing real estate management and Buildings and Grounds. As Joelle liked to pontificate, no one could beat a southern gentleman when it came to sexy charm. And class. From the vantage point of her desk she checked him out approvingly: his easy stance, one hand resting lightly on his hip, dark blue blazer tossed casually across his shoulders . . .

Turner Van Voorhees dismissed his employee with a friendly nod and entered the building, auburn hair catching a glint of sunlight as he removed his panama hat. As was his custom, he came over to the receptionist's desk. Joelle fiddled nervously with the heart pendant on her necklace.

"Welcome back, Mr. Van Voorhees. How was San Francisco?"

Turner's only answer was a smile, which was more than good enough for Joelle.

"I suppose you've cooked up a storm for the festivities this afternoon, Joelle. What temptations have you concocted this time for my dietary downfall?"

Joelle's nervous right hand went from necklace to hair as she began to go into details about the party. (Why did she always babble on in his presence?) Without seeming to interrupt her, though he had, Turner dazzled her with another smile and headed for the stairs.

During the next several minutes the singleton arrivals expanded to group entries as administrators and staff for the services of the college, from Admissions to Word Processing, began to pour in. The Hall was beginning to settle down for the morning.

Joelle glanced at her watch; 8:45. She quickly shoved things from the desk top into one of the drawers, put her phone on call forward to the secretary in Admissions and hurried toward the stairs. She paused a second before a glass-fronted display case that housed college memorabilia. The sales person had been right; the blue of her new Laura Ashley did great things for her eyes. The cut did nice things to her bod too. Perhaps Phil's hormones would react for once — if he could get his mind off his boss.

Upstairs in suite 201 Phil Gertmenian, checking through the monthly printout of office expenses, picked up on the sound of high-heeled size 10s coming up the stairs. "The Boss," he shot across to Joelle who immediately stopped typing.

"Greetings, you two." Both stood up as Anne Parker-Brown came through the door.

"Welcome back." This from Phil as he shook hands with his dean while Joelle waited her turn with a fixed smile.

"Joelle." The dean extended her hand. "I wondered why you weren't on guard downstairs."

"I'm filling in," Joelle said needlessly, then blurted, "That's a great new hair-do, Dean Parker-Brown."

Phil shot her a reproving look. The dean hadn't changed her hair style since she had joined the History Department eighteen years ago as an assistant professor with a specialty in French history. There was, in fact, little to be done with such a lavish mane of tightly-curled red hair. But there was something different about her, the clothes perhaps; they were graceful, even smart — a far cry from the well-made but unimaginative apparel she usually grabbed off a rack in the Tall Woman's department.

"You look great, dean. Very elegant."

"All credit goes to the rue Bonaparte — and a reckless attack on my bank account."

Not wanting to be left out, Joelle saw fit to volunteer, "I love your shoes. You sure can tell they're French."

Strike two for Joelle, Phil thought. Parker-Brown was sensitive about the size of her feet — or so college lore would have it. The tale, possibly apocryphal, had circulated through four generations of students that the bilingual Parker-Brown, standing in for a friend in the French Department felled by Asian flu, had entered the classroom to be greeted by a recording of Fats Waller's "Your Feet's Too Big." Without a change of expression, she had coolly instructed the class to keep playing the tape and to put the words into idiomatic French. Panic in all its various mental and physical manifestations gripped twenty students in intermediate French as they struggled with "Your pedal extremities really are obnoxious."

"Thanks, Joelle." Unperturbed, Parker-Brown began rummaging in a capacious tote bag, handed a package to Phil.

"I thought you might like a Nepalese hat for the Gertmenian collection."

Phil ripped open the paper, jauntily stuck the bright-colored cap on his head. Joelle's voice rose a notch to shrill. "Kee-ute. I dare you to wear it; I'll treat you to lunch at the Student Union."

Phil, who had never had a date with Joelle and never intended to, ignored her.

"Why didn't anyone tell me the dean was back?"

The voice was strong but petulant. Its owner appeared in the door as the last reproachful words sounded and almost before Phil could shift his heaven-cast eyes to a neutral position.

"Anne, wonderful to have you back." Julian Merton beamed. "You look splendid."

Anne winced at the self-conscious heartiness, but extended her hand for the required formality.

"We were all extremely concerned at the news of the disturbances in New Delhi. Miss Taper called, but the hotel said you had checked out. Did you run into any difficulties?"

"No, Julian, none at all." She would wear the public face the game required. For now. "Don't you suppose the media exaggerated the situation? They usually do."

Anne considered the tall blond figure before her, the ruddy flush he referred to as his Viking heritage on his mother's side and the slight increase of girth, all signs that he had dropped out of his exercise program yet once again.

"And how was Paris?" Then without waiting for an answer, "You really should have had someone from the office meet you at the airport, Anne . . . "

They were drifting toward the door when Beulah Taper, the president's executive secretary, joined them with a nervous look directed at her employer, followed by a hasty nod in Anne's direction. "Sorry to interrupt, President Merton, but Mr. Weinert is on the phone."

"Back in a moment, Anne. I asked you to screen all calls from the Weinerts this morning, Miss Taper. That would seem simple enough to remember." Then he was on his way, calling back over his shoulder with a grin, "So long as it isn't Frau W. Dora Weinert has been deluging me with religious and political tracts — all highly dubious."

"A small price to pay for a remodeled gym," Anne called after him. With her employer out of earshot, Miss Taper lingered long enough to press Anne's hand and thank her for the card from India, adding in a whisper, "Thank heavens you're back, Anne."

Reluctant to pursue the possibilities suggested by the remark, Anne reached into her bag for Beulah's gift, a small Limoges plate for her collection of china. She smiled as Beulah hurried off a moment later in a familiar swish of girdled thighs.

Anne lingered at the entrance to her private office, listening to other remembered sounds: Phil was on one phone being diplomatic to an irate caller

— probably a faculty member — and Joelle's typewriter was producing a slow but steady tapping. How quickly the routine began to close in. Was it possible that only two weeks ago she had been trekking in Helambu at twelve thousand feet? That she had walked past sherpa villages and ancient Buddhist stupas as her group made its way through a rhododendron forest with the Himalayas looming behind them? And that three days ago . . . Why hadn't she learned by now? Anne considered herself to be lucid, to have few illusions about her character. She chided herself for her susceptibility, her feeble resistance to a childish avidity for affection and approval. Her "heart too soon grown fond." Yet self-understanding was no guarantee of self-control. In fact, she often wondered whether it wasn't synonymous with self-indulgence. Everlasting hope. Always searching, never finding. She shivered, remembering. Or was it Wyndham Hall's antarctic air conditioning?

Phil, glancing up from the phone, gave her a questioning look. Anne mouthed a "No hurry," and closed the door of her office behind her. She stood leaning against the door a moment, then went to a small closet and took out an embroidered Indian jacket, a garment she called her in-house coat. Anne slipped it on and went over to the large window overlooking a small enclosed garden and much of the Thorndyke quadrangle that lay to the west of the Hall.

Usually, after a prolonged absence, this particular view of the campus with its trees and bosky areas offering protection against the July heat erased any lingering sensation of being elsewhere; it brought her fully back to the campus that had been her professional home and personal refuge for the past eighteen years. Not so this morning. Favorite things had lost their totemic magic to soothe or delight: the fireplace, whose uselessness was redeemed by the graceful Adam mantle, her own Bessarabian rug with the Savonnerie pattern, the two very small but exquisite Callot etchings, and the framed caricature of herself as Louis XIV, done ten years ago by a favorite but lazy student to whom she had given a D in seventeenth-century European history — all nothing now but dead objects, empty of meaning.

She sat down at her desk, grateful for the responsibilities that would soon engulf her. Anne grimaced at the pile of mail, stacked and waiting, and the green slips of telephone messages, neatly arranged in staggered rows. She checked to see that Phil's light had cleared, then buzzed.

Gertmenian entered, closing the door behind him.

"Phil, how is your father?"

"About the same, Anne. As cheerful as ever, and in as much pain as ever, it seems to me. There's a new drug out that's being touted for crippling arthritis. We can but hope." He flipped open his notebook.

"Phil, would you call maintenance and ask them please to do something about the air conditioning in this office."

"I have, Anne. They said they would. Again. It's a losing battle, I'm afraid." He jotted something down then asked, "Do you want to go through the mail first or hear a news report?"

"The choice is yours." Anne smiled at the young man. She had hired him for his competence and brains, but she also derived no little satisfaction from disconcerting the *phallocrates*. As the only top female administrator in the Hall, Anne felt it a small triumph to have a male executive assistant. It amused her too that his dark good looks (what he called his Armenian mug) was as unsettling to the "old boys" as his secretarial skills.

As Phil leafed silently through some notes, Anne waited for an opening quip from the Gertmenian repertoire, perhaps one of the standbys regarding Fred Zumholtz, chairman of the three-person Religion Department, whose reports by their length would do justice to a department five times as large and who, according to Phil, couldn't take a pee without first checking with the dean's office. But Phil, still studying his notebook, seemed at a loss where to begin — an anomaly that Anne found puzzling. Then he looked up with a smile.

"How about some good news first — a major event."

She kept her voice light: "That bad, eh?"

Phil ignored her. "The college has had an unexpected windfall."

"More Weinert money?"

"Not money. At least not directly. Vincent Riley unearthed a lost collection of Asian art objects — mostly rare jade. Found them about a week ago in cleaning out an old store room. Apparently no one knew they existed — or where they came from. And very valuable."

She raised her eyebrows. "Impressive."

"Victor Laszlo's nose is out of joint, however, because Riley's boss gets the credit for the find. And I guess Turner didn't rush right up and inform Victor."

Anne raised a hand to stop him. "Spare me. I'd rather hear the bad news than a report on the eternal bickering between Development and Turner's office. So tell. What am I not going to enjoy hearing?"

The question had barely been put when a rap at the door was followed by Joelle's entrance with a folded note. Anne flicked it open and turned to Phil: "We'll have to delay our visit; Claire Tidwell needs to see me a moment."

Phil's quick and wordless departure seemed like another sign to be read. It was of no importance, Anne told herself, yet she missed the small rituals,

the set comments that inevitably greeted her return to campus after a prolonged absence and, like
the click of a well-fastened seat belt, made her feel
secure. This slight sense of unease vanished immediately as Claire, her oldest friend on campus
and disheveled as usual, strode into the room and
embraced Anne enthusiastically *à la française*.

"I couldn't believe it when I spotted your car in
the parking lot. Did something go wrong? You look
great. Are you OK?"

Anne smiled at the familiar Tidwellian burst of
questions. "No; thank you; and yes. I grew restless once I got back to Europe — five weeks
seemed long enough to be gone."

Claire flopped into a chair with a resounding
thump, then eased up to straighten out the float
she was wearing and that Anne recognized as coming from her heavy-side wardrobe; during thinner
incarnations she preferred slacks.

"You look flourishing, Claire. Have you had a
relaxing summer?"

"Can't you tell?" She gestured towards her hips.
"Of course it's been a blessing to have such quiet.
No students, and above all, no faculty meetings."

"But?" Anne smiled, waiting for Claire to go on.
Her opening pronouncements were usually worthy
of high drama, as though her exceptionally beautiful voice hadn't been created to speak of mundane
things. This morning, however, there was an anx-
ious look in her eyes that bore out the urgency of

the note she had sent in: "Must see you pronto. *Motus.*"

"I take it we'll skip the chitchat. Departmental problems? Don't tell me something's wrong at home? Not with my favorite emeritus professor in charge?"

"He'd love to hear you say that. No, Mark's fine, the boys are off doing something ecological in Alaska, and my fellow psychologists are either away on vacation or lolling around waiting for the cocktail hour; one may be doing some research, though it's questionable. Except for working on the application for the Payton grant, I've been a fearful loafer myself." Claire Tidwell fidgeted with her shell necklace then leaned forward earnestly. "I hate like sin to greet you right off with bad news. Has anyone talked to you yet, or did you get any letters about what has been going on here this summer?"

"No, and I'm getting the impression that it is just as well that no one has and that I didn't."

"Anne, Mark and I think you are about to be screwed."

The dean walked slowly back to her chair and sat down. "Metaphorically speaking, no doubt. Alas."

"Don't joke. Believe me, I'm not exaggerating."

Anne heard her voice saying brightly the first thing that came into her mind, "You mean that I'm about to be fired." Claire looked pained. Anne aimed for a reassuring smile. "I'm sorry, Claire. I'm not yet up to battling campus undercurrents."

Claire looked glum. Anne's own expression grew somber as she listened incredulously to her friend's report: sub rosa meetings; a graduate program proposed for Tipton; Milton Weinert — a high-handed donor who would interfere in the curriculum and staffing; the beginning of a new era to which she would be excluded. It sounded like the scenario for a nightmare, and equally unreal. Yet, as Claire spoke, Anne received another inner jolt. Julian hadn't returned as he inevitably did after she had been away to sweep everyone out of her office and settle in for what he called a *tour d'horizon* of campus affairs. In light of what Claire was telling her, if true, wasn't the urgency greater than ever this time? And hadn't there been something in Phil's manner that was out of kilter?

A short time later Anne accompanied her old friend to the head of the stairs. On the way back to her office, she looked across the foyer to the president's office; the door was open. Julian, swinging slowly back and forth in his tapestry-covered desk chair, was dictating from some notes before him. He looked up, stared blankly at her, and turned away.

The apparent snub was a typical Mertonism, but Anne felt the flush spreading over her face. She took a calming breath and returned to suite 201 where Phil was waiting for her. Notebook in hand, he followed Anne into her office, closed the door and took his usual place in one of the Tipton College Hancock chairs placed at the visitors' side of the desk.

"To pick up where we left off," she began, "I would guess that you had something dire to tell me. Such as that I am about to be plucked from this garden of delights and sent packing back to the History Department."

Phil looked at her a moment, then shook his head. "Claire Tidwell. That's alarming. I had hoped the rumor hadn't made headway."

Anne shrugged an indifference she was far from feeling.

"I don't think you should feel blithe about it, Anne."

"I don't. I have been looking forward to returning to Fiedler Hall in due course, but I don't care for the suggestion that I might be booted back. That idea has got to be scotched."

At Phil's noncommittal expression, Anne went determinedly on. "According to Claire, Victor Laszlo is the source of the rumor. His position is in jeopardy, as you and I know. He must know it too, for that matter. Conceivably he thinks that, as one of the old régime, I'll be swept out with him."

Phil studied the rug for a moment, then looked up. "Maybe. But you'd best hear it all. This comes from Beulah."

"Who was being indiscreet."

"Don't be hard on my pal Beulah, Anne. She needs some outlet, and better me than others I might mention."

"Sorry. What's the problem?"

"The president called a hush-hush meeting for last Saturday morning — unusual in itself. Furthermore, it was done at the request of the chairman of the board and Daddy Warbucks."

"Milton Weinert?"

Phil nodded. "The invitation to join the president, Weinert and Leslie Filmore went out to a select few: the chairs of Econ, Government, and International Relations."

So Claire had been right. Anne sought to put a good face on it. "Well, they're all members of the president's council."

"Right, but so is the chair of Classics. George Macready is very much with us, and he wasn't invited."

Anne listened in unhappy silence as Phil continued his report — a detailed confirmation of Claire Tidwell's news. At its conclusion, she stared thoughtfully at the opposite wall a long moment, then reached for the phone and dialed the president's number.

Phil drew daggers on his pad, half-hearing the murmur of Beulah's voice and Anne's noncommittal responses. He looked up as she replaced the phone in its cradle.

Anne kept her voice steady. "The president is not free. He is meeting with the chairman of the Board and the chairs of Economics, IR, and Government."

"And you're not to be included?"

"Obviously not. I can see Julian at eleven."

Phil Gertmenian returned from lunch at a few minutes past one to find the dean at her desk, apparently lost in contemplation of a sandwich box and milk carton. "Did you take up self-hypnosis in Nepal?"

With only an absent look for an answer, Phil scolded, "Why didn't you tell me you were going to eat in? I would have made the Jolly Belly Deli run for you."

"I needed the walk. I had an unexpectedly long session with the president." Phil waited for her to continue, but Anne remained silent, still hearing Julian's voice, still seeing the hard expression that accompanied his quick dismissal of the incident in San Francisco. The familiar stratagem: indignation as a means of gaining control; the suggestion that a proposed meeting had been her foolish idea; the question of *her* 'expectations' quickly dismissed with an impish grin designed to turn a self-deprecating admission of unconscious complicity into a joke. Then the change of mood, the intimate conspiratorial tone, the need for her understanding. For them to pull together. His hands on her shoulders, lightly, briefly drawing her closer. The importance of separating the personal from the professional. And the tender smile. How odd that she had once found that smile endearing. Finally, the unsatisfactory explanation of her exclusion from this morning's meeting and for the delay in telling her what he now put forth with all the earnestness of bad faith. "I hope I have your support, Anne. The decision to resign is entirely up to you — entirely."

Phil cleared his throat and Anne gave herself a little shake. "Sorry. I'm woolgathering." She assembled the trash from her lunch, tossed it into the wastebasket.

"We'll talk later, Phil." she said briskly. "I'd better start on this pile in my box."

"Sure," Phil said, not taken in for a moment by the business-as-usual tone. "I'll hold all calls until further notice."

After he had gone, Anne stared blankly at the closed door. How, she wondered, could she have been so blind? Why couldn't her competence and common sense extend into her private life?

Her loving parents had done everything right. Hadn't they seen to it that her teeth were straightened, medical checkups arranged on schedule and her wardrobe handsomely provided? Hadn't they always encouraged her? Supported her interests and applauded her scholarly success? Yet she had always known that she wasn't the daughter they wanted, known that they had hoped for a "dainty little girl." Instead, some rogue of a genetic model had produced a gangly youngster who had been mercilessly teased about her height, humiliated during adolescence for her boyish shape, and, at 6'1", enthusiastically recruited for basketball, a game in which she had no interest. In college, her response to the wooing of the coaches was to go out for the most sedentary sport she could think of: the rifle team.

At the university, when she had married Michael Parker, Anne believed her emotional malaise was a thing of the past, obliterated by a love that was deep and true. But Vietnam had the final claim. Two months after his death, with grief still her constant companion, she had discovered that the old restlessness, still in hiding, was waiting for her: a vaguely defined but compulsive yearning that was a trap in which physical desire and spiritual hunger were inextricably confused. She had paid for past errors in judgment with sorrow or disappointment. This time the price was higher: bitter and demeaning humiliation. A price she refused to pay.

At his desk, Phil Gertmenian busied himself putting together the dean's folder for Friday's board meeting, but his mind was elsewhere. For the first time in the five years of their association Anne had been evasive with him. Something had gone very wrong during her interview with the president. At the thought, his adrenalin began to pump.

WEDNESDAY, JULY 19

WORD OF ANNE'S RETURN TRAVELED fast; the next hour went by in a flurry of drop-ins from faculty and staff.

At two, the chairman of the Music Department came by the dean's office to discuss a replacement for the choral director who had resigned without warning to accept an offer from Brown University. At a little before three, the president bounced into the outer office to rummage in the jar of trail mix that stood on a filing cabinet and bounced out again after jokingly chiding Joelle for picking out all the cashews. Turner Van Voorhees and Victor Laszlo arrived hard on Julian's heels to welcome back, in Victor's words, "the Muse of Wyndham Hall." Phil scowled as Victor descended on Anne, arms extended. Clasped in his vigorous hug, Anne looked over Victor's shoulder at Phil and winked. He did not find the signal reassuring.

At 4:15 Phil interrupted to call "time." Anne hung her embroidered cotton jacket in the closet, ran a comb through her hair, then walked down the hall towards what would now be called the Ward Finlay room. She would miss Ward, his vast knowledge of Tipton's past and, above all, his wry sense of humor. He richly deserved the title of Grand Old Man. Over the past thirty-five years Ward had sold the tax advantages of a gift via Tipton's annuity and trust program to more widows, retired corporation executives, and just plain rich folks than the rest of his department put together.

Anne paused at the archway to take in the scene. It was a spacious, almost square room, lined on three sides by suites of offices belonging to the Development staff. The arrangements for the Hall's office parties rarely varied. The bar for mixed drinks had been set up in one corner of the room, and a long table decorated with flowers extended down the center. Every inch of space was taken with handy-to-reach bottles of wine and apple juice, trays of fruit and cheese and examples of the considerable culinary talents of the staff.

The reception was already gathering momentum. Anne could see Priscilla Merton's blond head with the distinctive chignon that never seemed to slip, no matter how much she drank. She caught drifts of the high-pitched voice and mid-Atlantic accent as Priscilla talked animatedly to the honoree, tanned and erect, and a regal-looking Sally Cochran, chairman (as she insisted on being called) of the trustees' Ways and Means Committee. Turner Van Voorhees was in a huddle with the chair of Economics and Trustee Neville Barnes (Academic Affairs), while his wife, Kitty, was the center of an admiring circle that included the impeccably turned-out chairman of the Board, Leslie Filmore (Filmore Oil). A number of staff and a sprinkling of old-time faculty had positioned themselves for the duration at the buffet table while various secretaries and an ostentatiously convivial Victor Laszlo bustled about filling glasses or offering hors d'oeuvres.

Anne resisted the impulse to bolt and moved resolutely forward to be greeted by Joelle Lieberman, who offered her a glass of wine while pelting her with questions about her "exotic adventure." Anne managed some kind of general statement before escaping into the party area.

With part of her mind still in thrall to Julian's brutally dismissive remarks, she began to circulate, operating on what Phil called her "automatic pilot," talking of mountain climbing with the seventy-six-year old honoree, himself an ardent if now somewhat restrained Sierra Club hiker, of changes in this fall's Parents' Day program with Priscilla Merton. Kitty Van Voorhees claimed her attention regarding possible summer camps for her two children next year in French-speaking Switzerland, and Anne listened patiently once more to Kitty's self-serving praise of Les Nénuphars and what two years at this most fashionable and costly boarding school had meant to her and the fellow student who would eventually become her husband. Reflecting on the economic status of the establishment's clientele, Anne clamped down a smile as Kitty rattled on about the importance of lowering class and national barriers through "foreign language acquisition."

With her auburn hair, long-legged figure, and air of accustomed privilege, Kitty could have been her husband's sister. The Heiress, as she was called by the Hall, was indeed the only child of an eastern industrialist. The head of the French Department, Pierre-Xavier de Grancey, who claimed an ancestry going back to the fifteenth century, had once said sniffily that Turner had no doubt married Kitty to *"redorer le blason"* of his aristocratic but impoverished Virginia family. A *canard* indeed, for the Van Voorheeses were prosperous and flourishing, not only as landowners but as one of the south's leading publishing families. Anne had once met mama and papa, who were proud of their youngest child, but who clearly considered his interest in the financial management of private education to be mildly eccentric, albeit respectable.

Anne glanced surreptitiously at her watch: 4:50. At least one more hour to go. Sipping her wine, her eyes caught Julian looking her way; he looked through and beyond her, his expression empty. Anne's grasp on her glass of wine tightened, then she calmly walked over to examine the new portrait of Ward Finlay that had been hung opposite the painting of Wyndham Hall circa 1880, the year of Tipton's founding. Turning away from Ward's smilingly benign portrait, she resolutely rejoined the party.

It was now in full swing as people flowed around the buffet table, wandered from group to group, circulated platters of food or served drinks. Laughter grew more frequent and voices rose. Escaping from Joelle and her crowd, Phil Gertmenian sought temporary refuge near the water fountain by the back stairs, where he was almost bowled over by Henry Norton as the Dean of Students raced by him, calling up something unintelligible from the stairwell. Anne was momentarily close enough for Phil to overhear patient answers to such questions as: "Was it dangerous?" "How high did you climb?" "What do the sherpas think of communism?" (from dear old Ward)"Any sign of the abominable snowman?" (Vince Riley). And from Victor, predictably, "What did those sherpa guys think of a gorgeous gal like you?" Anne retrieved a bowl from a small table, offered it to Laszlo. "Nuts?" Phil mentally applauded.

As Phil moved away to mingle once again, he noticed Claire Tidwell standing by the door of the women's room just outside the reception area, seemingly indecisive as to whether to come or to go. Phil was considering rescuing her when his attention was drawn to a new arrival: Terry Logan. Ignoring everyone, Logan made straight for the buffet table. The phrase "funeral baked meats" trotted unbidden through Phil's head. He caught sight of Beulah setting a course toward the chairs placed against a section of wall and elbowed his way through the press to join her.

Beulah, who shunned Kleenex as ungenteel, dabbed at her perspiring forehead with a lawn handkerchief. Despite the overactive airconditioning, she was warm. Tension, no doubt. But she could now relax. Dear Ward seemed pleased, and the handsome luggage he would receive from the college, along with a ticket for an Alaskan cruise, a gift from the Board, would go down well, she thought. Both gifts had been her idea, and President Merton had even expressed something close to approval of her choice.

Phil Gertmenian sat down beside her. "Good party, old chum."

"The liquor store made a mistake and delivered a rosé instead of the Blanc de Blancs I ordered, so the white-wine drinkers are out of luck. But I don't intend to worry about it."

"That's the spirit. And don't let it upset you if His Nibs gives you his Thunder Scowl. Tell him white wine is no longer chic."

Beulah smiled indulgently at her young colleague.

Phil observed Julian Merton for a moment — Merton being his most charming with the very rich and very influential Sally Cochran. Phil caught himself grinding his teeth. He was brought back to the moment at hand by Beulah's voice.

"Don't forget to say something nice to Joelle; she has been most helpful."

Phil's grunt was not promising of follow-through.

"It does seem to be a success so far, doesn't it?" Beulah went on. "Not many faculty, of course, but even a few unexpected guests."

"Yeah. Terry Logan doesn't even know Ward. Your boss won't be overjoyed to see her. Nor mine. Where is she by the way? Victor had her cornered a moment ago."

"I think I saw her going toward the ladies' room."

"Women's room."

Beulah ignored the correction. "She looks tired, Phil. Fit but tired."

"Paris to LA is a killer at best. And she's too tall for those tourist class seats." Phil stretched his own legs at the thought and seemed to be studying his rumpled chinos. "And maybe her welcome back wasn't exactly all it might have been." He waited for Beulah to volunteer a comment. With none forthcoming, he persisted, "She's putting up a good front, but I think the talk she had this morning with His Nibs took the starch out of her."

Beulah struggled toward loyalty: "He's always a bit prickly the first day a close associate returns."

"From what you told me about that meeting last Saturday . . . "

She interrupted hurriedly. "It's too early to speculate, Phil — and certainly not here."

"If that so-and-so does fire her, I'll give him a pain where he should have pleasure."

Beulah cleared her throat. "Phil, this is no time to be joking. I confess I am worried for Anne. But don't ask me any more. Please. Not now."

The two fell silent; the easy silence of two congenial colleagues, Beulah thought, not noticing how Phil's expression had darkened. She wondered, as she always did, why supervisors and staff inevitably gravitated toward each other to talk business at office parties. The housing director and two young assistant deans were powwowing with Henry Norton, who had returned to the scene; the registrar and the dean of Admissions were in a huddle, and Vincent Riley, who stood at just a hair over five-six, was looking up at his six-foot-two supervisor, a patient Turner Van Voorhees, and talking a mile a minute. Vince could be tiresome, Beulah thought, he was obsessively finicky on the job, but he was thoughtful and a gentleman, which put him high on the plus side in her ledger. As for Turner, she hadn't made up her mind about him, even after two years.

"Phil, do you think Mr. Van Voorhees is . . . well, aloof?"

"You mean a snob?"

Beulah made a vague gesture with her handkerchief.

"I'm suspicious of anyone who shows off his genealogy with a crest on his blazer," he said.

"That's not a family crest, Phil; it's a preparatory school emblem."

"Almost as bad. He and Madame Van V. would certainly never win the hospitality award."

"They are private people."

"That's a polite way of putting it. Right now he seems happy enough to be with the proles."

"I think he genuinely appreciates Vince."

"He should." Beulah looked puzzled. "The way Vince is handling the inventory job, I mean. And unearthing that long-lost Asian collection."

"Mr. Van Voorhees made sure Vince was recognized for that," Beulah said, stoutly fair. "And he couldn't have been more helpful when Vince approached him last fall about buying his house. It wasn't easy to persuade the Board to let go of a college property."

They both looked in Turner's direction, as though expecting some signs of virtue to appear miraculously — like the stigmata. Now doing a turn at the bar, Turner was busily pouring drinks for a group that included a vivacious Joelle and Julian Merton.

"Well, well, His Nibs has put a foot up on the rail. Must be about time for the ritual party drink. I had an uncle who always said never to trust a fellow who didn't enjoy booze."

Beulah laughed. "How many wise Armenian uncles do you have anyway?"

He grinned at her. "As many as I need."

"That's what I thought."

Observing Claire Tidwell engaged in solitary stuffing at the buffet, Phil said something about the sociological study that could be made of the drinking and eating habits of the academic community, but Beulah didn't respond, her attention now focused on her employer as he entertained the noisy group clustered around the bar at the far end of the buffet table. He was so handsome, she thought, brilliant, charming — and unkind. Her feelings on any given day swung wildly with his changes in mood as he showered her with smiles and included her in little jokes one moment, or reduced her to tears the next — tears held back until silently shed in one of the stalls of the ladies' room. Recently Beulah had begun to wonder whether she could keep going one more year to retirement. Mixed in with a resentment that so often discouraged sleep was the fear that she was slipping, that her legendary memory had begun to misfire. Her morale had deteriorated to an all-time low. She didn't mind criticism, went her bedtime soliloquy, it was the harsh treatment, the cutting insinuations as to her competence that were undermining her self-confidence and her self-respect.

Beulah's eyes fastened on Priscilla Merton, who had now joined the group at the bar. At least her boss got as good as he gave at home. Beulah was aware that the incidence of quarreling at the president's house was on the increase. Snippets of overheard conversation, the repeated phone calls from Mrs. Merton she put through, sometimes as many as three in a fifteen-minute period, had given her a glimpse of the Mertons' conjugal life that she alone was privy to. Beulah suspected her employer of being a womanizer, but so far as the dean was concerned, had anything indeed occurred, she was certain that, somehow (the method was vague in her mind), the dean had been taken advantage of.

Like a couple at a sidewalk café, Phil and Beulah watched the scene being played out before them, each aware of many of the true feelings that lay behind the laughter and animated gestures and idly guessing at others.

"Old Victor already looks half-seas over," Phil opined. "The poor sod had better get himself pulled together. Isn't he to take part in the presentations?"

The crowd had parted sufficiently for them to see Victor look around vaguely before going into his office.

"He's very depressed these days, Phil. Ward's departure leaves him stranded, without one real friend or supporter."

Phil nodded and lost interest in the subject. He saw the dean coming back down the hall to rejoin the party. With partisan pride he remarked to Beulah that Anne was the most stunning-looking

woman in the room. Beulah accepted the comment
as rhetorical and got to her feet.

"I think I shall reward myself with a glass of
wine."

Phil started to get up. "Let me . . . "

"No, no, thank you. I want to check the table
anyway."

The dean came toward him now, a bottle of wine
in one hand, and a plate of what looked like cheese
sticks in the other. "If you want a cheddar high, I
can recommend these."

"Thanks, Anne. Want me to take over?"

"No need. Haven't done my share yet." Then, as
he just stood there, "Circulate, Phillip. I think
Joelle is headed in your direction."

He took off. Threading his way through the
crowd, Phil found himself momentarily wedged in
behind the chairman of the Board and Julian Merton. He heard Merton say, "She will be manage-
able. Anne will do . . . " Merton broke off, aware
that someone was behind him. Putting a hand on
Filmore's arm, the president steered him out of
hearing.

Claire Tidwell's hand was hesitating between the
Mexican wedding cakes and Beulah Taper's justi-
fiably renowned double chocolate cake when she
heard the elevator doors open.

"Hi, Claire." Mary Walker from the News Bureau
rolled her chair forward. "What a crush."

"Can I get you something, Mary?"

"No thanks." She craned her neck, apparently looking for someone, saying absently, "I'm just staying long enough to take a picture of Ward with the bigwigs and wish him godspeed."

"I'll get him for you." Claire started to leave, then turned. "I've been meaning to tell you, Mary. That was a slick editing job you did on Charlie Peese's article for *Tipton Topics*."

"Thanks. I had a nice note from your husband, by the way."

Claire nodded. "A damn shame poor Charlie didn't live long enough to see the article printed. He always fussed that the college didn't recognize the importance of his work with those toxic waterblooms he was so nutty about. Oh, there's Ward." Yoo-hooing and waving, Claire took off.

Balancing a plate of food in one hand and carrying a glass of wine in the other, Terry Logan edged around to a spot near the back stairwell where Priscilla Merton stood alone. The president's wife greeted her warmly. She was already in a mellow mood, and she liked Terry Logan, in part because the Psychology professor took the view that a college president's wife was a working partner, not a mere social appendage. It was Terry who had been largely responsible for Priscilla's appointment to the Faculty Committee on Women's Issues. In addition, Priscilla enjoyed championing someone whom Julian disliked. During the past year and a half Priscilla and Terry had become allies on committee matters, meeting occasionally for lunch or a drink to discuss committee affairs in particular and feminist concerns in general.

Such preoccupations were new to Priscilla Merton, convent reared and the only child of a domineering mother whose values and moral code she had docilely accepted. Priscilla was comfortable with Terry, though sometimes, when the drinks had worn off, she felt guilty at having shared personal feelings about married life.

"Terry, hello. This is a surprise. I thought you were spending the summer in England."

"Yeah, well, I wound up my work sooner than expected. The more I thought about the future, the more urgent it seemed to get cracking on making contacts and to finish sending out my CV."

"Is it really a dead issue here — with your department?"

Terry was amused by Mrs. Merton's naiveté, but it was predictable. She had learned that Julian rarely took his wife into his confidence. Terry shrugged. "Looks that way."

"I'm truly sorry. I wish there were something I could do."

"Listen, I know that — and appreciate it. Anyway, you shouldn't get involved with campus politics. It stinks."

Priscilla saw Julian look her way and frown. She smiled and raised her glass to him. A gesture mistakenly read by outsiders as a signal of marital complicity.

"Say, Priscilla, I'd like to see you about something. Any chance of your being free sometime early tomorrow morning? Around nine?"

Priscilla's affirmative reply trailed off as she saw her husband go up to Anne; she was hardly aware of Terry's departure, fighting futilely against the old sick feeling she always had when she saw Julian and Anne together; trying to erase from her mind that intimate moment when she had asked him point blank whether he was having an affair with Anne. His answer had been to laugh and hug her to him.

Priscilla downed the remains of her wine without tasting it and walked over to join her husband and the dean. "Sorry to interrupt, but it's almost six, Julian, and I promised Cissy I'd be home to help her get ready for the party. Her first date," she added, turning toward Anne. "She was fifteen last week."

"Congratulations, Priscilla. You did hold out against peer pressure."

"I often wondered whether it was worth it, but I think Cissy is glad of it now — though her indulgent father wasn't much help."

"I'm a weakling, Priscilla," Julian said lightly, putting an arm around her shoulders in a quick hug. "You deserve a medal."

"In lieu of that, a gold bauble from Rodeo Drive will do nicely."

Good for Priscilla, Anne thought; she should be spunky more often.

"About the time, Julian . . . "

"I go, I go. Let me round up Victor and Leslie. Anyone seen Sally Cochran? You should be out of here in ten minutes."

"Will you be home to admire Cissy in her finery before she leaves?"

"Not likely. I'm expecting a call. And I have some work to finish. Don't wait dinner. I'll pick up a bite when I get in."

Embarrassed by these details of family life, Anne had discreetly stepped back, but Julian moved toward her as he went on cheerfully to his wife: "Tell Cissy to go easy on the makeup and say all the usual cautionary things." He laughed. "And to be home absolutely no later than eleven, right?" Evidently convinced that no answer was called for, Julian headed in Leslie Filmore's direction, beckoning to Victor Laszlo as he went.

Shortly after six, toasts having been proposed and responded to and gifts presented, the party began breaking up. After asking around in vain for Vince Riley, Turner joined Henry Norton as porter for the new luggage, and Ward departed in a flurry of well-wishing and heavy-handed recommendations from Victor to look for romance ("You old rascal") aboard the *Alaskan Queen*, and redundant expressions of appreciation from the trustees, each one of whom seemed eager to have the last word. Joelle and the secretarial staff began tidying up so as not to leave too great a mess for Jeff, the custodian. Claire Tidwell broke away from the buffet to follow Anne down the hall to her office door.

"Anne, I do wish you would stop off at the house and let Mark fix you a decent drink. We could have a light supper and see that you got home early."

"May I play it by ear, Claire? There are a couple of things I want to clear up here first."

"Good grief, what? You sound so grim."

"Just a touch of fatigue, *mon petit*. Look, I'll try to stop by for a few minutes. I would like to say hello to Mark. But if you don't see me by seven, don't worry. OK?"

Claire nodded, and with a look wistful enough to accompany condolences, squeezed Anne's hand and strode off toward the stairway.

Phil, who was straightening some papers on his desk, saw that the president was about to follow Anne into her office when he was stopped by Beulah.

"It's Mr. Weinert, President Merton."

"Hell." He glanced at his watch. "He's early; I haven't the materials . . . "

"Do you not wish to take the call?"

"Of course I'll take it. Tell him I'll be right there. Anne, see you tomorrow morning, if I can't wind things up with Milton before you leave. 8:30 too *matinal* for you?"

"Not at all."

"What you need," said Turner to Anne — followed by Kitty, he had come up behind Julian — "what you need to offset jet lag is a good workout in the weight room."

"Don't be a show-off, Turner." Kitty gave him a playful punch. "Honestly, if he develops another set of muscles, I'm going to get hugely fat in protest."

Enjoining Anne to get a good night's rest, the Van Voorheeses trailed after Julian into the foyer of the presidential suite. At her desk, Beulah glanced up briefly from studying the appointment book as Kitty and Turner went on into the latter's office, to the east of the president's. They were both back in a short while, with Turner flourishing his gym bag in Beulah's direction. "Time to relax, Miss T. The party was a grand success. Go home and treat yourself to a glass of champagne."

Beulah glanced toward the phone; the button for the president's private line was still lit.

"My judgment is that Milton isn't going to let him go very soon. When I poked my head through our communal washroom he raised his glass in dreary resignation. He'll need that drink before Milton is through with him."

Kitty nodded and giggled. "He's so funny. President Merton I mean."

Beulah looked blank, but elected not to enquire into the reasons for Mrs. Voorhees's remark. It was soon elucidated.

"The faces he was making. He should have been an actor."

Beulah silently marveled at such silliness, and Turner tugged at his wife's elbow. "Come along, darling, Allison and Jamie will be getting impatient, and I want to get my grunt and groan over with.

Beulah watched the couple as they hurried toward the stairs, laughing and chattering. The light on the selector button was still on, and a low murmur reached her through the president's door. Beulah checked her watch: 6:25. She got up, retrieved her purse from a file drawer and, joined by Phil who also was just leaving, walked slowly down the stairs. She hadn't realized until just this moment how tired she was.

In the main floor reception area, Jeff Colton turned off his vacuum cleaner. "Good evening, Miss Taper, Mr. Gertmenian."

"Good evening, Jeff." Phil chimed in too, raising his voice a notch, for the old man was hard of hearing.

"There are some sandwiches and cake on the buffet upstairs, Jeff, if you'd like a snack later on," Beulah said.

"Thanks, Miss Taper, I sure would." Jeff watched the two leave. Some folks thought that the friendship between Mr. Gertmenian, thirty-two, and Miss Taper, sixty-five and then some if she was a day, was something to poke fun at. Not so Jeff Colton, who knew what loneliness was.

It was a little past seven-thirty when Jeff Colton rode the elevator to the second floor. He wheeled his cleaning cart toward the president's office and stopped with a muttered "Shit." The light was on. He'd empty the wastebasket, then have to come back upstairs later to vacuum. Jeff walked around his cart, knocked lightly as he opened one of the doors, then stood there, staring, his hand on the knob. Dean Parker-Brown was bending over the president, her mouth on his. As she glanced up, unseeing, Jeff knew he wasn't witness to an embrace. Jeff Colton had landed on a Normandy beach in '44; he knew a dead body when he saw one.

WEDNESDAY, JULY 19

As SHE LEFT THE WOMEN'S LOCKER room at Pusey Gym, Mary Walker called goodnight to Coach Beeson, who was locking up his office, and waved in the direction of Turner Van Voorhees as the latter emerged from the Nautilus room. Mary wheeled her way across the parking lot to her specially equipped Acura sedan, a vehicle purchased with monies from the insurance settlement; exceptionally, the teen-age driver had been adequately covered. Mary raised the steering wheel, deftly slid in, then folded her light-weight chair and pulled it in after her, wondering why, after nearly four years, it was still such an all-fired effort to come in for her thrice-weekly sessions at the gym when she felt so much better for it afterwards.

Mary had hoped for a quick stop at the supermarket but was waylaid by George Macready, chair of Classics. She listened dutifully to her former professor's comment on a typographical error ("Two t's in the Italian *dilettare*, Mary") and his usual criticism about the selection of articles in the latest edition of *Topics,* the college alumni magazine of which she was an assistant editor.

It was going on eight when Mary turned into the driveway at 111 First Street. She smoothly maneuvered her chair out of the car, swung herself into it and rolled up the ramp to the kitchen door. Something unintelligible from the front of the house answered her "Thad, I'm home. Groceries to collect, if you would be so kind."

Mary took the prepared makings for a mixed salad out of the refrigerator and placed them and the salad bowl on the table in the bay window that overlooked the back garden. Spinning her chair briskly around, she rolled across the kitchen floor to retrieve the bottle of Brouilly Thad had brought up from their small but thoughtfully stocked cellar. She uncorked the bottle, appreciatively sniffed the characteristic bouquet of plum and peony and poured herself a small amount. It would go nicely with the slice of morbier she had picked up at the market.

Her brother's voice came to her from the front of the house; Thad was talking on the phone to someone. Moments later, Thaddeus Walker strode into the kitchen, struggling into a rumpled seersucker jacket.

"Oh no."

"Oh yes. The department just got a call from Campus Security."

"What?"

"Julian Merton was found dead in his office half an hour ago."

"Thad! Good Lord . . . How . . .?"

"Cardiac arrest, apparently."

"But I saw him — only a couple of hours ago."

"Oh?"

"There was a reception in the Hall this afternoon. I took a few shots for the magazine; he looked so — so vital. But why are you called in?"

Thad shrugged. "Captain Brown is on vacation and Commander Dexter is in the hospital. Will that satisfy you?"

"I guess that leaves the old Chief of Police right enough."

"Thanks." Her brother reached for a Greek olive from among the salad makings. "I think I should show up on general principle — and for courtesy's sake. The man *was* Altamira's most illustrious citizen." He bent over and planted a kiss in the vicinity of an ear.

"What's that about? Good-bye forever?"

"Only a burst of fraternal affection. Which a prickly pear like yourself doesn't deserve."

She grinned up at him. "How true."

With her pert face and short curly hair, Mary still looked to Thad like an impudent choir boy. Only the premature streaks of gray and the light shadowing under her eyes testified to what she had gone through — and to his own personal loss. That and the damn chair. Even now, four years after a drunken kid in a souped-up dune buggy had killed his adored Fiona and transformed his graceful quick-moving baby sister into a chair-bound woman, his stomach knotted at the sight of the metal and cloth contraption.

"But isn't someone from the station already there?"

"Patrol Officer Rodinsky answered the call. And Pete Wiggins is securing the scene."

Checking his pockets, Chief Walker went to get a notebook from a cupboard reserved for what he called his "cop junk."

"Well then."

"Pete's just been promoted to investigation, Mary. This will be his maiden assignment. I don't want him to have to face the college hierarchy alone. Rather intimidating the first time 'round."

"What's to face? This is a routine matter, isn't it?" Thaddeus shrugged. "The truth of the matter is that you're just plain curious."

"And you're being difficult. What's the idea of all this opposition?"

"I'm hungry."

He laughed. "What a brat you are."

"I'm also a concerned sister. You work too hard and you let people take advantage of you." Thad grinned at her without answering .

"I wonder if Vince knows." Mary turned to stare out the window toward Vince Riley's bungalow next door.

"I'm sure I couldn't say." He gave her a pat on the head and left the kitchen.

Mary and Vince. An unlikely twosome. But it was Vince who had succeeded where he, Thad, had failed. After the accident it had been Vince more than anyone who had been able to help her through the long period of adjustment.

Caught up in his own grieving, Thad was paralyzed in the face of his sister's physical and mental suffering. Vince Riley, however, had stopped by once or twice a day to talk, or just to sit quietly with her. It was Vince who, one day, had brought a sketch pad from the sunporch that had served her as a studio and thrust it into her hands. When she threw it to the floor, he picked it up again — a procedure that was repeated until she finally burst out laughing and drew a cartoon of him as a skinny cowboy chewing on a carrot. Vince had known what to do, while he, Thad, had struggled with his rage and his feelings of helplessness. He understood with both gratitude and regret that Vince Riley had become Mary's Paladin, the only person with the key to that very special part of her life labelled "handicapped."

Thad called from the backdoor, "I'll put the groceries on the back porch, OK? And don't bother waiting for me, greedy guts."

"I shall let my conscience be my guide," she answered back, then cut herself a piece of cheese.

Mary munched reflectively and took another sip of wine. As she heard her brother's car drive off, she began to put away the food she had gotten out for supper. She rocked her chair back and forth for a moment, then, her mind made up, put away the groceries and quickly scribbled a note to leave on the refrigerator door. Fifteen minutes later her car was in the Wyndham Hall parking lot, and she was expertly negotiating her chair down the ramp leading to the basement offices.

The door to the News Bureau, where she worked part-time, was open, as was the door to the Buildings and Grounds offices across the hall. As she propelled her chair toward the News Bureau, a weary-looking Vince Riley came into view.

"You've heard?"

"Thad was home when Security called. I thought I could give my boss a hand."

"I'm sure Tom'll appreciate it." Vince rubbed his forehead and sat down on one of the benches placed here and there the length of the hall.

She turned her chair to face him. "I went upstairs to Ward's reception for a moment this afternoon, but I didn't see you."

"When was that?"

"Close to six, I think."

"I must have just left — got a call to go to the campanile." He shook his head. "I still can't take it in. No one can."

"How did you hear about it?"

"I was in my office, writing up a list of things for Max Dingam to do while I'm away — and trying to sober up with a cup of rosehip tea." Vince's weather-beaten face crinkled further into a grin.

"Vincent! You gave in to Demon Rum?"

"There are times when carrot juice won't cut it, kiddo. And saying good- bye to Ward this afternoon was one of them. I may have toasted him a couple of times too many. Or maybe it was the wild-goose chase some joker sent me on that gave me the headache."

"Wild-goose chase?"

"One of the secretaries took a call that came in during the party. Supposedly from one of my crew at the plant reporting an act of vandalism in the campanile — some anchor bolts removed from the bell supports. One hundred and seventy-five steps — and for nothing."

"Oh Vince, that's rotten."

"I'm only sorry to have missed Ward's send-off. Turns out none of my people knew anything about the phone call. Some kid's idea of a practical joke, I suppose." Vince paused reflectively before going on. "I'd just gotten back to the office when I heard Jeff hollering."

"Jeff found him?"

Vince shook his head. "Hunh-uh. The dean. Parker-Brown. Tom and I tore upstairs. He was at his desk. President Merton, I mean." Absently, he took hold of Mary's hand. "Jeff Colton phoned for the paramedics; the dean was trying CPR. Tom took over in pure desperation, but you could tell the man was dead. Cardiac arrest. At least that's the way the paramedics called it." Vince kissed her hand and got to his feet. "I'd better go back upstairs — just came down to get some aspirin."

Mary made no comment on the efficacy of rosehip tea; this was not the time for the non-stop teasing that punctuated their conversations. His distress was evident. "You look beat. Do you really need to stay, Vince?"

"I think so. Turner hasn't gotten here yet, and . . . I'll let Tom know you're here."

"Thanks. Tell him I'll pull the file on the president and have it ready for him."

"OK. And, Mary?"

"Yes?"

"Do you feel like coming over later tonight ?"

"Depends on what you have in mind."

Vince smiled and touched her cheek. "The pleasure of your company."

"A *femme fatale* at last." Mary put her hand over his, looking up at him. "Count on it. I'll be there."

As she made her way toward the News Bureau, Mary paused a moment at the open door of Vince's office, shaking her head at the clutter on his desk, one pile of papers precariously weighted down by a small plaster cast of three crudely painted monkeys. Next time Vince criticized the disorder of her own office, she'd be ready for him.

Mary Walker wheeled into the News Bureau, checked Tom Donaldson's desk, then plucked the folder on Julian Merton from the file. Studying the last official photograph, the well-defined lines of the face, the youthful yet dignified smile, the artist in her appreciated the beauty of the head and the clever lighting that concealed what she had always viewed as a ruthless expression in the eyes. In her estimation, Julian Merton was a cold and calculating fish. Who, she wondered, who outside his immediate family would mourn him? Or should the question be turned another way? Who would be relieved to have him dead? He would not, she suspected, be remembered as a beloved president.

Mary returned the photograph to its folder and picked up the CV: Born, 1945, Fort James, Ohio; High School Valedictorian; B.A. Yale University '67, Summa Cum Laude; Marshall Plan Scholar, University of London School of Economics; PhD Yale, Philosophy; Fulbright and Guggenheim Fellowships; two-page list of articles and three books, including the one on a philosophy of economics that had rocketed him to some national as well as academic prominence. Assistant Professor, Fitzwilliam College, 1970-1973; Associate Professor then Professor of Philosophy, Staunton University, 1973-1983; President, Ludlow College, 1983-1986. President, Tipton College, 1986-.

Married, Priscilla Lavery Farrington, Radcliffe '70; one daughter, Priscilla, born 1974. So much effort spent, so many words spoken and written, so much striving, so many compromises — and how many lies? At what point, she wondered, had a passion for the life of the mind turned into a passion for exploiting it?

Mary slipped the last page of the CV into the machine and typed the phrase that cancelled all the others: Died, July 19, 1989.

Tom Donaldson of the News Bureau and Héctor González, head of Campus Security, stood at one side of the open double doors to the president's office. At the northern end of the room, the city patrolman who had answered the call and an officer with a camera were completing the routine of recording a sudden and unattended death. In the reception area, from her position at Beulah's desk, Anne Parker-Brown could see into the office beyond, her eyes drawn unwillingly to the grotesque scene that dominated the room.

Seated at his desk in front of the large bay window, the late president of Tipton College seemed reluctant to let go of the position: arms stretched out on the desk before him, head thrown back, mouth slightly awry, Julian stared up at the coffered ceiling as Tom Donaldson had left him. She found herself expecting him to sit up and transform this scene of horror into a macabre joke. Every lamp and overhead light had been turned on. The office, normally so inviting, with its genteel shabbiness of old leather and much polished wood paneling, had taken on a harsh and forbidding air. The glass protecting the portraits of seven past presidents and the crystal base of the desk lamp glittered with shafts of light that seemed to point at the still and now livid form in the tapestry-covered chair. Anne broke her stare with a shudder. She closed her eyes, realizing suddenly that she felt nothing at all.

Thad Walker noticed the red-headed woman sitting with head bent at a desk outside the door to the president's office and identified her as the dean. He glanced over to where Priscilla Merton and Dr. Simon Lowenthal were conversing side by side in a quiet corner of the outer office. He hesitated, then chose not to disturb what was clearly an emotional tête-à-tête. He nodded toward Tom Donaldson and stopped to speak briefly to Héctor González. After a quick appraisal of the figure at the desk, Thad gave the patrolman an order to cover the body and headed toward the officer with the camera at the far end of the room.

"What does it look like, Pete?"

"Pretty routine, I guess. There was a big office party here this afternoon. Broke up a little after six. President Merton was called to his office for a phone call and was found dead about an hour and a half later." He glanced at his report book. "About 7:30, she thinks."

"She?"

"The dean of the college. She found him and had just started CPR when the custodian came in. She told him to call the paramedics and get whatever help he could find in the building."

"And?"

"Rodinsky here arrived a few minutes after the call came in from Héctor González, about the same time as the paramedics. It was too late to do anything."

"Did the paramedics offer anything significant as to cause?"

Agent Wiggins shook his head. "Only that it appeared to be cardiac arrest — maybe a stroke. Dr. Lowenthal is of the same opinion."

"Has he already signed the death certificate?"

Agent Wiggins seemed embarassed. "Well, no. The coroner's office will probably order an autopsy. The doctor wasn't too jazzed to hear that."

"I bet." Thad was aware that Simon Lowenthal, also Mary's doctor, never suffered his opinion to be challenged. "How come? If Lowenthal is willing to sign the death certificate . . . "

Ill at ease, Pete shifted the camera from one hand to another, then said firmly, "I guess what I said to the coroner made the difference."

Thad tried to keep the annoyance out of his voice. "Given their case load downtown you must have really turned on the zeal. What the devil did you tell them?"

"Look, Thad. The man was only forty-four years old. On the young side for falling over dead. And Merton hasn't had a physical since the one Lowenthal gave him when he came here three years ago. It's true he suffered from hypertension . . . "

"Well, what more do you need?"

"Some fingerprints."

"What?"

"I spoke with Mrs. Merton. Briefly. She was pretty incoherent, but I managed to pin down a couple of things. Merton was talking to someone on his private phone when the attack occurred. He hung up on the man."

"Yeah?"

"But" — Pete raised a finger to get his Chief's attention — "but the phone was off the hook when I got here. According to Héctor and the dean nothing had been touched."

"I'm still waiting for the punchline. Merton could have knocked the phone off himself."

"Possibly. But I can only pick up one badly smudged latent from the phone. Might be a thumb."

The Chief looked solemn. "What about the second phone?"

"Lots of prints on that one. It's the phone the custodian used to call the paramedics."

"I see." He looked around the room, then out the window before saying, "Pete, I'm glad you're being careful, but Merton may have smeared his prints himself when he grabbed for the phone — knocked it off." He put a hand on his young colleague's shoulder. "But look, if the coroner bought it, go with it."

Pete looked disgruntled. "You've always said . . . "

"I know: 'Never assume that a situation is what it seems.' You did the right thing, Pete. It's OK. It's your investigation."

Pete Wiggins brightened considerably. "The tech boys and the deputy medical examiner ought to be here in about forty minutes. Doc Rooker'll make the final recommendation."

"Good. Any other problems?"

"I think we've got the scene well contained, Chief. Thought I might as well begin to get statements from the people who attended that party."

Thad nodded. "That could be quite a job; I'll give you a hand."

Pete Wiggins' thanks showed his obvious relief. He was an Altamira boy, but he had never been able to psych himself out of a feeling of diffidence where the college community was concerned.

Thad walked over, turned back the sheet to study again the rigid figure in the desk chair. Except for the twisted mouth, the face seemed curiously blank, as though no emotion had passed over it at death. "Was the body moved?"

"He was found slumped over in that chair. The head was pushed back when they tried to give mouth to mouth resuscitation."

"They? I thought you said the dean . . . "

"First the dean, then Tom Donaldson of the News Bureau."

"She found him at about 7:30? Is that right?"

"Yeah." Pete Wiggins tilted his head toward the open door. "She's outside."

"Is her office on this floor?" Pete nodded. "Ask her to be good enough to wait for me there. Oh, and Pete."

"Sir?"

"What about that plastic goblet on the desk?"

"Couldn't pick up any prints on that either; had that cocktail napkin wrapped around it. But I'm sending it and the napkin to criminalistics just the same. It looks like it contained water. Some was apparently spilled on the desk pad. The desk was damp underneath. As you can see, there's a little left in the cup."

On the couch around the corner from Beulah Taper's desk, Priscilla Merton and Dr. Lowenthal were now silent. Priscilla, head bowed, was clutching one of his hands as if it could rescue her from grief.

Pete Wiggins came out and spoke briefly to Anne. She nodded and rose, stopping in front of Priscilla and Simon Lowenthal as she passed. Priscilla glanced up. Except for her reddened eyes, she looked as immaculately groomed as always. For a moment Anne had the impression that Priscilla was smiling at her.

"There's nothing like the old home truths, is there Anne? Like, 'Every cloud has a silver lining.'"

A startled Simon Lowenthal began to make comforting sounds, but Priscilla persisted. "Well, won't it be just wonderful to be acting president? Isn't that what the bylaws . . . " With a choking sob, Priscilla Merton buried her face in Dr. Lowenthal's shoulder. The doctor looked helplessly at Anne, who remained impassive.

"Priscilla, we'll all be standing by to do whatever we can to help."

Priscilla Merton nodded, dumbly, face still hidden. Simon put in, "Don't stop by before tomorrow morning, Anne. I'm taking Priscilla home and giving her a sedative as soon as Thaddeus Walker has a few words with her. My wife is on the way to the house now; Ruthie'll spend the night."

"Look." Priscilla sat up. "There's no point talking as if I weren't here. I know we have things to discuss, Anne, arrangements . . . " She stumbled over the word, unable to go on.

"Whenever you say, Priscilla."

"There's no hurry, I guess." The tone was bitter. "Can you believe it, Anne, they're planning to do an autopsy. Oh God. The very idea of someone . . . As if this isn't awful enough."

Simon Lowenthal put his arm around her. "I'll speak to them, Priscilla." He looked up at Anne over Priscilla's bent head.

She took the cue. "Simon, we'll talk later."

As Anne walked toward her office, Priscilla's high-pitched voice trailed after her. "Why weren't you firmer with him, Simon, about coming to see you? Damn it, why couldn't you convince him he wasn't immortal . . . "

As Priscilla entered the Burckhardt Room down the hall from the president's office, Simon Lowenthal drew Chief Walker aside. He was at his most ingratiating.

"Thad, about this autopsy business . . . For heaven's sake, leave the man's death some dignity. What happened here this evening was totally predictable. You have my word on it. That over-eager young cowboy of yours in there is out of line. It's criminal to ask Mrs. Merton and her daughter to accept that procedure."

"When did you last examine Merton?"

Simon looked uncomfortable. "A little over three years ago — just before he assumed his duties as president. Julian was very stubborn. But I know his history. I know where he was headed without some serious revisions in his life-style. The stress EKG I did at the time showed that."

Thad was equally smooth. "I sympathize, Simon, but it isn't up to me."

"Look here, I know the weight of your influence—"

Thad cut him off. "Influence has nothing to do with it. Sorry, Simon. I can't change a coroner's decision — if it goes in that direction. A deputy M. E. will be here soon. I expect he'll be in agreement with you as to the apparent cause of death." Simon gave a tight-lipped smile as though anything else would be unthinkable. "However, I wouldn't be too optimistic about avoiding the autopsy if I were you."

Simon's eyes narrowed. "You've discovered something?"

Thad smiled. "There's no call for suspicion, Simon. Talk it over with Dr. Rooker, of course. I'm sure he'll find your opinion helpful."

"He'll get it, that's for sure."

"I hope the reporters won't, Simon."

"What do you mean?"

"It's up to you, of course. But you might remember the Liberace case. A difference of opinion between the attending physician and the coroner can fuel some wild speculation on the part of the media. Make it all the more difficult for the family."

Disgruntled, Lowenthal gave in. "Perhaps you will do this much: go easy with Mrs. Merton, Thaddeus; she's on the ragged edge."

Priscilla looked lost at the large mahogany table that served for administrative meetings, most regularly those of the president's council. She smiled at the policeman, a tremulous smile that vanished as her glance flicked momentarily to the far wall. The four walls of the Burckhardt Room presented a photographic history of the college, its presidents and academic officers, both past and present. At one end of the room, facing Mrs. Merton, was an imposing photograph of Julian in full academic regalia; beneath it hung a similar, though smaller, one of Dean Parker-Brown. Thaddeus noted the direction of her glance and the nervous twisting of her hands that accompanied it.

"I won't keep you long, Mrs. Merton."

Again, the tremulous smile. Why did he have the unkind thought that it was artificial? Thaddeus placed his notebook on the table and uncapped his Mont Blanc pen, one of his few indulgences.

"I'm deeply sorry about what has happened, Mrs. Merton. I know how distressing it is for you to answer questions right now. I'll try to be as brief as possible."

Priscilla looked at him dully, nodding her head.

"Did you consider your husband to be in good health?"

"He drove himself, Chief Walker. I can't tell you how hard he drove himself. No one appreciated it."

Thad looked sympathetic but persisted. "About his general health . . .?"

"Julian insisted he had the arteries of an astronaut. But I know he didn't take enough care of himself. So much stress in his life. And envy, resentment, hatred . . . "

"Are you saying your husband had enemies?"

"You don't know much about the academic world, do you?"

"I guess not."

"So much pettiness. Always ready to snipe at you. To criticize. And never appreciative." She wiped her eyes carefully with the wad of Kleenex clutched in her hand.

Thad wondered whether she was referring to her husband or to herself.

"Did your husband give any indication of late that he wasn't feeling well? Any specific mention today of pain, discomfort, fatigue . . .?"

As he led her through what she knew of the president's day, Thaddeus remembered what Mary had once said about Priscilla Merton: a small woman with a very big problem.

Outside the Burckhardt Room, Vince Riley and Héctor González were assisting Agent Wiggins by drawing up a list of those in attendance at Ward's farewell party.

"Good thing Ward has already left town," Vince said, turning toward Héctor. "This would be hard on him."

Héctor González nodded, concentrating on the list. "Well, it looks like there were around fifty people here at one time or another." He looked questioningly at Vince. "That seem about right?"

Vince agreed, then turned to Pete Wiggins. "Are you going to have to interview everybody?"

Agent Wiggins flipped his book shut. "Don't know yet. Mainly, we want to know if President Merton had mentioned feeling bad to anyone recently, or at the party — if he had any warning."

"If talk in the Hall means anything, the man was a walking time bomb, worked too hard, lived too hard, worried too hard. Right, Héctor?"

Héctor remained discreetly silent.

"I can begin with you two guys right now. Did either of you notice anything? Did you hear him say anything about not feeling well?"

Héctor shook his head. "I wasn't at the reception."

Again Vince answered for the two of them. "President Merton didn't confide in the troops, Pete. But he struck me as the kind of man who would never admit to being sick. Ask his secretary, Beulah Taper. She'll know, if anyone does."

A breathless Phil Gertmenian strode into the dean's office. "Sorry, Anne, I was out to dinner.

Dad gave me the message. And I ran into Tom Donaldson just now . . . God, Anne, it's, it's unimaginable."

Anne sketched a dismissive gesture, but remained silent. She still couldn't find a reaction to Julian's death. She felt nothing except regret for a failed life. A picture had burned into her brain, the image of a charnel-house figure seated at an imposing desk, ambition that would decay to dust. Anne broke loose from her thoughts. "We'd best get to work, Phil; there are innumerable calls to make."

"What about Filmore?"

"I've spoken with him. He's going to phone Weinert" — she spoke the name with distaste — "and see that the officers of the board are notified right away. Tom Donaldson was able to reach Henry Norton; he'll call the other VPs; I'm setting up a meeting here with staff in a few minutes. Filmore plans to get here about ten — he's at his beach house."

"Has someone called Beulah?"

"Yes, but she's out. Keep trying, will you? If you can reach the registrar and dean of Admissions, ask them to join us. And here's a list of some faculty to notify by phone — the department chairmen, plus the president's council."

"What's the story going to be?" Anne's expression told him that his choice of words had been an unfortunate one.

"The truth. That the president died in his office this evening, apparently from a heart attack. I want to meet with the council at eight tomorrow morning."

"OK. Shall I draft a notice to go out to faculty and staff?"

"Please."

"What about the trustees?"

"Let's wait and see what Leslie has to say."

As he rose to leave, Phil gave his boss a long appraising glance. "Are you all right?"

"I don't know how to answer that, Phillip."

"Then how about something to eat?"

"A cup of coffee would be a godsend. Oh, and ask Tom Donaldson to join us."

Phil Gertmenian almost collided at the door with Victor Laszlo. Behind him came a white-faced Turner Van Voorhees and an unperturbed-looking Henry Norton. Crises with students, from simple homesickness to suicidal depression, were part of a Student Dean's daily diet and had prepared Norton to meet any emergency with at least an outward show of exceptional calm.

As Tom Donaldson slipped quietly into the office some minutes later, the meeting was underway and Victor Laszlo was saying ponderously, "Hold the phone, Anne."

Henry Norton sat up straighter, startled. "Good Lord, Victor."

"Sorry, bad joke. What I mean is, I don't get the business about the phone and Weinert." Turner looked up at the ceiling and Henry Norton, always restless at meetings, jiggled his feet.

This was Donaldson's first session with the executive group; during the three years Merton had been at Tipton the president had not found it necessary to include him. What Tom now observed bore out what he had heard: that Laszlo had become a barely tolerated nuisance.

Anne was conciliatory. "I may not have explained it very well, Victor. From what I've been able to learn, Milton Weinert was on the phone with Julian sometime around six-thirty when Julian hung up on him."

"Oh boy." Victor shook his head despairingly, wise in the ways of donors. "That could sure tear it."

"I understand he called back a couple of times and kept getting the busy signal on Julian's private line. He tried the college extension, but got no answer. Finally he phoned the president's house and reached Priscilla. And you're right, Victor, he was angry."

"A polite understatement is my guess," Turner put in dryly.

"Well, yes. Priscilla referred to it as a towering rage. The college phone didn't answer, and the private line rang busy. So she walked over from the house."

"Were you the one who had to tell her?" Turner asked.

Anne shook her head. "The paramedics. Priscilla met them downstairs as they were leaving."

There was a long silence, which Turner broke. "I guess Kitty and I were the last persons to see him alive. He bowed his head, shaking it in disbelief.

Victor pulled at the lobe of one ear, his mind still on the earlier subject. Finally he blurted out, "But why didn't Julian ask Milton for help, before he hung up? And why was the phone found off the hook?"

Tom Donaldson smiled to himself. Old Victor wasn't such a dolt.

"The man must have been in dreadful pain," Henry Norton suggested. "Breaking the connection could have been an accident. Then he may have grabbed for the phone, to try to call for help — and couldn't make it."

"Poor bastard."

All eyes fixed on Victor. No one said anything. Victor, Tom Donaldson thought, had probably stated what everyone was thinking.

The next twenty minutes held no startling surprises for the director of the News Bureau: Victor was concerned about alumni and donors, and Milton Weinert in particular, though testy about having been left out of "recent developments"; Henry Norton discussed the possible effect on students and parents, while Turner wondered about the board's reaction and what could be done to help Priscilla. Anne tried both to answer questions and to keep the meeting on track for setting up a list of priority actions. Phil had just buzzed to say that the dean of Admissions and the registrar had arrived when Turner interrupted.

"Could you ask them to wait a moment, Anne?" After Anne had done so, Van Voorhees continued. "We've been remiss under the shock of this dreadful business. I'm sure I speak for all of us when I say you have our fullest support."

"Absolutely," Victor put in heavily. "Dreadful responsibility, Anne, for you to have to step in as acting president. I think I can say we're all team players."

Henry broke the embarrassed silence. "Of course, Victor. Absolutely."

"I'll need your help, no question about that. But you're rushing things in assigning me a change of title. The Board may have something else in mind."

In the midst of protestations and the unthinkability of any other solution, Tom got Anne's attention. "If I may be excused a moment, Anne. I should call Willie Hefner, though I suspect he already knows."

Anne grimaced. The editor of the *Altamira Ledger* was persona non grata at Tipton. She did not care to consider how he might handle the report on her discovery of the body or the intimacy of the attempted resuscitation. Even the taciturn Jeff Colton couldn't protect her from Willie's gossipmongering or his insinuating style.

Willie Hefner had heard. A reporter in the *Ledger's* office had been listening to a scanner and had picked up the call from the police department to the cruiser. Willie had arrived on campus in time to catch George Rodinsky as the patrol officer was leaving the Hall and had now buttonholed Chief Walker as he finished talking to Héctor.

"What do you make of this mess, Thad?"

Those who had known Hefner senior were always startled at Willie's physical resemblance to him. But there all similarity stopped. The owner-editor of the *Ledger* was a washed-out copy of his father. Upon Hefner senior's death, Willie had set out to change what had been a cozy, small town bi-weekly newspaper with well-written editorials into one that reported major news events as well as town happenings in a more "analytical and interpretive fashion." Willie's words were a euphemism for a confrontational attitude and an investigative style of reporting. This was a challenge in a town of 32,500 inhabitants, and one generally as tranquil as Altamira. Willie met the challenge well-bolstered by supreme self-confidence and an imagination fueled by town gossip.

"I imagine you know as much as any of us by now, Willie."

"I know what people are saying. I hear there's to be an autopsy."

Thad shrugged. "Possibly. Fairly standard procedure for a man who hasn't had a medical check-up in a long time. As you should know."

"Sure. I just figured that given your big-time background you might be looking beyond the obvious."

Thad's irritation showed. "My big-time background also taught me to respect the obvious, Hefner." Which was only partially true. Thad's years with the LA Police Department had also taught him to take nothing on faith.

Hefner wasn't to be put off. "I'm not saying Merton didn't die of a heart attack, Thad, but you gotta admit it's come at a funny time."

"I'm not laughing."

"Well, I mean, right when the faculty power brokers are up in arms about this Weinert business . . . " Willie paused, waiting to see whether Thad understood what he was talking about. Thad didn't cooperate.

"Then you've got the female angle. What you might call 'the woman scorned.'"

Thad had had enough. "Oh, come off it, Willie."

As he began to walk away, Hefner gave it a last shot. "The I-hate-Merton list makes interesting reading, Thad. You oughta at least give it the once-over."

WEDNESDAY, JULY 19

JOELLE, CALLED IN TO HELP GET OUT the faculty notices, looked up as Chief Thaddeus Walker came in and went over to Phil Gertmenian's desk. Her glance was brief, but long enough to file away her impressions: tall and lanky, great cheekbones, sexy brown eyes, long lashes. Not exactly Tom Cruise. More like that guy who was in the old movie she had watched last night; Cary something.

"Is the dean free, Phil? I believe she's expecting me."

"Sure, Thad . . . " Phil buzzed and delivered the message. "She's winding up a meeting with the VPs and some staff. They'll be right out."

"How's your father, Phil?" The Walkers lived across the street from the Gertmenians ."I haven't seen him of late."

"Little change. However Dr. Lowenthal is trying out a new prescription . . . "

He broke off as the door to Anne's office opened and five people filed quietly out, nodding to Thad as they went by. Only Victor stopped, to put a hand on his shoulder, adding inexplicably, "Thank God, Thad. Thank God you're the man on the job."

A voice from somewhere said, "Please sit down, Chief." A second later the dean stepped out from behind an open closet door, slipping into a brightly embroidered Indian jacket as she did so. "It's freezing in here, don't you find? Wyndham has always resisted modern technology."

Thad nodded an absent-minded agreement. "Sorry to bother you, Dean. I have a few questions you might help me with."

"Héctor explained to me — it's good of you to take over this investigation in person."

"I don't know about taking over. I'm only helping out some this evening. We're a bit short-handed at the station right now."

Thaddeus folded his rangy frame into one of the Tipton chairs and rummaged in a gaping coat pocket for his pad and pen. Anne recognized the make and the elegance of the latter. Given the officer's rumpled attire, as well as his possible salary, it seemed something of an anomaly. But then, the policeman himself didn't seem to be cut from the traditional boys-in-blue cloth.

In keeping with a hundred-year-old tradition, the college handled its disciplinary cases and misdemeanors internally, whenever legally possible. Altamira police rarely came on campus. Anne had met Chief Walker once professionally, when two members of the housekeeping staff had been caught after a long series of robberies that included ripping off an elaborate stereo and video system in the Dance Department. She knew he had lost his wife in a catastrophic automobile accident that had left his younger sister a paraplegic. Mary, with whom she lunched occasionally at the round table at the faculty club, seldom mentioned her brother. Phil Gertmenian, on the other hand, was eloquent in his admiration of someone who had had the nerve to exchange the expectation of promotion — and burn-out — in the Los Angeles Police Department for hope of a more tranquil and interesting life in a college town. In fact, Thad Walker had become a regular at Tipton's musical events and science lectures in particular. As he uncapped his pen and opened his report book, Anne found herself staring at his hands: slender, strongly articulated with tapering fingers and well-kept nails, they didn't seem made to grasp the butt of a gun, much less pull the trigger.

"I know how painful this must be for you, Dean Parker-Brown. You and the entire college community have the Department's sympathy."

"Thank you."

"Pete Wiggins will drop off a list; we're trying to put together the names of all the people who attended the party this afternoon. If you and your staff will look it over and add any names we may have omitted, I'd appreciate it."

"We'll do our best. Though I don't understand the necessity."

Thad patiently ticked off the official reasons, concluding, "It's routine procedure, particularly for the sudden and unattended death of a man his age."

"I see. Well, as you know, I only returned to town this morning. All I can say is that he seemed much as usual."

"You weren't aware of any particular tensions or physical malaise of any kind?"

Anne hesitated. "No."

"How well would you say you knew the president?"

A slight stiffening of her posture reminded Thad of Hefner's insinuations; he hurried on. "You've worked very closely with Merton ever since he became president, is that right?"

"Of course."

"Would it be in the nature of things for him to mention any health problems to you?"

"Since he never did, I can't say."

Thad was acutely aware of the dean's mounting displeasure, and opted for a more direct approach.

"What I'm trying to find out, Dean, is whether President Merton lived as hard, and worked as hard as people say."

"Julian Merton had enormous energy, Chief Walker. In endless supply, it always seemed to me. He did indeed work very hard. But no more perhaps than any conscientious president of an institution like Tipton where the responsibilities are so vast: administrative, financial, curricular — and heavily social as well."

"Then, so far as you know, it was business as usual?"

"Yes."

"No undue stress from any new projects or problems?"

"As I said, I just got back this morning."

Interesting, Thaddeus thought. Mrs. Merton saw her husband as being on the ragged edge, while Anne Parker-Brown seemed determined to give him a clean bill of health. The contradiction was not necessarily significant, nonetheless he automatically noted it.

"I understand that there might be some tension between the president and the faculty."

"There usually is at any college."

"Something to do with a Mr. Weinert?"

"I don't know how you could have heard that. But it's true that Milton Weinert is a donor who is interested in initiating a new program. As with any possible curricular change there's bound to be divided opinion. It is all very tentative at the moment. And certainly not for public discussion."

"I see."

To Chief Walker's questions about discovering the body the dean responded clearly and economically. His sister Mary said that the Wyndham Hall staff considered Parker-Brown one of two "real human beings" among the administration, Henry Norton being the other, and dismissed the underground gossip about an affair with Julian Merton as the work of the disgruntled or the envious. The dean might well be a "real human being," Thad thought as he rose to leave, but she was also one impressively assured customer. And a handsome one. As he turned toward her once more, his hand on the doorknob, her expression indicated that she wasn't viewing him with any favor.

"By the way, Dean. Do you know who was the last person to see the president alive?"

"Mr. Van Voorhees believes he was. He and his wife. Or perhaps the president's secretary, Miss Taper."

Beulah Taper, looking haggard beneath the discreetly applied make-up, stood up as the Chief approached her desk. "I've finished checking over the guest list, Chief Walker."

He took it from her, glancing at it only briefly. "Thank you. Has Agent Wiggins spoken with you?"

Beulah nodded. She was a sturdy woman, he noted, square in shape: square body, square face and determined chin. The blemish- and wrinkle-free complexion was of the kind that used to be compared to porcelain. The only soft touch was the gently waved and artfully dyed ash-blond hair. What, Thad wondered, what the devil was going on behind that impermeable and invincible-looking exterior?

"Just a couple of questions. Do you know who was the last person to see him alive?"

"Mr. and Mrs. Van Voorhees, so far as I know, Chief Walker. His office is next to Mr. Merton's — right over there."

He turned to follow the direction she indicated, to the east of the presidential sanctum.

"There's a connecting closet-washroom. The Van Voorheeses looked in on him before they left."

"Do you know whether they spoke to him?"

"He was on the phone. I believe they just waved at each other."

"And how do you know this?"

"I was still here — when the Van Voorheeses left. They mentioned it to me."

"But you didn't see the president?"

"No. His phone light was still on, so I picked up my things and left. With Mr. Gertmenian."

"What time was that?"

"Almost 6:30. 6:25 to be exact."

"I see. Was there anybody else on this floor at that time, except the dean?"

"There was no one at this end of the floor. But as for the Development people — I couldn't say."

"And in the basement?"

She shook her head. "No idea."

"Did you have any notion that the president was not feeling well today, Miss Taper?"

"No."

It was clear that Beulah Taper was not a woman who volunteered information. Thad pressed on. "You've been in this position for some time, I understand."

"Forty-one years, Chief Walker. And two former presidents."

"That's impressive." He smiled; Beulah waited, impassive. "I'd be interested in hearing whether, in retrospect, this sad business strikes you as totally unexpected."

Beulah didn't pause. "No."

"Could you explain that?"

"President Merton was a very highstrung man. An agitated man. Sometimes," she was quick to add.

"Agitated by what? Or by whom?"

"By the pressure of the job. And by his ambition. For the college." Another hasty addition.

"Could you be more explicit, Miss Taper?"

"Well, really, what more is there to say?"

A lot more, he thought, but she had clearly backed away from any further confidences, and Thad decided to let the matter drop. His early training to be constantly suspicious during any investigation could be carried too far.

"Could you give me an idea of what his day had been like? What people he saw?"

She handed him the open appointment book.

"Looks like a light day. Only one entry: Leslie Filmore *et al.*"

"The chairman of the Board. That was his only scheduled appointment. At ten."

"What about *et al?*"

Beulah cleared her throat. "Professors from the Social Sciences. A discussion of some curricular matters."

"That was it?"

"The dean spent some time with him, and the other VPs drifted in and out, but President Merton spent most of the day alone in his office, dictating, to catch up on his correspondence. He had been in San Francisco for a few days."

"I see. Would the ten o'clock meeting have been trying in any way? Or his meeting with the dean?"

Beulah hadn't the slightest hesitation in deciding to say nothing about Julian Merton's momentarily raised voice during the meeting with Anne, or about the tight look on Anne's face as she left the office.

"If anything did upset him, he didn't mention it to me."

"So nothing happened during the day that might have created unusual tension?"

"Why no. Nothing unusual."

Which could mean, Thad thought wryly, that tension was a standard condition. "Do you know of any particular worries he might have had?"

She shook her head emphatically. "No. Except for the usual ones that come with running a college."

He returned the appointment book to her. "Thank you, Miss Taper."

"Chief Walker, about the man on the door." She gestured toward the closed door, sealed off now by a tape and guarded by one of Héctor's men. "Is that necessary?"

"Only until the autopsy has been completed. If, in fact, one is ordered. We'll know in a little while."

"Oh my. Is that usual?"

"It will be the coroner's decision, Miss Taper. Your president was a comparatively young man."

"And how long will that take?"

"I hope no more than two or three days."

"I do need to get some files. Will that be possible?"

"I'm sorry, but the president's body hasn't been removed."

"I've seen dead bodies in my time, Chief Walker. And I would like my files."

Thad started to tell her she would have to wait. Then some leftover instinct from the old LA days caused him to change his mind, to want to get her reaction before the scene was neutralized.

As Thad switched on the inner office lights, Beulah didn't make a sound. She removed the handkerchief tucked in her belt and held it to her mouth for a moment, then resolutely walked up to the desk. His body covered by a sheet, Julian Merton was a ghostly presence.

"Please don't touch anything, Miss Taper. I'll hand you what you need."

She nodded.

"If I understand correctly, President Merton was found just like this? In his chair?"

"Yes."

She studied the desk a long moment. "Is everything just as it was?"

"Yes. Why do you ask?"

"I was wondering about that stain on the desk pad — on the leather."

"A water spill, Miss Taper. Does that surprise you?"

"Oh, no; I guess not. He did have a glass in his hand when he came to take Mr. Weinert's call. I presume it's that one." She pointed toward the plastic goblet.

"You're very observant."

Thad waited for her to go on. She seemed hypnotized by the desk. "Is something wrong, Miss Taper?"

"I'm concerned about the spill — if it went through the blotter . . . It's a valuable desk, you know."

"We've been careful, Miss Taper."

She seemed about to make a comment, then indicated the pile of papers on the right far side of the desk. "May I take the folders?"

"I don't see why not. However, not the one right in front of him." He craned his neck to see better: "'The Weinert Proposal.' If you'll just identify the others."

"I only need two of the three, Chief. Signed correspondence and unanswered correspondence."

"There *are* only two folders, Miss Taper."

She blinked. "Oh. Of course. I miscounted."

Thad looked through each one, made a few notes in his book, then handed them to her. Beulah thanked him and quickly left the room.

Alone at her desk moments later, Beulah dialed the Buildings and Grounds office. Not getting an answer she hung up and noted on her calendar for the next day: "B & G annual report — locate." As she put down her pen it struck her that it was a curious thing to worry about at this time. All too true, she mused: old habits die hard.

Dr. Rooker, the deputy medical examiner, and the technical crew arrived from Los Angeles at nine; by 10:30 they had completed the job. The office had been vacuumed and dusted for prints; the deceased's pockets had been emptied of their contents, the items on and in the desk and the folders Beulah had removed had been inventoried. The M.E. tentatively estimated the time of death between 6:30 and 7:30. As always, Thad noted, Doc Rooker was fast, efficient, and decisive. He listened patiently to Simon Lowenthal's assessment of Merton's health, the reminder of Julian's position and connections and his plea to "for God's sake allow the man's death some dignity." Rooker agreed with him that yes, the coroner's office was overloaded; nevertheless, he believed that the circumstances justified an autopsy. As Rooker was about to leave, he turned one of Simon Lowenthal's arguments against him. "President Merton was an important man, as you indicated, Doctor Lowenthal. I think we will all be more comfortable if his death is handled carefully and correctly." He said nothing about missing fingerprints. That lacuna was not yet for public consumption.

Pete Wiggins stood by as the remains of Julian Merton were carried out in a body bag, the stretcher loaded into the coroner's ambulance parked at the front door of the Hall. As the doors closed Pete glanced up. Someone was standing in dim light at a second-floor window, watching. The figure raised a hand in a kind of salute and disappeared.

Leslie Filmore bustled into Anne's office at 10:40, self-assurance and presence triumphing as always over his small stature. "Sorry to be late. I was detained by that policeman fellow — Walker."

"So I heard."

"Damn nonsense." His tone was peremptory. "Don't call the others just yet, Anne. We have some important business to discuss first."

It did not bode well, Anne thought, as she gave instructions to Phil. Hanging up, Anne turned to face Leslie who, even at the end of a day such as this one had been, looked as though he had just emerged from the hands of his barber and tailor. His crisp appearance made her feel all the more rumpled and drawn.

Putting the tips of his elegant and manicured fingers together Leslie looked straight at her with his most disarming smile. No, it definitely did not bode well. Anne had always respected Filmore, now in his tenth year as chairman of the Board, but over the past several months she had become aware of a change in him that seemed to accord with the modification in Julian's behavior. Or had each brought out in the other traits waiting for the appropriate catalyst?

"I'm not going to waste time discussing Julian's death with you, Anne. It's tragic, but it has occurred. It's the precarious situation we find ourselves in that must be our primary concern."

"Precarious, Leslie?"

"You know of course about the Weinert proposal."

"As of today, yes."

"I hope you understand the reason for the secrecy that surrounded Julian's and my dealings with Milton."

Anne matched his smile with her own. "Not to put too fine a point on it, Leslie, I consider that secrecy an insult to this office. As was your meeting with Julian and the others this morning."

"This morning wasn't the moment to bring you up to speed; the meeting was already arranged."

"Not good enough, Leslie."

"Be reasonable, Anne. You've been gone nearly six weeks. Of course you would have been brought into the picture, had you been in town."

"Apparently this was in the works sometime before I left. Or so Julian admitted to me this morning."

Leslie said nothing.

"Had I been in town, Leslie, I would have opposed the idea of an M.B.A. at Tipton with everything at my command."

Filmore's expression chilled by several degrees. "That would have been very foolish of you."

"It's this proposed graduate program that is foolish. The Weinert School of Business. Good Lord, Leslie. Seed money for a fancy building and a chair in business administration doesn't add up to a program. What the college would have to contribute in money and faculty time would weaken the undergraduate curriculum. And only to end up with a half-baked M.B.A. program and a second-class degree? Tipton couldn't possibly compete with UCLA or Stanford — to name only two institutions."

"Julian told me of your opposition. You disappoint me. I expected more vision on your part, Anne.

"Well, the question is academic at this juncture. Here are some drafts I've had prepared for you, announcing Julian's death to the faculty, and one for the Trustees . . . "

Leslie waved the proffered papers aside. "The question is not academic. I realize you have been hurt."

Anne stifled a protest.

"But you must understand," he went on, "that Julian's death changes nothing. In other words, as much as he admired Julian, Weinert's gift is not tied to the man himself. So long as nothing occurs to rock the boat."

Taking advantage of her stunned silence, he continued. "I learned this afternoon that some faculty are stirred up by the Weinert proposal. There's been a leak, evidently. I doubt that we will have a serious problem getting everybody on board, but your endorsement will be crucial, Anne. I trust you will decide to keep an open mind." He flashed an appealing smile.

She could almost admire him; Leslie Filmore at his most charming. Clearly he expected his hope to be confirmed, but Anne would not oblige.

"It's a question of keeping a rational mind, Leslie. The idea of springing a major curricular change on the faculty as a *fait accompli* is appalling. Indeed I do have the most strenuous objections to circumventing normal procedures where a major program is envisioned, particularly one with significant staffing and financial implications."

"Those questions have been thoroughly examined, Anne. How could you think otherwise?"

"Fritkin and Mayhew. I heard."

Filmore caught the sour tone. "The absolute tops in higher education consultants," he said defensively. "They did the study for Fremont College five years ago, and I needn't tell you that their new pre-med program is one hell of a success."

"I'm surprised, given the firm's reputation, that they would take the assignment. And not consult with the full faculty?"

Anne recognized the futility of further argument. She only half listened as Leslie went on about Weinert's conditions before he would commit, the sub rosa cooperation of the chair of Economics and those of Government and International Relations; the files Julian had made available to the consultants, and at last the clincher that was supposed to legitimize the subversion: "And of course there will be a full faculty discussion and vote before the final implementation of the program."

"After the fact. And if it doesn't go your way?"

"I hardly need to remind you of the power given to the board by the charter, Anne. But it won't come to that, I'm sure."

Anne listened in consternation as Filmore proceeded to outline his strategy for the timing of the announcement on the Weinert gift — tied in to an announcement of a donation of his own to establish a fund in memory of Julian Merton.

"Something to assist the humanities, I think, so they won't feel left out. Something in the neighborhood of three hundred K, in Julian's memory, to get the ball rolling."

"That's blackmail, Leslie."

"It's diplomacy, Madam Dean."

She stood up in irritation, walked over to the window to look out on the grounds whose darkness now seemed like a leaden pall.

Leslie crossed his small feet at the ankles and considered the tips of his bespoke loafers. "I'm sorry you're not with me on this. Under the circumstances, then, don't you think it would be wise for you to step aside as a possible acting president?"

Ah. There it was. What he had been intending from the start.

"In favor of whom?"

Leslie looked straight at her. "I intend to propose that the Executive Committee, represented in fact by the chairman of the Board, use the extraordinary measures available to it under the bylaws and constitute itself president pro tem. I've called an emergency meeting for tomorrow."

Anne could imagine the conference call: "Under the circumstances, Sally and fellas, I'm sure that Anne will be the first to agree . . . "

"So that's that."

"I deeply regret, Anne, that we're not of one mind. I'm a pragmatist. You know full well, Anne, that, as trustee and chairman of the Board, I have a duty to ensure the educational and financial welfare of the college. There's too much at stake, and we are too far along with Milton to risk anything going wrong."

"Perhaps the best way to ensure that would be to accept my resignation as dean."

"Julian told me you were considering going back to the History Department," he said easily, "but now is not the time to make changes in administrative structure."

So Julian had put words in her mouth. Leslie went on earnestly, "Tipton and its good name must be protected. It's imperative that we get through the next several months with a show of harmony. Are we agreed on that?"

"And if I refuse? You have considered that possibility?"

"Not seriously. Just think this through. What reason could you give the college, and the media, for stepping down as dean at this point? I can't think of one that wouldn't be embarrassing to you or damaging to the institution. Can you?"

"You understand that I would continue to oppose the Weinert proposal."

"And split the college into two warring camps? That wouldn't be like you. All I'm asking is commitment to your decanal duties — and cooperation — for one semester. So think about it for a few days. At least do that."

She widened her eyes and smiled at him. Filmore misread the expression. It was not a smile of reluctant admiration. Anne was smiling bitterly at the ease and rapidity with which Leslie Filmore had relegated Julian Merton to the dustbin.

WEDNESDAY, JULY 19

AT 100 TIPTON WAY PRISCILLA MERTON awakened a moment from her drugged sleep to be engulfed in a wave of sorrow and remorse. The recent past with Julian was swept away by memories of brighter days: their early marriage, the affectionate enthusiasm with which he shared his work with her, the high energy of an ambition that included her and was tempered by humor, not driven by hunger for acclaim. Happy moments flashed through her mind to give way to the self-accusing refrain, "You fool." Before the drug claimed her again, Priscilla heard Cissy's voice, saw her daughter's rigid and hostile stare. "Why don't you cut out the bereaved widow act. You don't have to pretend any more; you've got what you wanted."

Sunk in a deep and shabby armchair, her legs crossed under her, Terry Logan stared at the flickering candle flame and took a long drag on the joint in its roach holder. Exhaling slowly, she removed her datebook from a jacket pocket, opened it to

July 20 and read the first entry: 9:00, Delmonico's, Pris. With a shrug she crossed it out. After a moment, she picked up a photo on her lap, studied it, then tossed it onto the table beside her. Obsolete. Terry leaned back and inhaled contentedly.

Victor Laszlo sat in the dark, a tumbler of whisky in his hand. Muffled sounds reached him from the bedroom across the hall from the den. She was crying again, the old cow. Wanting his attention, his sympathy; wanting him to come to bed, to hold her, touch her. To hell with her. To hell with all of them. He reached over for the edge of the door, swung it shut. The sound reverberated through the darkened house.

In the large old Spanish-style house the college provided its dean of students, Henry Norton slipped into bed and curled around the body of his sleeping wife, then, with his usual restlessness, flopped onto his stomach. In his cool-headed, methodical way he was going over the events of the evening and considering their implications for the future, both near and distant. The coming year would be a rough one for Tipton. His job was in no danger, and he was good at it; he had nothing to fear, yet . . . Henry rolled over to his side of the bed. As he drifted off to sleep he wondered whether Lucille and the kids would rebel at living in the northeast. He could always go back to teaching chemistry. Given the present circumstances it might be prudent to re-explore that possibility.

Pushing aside the sheet, Turner Van Voorhees got up to get a drink of water from the bathroom. Making his way carefully back, he could dimly see Kitty sitting up in bed.

"I can't sleep either, Turn."

"Let me fix a cup of warm milk."

"You know I hate warm milk. I'd better take the pills. Unless you've got another solution."

Turner leaned over and kissed her. "I've got too much on my mind, Kitten."

Kitty pouted, then opened the drawer of the nightstand.

"Go easy on the pills."

"They're mild, Turn."

"Yeah, but no more than two, OK?"

Kitty nodded as she lifted off the bottle top. "See? Just two." She reached toward his water glass. "Gimme." Kitty took a long drink, then let out a long sigh, heavy with compassion. "I keep seeing him talking on the phone, making those funny faces. He was such a great guy. And so brilliant."

"Don't I know it. Amazing grasp of every aspect of college life."

"Poor Priscilla — and Cissy."

Turner lay back and closed his eyes as Kitty proceeded to give her view of the Mertons' conjugal life in general and Priscilla's idiosyncracies in particular before moving on to discuss possible changes in his career.

"Of course, what's happened is perfectly dreadful, but it will mean an opportunity for you, Turn. I mean, for you to move forward with your idea for bringing part of Development under the umbrella of your office. Leslie certainly thinks the world and all of you."

"Kitty, please . . . "

"It's true," she interrupted. "Leslie was telling me again at the party about the great job you were doing with the college's investments. And as soon as Victor is out of the way . . . Turn, you're not listening."

"Sorry, Kitten, but your timing's wrong. I can't get Julian off my mind. I just can't believe it."

"I know." She snuggled up closer. "I wonder what Anne feels. Terribly rebuffed, I imagine."

"Rebuffed?"

"Yes. Isn't that what you said happened at her meeting with Leslie?"

He sighed wearily. "It was her choice, Kitten."

"Turn, even I know better than that. And if it doesn't fool me who am dumb-o about campus politics, it won't fool anyone. As a matter of fact, I don't see why the Board doesn't put you in that position."

He gave a short laugh. "You're right. You are 'dumb-o' about campus affairs."

"Well, why not? You would be a neutral choice, it seems to me; you aren't involved with any faction."

"And here I was agreeing that you were dim about campus politics."

"Not that dim. Furthermore, you're like that with Weinert." She twined her fingers together. "You would be a great leader for the business school — and you're the smartest of the whole lot, in or out of Wyndham."

With that, Kitty turned his face to hers and planted a long kiss on his mouth with accompanying body rubbings that held no appeal for him at the moment. He pushed her gently aside.

"You forget one decisive point, my darling: I haven't the academic credentials."

"Pish, tush, and poo on academic credentials," Kitty said, with a big yawn.

Turner slid down in bed and turned on his side. "I've got a heavy day ahead. And you need to relax and let that pill work. Goodnight, Kitten."

Anne turned off the hot-water tap and stretched out full length in her over-sized tub. Five minutes more, she told herself, and she would get out. If only she could stay like this. Soothed by the water's warmth and the faint odor of tuberose, she had managed to block out for the moment the last picture she would have of Julian, the feeling of his body as she forced his head back with the absurd notion of reviving him — a body still yielding within the soft folds of his jacket.

Anne looked down at her two nipples poking up out of the foam: her absurdly childish nipples that had enchanted her husband, despite her insistence that they lacked erotic interest. Now they lay flaccid, depressed. Anne, suddenly annoyed, gave each one a vigorous pinch. "Let's have a show of character." A show of character. What she had shown with Leslie Filmore was the white feather. What she had shown since her return to California was confusion and poor judgment.

"Oh, to hell with it." Anne rose in a large whoosh of bathwater, grabbed a towel and began a brisk rubdown, repeating rhythmically to herself, "Take it one day at a time, one day at a time."

Anne pulled the plug, turned off the light and headed for her bed, slipping into a pajama top on the way. She set the alarm for 5:30, switched off the lamp, and, contrary to her expectations, fell immediately to sleep.

Claire Tidwell sat bolt upright, turned on the lamp and reached for the pad and pen on the nightstand. From Mark's side of the bed came a drawn-out sound of complaint. "Claire, for cripes' sake . . . "

"I've just thought of something important for our division meeting tomorrow. If I don't write it down, I'll forget it."

Mark turned over to lean on an elbow. "You're surely not going to hold that meeting under these circumstances?"

"You know the scientists, Mark. They'll see no reason to cancel it. There are enough people in town for us to get a jump on dealing with some important issues. Besides, it's not until late afternoon; we have the entire morning to observe respectful inactivity."

"And you're gung-ho to get started. Being the new chair for Psychology *and* the Science division has gone to your head."

"Nonsense. The question of security is a large and pressing issue, Mark. And we only have five weeks until classes begin."

He sighed and flopped over onto his back. "I should have known better than to say anything to you."

"It's not just the security in the Chemistry Department. I've discussed the question with Vince Riley, and the problem is wide-spread throughout the college. I wish I'd had the chance to speak to Anne about it, but there was such a crush at the party . . . "

"Don't tell me that stopped you. What is this passion of yours, Claire, for finding a cause then bulling ahead? I bet you didn't even talk to Ewen as I asked you to."

"Not yet."

"If you bring up your ideas in an open meeting of the division on the so-called poor security in the Chemistry Department, when we've gotten along just fine, thank you, for fifty years — you'll embarrass Ewen as chairman and my name will be mud. Cool it, Claire.

"The point is that there is no reliable record of withdrawals from the substance rooms."

"People may be a little forgetful some of the time."

"Most of the time, if you ask me."

"Jeez, Claire, are you turning into Miss Bureaucracy? We know what we're doing and have known . . . "

She chimed in with him, "For fifty years. It's sloppy, Mark, and maybe even dangerous."

Mark Tidwell heaved himself to a sitting position, and with the twangy accent his French-born wife usually found endearing, *"Ma petite chérie, tu as perdu le nord."*

Claire remained stubbornly silent. Mark sighed. "At least promise me one thing: have a tactful, repeat, tactful visit with Ewen before you bull ahead on this project. Agreed?"

"I'll think about it."

"And don't go running to Anne. She has enough worries right now."

"That cautionary note was totally uncalled for."

"Good. Now that you're virtuously indignant, maybe we can get some sleep. That is, if you still intend to get up at dawn and fix breakfast for our favorite neighbor."

Claire obediently turned off the light, but before settling down she leaned over to whisper in his ear, *"Tu sais, mon petit vieux, je ne suis pas née d'hier."*

In the Walker bungalow on First Street, Thaddeus Walker was in bed, unable to get to sleep. A light from Vince Riley's house next door threw leafy shadows on the ceiling. He glanced at the luminous bedside clock. Past midnight. Was Mary still over there, he wondered. What did those two find to talk about? Should he get up and get something to eat? Start the biography of Linnaeus Mary had given him for his birthday? Or just wait it out? Wait for the sense of unease to subside? The feeling that there was something not quite right about Julian Merton's death?

Thad reminded himself that he always felt this suspicion when investigating a sudden and unattended death — or had, when such moments were more frequent in his professional life. It was a reflex developed during his rookie days. He recalled Red Harris, his first captain — Lord, how many years ago — cigar clamped between his teeth, blunt finger stabbing the air, an educated man who affected a caricature of hayseed comportment: "Remember, Walker, suspicion, S - U - S - P - I - S - H - U - N. Engrave those letters in your thick skull. Doubt everybody and everything, and always listen to your gut." What was there to doubt this time? He had gone over his notes and reviewed all the information on his own and with Pete Wiggins. Tomorrow, he and Pete would finish their routine interviews. It seemed unlikely that anything significant would be added. Yet several things kept nagging at him: was it the rumpled paper cocktail napkin that explained the apparent lack of prints on the plastic cup? Could panic or a convulsive movement from a man in the throes of a heart attack explain why the phone had been slammed down in its cradle then knocked off? Leaving a solitary smudged print? Possibly. Then there was Willie Hefner's reference to the Merton hate list. But that should be considered in the light of Hefner's affection for gossip. Yet, with the possible exception of Mrs. Merton, no one he had spoken with so far seemed ready to go into deep mourning. They were a smooth lot at the college. Unfailingly polite, civilized, yet a closed corporation. What was it Willie Hefner had once said? Oh yeah, he had called the place a zoo, adding, in a vertiginous mix of metaphor, with enough intrigue going on to fill a couple of Italian operas. Hefner was a worm. On that conclusion Thaddeus fell asleep.

The soft light from the hall cut diagonally into the bedroom, reaching as far as the sheet pushed down to the foot of the bed. Leaning on an elbow, Vince smiled down at the young woman beside him, bent over to kiss her stomach, then her breast.

"You do have the most beautiful . . . "

"Don't you dare." Mary Walker's head came up off the pillow as she glared at him.

"Don't dare what?"

"You were about to use that word. I could tell."

Vince Riley stretched out on his back, picked up the near-side hand and kissed it. "A calumny. I'm too old-fashioned; I never say boobs."

"You know what I mean — the t-word.'"

"Problem is, I've always had trouble saying 'breast' — ever since I was a kid. I can't even hear it without seeing the eternal plate of fried chicken at Sunday dinner on the farm in Mangum. And hear Mama saying, 'Vince, leave some of the breast for little Georgie.' Little." Vince snorted. "At age ten the kid weighed over a hundred and fifty pounds. So you see we're stuck with 'tits'."

"I don't believe a word of it."

Vince laughed and kissed her again, on the mouth this time. "Anyway they are beautiful, darling Mary. They and all the rest of you make me very happy. Sorry to have been a shirker tonight." He smiled down at her. "Too rough a day, I guess."

"I thought you were extremely well up in your part. Or parts."

"Well now, look who's being salty."

Mary pivoted her torso as far as she could, put one arm across him, her head buried in his neck. "Oh Vince, you are so dear to me. And such a wonderful lover."

"How would you know?"

"I was hardly Miss Promiscuity of the year — before the accident — but I know. It may not be your full blast orgasm, but I swear I can feel it in my toes; you make me feel so — so whole."

"Maybe we've discovered a new kind of re-education. How about telling Dr. Lowenthal?"

Mary laughed. "Shock him out of his socks. He's not quite as hip as the gang at the rehab center with their sensate focusing. I remember his telling me, oh so delicately, that with an L1 lesion I might have spotty sensation, but could not be expected to have a complete, ahem, sex life. There are times, though, when I would like to shout it to the world. About us I mean."

"You may, so far as I am concerned, kiddo. And I'll shout right along with you. Did it ever occur to you that I'm flattered? Don't you know how beautiful you are? And the locker room machos would never vote me the greatest cocksman on campus."

"Only because you've been hiding your talents under Fruit of the Loom."

"My natural modesty."

"Ha!" She smiled at him, then grew solemn. "Vince, I couldn't bear to think of people wondering about us, picturing us together as something grotesque. And of course speculating on how we 'do it,' how I manage . . . "

"They're more likely to wonder what you see in a sawed-off, scrawny old geezer like me."

"Correction: handsome sawed-off old geezer. Anyhow, I like it this way. My secret. Our secret. Help me turn over, Vince, so that I can lie against you."

Uncertain whether he was dreaming or not, Thad thought he heard a door close next door. A moment later the soft swish of tires moving down the sidewalk reached him through the open window. Mary on her way home. What time was it anyway? The question remained unanswered as Thad sank back into a deep sleep to pursue fruitlessly an ephemeral vision of a woman with clouds of red hair.

Mary paused a moment at the side entrance to Vince's backyard to listen to the night sounds of crickets. In the far distance a dog barked once and fell silent. How fresh the air was at this hour. The very best part of the day. Someone else was in agreement with her, she thought, as she first heard then saw the jogger headed her way. A man, she thought idly. As he approached the street light in front of her brother's house he crossed over to the other side. Mary stayed still a moment admiring the runner's loose and easy form, then rolled on toward home. At the front walk she turned, looked back down the street. She noted half-consciously that the runner was now crossing back over, no doubt to avoid the MacPhersons' Labrador, quick to be roused. Mary thought no more about it, eager to keep alive the feeling in her body, the imprint of Vince's tenderness that blotted out the fear that was always just below the surface, the fear that this happiness would slip away. As silently as possible she let herself back in the house.

At the end of First Street Angel's friend turned and headed back. The street was now empty. The sight of Mary Walker at the entrance to Riley's backyard had been unexpected. What was she doing there at nearly one o'clock? A lucky warning; something to watch for tomorrow — or rather today. Angel's friend checked the time. The round trip would take fifteen minutes plus another twenty to twenty-five maximum for what needed to be done.

Phil Gertmenian stood at the door of his father's room, listening for a moment to the sound of the old man's breathing. Back in his bedroom he stretched out on his bed, hands grasping the head-board. Phil stretched long and hard. He was bone-tired, yet keyed up. The Royal Bastard was no more. There was a bad patch ahead for Anne, and that was a damn shame; but the worst was over for her. All things considered, Julian Merton's exit was the best homecoming gift she could have had.

Feet propped on his desk, chair tipped back, Willie Hefner began to reread the story he had keyboarded for tomorrow's special edition of his bi-weekly paper. He had kept his promise to Tom Donaldson: the announcement was dignified and straightforward, but he was vacillating about the headline. "Sudden Death of Tipton's President" certainly had less of a shock than "Unexplained Death of College President."

Hell of a way to go, Willie reflected, even for a snotty prick like Merton. Willie ticked off the names of those who might be rejoicing: the long-suffering Beulah Taper? Victor Laszlo? In his cups at the Grapevine Bar, Victor had been explicit about the harm he thought Julian Merton was doing the college. Then there was the neglected wife — and the faculty: Terry Logan, for instance who had spilled her guts over the phone when interviewed about her terminal contract. And what about Anne Parker-Brown? Was she his mistress or a has-been? Whichever, he bet she was a hot lay. Isn't that what they said about redheads? Blondes, on the other hand, were ice maidens. Crystal Mathews, his blond and current girl friend, was aptly named, he thought. Hefner smiled as he typed, "Dean Anne Parker-Brown, who discovered the body, tried applying the kiss of life." He erased it from his computer screen, made up his mind and wrote, "Sudden death of college president" at the head of his story and hesitated only a moment before adding the sub-heads: "Julian Merton dead at 44. Selection of acting president awaits decision of Board of Trustees." Willie complimented himself on being Mr. Nice Guy.

Thursday, July 20

LESLIE FILMORE AWAKENED AT PRE-
cisely 4:45. As he did every morning he glanced
briefly at the next bed where Bernice was still
sleeping and thought unkind thoughts. Her gone-
to-fat figure was a personal insult. His own slight
but perfectly proportioned body, taut and muscle-
toned, would never follow suit. Leslie would
stretch for a couple of minutes, then get up, slip
out of his Charvet pajamas, step outside, and dive
naked into his pool for the daily twenty-five laps.
After his usual breakfast of decaffeinated tea, dry
rye toast, bitter orange marmalade, and two strips
of crisp nitrate-free bacon, he would be ready to
face the day.

Leslie was looking forward to it, to getting the
messy situation caused by Julian's death "coopered
up." The executive meeting and the meeting of
the full Board should sail along as planned. Anne
would be dignified and discreetly supportive;
Turner, prepared and concise; Henry Norton
would probably not show, he rarely attended Board
meetings; Laszlo had nothing to contribute and

would keep quiet anyway. Leslie felt a twinge of excitement. The prospect of running the College and putting together the new business program was exhilarating. Implementing the M.B.A. program would provide him with a needed change of pace and be worth a few articles in the likes of *Business Week* and *Time*. Milton, thank God, showed no signs of being unduly perturbed by Merton's disappearance from the scene. Brilliant fellow, Julian, but there were obvious signs of instability. Yes, all in all, his death was for the best in the larger scheme of things, and Leslie Filmore never wavered in his conviction that he was always and fully in touch with the larger scheme of things.

Still in a daze, Anne turned off the alarm, switched on the light and got out of bed. It wasn't until she was groggily slipping into her jogging outfit that the events of yesterday rushed back into her mind, laid out in clear detail like a monstrous spread-sheet.

In the kitchen, she had just turned on the gas under the kettle when there was a knock at the backdoor. A moment later Claire and Mark Tidwell were setting the kitchen table and laying out the contents of a picnic basket.

Mark handed her a glass of orange juice. "Try this, Anne, fresh squoze."

She smiled gratefully. "This is too much. It's not even six o'clock."

"Claire opted for a *nuit blanche* for both of us. She's been hovering like a vulture at our kitchen window for half an hour, waiting for yon light to break."

"Don't be silly, Mark. Vultures don't hover; they lurk — and circle. Anyway, who got up betimes to make bran muffins?"

"Don't fuss, you two. Whoever did what, it's a godsend." She sniffed at the coffee pot. "I could get drunk on this coffee, Claire. It will be the first decent cup in almost two months."

For the next half hour recent events were carefully avoided as Mark steered the conversation to Anne's trip. Finally Claire broke in.

"We're calling on Priscilla later this morning. I dread it. Mark always knows what to say, but I'm such a dud at that kind of thing."

"I think she'll be grateful to have people around her. Particularly since she has no family."

Mark carefully buttered another muffin. "Isn't Julian's father still alive?"

Anne nodded. "Lives in Arizona. He may be here by now." She gathered up some dishes and headed for the sink.

Mark was on his feet, taking the things from her hands. "None of that. Cleanup is fully programmed. You go ahead and get ready." He looked her up and down. "I guess we interfered with your morning run."

"I wasn't planning to go out. This was just handy."

"I must say, Anne, for you to go jogging today in a black getup would certainly have been the height of *raffinement.*"

"Ignore her, Anne. But look here, you will let us know, if there is anything we can do to help? There are heavy seas ahead for you."

"Oh I don't know, Mark. The Executive Committee of the Board, that is to say, Leslie Filmore, will be assuming presidential responsibilities."

Predictably, the comment was met with shocked silence. Anne went on, "That's off the record. Though after the council meeting this morning the news will be all over the campus in fifteen minutes. I don't want to talk about it. What you can really do to help right now is to pour me another cup of coffee, please Mark — and tell me what you've been up to."

"Mostly trying to keep Molly Chandler quiet."

Anne looked blank.

"Charlie Peese's daughter."

Claire looked over the rim of her coffee cup. "I just realized. Do you know Tipton has had two deaths this summer? Charlie, quietly, in May, at the splendid old age of eighty-six, and now Julian, so unexpectedly, just two months later."

Mark frowned. "What does that contribute?"

"Well . . ." Claire returned to her coffee cup.

"Go on about Molly, Mark."

"Molly has requested a complete collection of her father's writings as well as what the college may have produced about him — and she's rather impatient, that's all. Keeps calling. And she's asked for twenty copies of this summer's *Topics*. I'm trying to rustle them up."

"Why that issue?"

"It has Charlie's article on his research — the toxic properties of blue-green algae."

"Oh yes. Good piece as I recall."

"Very. Mary Walker did the illustrations — and a swell job of editing, I thought. She made it understandable to the reader without turning it into pop science."

Claire piped up. "Provocative title too: 'The Very-Fast-Death Factor.'"

Beulah Taper finished washing and wiping her breakfast dishes and spread the blue and white striped towel to dry on the rack. She sponged off the already immaculate counter before suddenly realizing that she had just done so. Beulah stopped off in the bedroom for a last check in the mirror, headed for the garage, then had to come back to get her purse. She tried convincing herself that this morning's forgetfulness was due to fatigue and stress following the horror that was yesterday. But this kind of absentmindedness had been occurring too often of late to be ignored. She had taken to making lists, to writing things down. When people sought her out for information ("You're such an encyclopedia, Beulah"), she often said, to protect herself, that she was busy and would get back to them; then wait for the desired information to rise from a memory that seemed slowly to be turning to sludge.

Last night she had awakened several times to be confronted by a nagging question and had drifted back to sleep telling herself it was nothing to worry about. Certainly not at a time like this. Nevertheless, her compulsive tendency to fret about any records out of place or errors in her work had been on the increase since Julian Merton's arrival three years ago. Now she had the additional concern for the reliability of her memory.

At seven Beulah pulled into her reserved spot in front of Wyndham Hall. Her next stop was room 2a in the basement.

Startled, Jeff put down the newspaper and got hurriedly to his feet in answer to Miss Taper's "Good morning." Her response trailed off somewhat as she caught sight of the wine bottle on the battered table that filled two-thirds of the cubby hole he called his office. She had never known him to drink on the job.

"What can I do for you, Miss Taper?"

"I think I'm missing something from the president's desk, Jeff. I was wondering when you last emptied the waste basket yesterday."

"Well now, that's just what that police fellow asked me. The last time was right after my lunch period, around 12:30."

"You wouldn't happen to remember whether there was anything bulky in it? Like a folder?"

Jeff reflected a moment. "No, ma'am, I don't recollect anything unusual. I'm pretty careful about emptying out the stuff from the administration offices ever since Dean Williams threw away her wallet by mistake that time."

Beulah nodded. She had heard the twenty-year-old story often enough. "Exactly. I know you're careful. That's why I thought I'd ask."

"Is there anything I should be keeping an eye out for, Miss Taper?"

"If you do come across a folder with documents addressed to the president, let me know." Her eyes strayed again to the bottle, this time Jeff caught the direction of her glance.

He grinned. "I'm not drinking on the job, Miss Taper. I got that there bottle from upstairs last night, for the label. But maybe you'd like it. There's still some wine left."

Beulah made a dismissive gesture with her hand.

"Look at this." Jeff held the bottle out to her so she could see the soberly elegant label with the aristocratic owner's laconic signature: Lur-Saluces. "I was in that area in 'forty-six. Château de Wykem. I biked around France some with a buddy after the war. He wanted to learn about wines.

Me, I just liked to drink the stuff." He grinned. "But I sure remember Bordeaux. Had what you might call a little adventure . . . " He broke off, embarrassed. "I thought I'd soak off the label, for my collection." Jeff jerked his head toward a bulletin board filled with dusty postcards and other memorabilia collected over thirty-odd years at the college.

"Where did you say you found this?"

"Upstairs, after the party for Mr. Finlay. It was in the trash can near the bar."

A few minutes later Beulah Taper was on her way to the second floor, a partially full bottle in a paper bag. Château d'Yquem. It didn't belong. She had placed the wine order from The Cork and Bottle herself: a case of a Beaulieu Vineyards' Cabernet and three cases of Wente Brothers' Blanc de Blancs that the liquor store had mistakenly replaced with a rosé. No, it didn't fit, any more than did the water from the plastic cup spilled on the blotter of the president's desk. Or the missing folder. She was positive she had put it on his desk herself. Back at her own desk, she checked her calendar and once again called the Buildings and Grounds office. Vince Riley, she was told, was not on campus. Was there any message? The matter, Beulah said, could wait.

Window blinds slanted to dim the morning light, Mark Tidwell was sleeping, comfortably stretched out in his office easy chair. He had intended to profit from the dawn breakfast at Anne's to get an early start on his work with the Peese papers, but even the lashings of coffee he had consumed didn't suffice to keep his eyes open. He jerked awake at the knock at the door, glanced at his watch. Almost eight. Damn.

"Come in . . . Beulah!" Mark eased out of his chair. "Good grief, girl, what brings you here at this hour? Come on in. Sit down."

Beulah carefully closed the door behind her. "You still get to the office early, don't you, Mark? I took a chance you'd be in."

He nodded, smiled, and waited as she removed a paper sack from a tote bag, then carefully lifted out a bottle by a string around its neck.

"Isn't it a bit early to ply me with drink, Miss T.?"

The bantering expression died as he noted the expression on her face.

"I'm sorry. Something's wrong?"

"I don't know. I was wondering if you could analyze what was in this." She held the bottle out so he could read the label.

Mark squinted his eyes, then whistled appreciatively ."Very special stuff, I would say. You taking up oenology?"

"Mark, someone brought this wine to the party for Ward yesterday. It was not ordered. I'm positive of it."

"Someone brought it as a gift?"

"I don't think so; that wouldn't be normal procedure for our office parties. And I'm quite sure it
wasn't on the buffet table. Or at the bar. That's
why I've come to you, instead of going to the
police."

"The police! Jumping Jehoshaphat, Beulah. What
are you implying?"

Beulah looked as though she were about to announce a death in the family.

"When President Merton left Ward's reception
to take a phone call, he was carrying a drink. I'm
quite sure it was a glass of wine. I'm not the only
one who noticed it. Mr. and Mrs. Van Vorhees said
good-bye to him while he was still on the phone.
He had a drink in his hand; they said he waved
with it."

"How do you know it was wine? Was it red?"

She nodded, then frowned. "I feel reasonably
sure of it." Mark's eyebrows shot up. She made a
dismissive gesture. "It sounds silly, I know. But I
tend to notice what the president is drinking."
Mark waited, with the very nasty feeling that he
knew where she was headed.

"When I went into the president's office with
Thad Walker yesterday, water had been spilled on
the leather desk pad. At least Chief Walker said it
was water. He said there was water in the plastic
cup they found on his desk."

"But isn't there a basin in that closet between Julian's office and what's his name's — Voorhees's? Couldn't Julian have gotten a drink of water after finishing whatever else he had been drinking?"

"Maybe. But I don't see how there was time for that. I understand he hadn't finished his phone conversation when the attack occurred." She paused. "I don't want to be a foolish old biddy stirring up a tempest over nothing, Mark. So I thought if you could . . . "

"How did you get hold of this bottle?"

"Quite by accident."

Mark listened attentively to her explanation. "I see. Well, there's one problem."

"Oh?"

"You said Julian was drinking red wine. Are you sure?"

She hesitated. "Pretty sure."

"Château d'Yquem is a white."

"Well — but this isn't. White, I mean."

"Let me see that again."

Mark reached up for the glasses perched on his head, settled them on his nose, then went over to the window to fiddle with the Venetian blinds. Protecting the bottle with his handkerchief, he held it to the light, uncorked it, sniffed, tilted it to look inside.

"You'd best take it to Thad after all."

"But then Willie Hefner is bound to hear of it. Mark, there must be some explanation. If they

don't find anything, Willie will report it anyway —
and in his insinuating manner. It would be dreadful
for the college," she added miserably. "That's why
I came to you first."

Professor Tidwell looked solemn. "OK, girl. It
could get us into trouble, but I'll see what I can
do." He placed the bottle gingerly back in the sack.
"One thing my nose can tell me, there was more
than Château d'Yquem in this bottle, Beulah.
Something that would color it pink. If I'm not mis-
taken, there's a definite odor of cassis. And that's
a damn funny thing to add to one of the noblest —
and most costly — of Sauternes."

Agent Wiggins put the guest list for the Ward
Finlay party on Thad Walker's desk. "Everybody
is saying about the same thing, Chief: President
Merton seemed as always. No sign he wasn't feeling well."

"Let's try to see all forty-eight, Pete. Don't spend
more than a couple of minutes with each one.
Unless you come across something out of the ordinary you should finish the sweep through
Wyndham Hall in pretty quick order. That just
leaves faculty; there weren't many of them at the
party. I'll check out the trustees who were there."
He studied the list a moment, then put his initials
beside some faculty names. Wiggins let out a sigh
of relief, which changed to a groan as his superior
added, "You take the others."

"Thanks a heap. I'm no good at dealing with those faculty types."

"Don't let it get to you, Pete. Just think of what you know that they don't. And you speak Spanish. Throw in a Spanish idiom or two — that will impress them."

"Aw, come on, Chief."

"I'm serious." Thad rose. "I'm off for my appointment with Weinert. Should be back in a couple of hours. I saw him on a TV talk show once. Take it from me, you can be thankful you don't have to interview that hard-nosed defender of the right, which in his case is always spelled with a capital *R*."

The offices of Weinert Enterprises had resisted the shifts in urban development of downtown Los Angeles. They were still located in the building at Sixth and Los Angeles Street that Weinert Senior had purchased in 1929. After having been passed along through several offices, Thad Walker was greeted at the door of Weinert's anteroom by an unexpectedly young and nubile executive secretary. Then he noticed the jeweled American flag pinned to the lapel of her smart, gray silk suit. Patriotism was after all the ultimate seal of approval.

The same emblem, but in enamel, graced the lapel buttonhole of the King of the Munchie Bar. Milton Weinert swiveled to sit sideways to an old rolltop desk as he gestured Thad to a captain's chair opposite him. The face that looked unsmilingly at Thad was round and rosy; the hair, a wispy halo of white around a pink bald spot, made his black shoe-button eyes all the more piercing. Weinert reached for a sheet of paper on his desk.

"Here you are, officer. I've got it all down. Save everybody time."

Thad studied the heading: "Report on last conversation with the late president of Tipton College, Julian Merton. Wednesday July 19, 1989."

"I'm sure this will prove most helpful, Mr. Weinert, but I would still like to ask you a few questions."

"There's no need, officer, it's all there."

Milton Weinert swiveled back into working position.

Thad didn't get up. Weinert's expression was not encouraging, but Thad pressed on. "Had you any idea that Mr. Merton was in ill health?"

"Of course not."

"You say you had told Mr. Merton that you would call at 6:30 p.m. sharp."

"If you used your eyes you would see that I had to call earlier — at ten after."

Thad remained impassive. "What I'm interested in is how long you spoke before he left the phone."

"Young man, if I knew I would have said so."

"If you could make an educated guess, sir."

"I never guess, officer." Thad waited. "Maybe thirty minutes."

"Could you tell me the subject of your conversation?"

"I could, but won't. Of no consequence to your investigation."

"You say he asked you to wait while he went to get some figures. Would he have had to leave his desk?"

"I think not. I heard . . . " He broke off as he noticed Thad studying the report, then continued testily, "No, it isn't there. I heard something that might have been a drawer opening. Then closing."

"Then the phone was banged down."

"As I wrote."

"Not dropped? Slammed down in the cradle?"

"Where else?"

Thad couldn't resist saying, "You didn't specify."

The Weinert pink was modulating to a darker tone at the implied criticism of his text. "I only wrote what I know."

"You're certain you didn't hear a gasp? He didn't say anything right at that moment?"

The hostile stare didn't budge.

"Before you were disconnected, Mr. Weinert," Thad continued, unperturbed, "were you and President Merton having an argument?"

After the briefest struggle between ego and taciturnity, the former won out. "Only an idiot argues with someone about to make a ten million dollar gift."

Thad was unimpressed. "You called back a couple of times on the private line and got a busy signal? Then you tried one last time." He checked his notes. "About ten minutes later?"

A stare as hard as petrified wood was his answer.

"Finally you dialed the college and asked for his regular extension, which rang, but there was no answer."

"Officer, are you trying to be funny? We were engaged in a straightforward business conversation when Merton had some kind of seizure. The man died of a stroke. Period. What's all this super sleuth routine?"

"Presumably it was cardiac arrest or a stroke, Mr. Weinert."

Weinert's eyes bulged. "Are you suggesting . . .?"

"I'm not suggesting anything. You were the last person to have talked with President Merton. And your report is important for clearing up the question of probable cause and helping to confirm the time of death. That's all."

"And I've given *all* the time I intend to. Good day, sir."

Thad gave another quick glance at the Weinert report and decided he needed nothing else for the moment. He said his good-byes and thank yous to Weinert's profile and was about to let himself out when he changed his mind. Feeling rather like Colombo, he said, "One more thing, Mr. Weinert. What time was it when you phoned Mrs. Merton?"

Weinert scowled. "About 7:30, 7:40. Why?"

"I only wondered why you waited so long."

Weinert threw his pen down on the desk. "Because I expected the man to have the courtesy to call me back."

"Did Mrs. Merton have any explanation to offer?"

"No. Now get out." This time he turned his back.

Thad gave a small salute to Weinert's back and went out into the reception area. As if in telepathic communication with her boss, the secretary's manner was chilly as he nodded to her and passed on through.

The policeman's lot might not be a happy one, he reflected, but the gods had smiled in having spared him the fate of employment at Weinert Enterprises.

Terry Logan's office didn't fit Agent Wiggins' image of the scholar's retreat. The offices of his instructors at the community college had been cubbyholes with metal furniture and erector-set bookcases full of paperbacks and dog-eared journals. An office at Tipton, he thought, should correspond more to what he had seen on a recent TV epic with an Oxford setting. Here, walls and furniture were largely invisible behind the bookcases, the cartons, the piles of books and papers that covered every available space, including much of the floor. Two chairs indicated the presence of a desk. In answer to his knock at the open door, Professor Logan peered around one stack of papers and pushed some other paraphernalia leaving an opening opposite her own chair.

"You're the guy who called this morning, right? Agent Wig something? Come on in."

"Wiggins." Pete Wiggins sat down, pulled his notebook from his pocket and jettisoned any idea he might have had about bolstering his nervousness with Spanish quips. This wasn't going to be easy.

"Things are in something of a mess," Terry Logan said in bold understatement. "I'm getting ready for my photography show — and getting ready to leave this dump, and sooner than later I hope."

A phone rang from somewhere amongst the spills of papers on the desk. Professor Logan's hand dived for the right spot. "Hello? . . . Oh hi, Ellen . . . " Pete Wiggins started to rise, but was motioned to sit down again. "When did they find the body? . . . And how long . . . ODed? . . . God . . . No, I hadn't mailed him the print yet; haven't finished developing the roll . . . Why're the cops bothering you? You didn't even know the guy . . . Yeah. Fuzz tactics. She winked at Agent Wiggins. "OK. Be talking to you, cuz."

She hung up. "Drama in Laguna, officer. A young guy who lives near a relative of mine there was found dead this morning. That's the second; we can expect a third."

"Ma'am?"

"Haven't you ever noticed? When you hear about one death, or an airplane crash, you usually hear about two more almost right away. Julian Merton, now this kid. Who's next? The rule of three. Well, what can I do for you?"

It was easy after all. Professor Logan answered his questions willingly, clearly. She knew nothing of any health problems Merton might have had, had had no conversation with him at the party, and volunteered only that President Merton's demise made one think that there might be a just God after all.

Pete Wiggins closed his report book. "Thanks, Professor, I guess that does it."

"Yeah? Well remember, Wiggins, around here things are never what they seem."

Seizing his chance, Wiggins countered with a smile, *"Dicen que la vida es sueño,* right?"

To which Terry replied in flawless Spanish, *"Sólo para los que se pillan dormidos."*

Agent Wiggins sighed and reopened his book to make a final entry: "Shit."

Joelle had just returned to her desk downstairs when she saw Pete Wiggins coming up the front

walk of Wyndham Hall. He had certainly changed
for the better, she thought, since their school days
at Altamira High when he could have modeled for
a Boy Scout in a Norman Rockwell poster. But life
was funny, Joelle sagely reflected: in the class
prophecy a theatrical career had been predicted
for her, while Pete the Nerd was destined, so it
declared, to become a monk. As things had turned
out, that would have been a loss to womankind.
Joelle moistened her lips and had her brightest
smile at the ready.

"Hi, Pete. I hear you guys are still interviewing."

"Well, there were a lot of people at that party.
May I sit down?"

"Sure. You mean I'm next? Right after Ms. Stuck-
up?"

Pete looked puzzled.

"The secretary in Psychology told me you had
been in to see Logan. Who just happens to be on
my shit list."

"I thought she seemed like a pretty neat lady."

"If you had been a cute girl she would have been
even neater."

"That's not nice, Joelle."

"It's the truth. Logan's a dyke. And she's one of
those snotty types who only speaks to the help
when it suits her. I know she's had a rough time
here, so yesterday morning when she came tearing
downstairs after seeing the president, I said hello

just as pleasant as could be and got a nasty look in return."

Agent Wiggins took out his book and made a note.

Anne was admitted to the president's house by a sullen and red-eyed Cissy. Before she had a chance to say anything, she found herself enfolded in Priscilla's arms.

"I'm so sorry for yesterday, Anne. Please forgive me."

Anne disengaged herself gently. "Of course." Automatically she added the ritual lie. "It's quite forgotten."

On the sofa in front of the bay window that overlooked the back garden, Julian's father and Leslie Filmore sat talking. The flow of visitors hadn't yet begun. Anne nodded to Dr. Lowenthal's wife, Ruth, who came in from the kitchen with a large pot of coffee, followed by the Mertons' housekeeper carrying a platter of miniature sweet rolls.

"You know Julian's father, don't you?

"Yes, of course."

"Then if you'll excuse me . . . " Priscilla turned to join the women who were arranging a side table with food and beverages. Cissy had disappeared.

As Anne walked toward the sofa, both men stood up and she was struck once again at how little Julian resembled his father. Mr. Merton was short and swarthy, with a Levantine cast to his features. Age had attenuated but not destroyed a certain resemblance to a Lower East Side tough. Not the kind of father, Anne reflected, that a Julian Merton would want to present to California society. Yet the hand that grasped hers was gentle, the voice that greeted her was cultivated.

"Anne, thank you for coming."

Strange that he should remember her name; they had met only once before. As they talked, after Anne had expressed the usual condolences, she was struck by Mr. Merton's references to "my boy." She had never thought of Julian the child. She was on the point of asking Mr. Merton about Julian's childhood, but he was distracted by people beginning to arrive: Mayor Paulson and her husband bearing a plant, Claire and Mark Tidwell, other faculty and staff members and spouses, some with flowers, others with platters of food in the old western tradition; the room was beginning to fill.

Leslie Filmore took the opportunity to draw Anne aside. "If you would do me a favor, Anne. I would appreciate your telling Miss Taper that I will be in a little later than I said. I plan to spend the morning in Julian's office — until we drive in for the board meetings."

"Of course. But you won't be able to work in Julian's office, Leslie. It's sealed off."

"By whom?"

"Chief Walker's order. Or I suppose it's the coroner's orders; I hear it's his case now. Héctor Gonzáles volunteered our security people to help out."

Leslie sputtered. "But that's ridiculous. There are documents from the Weinert file that I need before our meeting."

"I expect they'll allow Beulah to get them for you."

"They had better. When will this autopsy nonsense be over with?"

"No idea. Why don't you ask, Leslie? I'm sure your name will carry weight with the authorities." Anne immediately regretted her flippant childishness — until she noted balefully that, in all seriousness, Leslie was nodding his agreement with her.

Pete Wiggins hung up the phone and made his way to Chief Walker's desk.

The latter was in an impatient mood. After hearing about the visit to Milton Weinert, Pete thought he understood why.

"I don't see why we should spend any more time on this, Pete. Other than the standard divergences in human opinion, nothing unusual has emerged. Did you talk to the Mertons' housekeeper?"

"Yeah. The only exceptional thing seemed to be that the Mertons had a quiet breakfast. Nothing happened to raise his blood pressure. I got the idea that that was not always the case — that mornings were often tense."

"Oh?"

"The housekeeper heard him say that he felt fine — had had a good night's sleep. And he seemed to be in a good mood, ate what he usually did when he was on a diet: cereal and a half of banana — with tea."

"And when he wasn't on a diet?"

"Went for cholesterol-heavy goodies — like pancakes and eggs. Said he yo-yoed between pigging out and sticking to his diet."

"That may explain something about his hypertension." Thad leaned back in his chair, hands locked behind his head. "Seems evident the man had no forewarning of what was going to hit him." Thad rocked back forward. "Do you get the idea, Pete, that most of the faculty we've talked to were less than enthusiastic about their president? Lots of oblique comments and damning with faint praise. They don't come right out and say so . . . "

"Except for Professor Logan," Pete volunteered. "She was pretty savage."

"Not surprising, if you remember the smelly business last spring that Hefner aired in the *Ledger.*"

"Kinda," Pete said and was about to close his book. "One thing maybe I ought to mention, Chief. Something Professor Logan didn't tell me when I interviewed her."

"So?"

"She was in the president's office early yesterday. Quite a stormy session, I gather. Could have raised his blood pressure."

Thad mulled that over a moment. "Logan. I don't recall that her name was in the appointment book."

"I think she just barged in."

"Miss Taper didn't mention it."

"She showed up before Miss Taper arrived."

"According to whom?"

"Joelle Lieberman."

"The Wyndham Hall receptionist?"

Pete nodded, deadpan. "That's the one."

Joelle glanced at her watch. She was supposed to have left for lunch ten minutes ago but had been called back upstairs to do some filing. She had responded with alacrity, but when Phil had taken off after curtly telling her what she was to do, Joelle began glumly working away at the pile before her, muttering a repeated "bor-ing" as folders found their place in the cabinet. The items remaining to be sorted and put away were ticket stubs, receipts, and documents from the dean's trip. Joelle opened the passport and was riffling through it, stopping to examine various exotic entry and exit stamps, when an entry stamp caught her eye. She looked again; there was no mistaking it. Joelle put the passport away and locked the file drawer.

She was solemn, and not a little uneasy. This was not something to gossip about; she could get in trouble. Nor did she dare tell Phil; he would accuse her of spying.

It was a silent group that had left at a little past eleven for the Los Angeles Metropolitan Club where the Board usually met as a convenience to the majority of the members. Anne and Turner, at Filmore's invitation, rode in his chauffeur-driven Mercedes: Turner up front, Leslie and Anne in the back seat. Leslie placed his Mark Cross briefcase on the seat between them. It struck her as appropriately symbolic of their relationship. Phil Gertmenian, who took the minutes, Victor Laszlo and Henry Norton, who had decided to attend after all, were in one of the college Subarus.

The agenda of the July meetings of the Board of Trustees was usually a short one. This noon, however, the business for the specially called meetings was serious indeed; the atmosphere at the Executive Committee meeting was leaden. In one of the private dining rooms of the Metropolitan Club, eight trustees plus the college administrators bent over their iced vichyssoise in silence as Leslie described the events of the night before with suitable expressions for the "loss of a loyal friend and a man of extraordinary vision who would have led Tipton College to new heights." Clippings from this morning's LA papers were circulated and satisfaction expressed at Filmore's statement, which had been extensively quoted.

With the preliminaries out of the way, they got down to business over the chicken salad. Phil Gertmenian's notes were sparse, for everything was indeed proceeding as Filmore had anticipated. "Moved and voted: That Leslie Filmore, representing the Executive Committee, serve as interim president of Tipton College until such time as a replacement be found for the late Julian Merton."

At the meeting an hour later of the full Board, old Harvey Gillespie, '35, an honorary but still voluble member, asked why the trustees were getting involved with running the college. He was quickly silenced by Jerry Lazeroff, an equally voluble but more intimidating active trustee who, as his courtroom performances usually proved, could persuade even the most intransigent that black was at least gray. In this case he pointed to the importance of disrupting as little as possible the serious business of the college; the dean and the other officers of Tipton needed to have their hands free to take care of their own highly sensitive and essential duties. He pooh-poohed the idea that the announcement of Leslie's temporary position would unleash faculty paranoia; the immediate creation of a Search Committee would make it clear to the faculty that there was no hidden agenda to menace its autonomy. Finally, with a shrug to indicate the obvious conclusion to be drawn, Jerry said the magic words: ten million dollars, the Weinert gift. Phil noticed the look exchanged between Helen Finch and Sam Bernheim and the sour expression on the basset face of Mort Krauter, an alumnus of the college. But no hand was raised, no objections put forth, or further comments made. Everyone seemed sunk in a morass of depression.

Sally Cochran chairman of Ways and Means, briskly moved acceptance of the Executive Committee's recommendation. The nomination was seconded after a fulsome but mercifully short speech by Neville Barnes, chairman of Academic Affairs, on Filmore's contributions and self-sacrifice. To no one's surprise he was voted president pro tem by acclamation. Leslie's gracious remarks of acceptance were followed by praise of the college's "splendid administrative team on which I shall rely heavily," and an encomium of the late president of Tipton. In conclusion, he requested a minute of silence in Julian Merton's memory. It was then moved and voted that the Board's deepest expression of sympathy be transmitted to the late president's widow and family. Phil checked his watch and wrote: "There being no further business, meeting adjourned, 2:45 p.m."

Beulah Taper came out of the Burckhardt Room wondering why she had ever thought of Julian Merton as erratic and difficult. Looking at the organizational plan Filmore had dictated to her, Beulah was tempted to tear it up. Such nonsense, when there was a thick folder of urgent matters pending: the deadline for signing the contract to bring the Arrington dormitory up to code; the revised plan for the new fund-raising campaign to review; the presidential OK urgently needed on the reorganization of alumni support groups — all matters now to be delegated to the Executive Administrators, who were to prepare summaries of their decision-making rationale. She was beginning to understand why someone had called Filmore a "big-picture man."

Leslie Filmore had dictated his own announcement of his election as acting president with instructions to send it to the News Bureau for general media distribution, including, of course, the *Chronicle of Higher Education.* As she typed it, Beulah reflected that other smart businessmen had been defeated by the mysterious ways of academic institutions. It cheered her up to think that Filmore might not be an exception.

At a little before six Beulah reached for the phone, intending to ask Phil whether he would like to come to supper, then thought better of it. If he were there, she would talk. She wouldn't resist telling him about the wine, and for the moment she would prefer not even to think about that herself. Once again, as she returned to typing what had been Julian's last dictated letter (for Mr. Filmore's signature, she thought bitterly), Beulah sent up a small prayer that Mark's testing would prove negative. The more she thought about it, the more she convinced herself that Professor Tidwell would find a logical explanation.

There had been one for the missing folder. After the group had left for the board meeting, Turner's secretary, Crystal Mathews, had dropped it off with, "The president left this with Turner. He said to give it back to you."

It was a copy of Vince Riley's annual report; his memo was still attached: "July 18. V. Riley to President Merton: Annual report, including information on Asian collection. Request meeting with concerned parties. Copy: T. Van Voorhees." "July 19. JM to TVV: Need to meet on this a. s. a. p.," Typical, she thought. The president has often done this, generated a memo on his personal computer and handed it directly to someone without informing her. Well, she wouldn't have to be concerned any more about Julian Merton's indifference to her efforts to have all documents routed through her. She riffled quickly through the report and placed the folder in the files. And that, Beulah thought, was that. She checked her watch. Time to call it a day.

As he rolled off an unsatisfied Crystal Mathews, Willie pontificated in the direction of the ceiling. "They're getting damned worried at TC, you know that? Something's up."

Crystal grabbed for her Virginia Slims on the nightstand.

"Something usually is where you're concerned. But it's a damned cinch it's not your prick. No wonder you're such a lousy fuck, Willie. You're always thinking about what people might be hiding in closets instead of what you ought to be doing in the sack, for Christ sake."

Hefner was unperturbed.

"I ran into Victor Laszlo at the Grapevine. When that old soak won't talk, they're really closing ranks. Nervous about this postmortem, is my guess."

Crystal lighted her cigarette, exhaled noisily.

"You're paranoid. You know that? Just because you didn't get admitted to Tipton when you were a kid."

Willie let the familiar jibe slide; his thoughts were elsewhere.

"It's ironic, Merton packing it in the day Parker-Brown gets back."

"If you say so."

Hefner chewed on that for a moment.

"How do you think your boss would bet now on the chances of Weinert's sticking by his offer?"

"Do chickens have lips? For God's sake, why don't you ask him? I'd just bet you would too. Get out of here, Willie."

"But what about dinner?"

"Go home and fix your own." Crystal got out of bed and headed for the bathroom.

Disgruntled, Willie watched her retreating rear. With her thunder thighs and non-figure she ought to be damned grateful to have him in her bed.

Claire Tidwell walked in the backdoor carrying two boxes of raspberries.

"I couldn't resist these at the market, Anne. I know they're your favorite berry."

"Thank you, Claire. Sit down for a moment, won't you? I'm about to have a touch of the grape. White OK for you?"

"Lovely. Then why don't we go out for a bite? Delmonico's maybe."

"Fine with me. But what about Mark?"

"He's already eaten and gone back to the lab. Seems to be excited about something, poor dear."

"Why 'poor dear'?" Anne handed Claire a glass of wine and joined her at the kitchen table.

"Sometimes I think he keeps at his research as a matter of habit. A way to stay alive. It's not often he seems really steamed up." She sighed.

"Well, that's good, isn't it? A breakthrough maybe? So what's there to sigh about?"

"Oh nothing, nothing. But he's being secretive. And you know my low threshold for tolerating that."

Anne smiled over the rim of her glass. "You'll worm it out of him."

"Oh sure." Claire set her glass down, made a few circles with it before asking, "Anne, are you grieving?"

Anne thought a long moment before answering. "I don't really know. So I suppose that means I'm not."

"He was a strange and complex man. It seems even stranger that he should die as he did."

Anne frowned. "What do you mean by that, Claire?"

The latter made a vague gesture. "Cardiac arrest . . . When you think of his ambition, his arrogance — and yes, his brains . . . It seems so — so banal."

Anne said nothing. They drank their wine in silence.

Mark Tidwell, wearing a lab coat and gloves, turned from his work table as the security chief poked his head in the lab door.

"Evening, Héctor."

"You're working pretty late, aren't you, Professor?"

Mark looked at the clock on the wall: 11:45. "You're right. We emeriti have to be careful not to get in the way of the active workers in the vineyard, Héctor."

"You've never stopped being active, if you ask me, Professor Tidwell. Unlocking the secrets of the universe."

"You're very poetic tonight."

Héctor laughed, stroked his luxuriant mustache. "My youngest told us that at dinner. He said that's what scientists did."

"I guess some of us try. Though some secrets may be more mundane than others."

"Well, good night, Professor. And don't work too late."

Mark took a syringe and drew off two hundred microliters of wine for the first injection. An hour later, three mice injected with graded doses of untainted wine were exhibiting various stages of inebriation; of the six injected with graded doses of wine from Beulah's bottle, three were actively running around in their cage; three lay dead before him. Mark picked one up in his gloved hands and carefully pinned it out on a board. With scissors he made a ventral incision, carefully removed blood from the aorta, and proceeded to take tissue samples from the heart and lungs. As he snipped out bits of tissue Mark kept thinking about how this specimen had died. It reminded him of something that kept tickling the back of his mind. He had pinned out the second mouse, when it occurred to him. He needed to check out the freezer in the organic substance storeroom. If what he was thinking of was still there, he would have to raid Zoology for more specimens. The security guard had been partially right after all. There was indeed a secret to be unlocked in this lab. It would reveal nothing about the universe, but it could lead to something very ugly hidden at Tipton College. To something and to someone.

FRIDAY, JULY 21

CISSY MERTON, WEARING THE SHORTEST of red shorts and a purple T-shirt emblazoned in sequins with the name of an "in" rock band, The Styrofoam, sauntered into the breakfast room and sat down opposite her mother. She answered Priscilla's good morning with something inaudible and, bracelets jangling, reached for her glass of orange juice.

Priscilla put down the paper, turned it over as though to hide the obituary page she had forced herself to read. She swallowed the remarks that came to mind on the bad taste of Cissy's get-up or the outrageous makeup and settled for what she hoped would be a nonconfrontational comment.

"Cissy, would you please take pity on the linen napkins and use a paper one."

"Huh?"

"Lipstick stains are so very hard to get out, you know."

"Isn't that what Super-Bright-O is for? OK. I'll dab genteelly." She proceeded to do so in what she took to be a killing take-off on elegant behavior.

"You're grotesque."

Cissy yawned. "Sticks and stones, as they say."

Priscilla took a deep breath. "I'm not fooled, Cissy. I recognize this rebellious behavior as a sign of your anger and frustration . . . "

"Don't give me that pop psych stuff, Mother."

"Oh, Cissy. We should be helping each other, supporting each other . . . "

The fifteen-year-old reached languidly for an English muffin which she began to butter with exaggerated care.

"If we can't talk, can we at least call a truce?"

"OK by me."

Mother and daughter continued their breakfast in silence, each staring unseeing out the window into the back garden where Julian's father was reading in the shade of the live-oak tree.

"Mom, when will we know about Dad?"

"Know what?"

"Whether he was murdered or not."

Priscilla went white. "Cissy, wha . . . " She put her napkin up to her mouth. "How could you?"

"Well, isn't that what autopsies are all about?"

"You know perfectly well . . . Don't you dare say anything like that again, to anyone. Ever. Do you hear me?"

Cissy shrugged. "Sure. If you say so."

"How is it possible for anyone, even a callow teenager, to be so insensitive to grief?"

"Oh I feel grief, Mother." Cissy's voice hardened. "Grief and disgust at your pretense. You wanted him dead. You and that creepy Logan. The way she was always hanging around you . . . "

Priscilla reached for her cup, threw the remainder of cold coffee in her daughter's face.

"I must have hit a nerve." Defiantly, her face dripping, Cissy left the table.

Phil Gertmenian followed the dean into her office.

"You're looking more rested."

"I went to the track this morning. And even worked out in the weight room for half an hour. That helped. Then I had a leisurely breakfast. What do you think of that?"

"Fine. But I never thought you'd join up with the Fitness Freaks. Some running maybe, but pumping iron . . . I don't know." He shook his head.

"A pretty desultory, off-and-on Freak I'm afraid."

She reached for the messages Phil handed her. "I suppose Mr. Filmore is already in?"

"You suppose right. He's been closeted with Turner since around eight."

Glancing through the slips, Anne noted that Leslie had not asked to see her, a state of affairs that she found more satisfactory than annoying.

"What's this message you have for me from Beulah?"

"Mrs. Merton would like to meet with the two of you this afternoon, if possible. About arrangements for the funeral and for the memorial service in September."

Anne glanced down at her open appointment book.

"Set it up for anytime. There are still tons of letters and phone calls to answer of course, but the afternoon is free. As a matter of fact, Phillip, I think I may find myself with a fair amount of free time on my hands before long. I might even get back to work on the seventeenth-century Jansenist community in Rouen. So, how do you like them apples?"

Phil grinned. This was the more familiar Anne, the spunky Anne he knew and admired. Everything was getting back to normal.

"If you ask me, Turner, most of these sabbatical requests for year after next are boondoggles." Filmore tossed the papers on the desk with a disdainful flip of the hand. "'Eighteenth-century rites of passage in Morocco.' An excuse to lie on the beach, if I ever heard one."

"It may sound suspect, I grant you, but Helga Frantz is a good scholar, I hear. I'm sure that when you go over the list with Anne . . . "

Leslie gestured the idea aside impatiently. "What I'm about to say mustn't leave this room, Turner. The dean has remarkable qualities, but she is too susceptible to special pleading on the part of faculty. I've always suspected it, and going over the few items I've been able to review since Thursday . . . Well, much too easy-going is my impression."

"I doubt that the faculty would agree with you."

"Oh well, faculty . . . " Leslie dismissed them with the wave of the hand. "You've been very helpful, as usual, Turner. If you would work up some models for financing the remodeling costs on the Pusey gym . . . I'd like us to meet with Milton Weinert on that by the end of next week. Possible?"

Turner nodded. "Can do."

Leslie checked his Piaget watch. "Well, fella, time to put on my other hat and head for town. I'm meeting with Milton this afternoon — to reassure him that the college will continue on course as usual."

Mary muttered as the right wheel of her chair caught on a corner of the stone bench near the ramp's incline. Quickly disengaging herself, she propelled herself on down into the basement of Wyndham, stopping at the door to the offices of Buildings and Grounds.

"Morning, Max. Is Vince around?"

Max Dingam, a smiling tub of a man, looked up from his desk.

"Hi, Mary. No, Vince has gone for the day."

"Again? He was in LA most of Wednesday and yesterday."

"Well, you know how it is right before leaving on vacation. They always put a lot on your plate."

Familiar with the ways of "them," Mary nodded. "But this wasn't scheduled, was it?"

"Nope. Turner asked him to check on the custodial services at Cal-Western and Greenleaf College. We're thinking about requesting bids from some new-fangled institutional cleaning services. The boss thought it would be a good idea for Vince to have a look-see at a couple of schools before he leaves town."

"You mean we wouldn't hire our own people any more?"

"Kinda leans that way; it's President Merton's idea. These firms provide the full service shebang and can do it better and cheaper. So they claim."

"Bad idea. I bet Vince doesn't go for that."

Max nodded his agreement. "Shall I give him a message if he does get back early?"

"No need. Thanks anyway, Max."

In the News Bureau, Mary visited a moment with Tom Donaldson, who commented that the media flurry following Julian's death was now subsiding. Or was at least on hold.

"If," he added, "the *Ledger* will follow LA's lead and not make undue inferences about the order for a postmortem."

"Hefner has never had even a nodding acquaintance with taste."

Mary went on into the area that served as her part-time office. An hour later she looked up from her drawing board to see Terry Logan standing there.

"You sure concentrate, Mary."

"Off and on. What can I do for you, Terry?"

"I don't see Tom around, so could I leave this packet with you?"

"Sure."

"It's publicity I've put together for my show at 'Reflections' — and I've included some glossies."

"Thanks. It's too late though, Terry, for us to get any publicity out for tomorrow's opening."

"That's OK. The show will run two weeks. And I sent out invitations myself for tomorrow. Did you get yours?"

Mary nodded. "I'll try to be there."

"Great." Terry started out, then came back. "Mary, do you happen to know anyone around here called Dodie?"

"Dodie? Don't think so. Sounds like a child's name."

"Believe me, it's not a kid, that much I know for sure. See ya."

Mary slipped the glossies out of the manila envelope. The photographs, black and white and harshly lighted, were relentless in their depiction of outsiders and outcasts. Her eye was caught by the picture of a young man whom at first she thought was beautiful in the manner of Michelangelo. But a closer look revealed a sullen look in the large, thickly lashed eyes, a slackness to the sensual lips, slightly opened in a come-on smile; the skin showed a grainy, flaccid quality that seemed to announce the beginning of decay. A typed label was attached to the bottom of the photograph: "Dodie's Friend."

Coroner's case number 95-00612 lay open on the stainless steel autopsy table; a member of the staff stood by, ready to take photographs. Pete Wiggins, representing the Altamira Police Department, had politely refused the examiner's invitation to observe the proceedings more closely and elected to sit on a stool in the corner. He kept his eyes averted from the cadaver, but the smell of formaldehyde and other noxious fluids was overwhelming. He tried thinking, with small success, of mountain streams, gardens, fields bright with spring flowers.

The medical examiner shoved his glasses back up on his nose and continued dictating into his cassette recorder. "The unembalmed body is that of a forty-four-year-old white male weighing one-hundred-eighty-four pounds and measuring seventy-three and a half inches. The scalp is covered with blond hair with a scattering of gray hairs at the temples and around the ears. The eyes are blue . . . "

Mary finished drying their supper dishes, then went down the hall and into the guest bedroom that Vince had converted into a home office. Hunched over his computer, he didn't turn as she rolled up beside him, stroked the back of his neck.

"Mm. That feels good." He leaned over sideways and kissed her.

"I'd better get on home. You've got lots to do if you still expect to get away by two."

"Sometimes I wonder whether it's worth it for a three-week vacation. But don't go. Stay and be my inspiration."

"That's a new name for it." She peered toward the screen. "'For inventory file: status report on Asian collection, Wyndham Hall.' Do you need inspiration for that?"

"A tedious job. And the Mac won't do it all, even though it's advertised as 'user friendly.' Which is more than I can say of you, Miss Feisty."

"I thought I was a very friendly user."

"I'm not talking sex. Something more important."

"What could that be?"

"Cooking. You had harsh things to say about my five-vegetable casserole."

She squeezed his neck. "Honesty compels. You and Thad are the only *cordons noirs* I've ever known."

Vince shook his head. "Your poor brother. He deserves better than to be stuck with an impudent child of the Sixties."

"An anachronism! I wasn't more than a first grader when the hippies began to sprout."

"You probably caught the spirit of rebellion by osmosis."

She was suddenly serious, her voice low. "I've got to rebel, Vince."

He took both her hands, kissed them. "I know, my darling, I know." He smiled at her. "Just the same, don't take it out on Thad."

"I'll be better. Promise."

He kissed her hands again. "Now, let me get back to work."

"You're pretty good now with your toy."

"Mm. Sure made writing the annual report a lot easier this year. And here's the printout of things to do while I'm gone."

"Bossy." Mary glanced at the paper he handed her. "Other than filling the sheet with x's and o's you haven't written much."

"You're a woman without sentiment."

Mary looked down at the printout sheet again. "I see I don't have to defrost."

"Nope. That's done. And I've stopped the paper."

"Then what's left to do? Check your mail?"

"Right. That is, if you want to collect examples of my passionate prose."

"And for that I need a list?"

"Insurance." Vince grinned. "By the way, I suppose you prefer that I write you at this address?"

"Absolutely. Discretion above all things."

"Mary, are you certain Thad hasn't figured this out?"

She nodded. "Brothers, I'll have you know, older brothers in particular, don't often think of sisters 'that way.' And in my case, well . . . "

"The latest Mary Walker theory on sibling relationships, huh? It will stand up as well as a thin reed in a high wind."

"I thought it sounded plausible." She hugged him, rubbing her face against his shoulder. "I'll be off. Since you've got so much to do."

Vince frowned. "I could have finished this earlier, damn it, if I hadn't had to go haring all over the map these last three days. I guess Turner is going ahead with Merton's idea — just plain foolishness. We've got good people working for us. Can you imagine replacing Jeff, as a for instance, with some member of an outside cleaning team?"

"No, I can't. Don't get excited. You'll win the argument."

Vince grunted his scepticism.

"As I said, I'm for home. I'll leave you with the mysteries of Baja Wyndham."

"You're not kidding. Mysteries is right."

"Mm. Intriguing. What's up?"

"I'm not sure. Nothing, maybe." He turned to her. "Honey, I've really got to finish this . . . "

"OK, OK, I'm leaving." Mary headed for the door, then stopped. "Might you come over before you leave?"

"I'm planning to. See what a romantic guy you've turned me into?" He got up, lifted her in his arms and held her to him for a long kiss.

"Oh mister. That's not nice. Not when a girl has to leave."

"You don't have to."

"I thought you were in such a rush with your work."

"I can change my mind, can't I? Certain things have a higher priority."

"I love it when you're greedy. But any more dalliance tonight and you'll still be here when the sun rises." He set her down gently. "You will write from brother George's? And tell me all about the hermit's life?"

"You bet. I may even telephone."

"You mean to say he'll let you leave the mountain?"

"Little Georgie isn't all that weird. He enjoys a weekly visit to Wild Harry's Bar and Grill. Gets local color for his stories."

"Has he ever sold one?"

"Well — not yet."

Mary laughed and blew him a kiss. "See you later. Oh, before I forget, if you do call, phone me at the office. OK?"

"Will do." He called after her. "Don't wait up, Mary. It could be awfully late. I won't stop in if I don't see a light at the back door."

"Fat chance."

"That's what I want to hear." Vince smiled and returned to his typing: "Part 3. Copy of original inventory of the Lawrence and Penelope Croft collection of Asian art objects. Report on missing items."

Mary Walker, waiting for Vince, sat in the dark near the living-room window that faced the street, her sketch pad held to catch some light from the street lamp at their front walk. As she drew, concentrating on the contrast between the aureole at the top of the standard, the concentric circles of light cast by the lamp, and the shadowy forms of the bushes and houses across the street, a jogger came by, head down, hands loose. Hadn't she seen him before? Night before last? Only this time he — or she — stayed on the Walkers' side of the street. He, probably. The runner seemed too tall and lanky for a woman. With rapid strokes Mary sketched the figure, eyes following the bobbing form as it disappeared out of the circle of light and around the bend of Vince Riley's hedge. Californians, she thought as she jotted down, "Dark suit, cap with colored stripe (orange? red?)," Californians are indeed the world's greatest kooks. Who else would be out jogging at one in the morning? Who else would be sketching after a midnight roll in the hay? She put her work aside, closed her eyes and thought about Vince. Her lover. She savored the word, saying it softly aloud like an incantation: "My lover." The words soothed her anxiety and soon transported her fretful mind into a world of remembrance, of images that gently slipped into those of dream.

The runner carefully circled past the kitchen door to a lighted window. The room was empty. A moment later, Vincent Riley, in his bathrobe, came in and sat down at his computer. The desk was close to the window, but the machine was placed so that the screen was hidden from view. Angel's friend was conscious of a constricted throat, a looseness in the bowels, a racing pulse. The same unexpected yet strangely exhilarating sensations experienced when Angel was dying. The friend started for the kitchen entrance, then stopped at the sound of a car braking in front of the house.

Someone knocked at the back door. Pulling his robe tighter around him, Vince went to answer it, returned, followed by Max Dingam. The latter took a chair and waited while Vince finished his typing. After about five minutes, Riley got up. At the window, Angel's friend could see a corner of the screen go dark. Max Dingam disconnected the machine. The two men chatted a minute, then Max left with the computer in his arms. Angel's friend swore silently. Tomorrow morning that computer would have to be checked out. Now, there was something else to be done. Something distasteful. But an efficient and straightforward way out of a spiraling entrapment. And Grammy had taught Dodie that the straightforward way was always the best way.

SATURDAY, JULY 22

Mary Walker was staring idly into a steaming cup of tea when her sleepy-eyed brother, his hair still tousled, ambled in to join her at the breakfast table Thad's mumbled good morning was swallowed by a mighty yawn.

"Well, big Bro, what sexy tonsils."

"Sorry, Miss Manners. How about a little gracious pouring out?"

"Would you rather have coffee?"

"No, that smells lovely. What is it?"

"Sorry to say it is not Castleton Special Finest Tippy Golden Flowery Orange Pekoe."

"In other words, First Flush Finest Lipton Tea Bag."

"Show off." Mary served her brother his tea. "Thad, did you hear Vince take off early this morning?"

"No. Why?"

"Well, it's just strange." Taking her brother's silence for interest, Mary went on to elucidate. "He always starts out before dawn this time of year — to beat the desert heat."

"Stubborn old coot refuses to have a car with an air conditioner."

"That's not the point."

Thad set his cup down and leaned against the back of the banquette. "Sorry, Mary, I'm lost."

"Vince was going to drop by. And I was up until after two."

"Silly thing to do."

"You may be right. My sketch doesn't look so great this morning."

He reached for a slice of buttered toast. "What were you working on?"

"Oh — a charcoal study I've been playing with a couple of days — street light and shadow. Damn it, I fell asleep. Can't believe I konked out like that. Still, I had the backdoor light on."

Thad put his cup down, looked curiously at his sister. "Why are you upset?"

Mary tried for a casual shrug. "I'm not."

"It would sure fool a stranger."

"There's no need to give me your copper's look, Thad."

Her brother returned his attention to his breakfast. "Maybe he was delayed and hasn't left yet."

"I've telephoned and there's no answer."

"Well then." Thad felt a surge of impatience. "For crying out loud, Mary. So Vince took off on vacation without stopping by for once. What's the big deal?"

The big deal, Mr. Policeman, is that I am madly in love with a fifty-two-year-old man who lights up my life. A man who loves me tenderly — the crippled me and the whole me that still lives on inside this battered, depleted body. But Mary didn't say that. She tossed it off instead. "Oh, you know me; like to keep the little rituals in order. It's not important."

Thad Walker hadn't been in his office very long when the call came through. He hung up the phone and punched in Pete Wiggins' extension. "Pete? It's now official. Some calcification of the aorta and a fair amount of arterial sludge, et cetera. What Dr. Lowenthal will call predictable. They're sending the autopsy report over by messenger."

"Have you heard from criminalistics?"

"About the trace evidence? Nothing on the plastic cup — the cocktail napkin explains that; nothing clear on it either. As for the phone, they could only lift the one thumb print; it was his."

"That still strikes me as odd, Thad."

"Oh, I don't know. It looks like the other prints were smeared. Could have been done by his coat sleeve."

"I guess."

"Cheer up. You'll get more than your fill of violent crime before you're through, Pete. Be glad we can put this case to bed."

A short time later, Thad placed the autopsy report in Julian Merton's file folder; the drawer rolled shut with the smooth sound of finality.

Priscilla Merton hung up the phone and went into the family room where her daughter and father-in-law faced each other over a Scrabble board.

"That was Chief Walker, Father Merton. He's received the coroner's report. There was absolutely no need to put us through all this. It was cardiac arrest, of course. The arteries were severely blocked."

Cissy looked up from studying her tiles. "By what?"

Her mother didn't look at her. "Cholesterol deposits. What else?"

Eyes swimming, Priscilla sank into the third chair at the table, absently fingered some loose tiles. After a moment her father-in-law suggested gently, "Priscilla, would you like me to inform the funeral parlor?"

She nodded, then looked up, automatically wiping around her eyes to avoid smearing her makeup.

Cissy made a harsh sound. "Oh brother."

"I suppose we need to set a date for the services. This is Saturday . . . Wednesday perhaps. Just a simple graveside service, I thought — after the cremation. Just us, the Lowenthals — and I think I should invite the trustees and . . . "

Cissy got up, knocking over her chair, and bolted from the room.

Neither her mother or grandfather commented on her departure.

"The funeral director can help you with all the details, Priscilla. Why don't I ask him to come by the house?"

"Oh please. And thank you."

Wednesday. Four more days to get through. Then it would be over.

Chief Walker got to his feet, extended a hand to greet the tall white-haired man who had just been shown into his office — an old acquaintance and his idea of the distinguished professor.

"Mark, please, sit down."

Mark Tidwell took the chair indicated, placed a battered briefcase on the floor beside it. "Feels good in here. Hot as the hinges outside."

Thad tipped back in his desk chair. "I never had the opportunity to tell you how much I enjoyed the Patterson Lectures this spring. DNA remains a mystery, I'm afraid, but it was a rare treat to listen to a scientist as distinguished as Barton Phelps."

"Glad to hear it. It's not easy to get a good turnout for such specialized talks. The Science Division appreciates your fidelity." Mark picked up the briefcase, opened it. "I've got a confession to make, Thad."

"Like priests, the police are always ready to hear one." His smile faded as he began to sense the extent of Mark Tidwell's discomfort. "Is this serious?"

By way of an answer, Mark removed a plastic sack from his case, placed it on the Chief's desk.

Thad brought his chair forward. "A bottle of wine?" He peered through the plastic. "Correction. A partially empty bottle of wine."

"What remains is a Sauternes heavily laced with crème de cassis and what I'm pretty sure is anatoxin-a. That's an alkaloid toxin isolated from *Anabaena flos-aquae*."

"What?"

"A waterbloom. A blue-green alga."

"You're 'pretty' sure?"

"Call it an educated guess. Toxicologists working in this area refer to it, the exotoxin derived from toxic strains of the waterbloom that is, as VFDF or very-fast-death factor."

"How fast?"

"That I couldn't say without further experimentation and study of the literature. Based on my calculations, the correct lethal dose could kill a man in as little as two to three minutes. Maybe less. Providing a highly toxic strain of *Anabaena flos-aquae* was used."

"And what would be the cause of death?"

"Shock, circulatory collapse, leading to cardiac arrest of course."

Thad's friendly expression had shifted to one that was less relaxed.

Mark plowed on. "The thing is, it seems highly probable that this cocktail was served at the party for Ward Finlay last Wednesday."

Thad stared.

"And most probably to Julian Merton."

"But that's not possible. I just spoke to the medical examiner. He found no evidence of any abnormal pathology — except what could be explained by Merton's physical condition."

"It's very doubtful that an examiner *would* come across detectable pathological changes, unless he knew what to look for. And even then, traces of the toxin may dissipate quite rapidly."

"Any chance this was just a bad bottle of wine?"

Mark shook his head. "Of course, there is the possibility that nothing was poured from the bottle at the reception — but that leaves us without an answer to two questions: why was it there and what was it doing in the trash can?"

Thad struggled with his irritation. "Maybe you had better tell me how you stumbled onto all this."

Thad Walker listened in glum silence as Professor Tidwell recounted Beulah's visit to his office and his subsequent experiments.

"I've been racing against the clock, Thad. And you understand I'm out of my field. So my methodology wouldn't stand as a textbook model."

Mark pulled at his collar as though to ease his professional discomfort.

"Go on."

"A pal in the Zoology Department gave me some of their snake food. Enough for my limited experiments and for a small control group. The mice I injected intraperitoneally with untainted Château d'Yquem may have hangovers, but they are alive. Of the ones I injected with varying amounts of that stuff —" he gestured toward the bottle on Thad's desk — "three survived, three are dead. One of those died in a little under two minutes. As a check, I experimented with three more animals, and got the same fatal reactions."

"So you have an idea of the sub-lethal dose and the minimum lethal dose?"

"Not highly refined, but, yes, an idea."

"But you didn't give any of your specimens oral doses?"

"That's right. So I'm uncertain as to any significant differences in time or amounts. There may not be much, if any. The thing is, the stuff works. And very fast."

Thad looked at him, unsmiling.

"You understand, Thad, I was unable to isolate and identify this toxin from the tissue samples I took. I suppose the crime lab will want to run a gas chromatographic-mass spectroscopic analysis. To separate and characterize the separate components."

"Oh. Then why are you confident that this poison is ana — what?"

"Anatoxin-a. To answer your question, I don't know whether to call it a hunch, a leap of faith, or a feeling of *déjà vu*. All three maybe. Something kept nagging at my brain while I was working. Then there was the behavior of the mice — the paralysis, tremors, mild convulsions. It finally hit me. I was reminded of Charlie Peese and his experiments."

"Peese? Do I know him?"

"Maybe not. Charlie retired some twenty years ago. Died last May. Professor Peese was primarily a toxicologist. He'd been working on the toxic properties of waterbloom for years. His cultures are gone, of course, but he had developed a procedure for isolating the toxin; some of the yield was still in the freezer of the organic substance storeroom."

"In what form?"

"A green syrup."

"Go on."

"The response of the mice I injected with that stuff was very similar to those I had treated with the tainted wine."

Thad frowned. "I suppose I should thank you, Mark, but tampering with evidence is hardly legal."

"Can't we refer to town-gown cooperation, Thad? Isn't Tipton always ready to have its resources serve the community?"

The chief's smile was on the sour side. "You're an old fox, Mark. You may have saved the crime lab some trouble, nonetheless the toxicologists downtown will need to run their own tests — if that's still possible. He tilted the bottle. "Is there enough left?"

"I think so. The bottle was about a fourth full when I got hold of it."

"Which suggests that it was partially emptied before the poison and cassis were added. And one drink poured out — unless he has kept some in reserve. Or she," Thad added grimly.

Mark nodded agreement.

"What I don't understand, is why the person didn't empty the bottle before putting it in the trash can."

"As Beulah described the set-up for that party, there wasn't any place to empty it — except in the trash can itself. For whatever reason, time factor or someone interrupting him, the killer just shoved the bottle way down in. If it had been me, I would never have dreamed that anyone would retrieve a bottle out of the garbage."

"Mm — maybe."

"Thad, you'd best keep the stuff under refrigeration." Professor Tidwell began to dig around in his briefcase. "Here's a copy of my findings — and some vials of formaldehyde with the tissue samples I snipped out, also some blood samples. You can tell the forensic people that I've frozen the carcasses of the mice I used in the tests — in case they're interested."

Thad drawled, "Looks like you've thought of everything."

Mark ignored him. "I've also included a Xerox of the article Charlie wrote for the college magazine and some of his lab notes that I thought might be useful."

Thad took the folder along with the vials and jars Mark handed him. "I suppose there isn't a prayer of lifting any prints off the bottle — if the custodian has handled it, then you and Beulah. But no doubt the inventor of the sudden-death cocktail would have taken the usual precautions."

"Beulah and I tried to be careful." Mark's bushy eyebrows went up as he smiled. "TV has gone far in educating us laymen in police procedures, Thad."

Chief Walker didn't appreciate the pleasantry. "I'm still missing an explanation, Mark. If you thought there was something suspicious, why the devil did you and Miss Taper go off on your own? Or did you get that idea from TV as well?" Mark Tidwell studied his L. L. Bean camp moccasins. "Damn it, Mark, you've thrown me for a loop."

"I'm sorry. But to answer your question. Beulah and I *were* uneasy. As a matter of fact we felt damn foolish. Hard to believe there was anything wrong, except with our aging imaginations."

"You folks will take quite a few risks to protect the good name of Tipton College, won't you?"

Mark looked thoughtful. "You might say we weren't keen for the media people, Willie Hefner in particular, to get hold of this. Everything eventually leaks out to that guy. The idea of a poison rumor starting, well . . . "

"Apparently it's more than a rumor, isn't it? Who else knows about the results of these experiments of yours ?"

"Well, Beulah, naturally. I phoned her first thing this morning. And she felt the dean of the college had to be told. Beulah's with her now."

"You might have left that up to us, Mark."

"Now see here, Thad. You couldn't expect her not to be up front with the Chief Executive Officer of the college ."

"I thought Tipton had an acting president."

Mark looked uncomfortable. "I tend to forget about that. Anyway, I hear he's out of town."

"But your dean will inform him?"

"Presumably." Thad Walker sighed. "I'm sure you needn't question the discretion of the officers of the college."

"Possibly not." Thad jotted down a note to himself before continuing. "It still means the word will be out before the coroner's official findings are. If you're right, that word will be murder."

The word was out and between them now, the one that both had avoided. Mark brightened momentarily. "There's always the possibility they won't confirm my experiments. As I said, whoever concocted this drink may have decided against using it."

"Yeah." The Chief didn't look or sound hopeful. "Any idea how someone could have gotten his hands on this stuff?"

"Afraid so." Mark Tidwell knew he had to take another header. "From the freezer in the organic substance storeroom — in my own department."

"You mean deadly stuff like that is just lying around?"

"Not any more."

"And just what does that mean?"

"As I said, I got the syrup I used for testing from the freezer in the organic substance storeroom." He hesitated before continuing. "I took toxin samples from one bottle. The inventory lists two bottles of anatoxin-a. If the record is accurate, a second bottle is missing. One labelled 'Anatoxin-a from NRC-forty-four.'"

"What's the NRC business?"

"A highly toxic *Anabaena* strain."

Mark Tidwell eased himself into the seat of the corner banquette in Solly's Coffee Shop, a café rarely frequented by the college crowd. A teen-age wonder in hip-hugging jeans, halter top, and a wind-storm hair-do set off by a large acid green bow, slouched over to take his and Beulah Taper's order. As she moved off, neither one seemed eager to begin a conversation. Beulah took a sip of water, Mark inspected the silverware, then finally, "You've seen Anne? What did she have to say?"

"Very little." She shrugged. "Anyway, it's done. What about you?"

"Thad's face did not light up with joy. The police have this strange preference for collecting and handling physical evidence themselves."

"I'm so sorry I got you into this."

He smiled reassuringly. "I'm a big boy, Beulah. Quite capable of saying no. I couldn't resist the temptation."

"What temptation?"

"Oh . . . Of a little laboratory adventure; of trying to solve a riddle. Even," he sighed, "if I had to rob my own small cellar of my one and only precious bottle of Yquem. Needless to say, I shall treat Claire and myself to what's left."

She would never understand scientists, she thought. "Mark, have you any idea of who could have gotten hold of this awful . . . stuff?"

"Too many people, unfortunately. The security in the Chemistry Department isn't as tight as it might be." He gave her a lop-sided grin. "Just ask my wife."

"But who would know about it, outside of . . .?"

He finished for her. "Myself? The entire department, lab assistants, some students. Plus any of the however-many-thousand people who receive *Topics*. Which includes the entire faculty and staff of the college."

"What are you saying?"

"Just that there was a very thorough treatment of Charlie Peese's work on blue-green algae and their toxic properties in this spring's issue of the magazine." Mark zipped off the plastic from a package of soda crackers and began to munch. "But to be sensible and narrow the field a bit, the most likely hypothesis is that it was one of us."

"You sound almost cheerful."

He shrugged. "Man is a perverse animal, girl. I guess we scientists are near the head of the parade. You know what odd ducks we are, Beulah. Puzzles turn us on."

"Well, for my part I am definitely not 'turned on.'"

Professor Tidwell nodded approvingly at her. "That's because you're that rare creature: a thoroughly nice woman."

Beulah let the remark ride. "Then someone, anyone among fifty-odd people . . . " She broke off, appalled.

"Time to get your photographic memory working."

Embarrassed, Beulah glanced down at her lap, smoothed out the paper napkin. "That's a myth, Mark. I — I may have a good memory, but no more than that. And there was so much coming and going . . . " She looked up to say with faint hope, "Maybe they won't find anything. Maybe President Merton wasn't poisoned."

"I wish I thought there was a chance of that."

Beulah hesitated before asking, "Don't they say that poison is a woman's weapon?"

"Yep, that's what they say. If true, then that narrows the field, doesn't it?"

Mark Tidwell knocked at the partially open door with the inscription "Stockroom Manager" and looked in.

"Got a moment, Ulrich?"

A short somewhat stooped man of fifty-odd years rose, wiping his mouth as he did so. "Sure, Professor." The German accent was as unmistakable as the manners. "Please, come in, come in. Excuse me, I was just finishing my lunch."

Mark glanced at the plate and cutlery neatly laid out on a red and white check napkin. "Ever true to pumpernickel I see, Ulrich."

"With a good Münster, it's the best, Professor. Please, have some."

"Thanks, no. Just finished lunch myself. Ulrich, I wonder whether you've seen anyone go into the organic substance room recently. Or seen someone near it. Someone not from our department."

Ulrich bowed his head in thought. "No, Professor. But nobody could without a key, *nicht?*" He smiled and wagged a finger at Mark. "During the summertime I can keep after you guys a little better and see that the door is locked."

Mark reflected that the "little better" was an exaggeration. "Right, Ulrich. Well, have you noticed anyone here on the second floor recently who doesn't belong in the building?"

"You mean someone suspicious?"

"Not necessarily. But an outsider. A non-science faculty member, or someone from Wyndham Hall, for instance."

"Mein Gott, Professor. How long ago are we talking about?"

It was now over two months since Charlie Peese had been taken off to the hospital where he was to die five days later. The murderer could safely have wandered in and out anytime since then. Still, Mark Tidwell felt compelled to persist.

"Well, let's start with this past week."

Ulrich thought a moment, then shook his head. "I just can't remember, Professor Tidwell. Except for Mr. Laszlo. He came to see the chairman. And he stopped and asked about my mother on his way out — like he always does. Then I think that, what's her name, a blond lady with a fancy hair-do that works for Mr. Van Voorhees?"

"Miss Mathews."

"Ja. That's the one. She came over looking for the Psychology Department — had some papers for Mrs. Professor Tidwell. She must be new, *ja?"*

"Fairly new, I believe."

"Dean Norton is in and out. But he still has his office here, so he can't count as an outsider, *nicht?*" Ulrich ruminated a moment longer. "Then I remember seeing Dean Parker-Brown. That I remember because she didn't stop to say hello like she always does. And I wondered if something was the matter."

"When was that, Ulrich?"

The man shook his head. *"Keine Ahnung.* I just couldn't say."

"Could it have been Wednesday, the nineteenth?"

"Maybe. Maybe not. I know it wasn't Thursday or yesterday. Tuesday or Wednesday maybe."

"Do you remember where you saw her?"

"Ja. Sure. She was just outside there — in the hall."

"How long was she there?"

"I don't know. I was over there by the files — happened to look up. Dean Parker-Brown was going by — just outside."

"Where did she go?"

Ulrich shrugged. "I was going to say hello, but she went by too fast."

"Any idea what time it was, Ulrich?"

Ulrich concentrated. "About this time, I think. *Ja.* I always catch up on the filing pretty soon after lunch."

"Well thanks, Ulrich." He added the customary admonition, knowing it wouldn't be heeded: "And remember it's Saturday. You ought to go home."

"*Ja,* but there are things to do. You know me, Professor, I'm not a union clock-watcher. That's what's the matter nowadays, too many union clock-watchers."

Mark Tidwell gave the customary agreement and left, grateful for Ulrich Geisler's trustful mind-set that would never question the reason for the inter-rogation. Professor Tidwell did not feel cheered by one of the answers he had received. Not Thursday or Friday, Ulrich had said. That left Wednesday, the day of Anne's return, as the only possibility. "Just outside," Ulrich had said. Just outside his office was the entrance to the organic substance storeroom. He shook his head as if to clear it, to get it back on a sensible track.

A dreadful thing had happened. The lives of a number of people at the college would now be wreathed around by suspicion. And he was largely responsible.

Mary Walker finished her late lunch and rolled over to check the window thermometer: 102 de-grees outside — and obviously smoggy. Mary briefly considered going to see *Waiting for the Moon* at the Criterion, then opted for finishing the Alumni News notes for the next issue of *Topics.*

Baja Wyndham would be a cool place to work, as would be the gym for an early evening workout.

Mary stashed the few dishes in the washer, grabbed her purse and a favorite dilapidated straw hat, and wheeled herself down the ramp at the front door. She looked toward Vince's place and felt the familiar tug of longing. Where was he by now? Better than half-way? She stopped at Vince's mailbox, retrieved a telephone bill and a couple of pieces of junk mail. She had reached the walkway that led around to the rear of the house when the automatic sprinkling system came on with a whoosh, blocking her way to the backyard and the ramp that was her access to the house. Quickly she backed off. There was nothing that couldn't wait.

Anne Parker-Brown had almost finished hosing down her driveway when she spotted Mark Tidwell coming across the lawn.

"Anne, do I owe you an apology?"

Anne turned off the water and sat down on a bench under the old deodar tree at the curb. She motioned to Mark to join her.

"That's for you to decide, Mark. Anyway, had you and Beulah consulted me first, I'm not sure what I would have done. It's Filmore who has blood in his eye."

"Lord, I didn't think of that."

Anne's smile was rueful. "It was not an easy phone call to make. Bad publicity is his main concern, of course — not whether someone wanted to kill Julian."

"Does that idea seem farfetched to you, Anne?"

Anne rose and wiped at the back of her jeans. "That bench is damp — you'd better not sit there."

She began to coil up the hose, and after an uncomfortable moment of aimless talk Mark headed back next door. Anne obviously didn't wish to discuss the ramifications of possible murder. A singularly unsatisfactory conversation. When he reached his own backdoor it struck him that Anne hadn't answered his question. Nor had she asked for any additional information about his discovery.

Reflections opened onto an alley that ran behind the first block of Main Street. A poster on an easel stood in the small patio that fronted the gallery. "MARGINALS: DESPAIR AND AFFIRMATION — A NEW SERIES OF PHOTOGRAPHS BY TERRY LOGAN." Thad Walker and his sister stopped to study the photo that Terry had selected to announce her exhibit: an ancient bag lady, a shapeless mass of heterogeneous garments and scraggly garden party hat, dozed on one end of a park bench; at the other end, an emaciated youth in a knitted cap sat staring dull-eyed into the camera. His hands, dangling between his knees, were covered with scabs, the nails broken and dirty.

Thad looked down at his sister. "Why do I think we're going to have more despair than affirmation and that this evening will do nothing to lift my spirits?"

"Strong stuff, I know. But you can take it; you're a copper."

"Et tu, disloyal one."

Ignoring him, Mary rolled toward the entrance. "Hi, Deirdre."

Deirdre O'Rourke, a large woman in a silver-embroidered black caftan further enhanced by an imposing Navajo squash blossom necklace in front and a heavy plait of black silver-streaked hair hanging down her back, greeted them effusively. "So glad you could come. You'll love it — wonderful gutsy work." Before they could reply, Deirdre had moved out of the doorway to greet new arrivals. "William, precious . . ."

"I intend to fortify myself with a glass of wine," Thad said. "Would you like one?

"Please."

Mary propelled her chair toward a corner of the main room to wait for Thad's return. The gallery was one large space divided into three by movable partitions. There was a surprisingly good crowd she thought — townspeople and people from the college, including strong representation from the gay community. She turned her chair a bit to study the photographs on the wall to her left. The print she had seen of "Dodie's friend" was hanging there, blown up to a two-and-a-half-by-two foot format. The grainy finish Terry had achieved in the developing process gave a coarse texture to the skin, deepening the contrast between beauty and dissipation. Looking more closely, Mary noticed that the photograph now had another title: "Fallen Angel."

"That's a malevolent smile, don't you think?"

Mary glanced up at a slender young woman with long blond hair.

"You're Mary Walker, aren't you? I'm Ellen Forsythe."

"Of course. Hello." As she took the proffered hand, Mary remembered. Terry Logan's cousin, who had taught some courses in Asian Art and who had shared Terry's house for a while, according to Joelle, just before Terry was caught up in the buzz saw of her review for promotion.

"Do you like the show?" Ellen asked.

"I just got here. But I agree with your comment; there is something evil in that smile."

"Mm. Sad case, this fallen angel."

"You know him?"

"No. Though he lived on my street. His name is Angelo. Angel to his friends."

"I see. Hence the title."

"Mm. Or rather that was his name. Poor kid was found dead just a couple of days after Terry spotted him on the beach and took the picture."

"Somehow it's not a face with a future, is it?" As she spoke, Mary glanced toward the far end of the room, where Thad was standing, a glass in each hand, surrounded for the moment by a group that included Henry and Lucille Norton, the Laszlos and the ubiquitous Professor Fred Zumholtz.

"You two have met, I see." It was Terry, wearing makeup and a skirt for a change, and looking, Mary thought, somewhat less breezy than usual.

"We were just talking about this photograph, Terry," Ellen commented. "I thought you were going to call it 'Dodie's Friend.' Much more suggestive and provocative than 'Fallen Angel.' That's too sentimental."

"Changed my mind. Decided to go for a theological angle."

"I don't believe you. You're up to something."

"Honest. I like 'Fallen Angel' better. Makes a stronger ironic statement."

"If you say so." She shrugged. "Incidentally, there was a short-lived flurry of interest in Angelo's death earlier this week. The Laguna police came back to talk to people on the street."

"Yeah? How come?"

"He had a lot of expensive stuff in the house — jewelry, VCR, stereo system — the works."

Terry nodded. "Figures. Did the fuzz bother you again?"

Ellen shrugged. "Just the usual. Had I ever talked to him, been in his house, et cetera."

"They come up with anything?"

"Not so far as I know. According to neighborhood talk, he was dealing." Ellen lowered her voice. "Did you ever find out who his friend was?"

Feeling out of it, Mary interrupted to offer congratulations to Terry and started to make her way around the room. About to pass Joelle Lieberman and Mitzi Krueger from word processing, she was hailed by the "nerve center of Wyndham Hall."

"Hi, Mary. Mitzi's trying to convince me that this stuff is art. I mean, just look at that." She pointed to a photograph of two elderly women embracing; the hand of one rested on the breast of the other. "I think that's disgusting."

Mitzi, looking avant-garde with a spikey coiffure, long feather earrings and smartly baggy earth-toned pants and jacket, was in sharp contrast to Joelle's curls and flounced green satin dress that accentuated perky breasts. Mitzi assumed a haughty air.

"The trouble with you, Joelle, is that you're a bigot. You have no understanding or tolerance for anything that is outside the confines of your narrow little world. Why can't you see what a statement of affirmation that picture is making? What it says about tenderness? About the deep human needs that exist at any age?"

Mary was about to push on and leave the two to their argument when she stopped on impulse, giving in to what she recognized as idle curiosity.

"Joelle, do you happen to know anyone at the college called Dodie?"

"Dodie?" She thought for a moment, then answered reluctantly, "No, I've never heard the name. Are you sure it's someone at Tipton?"

Mitzi sniffed. "Joelle can't stand the idea that there is anything or anyone at TC that she doesn't know about."

"Hello, Mary." Mary looked up to see Kitty and Turner Van Voorhees smiling down at her.

"Great photography, isn't it?"

From the sound coming from behind her, Mary thought Mitzi must be enjoying a small triumph at Turner's remark.

Before she could answer, Kitty Van Voorhees took up the thread. "I was just telling Turner that my judgment has been confirmed. I already have two Logans, but after seeing this show, the word is 'buy.' It will be a good investment. They'll make great gifts too. I just know Terry is going to make a name for herself."

"I agree with you there."

"For once." Kitty punched her husband playfully. "Mary, did you know that a critic from the *LA Times* is covering the show? That's very significant. I was just talking to him; I'm positive Terry is going to get a smashing review. A nice revenge, if you ask me."

"Revenge?" Turner was frowning.

"But of course. For getting fired. I bet TC is going to feel terribly embarrassed."

Turner took a swallow of his drink. "I doubt that. And she wasn't fired."

"Same as."

Turner ignored the correction. "May I get you something, Mary?"

"Thanks, Turner, but it looks like Thad is coming to the rescue."

Some twenty minutes later Mary took pity on her brother and proposed that they go on home. As they were leaving, a departure frequently cut into by exchanges of greetings and brief conversations, Mary noticed that a number of round red stickers had already been placed by certain photographs, including the now retitled 'Fallen Angel.'

Deirdre O'Rourke bustled over, a box of stickers in her hand. "Isn't this wonderful? They're going like hotcakes. You should buy one, Thad. The one of the two wistful beggar children would make a great statement for your office."

"Oh sure. Walker the sensitive cop. Thanks, Deirdre, but I've seen too many sad marginals in my profession as it is. Afraid I'm a seascape man."

As Thad finished stashing her chair in the back and slid into the driver's seat, Mary noticed a small group consisting of her boss, Phil Gertmenian, and

Dean Parker-Brown walking down the alley toward the gallery.

"Tipton is nothing if not genteel."

Thad turned on the motor. "What?"

"When you think about it, the high tide at which emotions were running last spring, Terry Logan threatening to sue . . . Now just about everybody is showing up for her opening as though nothing had happened."

"Isn't that what civilized people are supposed to do?"

"I guess. Sometimes the nicey-nice veneer gets to me."

Thad finished backing around and headed out the alley. "If you were fifteen years older I'd say you were a child of the Sixties."

"I think I like that." That was what Vince had called her. She looked at her watch. Almost five-thirty. He should have gotten to Chimayo by now, and in another hour would be at brother George's mountain retreat. Tomorrow, she vowed, she'd hang around her office phone, even though it was Sunday.

The gallery was almost ready to close when Angel's friend sought out Terry Logan.

"Splendid show, Terry. Congratulations. But how do you persuade your subjects to pose for you? Like those transvestites in the pub, for instance . . . " The friend listened to the explana-

tion, congratulated her again and moved on —
dissatisfied. Terry had acted as though she knew
nothing, suspected nothing. But as they said good-
bye she had smiled in a funny way. A warning
buzzer went off. Watch it. Watch her.

Back home, Mary called to her brother that she
was going to check next door and rolled down the
walk to the Riley mailbox. Nothing for her from
Vince. Of course not. She had already looked once,
and it was much too soon anyway, but lovers were
given to useless gestures. She checked out the
backyard, where everything looked green and well-
watered, and decided against going on into the
house. Tonight its emptiness would be too hard to
bear. Backing out to the sidewalk she noticed a
corner sprinkler had puddled; she would ask Thad
to fix it tomorrow. A few inches from the puddle
was the imprint of one of her wheels that had rolled
off the walk; planted firmly over it and pointing
toward the backyard was the ridged print of a left
foot running shoe. It looked odd to see a single
print. Surrealistic. Or Zen maybe. Like the sound
of one hand clapping. Muttering "Drop that other
shoe," Mary gave a quick look around for the print
of the right shoe. Failing to find it, she lost interest
and headed for home.

Sunday, July 23

THE SOUND OF THE DOORBELL STARtled her. Beulah grabbed for a paper towel to mop up the spilled coffee on the breakfast table and, tying her housecoat more firmly around her, went to answer it.

A jaunty Phil Gertmenian greeted her. "Well, where have you been keeping yourself the last couple of days?"

Beulah motioned him in.

"You're either tied up with someone at the office, or your home phone is busy — like this morning."

"I was talking to Mrs. Merton. She has another stack of sympathy letters for me to answer. And she wanted to discuss the graveside services."

"Wednesday, right?"

Beulah gave a vague nod, turning away from him to pick up the coffee pot. "Would you like a cup of coffee? I was going to have another."

"I was about to suggest a jaunt to Solly's for Sunday waffles and gossip. But I won't say no to one for the road."

The cup rattled slightly on the saucer she handed him. Phil took it and gave her a searching look.

"You don't look so great. What's the matter, Beulah?"

"This past week — everything . . . "

"It's been hard on you. But everything is settling down OK." He took a tentative sip of coffee. "You don't think so?"

Beulah sat down at the breakfast table, took a handkerchief from her pocket and blew her nose.

"Working for Mr. Filmore is not going to be easy."

Phil took the chair opposite her and reached for the cream pitcher. "You can handle that pompous little fella." She didn't laugh. "Hey, Beulah." Phil reached for her hand, but she drew back.

"He telephoned here last night. I certainly understand why he was angry, nevertheless . . . "

"The s. o. b. didn't fire you?"

She shook her head. "Only because he can't afford to at this time. Phil, I have made such a mess of things . . . " It all came tumbling out then. As she feared it might if she were alone with this particular young friend. Everything she was supposed to keep to herself, everything she had vowed to keep to herself.

When she had finished, Phil was solemn. Damn it, she should have asked Anne's advice. But he couldn't say that to her now.

It was Beulah who said it. "I should have gone to Anne first."

Phil's tone was soothing. "You didn't want to sound the alarm. That's understandable. Pretty wild."

"But don't you see what an investigation could do to Anne? If the coroner agrees with Mark's findings?"

Phil stiffened. "What are you talking about?"

"You know the rumors."

"Oh, that. Sure there will be an embarrassing question or two, but there's nothing to substantiate foolish talk." Beulah said nothing. "Or do you know something I don't?"

"The police can always twist the most innocent thing into, well, something ugly."

"What is there to twist?"

At last she looked him full in the face. "Don't you know, Phil, that Anne got back to the States, to San Francisco, three days before she returned to Altamira?"

"That's nonsense."

"Joelle noticed the entry stamp in her passport, when she was doing some filing for you the other day."

"What! What the hell was she doing poking around? Why didn't she tell me?"

"I think she was afraid to."

"But she told you."

Beulah picked up her coffee cup, then set it down again. "Joelle considers keeping me 'well-informed' as part of her duties."

"I bet. A real little news hen. With a big mouth."

"I'm confident she won't repeat this, Phil. She understands how serious it is."

He looked skeptical. "I wish you'd told me."

"I only heard late Friday afternoon."

"Damn it all. She should have informed me." Phil reflected on the news for a long moment. And why hadn't Anne said anything to him? But then, why hand over the passport for filing if she were concerned about secrecy? As for what lay behind Beulah's distress . . . Phil thought about that a moment, then gave her a searching look.

"Beulah, are you thinking that the president wasn't where he was supposed to be?"

"Of course not." Beulah hoped her tone was convincing.

At 2:30 on this Sunday afternoon with the temperature standing at well over 100 degrees, activity on the Tipton campus was at a complete standstill. Except for Héctor González, no one was around when the van from the LA Coroner's Office pulled up in front of Wyndham Hall. The head of security unlocked the main door and led the three men carrying cases and photographic equipment into the building. When they finished, a college security officer would be stationed in the second-floor foyer and a yellow tape stretched across all entries to the president's office: "Sealed area. Police line. Do not cross."

From his desk in the offices of the *Altamira Ledger* a self-satisfied Willie Hefner dialed Crystal Mathews.

"Guess what we picked up on a scanner just now. 'Death at the hands of person or persons unknown.' . . . Merton, who else? . . . Someone at the station putting out the word to a patrol car. He wasn't shot, stabbed or strangled, so what's left? . . . I'm not gloating. But you gotta admit, babe, I was on target. Things oughta begin to hum in old Altamira. Hottest story since Teddy Roosevelt gave a speech here under the Founders' Oak . . . Now listen, babe, I'm working on an item for tomorrow's edition, and there's something you can do for me . . . "

Priscilla deposited the sack of groceries on the kitchen table and went on through into the family room where the television was blaring.

"Cissy, turn that thing off right now." At the click, Priscilla turned to her father-in-law. "You shouldn't let her inflict her subliterate video shows on you, Father Merton."

Cissy looked up with the expression of sullen defiance that now seemed permanently etched on her face. "I wasn't. I thought there might be a news flash."

Charles Merton went up to his daughter-in-law, put his hand on her arm. It was only then that she noticed how gray he looked.

"What's the matter?"

"We had a call from Chief Walker while you were at the market."

"I was right. I knew I was right."

Her grandfather turned on her. "Cissy, shut up."

"Oh my God. What are you talking about?"

"He wanted to prepare you for the coroner's call. There's some new evidence."

"I — I don't understand."

"The coroner has opened an investigation. They're saying Julian's death . . . " He swallowed hard. "Priscilla, they've found evidence of poison."

"Food poisoning? But that's impossible . . . "

"No, you dope. Daddy was murdered."

Charles Merton took his granddaughter by the shoulders and shook her. Cissy collapsed sobbing against his chest. "Oh, Gramps. Why did she hate him so?"

Priscilla Merton ran from the room and up the stairs. Locking the door behind her, she sat on the edge of her bed, hugging herself like an autistic child. Then she reached for the phone.

Terry Logan was folding laundry when she heard the phone ring. She finished folding the pillow case, then reached for the phone on the kitchen wall.

"Hello?"

"Terry . . . "

"Yes? Hello? Look, wise ass, answer or I'll hang up."

"Terry. It's Priscilla." The sound was choked, barely audible.

"Priscilla — what's the matter?"

"It's Julian. They say he was murdered."

"Priscilla, have you been drinking?"

"It's the police. They say so."

"Is this for real?"

"It must have been at the party. He was poisoned, Terry."

"Do you want me to come over?"

"No." It was almost a screech. Then, calmer, "No, you mustn't."

"Well, what do you want me to do?"

She could hear Priscilla breathing hard over the phone. "Did . . . did . . . I know how much you detested him."

Professor Logan didn't answer.

"I'm sorry — I don't know what I'm saying. I'm sorry. Sorry." Priscilla hung up.

Terry studied the phone in her hand. "The hell you don't know what you're saying, lady." She put it slowly back in its cradle.

Laid out against the foothills some eighteen miles northeast of Pasadena, the town of Altamira had retained something of its "Boom of the 80s" character, though its population had more than quadrupled, to 32,500, since the end of World War II. The orange and lemon groves had all but disappeared. Some of the larger homesites and former grove houses still kept token trees whose fruit was usually left to fall and molder on the ground. A scattering of Victorian-style houses, solid blocks of well-kept homes, lush yards, gardens and flowering trees abounded in the older sections.

Altamira had remained a pretty city, particularly in what was called Old Town, with a largely homogeneous population, and one that was less transient than the usual Southern California model. A sprinkling of Hispanics in the barrio, a narrow strip of land near the old disused railroad tracks, insured the presence of domestic help and gardeners, as did a small number of refugees from Central America. The Asians who had arrived after the end of the Vietnam war had almost all entered the middle class by now and had either moved away or purchased homes in one of the developments to the east.

Altamira was no stranger to violence, though the town prided itself on a strong neighborhood watch program and a crime rate that was lower than its surrounding neighbors. There were the usual break-ins, vandalism and petty thefts. Child abuse cases and cases of battered wives were blessedly rare, rape significantly less so, particularly when the college was in session. As for the murders that had occurred over the past twenty years, they could be counted on the fingers of both hands. With two exceptions they had been banal affairs, dissociated from the Old Town gentry or from the life in the Mediterranean-style buildings of Tipton College.

As Sergeant Brandon Blessing turned onto the Sunday afternoon quiet of Main Street and drove along in the shade of the old pepper trees, he noted that the town had apparently changed very little since his last visit of two years ago. Brandon checked his watch: 2:40; the town hall clock was still running slow.

Brandon Blessing found Wyndham Drive, spent about an hour with the technical crew at the Hall, then headed back toward the center of town. He drove his old Mustang into the parking lot of the police station, collected the materials he had brought with him from the coroner's office, and went in the back door. A new traffic officer, young and female, grinned and mouthed "Swish" to the shift commander, only to receive a scowl and a short but impressive rundown on Sergeant Blessing of the Los Angeles County Sheriff's Department. Wavy brown hair divided by a middle part, a somewhat pouting red mouth, pink cheeks and a mincing tight-assed walk were misleading signals. Sergeant Blessing was more than comfortable with his sexuality, as Mrs. Brandon Blessing could testify. After the arrival of the seventh little Blessing, she had first proposed, then insisted, that her husband have a vasectomy and had driven him to the hospital herself before number seven had progressed to baby food.

Sergeant Blessing accepted the coffee offered by Agent Wiggins with a nod and a sigh and continued to study the documents before him: photographs and reports gathered earlier by the Altamira Police Department. Thad Walker smiled at what the un-informed might interpret as an early sign of dis-couragement. Brandon and his partner had been assigned by the LA County Sheriff's Department to four of the nine homicides Thad had encountered during his eleven years on the Altamira police force; he was now reminded that Sergeant Bless-ing sighed a lot. Blessing was known as a "char-acter." He was invariably in a state of gloom over his cases, yet had the reputation for solving a high number of them in his plodding way — in spite of himself, as it were.

The sergeant frowned, removed a folder from his briefcase and glanced through the documents he had brought with him from the coroner's office.

"No clear latents on the plastic goblet, I see."

"We found a paper napkin stuck around it. Doesn't the report show that?"

Brandon muttered something approximating an affirmative.

Thad continued, "Given the new evidence, looks like the murderer rinsed out the cup, leaving some water in it. That would have been easy enough to do. There's a washbasin in the closet between the president's and the treasurer's offices."

Brandon nodded but looked sour. "I don't know, Thad. When you consider the condition of the aorta . . . Was it a nasty substance that triggered the cardiac arrest? Or did that occur before the poison acted upon his system? That's not clear from the medical examiner's report. We needn't worry about that now, but there's a neat legal distinction to be made there.

"As I hear it, no one knows much, if anything, about the pathology of this toxin in humans."

"Right. We've got a real cutie on our hands." He sighed again. "And look at this list of people who were at that reception. Must be fifty names."

"Perhaps I can be helpful, if you'd like to set some priorities."

"Thanks. Later maybe. I'm going back for another look-see where Merton died, and I want to check out the Chemistry Department. I've ordered a sweep of that Professor Peese's office and the room where the poison was stored."

Thad nodded.

"Though," Brandon complained, "the professor's office was probably cleaned up after his death."

"They've got a very dedicated German-born stockroom manager over there; likes everything spick and span."

Brandon gave him a baleful look. "Just my luck. Then," he sighed, "then maybe I'll begin with . . . " Brandon looked down at the notes. "With this Miss Taper."

"Wise move. She's been at Tipton in the president's office since the year one and is reputed to have total recall."

"Let's hope she noticed something worth remembering. We'll see what kind of new info, if any, the tech boys come up with." He looked up at the Chief. "Good thinking, Thad, to have called them in Wednesday night."

"Good thinking, Pete," Thad said.

Pete studied his desk top, embarrassed.

"Well, whoever. This time they're making a sweep through that entire party scene, and the basement area where the trash cans are stored. I want some additional pictures too. Do I have it straight that nothing's been touched in the president's office since the body was found?"

Thad nodded. "Campus Security has kept someone on duty, though not through the night. We've had to rely on their assistance; like you, we're short-handed right now. The two entries to the presidential suite of offices have been sealed at the end of the work day, at five o'clock. The building is locked up then also."

"But people have been allowed in? To the president's office?"

"Under supervision. Miss Taper and a few officers of the college have had to retrieve some files. But we've kept track."

Brandon reached into his pocket, took out a sack of chocolate-covered M & Ms, held it out toward

Thad, who declined. Brandon popped a few into his mouth.

"Still a chocoholic?"

"Keeps me from swearing. But I stick to a two-pack-a-day limit for M & Ms."

"That's what I call great self-control." Brandon grunted. "What does your dentist say?"

"He's given up." Blessing put the package back into his pocket. "This is make-do stuff," he complained. "Weather's too hot for the real thing."

"It's a tough life for a gourmet."

Brandon Blessing responded to the pleasantry with a solemn nod, adding a near-miss of a smile. "Your interview notes are first-rate, Thad. Big help."

"Thanks."

"You had a hunch, didn't you?"

Thad rubbed his chin. "I'd say the hunch was Pete's. He picked up on the absence of prints on the phone. But, yes, it's true . . . It didn't smell right somehow."

Brandon sighed in regretful agreement. "Well, in light of the M. E.'s second post, is there anything you would add to your observations? The way people acted, anything?"

"I'll have to think about it, Brandon. All I can say offhand is that there was a significant lack of regret."

"No loss to the college?"

"That's the general idea."

"Complicates the picture, doesn't it? If he had more enemies than friends."

"As to enemies, he seemed to be more the target of irritation rather than aggressive hostility. That's how it struck me."

"Yeah? Well, this killer sure as heck isn't going to share his secret fantasies with us. Do you know whether the guy left any real dough?"

"As a matter of fact I've made a couple of phone calls. Apparently Merton didn't leave a large estate. A hundred-thousand life insurance policy and three hundred-thousand maybe in conservative investments, like blue chips and CDs. And he owns outright the house his father lives in, near Phoenix."

"Who inherits?"

"His wife."

"Praises be for small towns who ignore red tape. When they die out, Thad," he sighed, "it means the end of the American way of life."

"Have faith, Brandon. There will always be an Iowa."

Blessing didn't react. "I suppose you've got a likely candidate or two, but I don't want to hear about that just now."

"I understand. You'd rather get your own impressions."

"You got it."

"I couldn't make any guesses anyway, Brandon."

"Too many possibles, huh?"

"Maybe."

"What about his married life?"

Thad shrugged. "Don't know. Mrs. Merton's re-action to his death was what could be expected from a shocked and grieving wife. If she was act-ing, it was a good performance."

"Women?"

"Again, I don't know. Nothing positive."

"What about the unpositive. Women near and far in his life."

Thad's answer came reluctantly. "One of the ad-ministrators, the Dean of the Faculty, is a beautiful woman."

"Married?"

"No. Widowed."

"Gotcha." Gathering up his papers, Brandon Blessing rose ponderously to his feet.

"Before you leave for the campus, a warning: you may find Willie Hefner of the *Ledger* on your tail."

"Willie who?"

"Hefner. Remember him?"

"Is he that runty, bald-headed guy who runs your local newspaper?"

"Right. He picked up something from a scanner."

Brandon looked cross. "What's wrong with his using the regular channels of the Sheriff's depart-ment?"

"Willie will use everything and everyone at his disposal. But he can be pesky. And he has his own private pipeline to the college. It could be worth something to give him a little attention."

"Buttering up to the press is against my principles." Brandon's forlorn expression creased momentarily into a fleeting grin. "OK. I can tell him that there's nothing to tell."

"You'll find that he's got plenty to tell you."

"That might make things more interesting. I always listen to gossip. How much should I discount?"

"About eighty-five percent."

"That still leaves fifteen doesn't it? See you later. And thanks for lending me Pete Wiggins. If that's OK. And OK with you, kid?" Before Pete could answer, Brandon had turned toward Thad again. "Our department can't spare my regular partner."

Thad started to remonstrate, but Wiggins, after a fast decision to shrug off the "kid," was already on his feet and holding the door open for Brandon. Thad's reluctant "OK with me" trailed feebly after them as they hurried down the hall toward Agent Wiggins' cubbyhole of an office.

Wiggins and Brandon had just settled down at Pete's desk when, simultaneously with his knock, Willie Hefner stuck his head around the partially opened door. Not the least put off by Pete's impatient frown, Willie barged on in and stuck out his hand.

"You're Sergeant Blessing, right? We met two years ago, when you were here on the Deblasio stabbing."

An indifferent nod accompanied Brandon's hand-shake.

Pete Wiggins piped up. "Look, Willie, we haven't a thing for you right now."

"Sure, sure. But I'm not here for information. I'm here to offer any resources of the *Ledger* that might be helpful."

Pete started to reply, but was cut off by Blessing who had decided to be hospitable enough to gesture Hefner toward a chair.

Brandon looked severe. "What do you have in mind?"

On anyone else, Willie's smile might have been endearing; on him, it turned into a leer.

"I figured a little cooperation might be in order. This is going to be a big story. Self-styled hot shots from LA and points east, west, north and south, will be crawling all over the place before long. I'm on the ground floor now, and I would like to stay there."

Brandon raised an eyebrow. "Good luck."

Unfazed, Willie continued. "I was born and grew up here. I know this town inside out. I guess Pete can confirm that."

Pete remained busy with a folder on his desk, then turned his back on the other to answer his phone. As he hung up, he heard Willie saying something about "insuring even-handed treatment of the press during the investigation."

Taking advantage of a momentary pause, Pete interrupted. "That was the desk officer. Our switchboard is beginning to get calls. There's been a TV and radio news flash. I'd better have a word with Officer Rodinsky."

As Pete left the office, Brandon studied Willie. Hefner's complacent expression was a turn-off, but he decided to overlook his annoyance.

"You think you've got some useful information?"

Willie looked wise and gave him a "maybe" shrug.

"This is a coroner's case. And my department has a very touchy public information officer, real zealous about his rapport with the media."

Hefner's grin began to look like an effort of will.

"Come on, Hefner, what do you want from me?"

"Just a little consideration."

"Such as?"

"For starters, what about the cause of death? Hear it was some kind of poison."

"We're not ready to discuss any possible evidence that we might have at this time."

Willie had expected this. He could wait. He had an ace up his sleeve. Spelled Crystal. Looking his most affable, Willie inched his chair up closer to the desk.

Pete Wiggins passed a smiling Willie in the hall as he returned to his office.

Sergeant Brandon had returned to his homework.

"Well, what did you get and what did you have to give?" asked Pete.

"It's not Christmas yet. As for what I got," Brandon shrugged. "Lots of 'everybody knows,' and 'people say' — what used to be called 'juicy tidbits.' Your boss was either being close-mouthed or else he's out of it, kid. The 'beautiful woman' he mentioned is a 'sexy woman dean' in Hefner's book, a lady who was shacked up with a married college president. Then there's the alcoholic wife; an eccentric billionaire donor whose proposed gift has certain faculty folks in an uproar; a mistreated administrative secretary, and an aggressive lesbian professor who was given a one-year terminal contract, but has decided not to return to the college next year. And finally, a hard-drinking administrator who is — or was — about to get the boot. That's the first course. Hold any surprises for you?"

"Most of it is town gossip."

"Yeah? How do you know?"

Pete looked mildly uncomfortable. "My mother." He hurried on, "Did Willie show any credentials for his list of candidates?"

"Don't be droll, kid. Confidentiality was invoked."

Pete snorted. "Well, allow me. Crystal Mathews."

"The pipeline, eh? Who's she?"

Pete shifted into the Hefner mode. "Everyone in town knows Willie is having it on with Crystal Mathews. She's Turner Van Voorhees's secretary."

Brandon studied the list of names in front of him. "Vice president and treasurer? Been here two years?"

"Right."

Brandon sighed as he jotted something down. "The twerp oughta be running a scandal sheet."

"Some folks in Altamira think he does."

Pete waited patiently as Brandon continued studying Thad Walker's report and then his own. Finally, he couldn't hold back. "Any questions, Brandon?"

"Not for the moment." He shuffled through the photographs again, then set them aside with a gloomy sigh. "This ain't gonna be easy. We're stuck with a mighty cold trail, kid. Four days old." His head drooped forlornly, then lifted with what passed for a show of resolution in the Brandonian repertoire of signals. "How about heading for Wyndham Hall — just to get rolling."

He crumpled up the now empty sack of M & Ms, made an accurate lob in the direction of the waste basket, and started for the door, mumbling as he went, "One down and one to go."

Sergeant Blessing sat at a table in the president's office making his own rough sketch of the office and notes on what reportedly transpired there between approximately ten after six Wednesday evening and the arrival of the medical examiner and crew. He glanced up as Pete came into the room.

"The custodian isn't there, but according to the schedule on his door he checks in for a while around eight p.m. on Sundays."

"OK. Find out all you can about that bottle, Pete — and whether or not any of the trash it was in could have come from some place else in the building." Brandon chewed on his lower lip for a moment. "Maybe he'll have a set of plans of Wyndham Hall. If not, get some tomorrow."

"Will do."

"Find out when Colton last dusted and vacuumed this office. And just generally noodle around."

"Jeff Colton's been here a long time. I bet he knows more than anybody thinks."

"Oh?"

"Most people treat custodians like they were invisible. Colton must have seen and heard plenty."

If Pete expected an encouraging reaction from Sergeant Blessing, he was disappointed. Brandon grunted an indifferent reply, then removed some photos from a folder. "Even dead, the president looks mighty impressive."

"Yeah. Well, it's that kind of desk — and that kind of room. I sure wouldn't want to come in here to ask for a raise."

Brandon got up and stretched, then walked over to the desk. He carefully opened a few drawers, glanced at the contents, and removed a checkbook from the center one. He flipped through it, then took out an envelope that had been underneath. Brandon lifted the flap, partially slid out a photograph and added the envelope to his folder. He walked around for a moment, then leaned over to turn up a corner of the rug. "Hand-knotted."

"Is that good?"

Blessing nodded. "I don't imagine any of these babies are coming out of Iran to the U. S. these days." He wandered on into the connecting washroom, turned the water on and off in the basin and opened the door to peer into Turner Van Voorhees's office .

"Are you looking for something special, Sergeant?"

"Wish I knew. This place isn't telling us much. At least not yet." He rubbed his eyes, made a selection of M & Ms. "A couple for the road. Let's drop in on the party room then make tracks for the Science building." He paused at the door. "And 'Brandon' will be OK with me, kid."

Brandon stood in the middle of the Development Department's foyer. Pete described where the table and bar had been set up, then fell silent as the sergeant began wandering around the room, stopping to read the name on each office door. He opened the doors of an ornate credenza against one wall, peered in, and shut them again. He walked over to the back stairwell, leaned over the rail and looked down. Brandon then stopped for a drink from the fountain in the corner and wiped his mouth with the back of a hand. "OK, kid. Next stop."

Mark Tidwell was waiting just inside the entrance of the Llewelyn M. Cooper Science Center when the two officers arrived. After names were exchanged and a few pleasantries engaged in with Pete, who had been a schoolmate of one of his sons, Mark led them upstairs and down a long empty hall to his office, past what appeared to be the open counter of a stock room, then on beyond a number of offices and closed doors with signs such as "Flammable Materials"; "Danger! Do not enter without wearing safety glasses." Or, "Caution! Radioactive materials." One laboratory door was open, allowing Brandon to read on the blackboard: "If you don't have something nice to say, say something nonsensical." A piece of advice he wouldn't mind passing on to certain brother or sister officers.

Mark Tidwell seated his visitors at the small round table in his office and drew up a third chair. "Ewen Miles, our chairman, said to tell you he will be completely at your disposal. However, since I'm probably the one most familiar with the late Professor Peese's research, he thought I might be helpful."

Pete Wiggins smiled while the older investigator continued to look gloomy. Mark was reminded of A. A. Milne's drawings of Eeyore. "Ewen said something about a technical crew coming in here?"

"That's right, Professor."

Mark waited, but no further information was forthcoming.

"You're retired, Professor Tidwell?"

"As of four years ago, yes."

"But you still come to your office?"

"As you see. Old habits hang on. And I continue to do research in my field."

"And what would that be?"

"Enzymology. It's a method for determining the relationship between the structure and the reactivity of the substrate."

Pete gave up on taking notes. Brandon looked intent.

"That is to say, the material catalyzed by the enzyme. A far cry, I might add, from Charlie Peese's work in toxicology."

Brandon cleared his throat. "I've gone over with Chief Walker your statement of how the toxic wine came into your hands, Professor, but I'd like to hear the story from you. What made you suspicious?"

"I certainly wasn't at first. I didn't take too seriously Beulah's contention . . . " He broke off as Brandon glanced down at his notes.

"She's the president's executive secretary? The lady who found the bottle?"

"Exactly. Beulah Taper. She was certain she hadn't ordered a Château d'Yquem, and equally positive none of the guests had brought any wine to the reception. I wasn't so sure about that. But it did seem damn queer that cassis liqueur had been added. No one in his right mind would want to make instant kir with that wine — even if 'eighty-four was a bit of an off year."

"This, uh, Yquem is something special?"

"You bet. Château d'Yquem is a Sauternes, in a class by itself. Connoisseurs wax poetic about it, describing it as 'a ray of sunshine concentrated in a bottle.' Ironic, isn't it? 'Blackout' would best describe what was served to Julian."

Brandon didn't appear to be amused. Nor did his expression warm up as he listened to Tidwell's description of the experiments he had run.

"Of course. To do things properly, tests should be run on at least a couple of dozen or so animals. What I did was a gross procedure, you understand. I was trying to get a handle on the thing in a hurry before turning over my findings to the police." Mark Tidwell was obviously unhappy at what he considered sloppy methodology.

Impassive, Brandon waited for him to continue.

"Well, three mice died from injections with the contaminated wine; I got an estimate of the minimum lethal dose. But it was the manner in which the animals died . . . As I mentioned to Thad Walker, it was one of those memory-triggering moments."

"What do you mean?"

"I observed Charlie Peese's work on several occasions — once when he was doing experiments with rats. And the symptoms were the same: gasping respiration, small convulsions, tremors, and finally death from respiratory failure."

Pete shifted uncomfortably in his chair and turned his attention to the view out the window.

"Something was nudging my memory. Then too, Charlie has been on my mind of late. His daughter wants me to assemble some articles of his . . . But never mind that. Anyway, I used some of the material he had left, and experimented with three more laboratory animals — with the anticipated result. I also dug out some of Charlie's notes on his work with anatoxin-a ."

"The M.E. reported Merton's weight at one hundred eighty-four pounds. So, in your estimation, Professor, about how much toxic wine would he have had to swallow for the effect to be lethal?"

"For a man of Julian's weight — that is to say, almost eighty-four kilograms . . . " Professor Tidwell pursed his lips in reflection. "Based on my calculations, it would take 0.25 milligrams of toxin per kilogram of body weight; then, figuring 0.4 of a gram of toxin per liter of wine . . . One very good gulp, or several sips ought to do the job."

"And there can't be any doubt in your opinion?"

"There are other potent neuromuscular depolarizing agents that elicit the same symptoms, curare for instance. You always have to leave room for doubt, Sergeant Blessing. But I question whether the toxin used was anything but anatoxin-a. I gave Chief Walker some vials of tissue samples in formaldehyde and some blood samples. I was unable to run the necessary tests to determine whether or not the poison was in fact anatoxin-a. I wonder whether your crime lab people . . . ?" He looked inquiringly at the detective.

"They have, Professor Tidwell; their findings agree with yours. Your Professor Peese's notes helped speed things up a lot, by the way. They identified the poison as having been isolated from a strain of waterbloom."

"*Anabaena flos-aquae.*"

"Yeah. That sounds right." He checked his notebook again. "From a highly toxic strain called NRC-forty-four."

Tidwell nodded.

"I understand your registry, or inventory book, listed two bottles of toxic material; but you only found one?"

"That's correct. However, one can't conclude beyond a shadow of doubt that it was stolen. We are not, alas, always as diligent as we should be about maintaining up-to-date inventory records."

Brandon groaned inwardly. Great. Just great.

For the second time since the death of Julian Merton the vice presidents of Tipton College gathered as a body to meet with the dean. They were joined by Beulah Taper and Phil Gertmenian. On this occasion, the meeting was being held away from the college, at Anne's home on Rexford Drive. The tension in the atmosphere clashed with the casualness of Sunday afternoon apparel.

Turner Van Voorhees looking tan and handsome in white shorts was the last to arrive. He broke the silence. "Sorry, Anne, I was playing tennis. Is this for real? That the police think someone poisoned Julian?"

"That's correct." Anne was standing in front of the fireplace, then moved to a wing-backed chair that faced the group. "We might as well begin."

Victor held up a hand. "Wait a minute. What about Leslie?"

"I spoke with him earlier today. He's tied up in town."

Henry Norton muttered something that sounded like "Convenient."

Anne continued, "According to our police, the coroner has opened up the case for further investigation."

Henry Norton leaned down to retie one of the laces in his new Sunday-go-to-meeting Nikes. "But on what evidence?"

Victor nodded vigorously. "Yeah. What could they have found? The autopsy report said it was cardiac arrest."

"No doubt we'll know more when we have the chance to talk to the officer assigned to the case."

"Who," said Victor, "will sure as hell want to talk to each one of us."

For a long moment no one said anything, reflecting on the prospect. Then Turner spoke up. "But how could that be? If the autopsy didn't show anything irregular . . . "

Henry Norton shrugged. "Obviously some new evidence turned up."

"But what?"

Anne and Beulah exchanged glances, then the latter cleared her throat. "I can explain that. I stumbled across it. The poisoned wine, I mean."

Anne broke into the silence that met Miss Taper's statement. "Before you begin, Beulah . . . I need to stress that her report is confidential. Until the investigating officers release information, we must keep the knowledge to ourselves. Chief Walker was quite definite about it. For the moment, all that anyone knows officially is that Julian was poisoned."

The heavy silence was shattered by the ring of the dean's telephone. As she returned a moment later, "That was Tom Donaldson. The community relations officer from the Altamira police station just called. A camera crew is already at the station. And there are cameras and media people milling around Wyndham. Tom says we can expect the first major announcement to be made on the seven o'clock news." She glanced at her watch. "In about an hour."

Once again all eyes, except those of Phil Gertmenian, were directed at Beulah.

At the conclusion of her account, Victor Laszlo blurted out, "I'm sure no one questions your motives or your devotion to Tipton, Beulah, but why you didn't notify the officers of the college is beyond me."

Anne put in smoothly. "I think that's been explained, Victor. And it wouldn't have changed anything."

They ruminated on that for a moment, then Turner spoke up, "Why would a chemist at a small liberal arts college want to fool around with poison like that?"

"Being at a college has nothing to do with it, Turner." Henry Norton rose to a former colleague's defense. "A good chemist is interested in research. Charlie Peese was a good chemist, and toxicology was his specialty. Pharmacological companies are interested in what we do, by the way. So are physicians. 'Fooling around' with plants and folk medicine has provided some extremely useful results."

Turner settled back in his chair, turned toward the dean. "Anne, it seems to me you should have invited Mark Tidwell to meet with us, so that we could get the complete picture."

"I did. He's busy with the investigating officer from the Sheriff's office. Would anyone care for something to drink?"

Victor was about to say yes, then decided to go along with the others.

"We are all going to be questioned of course by reporters and the police," Anne continued. "To the former we have nothing to say."

Turner's "Of course not" was echoed by Victor.

Henry Norton slouched down a bit more in his chair and scratched behind his ear. "Incredible."

Anne went on, "Tom will deal with the press and do all that he can to keep them out of our hair. He's putting out a directive to the Hall staff to refer all inquiries to his office. Obviously we need to do our best to keep a lid on rumors and speculation."

Henry Norton gave a short laugh. "Good luck."

Anne glanced his way, smiled, and shrugged.

"But you'll have to make some kind of statement, won't you, Anne?"

"I'm not going to volunteer one. Leslie is the appropriate person to speak for the college. As for faculty, I've asked Phil to prepare a memorandum; it will be hand-delivered to office mail boxes."

Gertmenian got up and began handing around copies of the memo.

"Though," Anne continued, "most of them will hear it on the news before we can get anything out."

Victor shifted heavily in his chair. "Do you all realize what this can do to the Weinert gift?"

A flash of anger crossed Henry Norton's usually placid face. "As far as I'm concerned, you can take the Weinert gift and shove it."

Turner Van Voorhees coughed. "Before we break up, Anne, I'd like to know whether anyone here has a notion of how this could have happened."

"I was going to ask the same thing, Turner," Anne said. "Seems to me I heard Julian order a Perrier at the bar."

Henry looked reflective. "I remember pouring him a glass of wine. He said something about having had enough water torture for the day and reaching for some apple juice, but the bottle was empty, so he settled for the vino. It was red wine, as I recall."

"He was drinking red," Victor confirmed vigorously. "Or rather rosé. He offered me a glass and poured one for himself at some point. Right before the toasts, I think. Say, does anyone even remember noticing a bottle of white wine — what was it? — Château something or other?"

Turner Van Voorhees answered the question: "The bottle couldn't have been left on the table.

Otherwise, anyone might have drunk from it. The wine had to have been served to him. By the murderer."

The word, spoken for the first time, dropped into an uncomfortable silence.

Henry Norton spoke up rubbing his left shoulder. "What we're toe-dancing around is the fact that any one of us could have poisoned Julian."

Turner nodded. "That's right. But so could have several dozen other people. And there's not one of us who benefits from Julian's death. Quite the contrary."

Henry nodded. "I expect the police to be interested in our policy differences."

"Exactly," Turner said. "But whatever policies Julian had in place, unpopular or not, will be implemented by Leslie. Julian's death doesn't change a thing on that score."

Sly bastard, Victor said to himself. He means Filmore is going to fire me. We'll see about that. Out loud he said, "Can you think of anyone who benefits from his death?"

Henry's response was immediate. "Yes. Tipton College."

"That," Turner said testily, "is a matter of opinion."

Henry piped up again, "What about his will? Anybody know?"

Anne put a halt to further speculation. As the group was filing out, she signaled Turner to stay.

He looked at her quizzically. "Something I can do, Anne?"

"You should know that when I spoke with Leslie he made it clear that I was to work closely with you in the days to come."

Turner looked impatient. "That embarrasses me, Anne. He called me to say the same thing. I'm ready to ignore it."

"I don't think we should do that."

"Look, let me take the heat from Leslie. His attitude toward you is patently unjustified. So far as I'm concerned, Anne, you're in charge."

Kind words, Anne thought, as she watched Turner head down the front walk. However, she wasn't certain that she felt up to being in charge of anything just now — certainly not of Tipton College. Ever since Julian's death Anne had had a feeling of floating — like a dream figure in a Chagall painting, remote, drifting, looking down indifferently at the Tipton microcosm from a great distance.

At a few minutes before seven everything was quiet at the Llewelyn M. Cooper Science Center. The technical crew had left, their sweep of Charlie Peese's office and the organic substance room completed. The chair, Ewen Miles, and Mark Tidwell had gone home. The only sign of anything out of the ordinary were the two men seated at a redwood table in the small patio to the north of the Science Building, report books in front of them.

Brandon leaned back for a stretch, staring up at the sky through the leaves of an overhanging branch. "One thing is certain. Anybody could have come into this building and walked around without being seen. Or noticed."

"Their security is sure spotty. The chairman, that Dr. Miles, didn't seem surprised that the door of the organic substance storeroom wasn't always kept locked. I'm not sure we can take his word that the entrances to the building are always locked up by five p. m. at this time of year, either." He paused. "Actually, that toxic material could have been lifted any time after Peese's death in May."

Pete's conclusion insured a lower-depth rumble from Blessing. "Better get a list, Pete, of everybody who has a passkey to this building and to that substance room."

"Will do. And I thought I ought to see if I can track down the source of that wine. There shouldn't be many liquor outlets around here that stock it — if we're in luck."

"Mm. Well, don't count on it. I want a word with that stockroom manager, Ulrich . . . "

"Geisler."

"Yeah. I'll leave Jeff Colton to you. Tomorrow I'll start questioning the people who work in Wyndham Hall."

"Starting with the big shots?"

"Right. And the Missus. The old saw about most murders being done by someone close to the victim is still pretty reliable." He got up. "I'll meet you back at the station. Want to review my notes along with yours and Thad's before I head back to the station."

Pete took a shot at anticipating the next reaction. "Don't imagine they'll tell you much."

Brandon nodded in weary agreement and reached for a candy.

In the study of his Hancock Park home, Milton Weinert turned off the television. His wife, Dora looked up from her knitting, a new sweater for the Chihuahua snoozing in her lap.

"This certainly changes things, wouldn't you say, Milton?"

"You can say that again. I smell a scandal. I'm sure as hell not going to have my money associated with a scandal."

Dora decided to let the "hell" pass. Also the "my" money. "The college has already invested a lot of money in the proposal, hasn't it, Milton? For consultation fees and architectural plans?"

Milton grumbled, "At their risk. No reason why I should throw my good money after their bad."

Dora measured her knitting against the small lump in her lap. "You know I was never too keen on this project. Julian Merton was much too glib for my taste. And too worldly. Every time I tried to talk to him about politics or the inspirational articles I sent him, he cut me off. As for that wife of his, well . . . "

"I'll call Filmore and tell him the deal's off."

"What about our commitment for the athletic facilities?"

"I've only given half the money. Under the circumstances they can raise the rest themselves. I'll let Filmore know that I don't want my name to be further associated with Tipton College."

Dora Weinert checked the row she had just completed before continuing. "Milton, I think we should give some of that money to the church's mission projects, particularly the one in India. The Roman Catholics have the monopoly there, if you ask me. Those poor Indians need to know they have a direct line to God. The RC's make sure they get all the media coverage too. And you know some of those priests are no better than communists. Not that Mother Theresa and her people aren't admirable, but . . . "

Milton wasn't listening. He got up to go fix himself a drink in the kitchen.

As usual, Dora would pretend that she hadn't noticed.

Mary Walker had turned on the television in the living room to catch the seven o'clock news, but after the first few dreary announcements had deserted it to do some straightening up in her small studio — what had once been a sun porch. She didn't hear the public information officer of the Sheriff's department answering questions about the murder with the expected "too early to say" and "there are no suspects at this time." The words "Tipton College" caught her attention, however, and she wheeled back into the room in time to catch a shot of Wyndham Hall and the brief descriptive comment from the newsman standing at the entrance. Without thinking, she turned to the telephone to call Vince, then laughed at her foolishness, at the same time chiding herself for an exaggerated sense of discretion. How silly to insist he not call her at home. Did brother George have a radio? Or did he get any newspapers? And speaking of brothers, she would have something to say to her own at what she considered an excess of official discretion, since table conversation had been at a low of late.

Mary began to play the guessing game much of Altamira was engaged in at this moment. Who would have sufficient motive? And what could that motive be? Jealousy? Revenge? Fear? Or something else? Something especially associated with the Byzantine and ingrown world of Tipton College?

At a little past eight, Pete Wiggins was having a cup of coffee with Jeff Colton in the latter's basement office. Jeff was shaking his head.

"Nope, the only trash in that can was from the party."

"Was the bottle on top of the trash?"

"Hunh-uh, it was shoved way in."

"How did you happen to notice it then?"

Jeff looked rather pleased with himself. "I was separating the bottles from the other trash for recycling. And like I told Miss Taper, I noticed the label."

"Is it college policy to recycle glass?"

"Not that I know of. Something I started doing on my own a little while back."

"So people here, or your supervisor, didn't know about it?"

He shrugged. "Far as I know."

"Did you pour out any of the contents ?"

The custodian made a vigorous denial.

"What did you do with it exactly?"

Jeff looked solemn. "I carried it to my office and put it right here on the desk, where Miss Taper saw it. So's I could soak the label off later. But I almost took a swig of it, for old times' sake." He shook his head. "Oowhee. Praises be something held me back."

"Why was that? Why didn't you take a drink?"

The old man didn't hesitate. He looked straight at Pete Wiggins. "I'm AA. Been sober for twenty-eight years."

"I see. But why didn't you empty the bottle?"

Jeff shrugged. "Kinda hated to waste all that wine" He hesitated a moment, then plunged ahead. "But that's not the main reason. I mean, if you were an alcoholic, you'd know. I would have emptied it in a day or two, I kept it as a kind of test. Of my resolve."

"Oh." Pete flipped his notebook shut. "I don't suppose you were in the vicinity of that party on Wednesday?"

"Sure I was. Just for a minute. I went up the back stairs not long before they broke up. Some time before six. I've always thought a lot of Mr. Finlay. He saw me and came over and shook my hand. Then I left. Mr. Laszlo was just starting to make a speech. "

"What time might that have been?"

"Hard to say. Maybe fifteen-twenty minutes before I saw Dean Norton and Mr. Van Voorhees coming down the front stairs with some luggage."

"Where were you standing while you were upstairs?"

"Kinda in the corner — at the head of the back stairs."

"Could you describe what you saw ?"

Jeff thought a moment. "Just a lot of folks milling around, eating and drinking. Pretty noisy. But come to think of it — there is something else. The president saw me. Darndest thing. He even came over and offered me a drink."

Agent Wiggins reopened his report book.

Brandon Blessing swallowed the candy he had been chewing, wiped his mouth with his handkerchief. "Let me have that again."

"Merton offered him the glass of wine he had in his hand."

"And this would have been about 5:45."

"Or thereabouts. Shortly before six anyway."

"Funny thing for a fellow like Merton to do, isn't it? I got the idea he didn't buddy with the help."

Pete shrugged. "One thing Thad and I picked up was that Merton had set comments he made to people. Like he had memorized one or two facts about each person. People joked about it. Seems the only personal conversation he had with Jeff was at New Year's — at the reception he and Mrs. Merton held for staff."

"And?"

"He always asked Jeff what he thought of this year's. . . . " he consulted his notes, "this year's Beaujolais."

Brandon made an explosive sound that passed for laughter. "You're kidding."

Pete shook his head. "Swear to God. Somehow Merton had cottoned to the fact that Jeff spent some time in France at the end of World War Two. Maybe he thought it was flattering to Colton to be treated as a wine expert."

Again the small explosion. "Just one gentleman to another?" Then, seriously, "At least we can assume that the president hadn't yet drunk out of that particular glass, if he offered it to Colton."

"One more thing, Brandon. I called the local liquor stores and hit it with The Cork and Bottle. It's the most popular with the college crowd; the other stores don't go in for high quality imported stuff. The owner said he had a special on six cases of that Château whatchamacallit last Christmas."

"And?" Brandon looked impatient.

"He sold almost a case of single bottles to local customers, he's not sure to whom. He said it wasn't a wine that many locals knew about. And not many people go for such expensive sweet wines. It was in the inventory when he bought the store last year and he was nervous about getting stuck with it, so sold it at a big discount. His records show one case delivered to Dr. Simon Lowenthal and four cases sold to college people." Pete paused to let the suspense build.

"Come on, Pete. Spit it out."

"The Mertons took three cases, Dean Parker-Brown bought a half case, and a French professor, de Grancey, bought half a case."

"Christmas-time, huh?" This brought forth a heavy Brandonian sigh that left Pete feeling deflated. "So any number of the bottles might have been given away as gifts." Brandon absently drew the outline of a bottle on the pad in front of him and added a large question mark. "Furthermore, the wine the murderer doctored could just as easily have been purchased outside of Altamira." He drew another and larger question mark.

"Well, it's a starting point," Pete said defensively.

"Yep. What about your theory that the custodian could give us a peek behind the false fronts around here?"

"Turns out Jeff is hard of hearing. Either he doesn't know much or else he's not telling. All I got was that people didn't much care for Merton — he intimidated them. And that he gave his secretary a hard time."

"No juicy gossip?"

"Hunh-uh."

"When was the last time he cleaned the president's office?"

"He vacuumed early the morning of the murder. Merton's wastebasket was emptied for the last time at noon, the day he was killed."

"OK. I'll pass that along to the lab. I've gotta check in at the station, then I'm for home, kid. Meet you tomorrow for breakfast at seven — at that coffee shop."

"Solly's?"

"Right. Maybe this evening you could start making the rounds — get to a few of the staff people on our list."

"Will do."

"We won't have to park in your office tomorrow. We can work out of Wyndham Hall. The college folks are letting us have our GHQ in the basement."

Sergeant Blessing heaved to his feet and headed for the door. Pete called after him. "What about that Geisler fellow?"

"Confirmed everything we heard about the security problem. Real organized type. Bothers him a lot that the faculty are careless about logging what they remove from the substance rooms — and about locking them up. The late Professor Peese was a particularly bad offender."

"What about noticing anyone in the building over the last week or so?"

"He threw out a few names of possible visitors the day of the murder, Laszlo and the dean, among the most interesting. Kinda tricky at this point to make much out of it, when you figure the poison could have been snatched two months ago. Not even a compulsive Teutonic type can be accurate that far back."

Pete Wiggins caught himself in time. This sighing business was contagious.

With one hand resting heavily on Crystal's pubis, Willie Hefner mentally reviewed once again the events of the day, the camaraderie with LA media people, the importance of his own role as editor-publisher of Altamira's only newspaper. His mind raced ahead to the stories in which he was sure he would be quoted, to the photos he had supplied that would give credit to the *Ledger.* His own piece for yet another special edition was already composed, the headline set in 60 point type: "PRESIDENT MERTON MURDERED." He savored the subhead, something he hadn't shared with out-of-town colleagues: "POISON TAKEN FROM CHEMISTRY DEPARTMENT."

MONDAY, JULY 24

AT FIRST LIGHT THE FRONT DOOR OF the president's house opened quietly. Julian's father, already dressed, stepped out on the front porch and picked up the *Los Angeles Times* from the top step. He opened it slowly. From below the fold his son's face looked up at him. "PRESIDENT MERTON OF TIPTON COLLEGE PRESUMED MURDER VICTIM. Story on page 5." Joseph Merton picked up a second newspaper and, without unfolding it, went back in the house.

Brandon Blessing and young Pete Wiggins rendezvoused at seven at Solly's Coffee Shop as arranged. The regulars at the counter sat before open copies of the *Times* or the *Ledger,* reading bits to each other, commenting and speculating in shocked tones. Brandon and Pete found a quiet booth in the back.

"Boy," Pete said, "Hefner's going to have a breakdown churning out special issues, trying to increase his subscribers by scooping the *L.A. Times.* What are you going to do about that guy?"

Brandon shrugged.

"Let him have his jollies this time. He may get knocked about some by our PIO and the folks at the college."

They ordered coffee and doughnuts, one chocolate, one plain, from a sleepy-looking waitress. Pete leaned forward. "I stopped by the homes of a few staff people last evening. One from each floor: the director of personnel, her office is in the basement; Crystal Mathews; and Joelle Lieberman. I figured them for three ladies who knew their way around Wyndham."

Brandon frowned to stop him as the waitress approached with their order. He bit into his doughnut, waited until the woman had moved off. "And?"

"Not real helpful about the party scene. The president seems to have been all over the place. Joelle remembers handing him a glass of wine. Rosé."

"When was this?"

"Towards the end of the reception she thinks."

"Yeah? Next?"

"I asked the personnel lady for info on the top brass. She said she'd pull their CVs, providing . . . "

"See what?" Brandon interrupted.

Pete took a note from his pocket. *"Curriculum vitae.* Here. Means something like your professional life's record." Brandon studied the note, gave it back. "But no soap, unless the court sub-poenas the files, of course."

Brandon sighed, thinking of less complicated days.

"I told her one was on its way. She'll get the copies ready. That will be a start."

"Good, kid. Get copies of those whatchamadoodles on the executive secretaries too."

"OK. I bet she knows a lot about buried bodies around here. You going to talk to her?"

"Not just yet anyway. Remember the privacy act, kid. Her mouth will be zippered shut tighter than a cow's ass in fly time."

Pete's head jerked up. Brandon mournfully continued. "'Just the files, officer.' That's all we'll get. Anything else?"

"Personal opinions. From Joelle mostly. Like Van Voorhees was the fair-haired boy but Mr. Laszlo wasn't in good shape."

"Days numbered, huh? And that woman dean?"

"Ms. Mathews was hinting that her position wasn't so secure either."

"The dean's a single lady, right?"

"Widowed."

"Does she fool around?"

"Gossip about her and Merton. And some raised eyebrows about her having a good-looking male secretary."

"And the wife? Mrs. Merton?"

"Boy, do they not like her."

"Why not?"

"They think she puts on airs. And they say she drinks." Pete got a far-away look in his eyes. "Do you ever get the idea, Brandon, that women can be awfully hard on each other?" Brandon managed to keep his lips firmly compressed. "I mean toward women who are ahead of the game socially or professionally?"

The sergeant didn't blink. "Pretty early in the morning for me to think about such heady stuff." He sighed and signaled their waitress. "You want another doughnut?"

Phil Gertmenian slowed down as he came abreast of Anne Parker-Brown at the corner of First and Mountain. "How about a lift, Anne?"

She got in with a smile. "Thanks, Phil. So much for my good intentions."

"Did you see this morning's papers?"

"Mm. If you could call Hefner's special a paper. More of a flyer."

"Makes hash of our efforts to cooperate with the police."

Anne kept looking at the passing landscape. "Predictable."

Phil gave a quick honk and a wave as he passed Henry Norton on his bike. He glanced momentarily at Anne. "Did you sleep well?"

"Shouldn't I have?"

Phil said impatiently, "You know what I mean."

"Sorry to be snappy. It was indeed a very bad day. I'm not thrilled about what today promises either. With police on the premises."

"What about Leslie Filmore?"

"He telephoned at five-thirty this morning."

Phil let out a whistle. "Ever considerate."

"Leslie has decided to make an appearance after all. He'll be here by mid-afternoon — wants to meet with the investigators."

"To tell them what?"

"That it's some kind of mistake. That Julian had no enemies and was a respected leader."

"He's whistling in the dark."

"I'm sure he's nervous about holding the Weinert deal together."

"Good news for a change. And better yet if the deal collapses."

"But not for our president pro tem, Phil. He's a man who does not readily accept any upsetting of his applecarts."

Phil drove on for a moment in silence, then pulled to the side of the road. Anne looked at him, a quizzical expression on her face.

"Anne, as you said, the police will be asking a lot of questions."

"Yes?"

"I think you should know . . . " he began with difficulty.

She laughed. "Come on, Phillip, don't tell me you have something on your conscience?"

"It's you I'm concerned about. A couple of people know that you returned to the States by way of San Francisco — some days ahead of schedule."

"I see."

"Joelle noticed the stamp in your passport when she was doing some filing for us the other day. She told Beulah. I'm awfully sorry, Anne. I didn't know . . . "

"Forget it." Anne sounded quite cheerful. "What a *panier de crabes* old Tipton is. Hornets' nest to you."

"Beulah thinks Joelle won't say anything; I'm not so sure. I'm planning to have a word with her."

"No, don't."

"But . . . "

She interrupted crisply, "I mean it, Phil. Let it ride."

Phil moved away from the curb, headed for the Hall. Her reaction left him unsatisfied.

"You were right to tell me, Phil. Thank you."

No further explanation was forthcoming. They drove on to the Hall in silence.

Mary wheeled down the sidewalk and turned in at Vince's, stopping briefly to pick up the papers lying near the front walk and peek in the mail box; nothing but a couple of circulars. The sprinkler Thad had repaired was no longer dripping; the footprint going nowhere had been largely obliterated by his activity. Given the heat predicted for the next several days, Mary made a mental note to check things out on Wednesday morning — make sure the automatic sprinkler system was working properly.

Mary maneuvered down the bumpy path that led around to the back of the house, receiving a shower of droplets from an overhanging bougainvillea that had been needing pruning for over a year. The profusion of plants and bushes in the backyard glistened with water, and she breathed in the fresh damp smell with pleasure. It was a contradiction that Vince, a stickler about the gardening at Tipton, should allow his yard to be so overgrown. His repeated declarations that he was going to attend to the backyard, now that he was a property owner, remained in the category of firm resolve only. "If it weren't for your demands on my time and energy, Miss Mary . . . " he would say to her.

Peering through the tangled growth, Mary saw that the garage door was closed. She rolled up the back porch ramp that Vince had built for her and retrieved the spare key to the backdoor from its hiding place in the mouth of a fire extinguisher. Entering the darkened kitchen, Mary glanced briefly around, gave an OK to the stove, and was starting to check the refrigerator when a sound caught her attention: water was running someplace. Outside? The bathroom?

Mary propelled her chair into the hall that ran from the kitchen to the dining and living rooms on the right and to the bedroom and study on the left. The carpet was sodden, running with water that flowed toward the living room. At the open door of the bathroom Mary braked so abruptly that she lurched forward. Her hands on the wheels of the chair began to shake. Water was spilling out of the tub, gently washing over the naked arm that dangled over the edge.

Beulah transferred her phone to Crystal's line before going into the Burckhardt Room where Sergeant Blessing was waiting. He gestured her to a chair, thinking that it had been a long time since he had seen a woman in a girdle; you could always tell by the packed look around the buttocks and waist. Miss Taper sat down, glancing at her watch as she did so.

"I'll not keep you long, Miss Taper." He briefly studied the squarely-built efficient-looking woman before him, then asked abruptly, "Have you any idea why anyone would want to kill President Merton?"

"None whatsoever." She folded her hands on the table before her. Exceptionally beautiful hands, Brandon noticed, at odds with the somewhat clumsily shaped body.

"Had he quarreled recently with anyone?"

"Not that I'm aware of."

"Do you know whether anyone had threatened him? In any way?"

"No."

"Not even in a burst of anger?"

Beulah shook her head.

"I've gathered that he was not a well-liked man."

"He was a difficult man, Sergeant. Erratic, unpredictable. I know that there are some faculty members who differed with him heartily. But to feel such hatred as to . . . " She shook her head again. "It just isn't possible."

"What about non-faculty people? Friends? Family? Members of the administration?"

Beulah gave him a stern look. "Inconceivable."

Brandon rubbed his forehead. "Well, it seems as though it has to be someone, doesn't it, Miss Taper? Somebody who was at that reception." He got up, walked over to the window, looked out for a moment, then faced her. "Were you fond of your boss?"

Beulah looked at him straight on. "I was not."

"Did you respect him?"

"Yes — at first."

"But then?"

"I expect I've been here too long, Sergeant, but my idea of what Tipton represents did not coincide with his."

He hadn't expected this directness. It encouraged him to ask the next question. "How far did this non-liking go?"

Again the steady glance. Brandon noted that along with graceful hands Miss Taper had uncommonly large and piercing blue eyes.

"There were times when I disliked him intensely." She brushed a speck of lint off the table. "I did not poison him, Sergeant Blessing."

His face was without expression. "And you can't think of anyone who hated him enough to kill him?"

He was watching for a moment's hesitation, but there was none. "Of course not."

"When you learned the president had been poisoned, some name must have popped into your mind."

She shook her head.

"Which one of the VPs did he see the most often?"

"That would be Dean Parker-Brown. Naturally."

"Would it also be natural for them to be more than friendly?"

She flared. "Sergeant, that is a horrid and unjustified insinuation."

Brandon remained dead-pan. "Then, were they friendly colleagues?"

"Mrs. Parker-Brown is a splendid dean. I'm sure the president appreciated her."

"But he was going to remove her as dean, right?"

"Idle speculation."

Brandon wondered whether she would be just as evasive about Mrs. Merton.

"How were things between Mr. and Mrs. Merton?"

"Mr. Merton never discussed his private life with me."

"Come on, Miss Taper. In your position you must have heard or seen things. Would you call it a good marriage?"

She clasped and unclasped her hands in an uneasy gesture, then rallied. "I'm told the best of marriages have their ups and downs, Sergeant. I have no proof that theirs was not a good marriage."

Yep, evasive. Brandon felt the M&M sack snug in his pocket and wondered what would happen if he offered her one. He doubted that she would be amused. Brandon sighed and switched gears. "Miss Taper, I understand that you have an extraordinary memory."

She made a dismissive gesture.

"I'm trying to get a picture of the president's movement during that retirement party. What he might have been drinking when. Who might have poured his drinks. Particularly right before the toasts and speeches."

As Beulah described what she could, Brandon took notes. "You think, then, that he was drinking soda water most of the time?"

"I think so. Mr. Gertmenian and I noticed that he went up to the bar at about, oh, the half-way mark, I suppose."

"That would be about five?"

"Probably a bit after."

"What was served at the bar?"

"Mostly hard liquor and mixers. But some wine was also available."

"I understand there were bottles placed around the buffet table?"

She nodded.

"The wine was ordered specially for this event?"

"Yes. I ordered a case of a Beaulieu red wine and two cases of white wine — Blanc de Blancs. They sent rosé by mistake."

"Where did you place the order?"

"The Cork and Bottle. Here in town."

"Could an odd bottle of another wine have gotten in with the rosé?"

"No. I checked the order myself. Joelle opened the cases for me. The boxes had been stapled."

"So they hadn't been opened earlier?"

"I don't see how."

"And what about the red wine?"

"There were only the dozen bottles."

"And you never noticed an odd bottle of wine?"

"No. And I did check the table from time to time. But then, it wouldn't have been displayed, would it?"

The old girl was pretty sharp. "Well, what did your president like to drink?"

Beulah chafed silently at the "my president." "He didn't care much for alcoholic beverages, but he would drink a little wine sometimes at office parties. And always, of course, if toasts were to be offered."

"White or red?"

"White usually. Or a kir, if available. President Merton liked sweet things."

"Do you know who was tending bar when you saw the president there?"

"Mr. Van Voorhees — but I'm really not positive."

"And later, just before the toasts were made. Where was the president?"

Beulah closed her eyes a moment. "I believe he was standing at the southern end of the buffet table. Vince Riley was talking to him for a moment. Mr. Filmore was there, and Mr. Laszlo. They both had brief speeches to make. I'm sure there were others coming and going. There was quite a crowd in that general area."

"Can you remember who was tending bar at that time?"

She studied her hands. "Dean Norton — no, I think it was Mr. Barnes, one of our trustees. But I'm not sure, Sergeant."

Brandon nodded. "Did you notice anyone specifically pouring him a drink?" A wild throw. He was not disabused. Brandon sighed and said, "Here's the list we have of people who were at the reception. We'll collect it later. Would you put a check mark by the names of everyone you saw talking with President Merton? And add any names that are missing."

"Yes, of course."

"Now then, did you see anyone leave the party and then return?"

"Yes, Dean Norton. Dean Parker-Brown went to the ladies room."

"How long was Norton gone?"

"I didn't pay any attention."

"And Dean Parker-Brown?"

"Just a few minutes."

"Was she carrying a purse or anything?"

"No." The rejoinder was sharp.

"Did you notice anyone with a large bag or a briefcase. Or a package?"

"No."

"Anybody else?"

She thought for a moment. "Yes, I saw Vincent Riley leave toward the end of the party. But he didn't come back. I don't recall anyone else . . . "

"I see. Now, Miss Taper, I'd like to know what you did, whom you saw, after you told President Merton he had a call from Mr. Weinert."

Brandon made notes as she carefully related her actions between approximately ten after six and her departure with Phil Gertmenian some fifteen minutes later.

When she had finished, he leaned forward, holding something out to her across the table.

"I found this in the top drawer of the desk, underneath the president's personal checkbook."

Beulah took the photograph and studied it without a word, turning it over to read on the back: "Trustee-Faculty Retreat, Arrowhead, April 1989."

"That is President Merton?"

Beulah nodded, her face expressionless.

"And is that Mrs. Merton with him?"

"No."

"Have you seen this photo before, Miss Taper?"

"No. I have no idea where it came from."

"Do you recognize the lady in the picture?"

"I think so. Of course the lighting . . . "

Brandon refrained from stating that the couple were standing in bright sunlight and waited.

Beulah shoved the photograph back across the table, saying almost casually, "That is Dean Parker-Brown with President Merton." Dean Parker-Brown, smiling at Julian Merton, his hands on her shoulders, his face close to hers.

"You didn't know it was in his desk?"

"Certainly not."

"Or why it was there?"

"No."

"And you still maintain that the Mertons had no marital problems."

"I said I had no evidence that theirs was not a good marriage, Sergeant."

To Beulah's relief, Sergeant Blessing lost interest in the photograph. He put it carefully back in a folder and studied his notes. The silence lengthened. At last he asked, "I suppose you're familiar with the college's auditing process?"

"Of course."

"When was the last audit ?"

"Our fiscal year ends on June thirtieth. The audit was completed just last week." She gave him a hard look. "There were no irregularities, Sergeant."

Brandon registered the volunteered remark without comment. "Who are the college auditors?"

"Colby-Forstman."

As he was writing, she added, "213-634-0028."

"Thank you." He repeated the number as he jotted it down. "Now about the partially empty bottle, Miss Taper. What was it that bothered you?"

Beulah repeated what she had told Thaddeus Walker, but her thoughts were tumbling about in confusion. The president and the dean. Was it true after all? It didn't fit with the image she had of Anne, nor with what she had overheard Julian Merton say privately to Filmore recently. Nor could she reconcile the idea of an affair with his attitude toward Anne Wednesday morning. And yet . . . Miss Taper's ideas on extra-marital love affairs had been formed by the two-hankerchief movies she had grown up with in the Thirties. Irene Dunne in

Back Street drifted into her mind, and the answer occurred to her: Julian Merton had repudiated her, betrayed her in some way.

"I think that's about it for now, Miss Taper. And thank you."

She looked relieved and rose.

"One more thing. Did you keep the president's calendar?"

"Yes, of course."

"I noticed one on his desk as well."

"For his convenience. I coordinated them as best I could."

"I don't understand."

"Naturally President Merton made some appointments on his own, and sometimes he would forget to tell me."

"Did he keep a pocket agenda also?"

"Yes."

"Did you also coordinate that with your calendar?"

"No. That was private."

"OK. That's all, then."

She got up to leave.

"Just a moment, Miss Taper. I'd like to take a look at the calendar you kept."

"Of course, Sergeant."

Beulah was almost at the door when she heard Blessing say, "Was the president having an affair with Dean Parker-Brown, Miss Taper?"

The beautiful blue eyes turned to ice. "That is an unseemly question, Sergeant."

"Maybe so, ma'am. I often ask unseemly questions."

"The idea is unthinkable."

"Problem is, a number of people around here seem to think it. I'd appreciate an answer from you, Miss Taper. A direct one."

"I know of no liaison between the late president and Dean Parker-Brown."

"Do you think you would have known if there had been one?"

Her chin came up. "Yes, officer. I'm quite sure I would know."

"What about Mr. Laszlo? I've heard that his position here was maybe a little shaky."

She finally made up her mind how to answer. "I believe there were areas of disagreement to be worked out. Mr. Laszlo has been at Tipton for a very long time, Sergeant."

"What about the other two VPs? Norton and Van Voorhees?"

"So far as I know, Mr. Merton had the highest respect for both of them."

And you know a lot more than you're telling, sister, Brandon thought. As she left the room, Brandon made himself a note: Rocky situation at home? BT protecting dean? Laszlo about to get the axe? Ditto dean? He made another note to retrieve Merton's pocket agenda from the coroner's office and dug in his own pocket for a pick-me-up.

Beulah returned with the blue leather-covered book that contained one entry she would have liked to erase: the trip to San Francisco. She handed it to him without a word.

The door to the Burckhardt Room opened suddenly and Turner Van Voorhees burst in. "I'm sorry to interrupt, but we've just received some dreadful news, Beulah. Vince Riley was found dead a short time ago."

Beulah's face crumpled with shock. She sat down heavily.

"Apparently he slipped in his bathtub, was knocked unconscious, and drowned."

"Horrible. Horrible." The words, buried in a handkerchief, were barely audible.

Brandon broke the silence. "Vince Riley worked for you, didn't he, Mr. Van Voorhees?"

Turner nodded. "Head of Buildings and Grounds. He was to have left Saturday morning on vacation."

Beulah gasped. "That means he's been lying there . . . "

Brandon made the quick and easy calculation: almost three days. The sergeant crossed a name off his list of people to question. A mean death, he thought, but, so far as his investigation was concerned, it didn't appear that he had lost a key witness.

As Brandon Blessing made his way down the hall in Baja Wyndham, he passed a knot of stricken people standing at the door of the Buildings and Grounds offices, Agent Wiggins among them. Pete disengaged himself from a conversation with Max Dingam and followed Brandon into their temporary quarters.

"Have you heard . . . ?"

Brandon cut him off with an affirmative.

"Sad business, but we can't linger over it. Anything on the pass key list?"

"You won't like it. Administrators, custodians, and a number of the Science faculty have pass keys. And so do students — unofficially."

"What?"

"Yeah. The word is that no matter how often locks are changed, students manage to snag keys to college buildings."

"What else is a good education for?" He shook his head. "What a mess. If we get through this, kid, we'll deserve a special commendation."

"How about a nice boost in salary and rank?"

"You youngsters are all alike. No idealism about our life's work."

Agent Wiggins was about to protest until he caught the unexpected and seldom- seen grin.

Brandon spread out some notes. There was a rustle of stiff paper and the now familiar package of M & Ms appeared and was placed beside them.

"Tell you what we're going to do, kid, since you're such a likable hometown boy."

Pete braced himself.

"It's obvious from your work last night that you've got at least a nodding acquaintance with a number of people in Wyndham."

Pete said he guessed so.

Brandon gave himself a chocolate fix. "Tackle the remainder of the junior staff. Get whatever poop you can. Find out if they saw anyone leave the party for a while, or if they saw anyone carrying a package or anything that could hold a bottle."

Pete was relieved. "Will do."

"Pass out the Xerox list to everybody who was at the party and have them check the names of people they saw talking to Merton. And when. And add any missing ones. We'll collect the lists at five. The big question of course is who poured a drink for the president during the last twenty to thirty minutes of that shindig." Brandon put down his pencil with a flourish. "We'll put the choreography of those two hours into the computer for a cross check and a look at contradictions or inconsistencies. Then maybe we'll have a notion of who was where and doing what."

"You don't expect the murderer to admit to serving any wine, do you?"

"If he or she is smart, he or she will. If not, it could show as an omission, given other testimony."

Brandon seemed to have shifted one small notch toward optimism. Pete ventured, "Maybe we'll get a break, Brandon."

Blessing sank back into the slough of despond. "Don't count on it. If the next hours go like the one I've just passed . . . "

"Wasn't Miss Taper cooperative?"

"Sure. Enough to make me think that there's a basket of smelly linen around this place and that people are going to keep it locked away if they possibly can." He took out the picture he had found in Julian Merton's desk and studied it. Then held it out to Pete.

"Does this look innocent to you?"

Pete examined it a moment, then shrugged. "Why not? I saw that photo when I went through Merton's desk Wednesday evening. I still wouldn't read anything into it necessarily."

Brandon repeated the word, breaking it into syllables. "Ne-ces-sa-ri- ly."

He heaved to his feet. "Let's see if this upsets the dean as much as it did Beulah Taper."

Pete Wiggins had planned to have a visit with Henry Norton's secretary, but was waylaid by Joelle, angling for a personal chat. Pete's score had risen since their high-school days and moved even higher since last night. He handed her a copy of the list of guests at Ward's reception and tried converting flirtatious conversation into something more official. Successfully, as it turned out. Joelle's struggle with her conscience had been brief. After all, this was a murder investigation. And it would impress Pete. A few minutes later Pete hurried upstairs to look for Brandon. He found him sitting in the waiting room to the dean's office and called him out to the hall.

Brandon listened in silence. Then he took Miss Taper's blue leather appointment book from his folder and opened it to the week of July 16th.

Mary Walker sat huddled in her chair at one end of the living room couch. Her brother looked on helplessly, his glance straying from time to time out the window, to the police car and ambulance in front of Vince's bungalow, the small knots of people on the sidewalk. Over an hour had passed since Thad, returning home for lunch, had heard his name screamed out from next door. Thad leaned over to put an arm around his sister, but she disengaged herself.

"Well, that's enough of that."

"Don't try to be brave, Mary."

"Oh, I'm not. Indeed I'm not. I'm . . . I'm so . . . so regretting him."

She kept her face turned away from her brother, but the frozen posture of her body, the tone of her voice had told him what he should have guessed months ago. So much was suddenly explained. How could he have missed it? Thad wanted to say he understood, but knew that for now Mary needed to keep the deep source of her grief as secret as she had kept her love affair. This was no time to ask her why she had shut him out. Why she so often did. He could do no better than say, "At least he didn't suffer, Mary."

"How can you know that?"

"The medical examiner says he hit the back of his head very hard when he fell." He refrained from mentioning the effect of the old-fashioned bristling metal fixtures.

"No."

Thad looked puzzled. "What?"

"He didn't slip and fall. He couldn't have."

"Mary, it's the most common household accident."

"Vince was murdered, Thad." She turned to face him, her face like stone.

"Mary, listen to me. People slip in bathtubs . . . "

"That's just the point. He couldn't have."

"What?"

"Oh, he could have slipped in the tub, but it wouldn't have been full."

"What are you talking about?"

"Vince never took tub baths. He used to complain about that antique shower, but he never got around . . . " She broke off, covered her mouth with her hand.

It came back to him then: Vince with his dietary notions, his ideas on holistic medicine; Vince holding forth one evening on the Japanese, whose many talents he admired but whose views on personal hygiene baffled him. Their custom of communal lolling around, as he put it, in a single tub of water seemed in direct contradiction with their aesthetic sensibilities.

Moments later Chief Walker was heading up the walk next door to give additional instructions to his officers.

Brandon Blessing was shown into Dean Parker-Brown's office and informed by Phil Gertmenian that the dean would be with him in a moment. Brandon took in the Bessarabian rug — the one bright spot to his way of thinking. The room was handsome but austere, he felt. The carefully arranged books, the lack of clutter bespoke professionalism and order. The only odd note was a funny drawing of someone in a wig. He had no preconceived notion of what a woman dean's office might be like, but this one struck him as impersonal. A few green plants, but no knick-knacks, no family photos. A setting for someone in control, he thought, not the office of an emotional personality.

The next moment Brandon considered changing his mind. The photograph that now lay face down among some papers in his lap hadn't prepared him for the sensual impact of red hair, gray-green eyes, and the graceful carriage of a woman not intimidated by her height. Willie Hefner's description had been accurate.

After brief preliminaries, the Sergeant handed the dean the list of the guests at the reception along with the now standard request. Then Brandon asked, "You've been on vacation, I understand."

She smiled easily. "Yes. To Nepal."

"When did you return, Dean?"

"On the nineteenth." To his surprise, she anticipated his next question. "To Altamira, that is. I flew from Paris to San Francisco three days earlier."

"Why the detour?"

"I wanted a few days to myself before returning to campus. San Francisco always revitalizes me somehow."

"And that's what you needed after a hiking trip?"

Her tone was patient. "Perhaps I can make this a little easier for you, Sergeant. Yes, after the trek and Paris and the long flight, I wanted a few days to myself before coming on home. And no, I did not tell people here that I was in San Francisco. Nor did I see anyone. I stayed at the Carlton Hotel."

"For three days? Just to be alone?"

"That's correct." Anne raised a hand to push back a rebellious lock of hair from her forehead; she was perfectly composed.

Brandon was lost in his notes for a while. When he looked up, he was frowning. "Did you know that the president was attending an event near San Francisco at that time?" He glanced at his notes again. "The Pericles Society. Something called 'The Summer Outing.'"

Anne spoke lightly, "Why? Should I have?"

"Did you, Dean?"

"I know that group meets in July — about this time of year, yes."

"I understand it's some kind of think-tank outfit."

"Correct. A very select group of people from education, business, and government. A few from the arts."

Brandon didn't press further. Each seemed to study the other for a moment, then Brandon asked, "On the nineteenth, when you got back to Altamira, did you go to the Chemistry Department?"

"No. That is, I passed through it. My destination was Psychology."

"What time would that have been?"

"Oh, around 12:30. I was looking for Professor Tidwell. Thought we might have lunch together. She wasn't in."

"Professor Tidwell is the chair of Psychology, isn't she?"

"Yes. Though she prefers 'chairman.'"

"I thought university women were all feminists."

"Sometimes you'll come across a quirky one, Sergeant." She was clearly amused.

"I see. Why didn't you telephone Professor Tidwell to see whether or not she was in?"

"A spur-of-the moment idea. I was on my way to pick up something for lunch — turned in at Cooper Science Center."

"Which door did you use?"

"Tipton Way."

"Then you went through the Chemistry Department?"

"Right."

"How long were you in the building, Dean?"

"Just as long as it takes to walk to her office on the second floor, look in at the Psychology library and leave."

"Did you encounter anyone in the building?"

"No."

"I take it you are familiar with the layout of the Science Center."

"Intimately."

"Were you also familiar with Professor Peese's research?"

"In a general way. Charles Peese had retired before I was employed by the college."

Brandon seemed to be giving himself time for that to sink in. "Have you any thoughts as to who might have murdered your president?"

"No."

Brandon gave a heaving sigh. "Look, Dean, the nicest people are capable of committing murder. I'm sure you're all nice people here at the college. But someone here wanted him out of the way."

"Someone wanted to kill Julian Merton. What makes you so sure it was one of us?"

"Because that person knew about the toxin, Dean. Where to find it and how to use it. That's why you college people are high on my list."

She thought a minute. "But there was that article in the college magazine . . . "

"Yes, but outsiders weren't at the reception. I'm planning to stick close to home for now, Dean. Wyndham Hall. And I think you could help."

"I would like to, Sergeant Blessing, but I don't see how."

"I hear that feelings were running high about a certain Weinert proposal." He looked at his notes. "For an M.B.A. program."

"Feelings will run much higher when more faculty hear about it, Sergeant. The president's death doesn't change a thing, if that's what you're thinking."

He frowned. "Seems that no one cared much for your president, but no one had reason to kill him. Well, I've got to find a reason, Dean. And I will."

"I hope so, Sergeant."

He seemed to be weighing her statement, then opened his report book. "I'd like to go back to Wednesday afternoon, Dean."

Brandon listened attentively to her observations on the reception for Ward Finlay.

"So you were there until the end?" he asked. "Until shortly after six?"

"Yes."

"And was that the last time you saw President Merton alive?"

"Yes."

"Did he have a drink in his hand?"

"I didn't notice."

"Then what did you do?"

"I went on into my office and talked with Mr. Gertmenian, mostly about a meeting I wanted to set up before the end of the week."

"Then?"

"He left and I attacked some more of the correspondence that had piled up during my absence."

"Do you know when he left?"

"Not precisely. He thinks it was almost 6:30."

"And how long did you write?"

"I dictate, Sergeant."

"OK."

"Maybe about thirty minutes. Then I started reading some reports, for a change of pace, and I fell asleep."

"But not from jet lag."

She smiled, as though humoring him. "No."

"Do you often fall asleep like that? In your office?"

"Rarely. But some academic reports can be powerful soporifics, officer."

Brandon remained deadpan. When he questioned her next about finding Merton's body, her answers corresponded with what she had told Thad Walker: Merton had been at his desk; she had started CPR when Jeff Colton walked in; while he called for the paramedics she continued the CPR, though she knew it was hopeless; then Tom Donaldson arrived.

"What flashed through your mind, Dean? What did you think had happened to him?"

"I thought he had had a heart attack — a stroke, something like that."

"Did you and the president get along?"

"Most of the time."

"And the other times?"

"We had differences of opinion, naturally."

"How did you feel about him, as a person?"

"He was a most interesting man."

And that, Brandon thought, could mean anything.

"Brilliant in his field," she went on.

"I've heard you were going to be removed from office, Dean."

No reaction passed over her face. She nodded. "I'm not surprised. But 'removed' is the wrong term. I never intended to stay on as dean for more than five years, Sergeant. I've been here seven, because of the changeover in the presidency. The president and I were in the process of discussing a time-frame for my return to the History Department."

"Then you weren't about to be fired."

She smiled, indulgent. "I hardly think so."

She got up and went over to adjust the blinds, to lessen the amount of sunlight that was coming into the room. It also, Brandon thought, gave her the chance to compose herself — if she needed it. Which he somehow doubted.

When she sat down again, he slipped something from his folder, reached over to put a photograph on her desk.

The dean barely glanced at it, saying, "What has this to do with the president's death, Sergeant Blessing?"

"I don't know, ma'am."

He waited; she waited. At last Brandon continued, "I like to understand anything we turn up that isn't self-explanatory."

Anne smiled. "And you don't think this photograph is self-explanatory?"

"I'd rather hear your explanation."

The dean shrugged. "I don't know what I can add. As you must already know, it was taken during our last Faculty-Trustee retreat at Arrowhead — during one of the bird walks, I believe."

"Do you know who took it?"

"Yes. Professor Logan. She's a talented — and enthusiastic — photographer."

"Did you know she was taking your picture?"

Anne shook her head. "Of course not."

"Any idea why she did?"

"You will have to ask her, Sergeant."

"Have you seen this photo before?"

A hesitation preceded the candid smile. "Yes. President Merton showed it to me when we were visiting in his office. The day I came back from my holiday."

"Why did he think it necessary to do that?"

Anne shrugged. "Oh necessary . . . Hardly. He thought it was quite good of me but dreadful of him. President Merton was a bit vain. He thought he looked, well, jowly."

Brandon studied the photograph, nodded as though in agreement, then put it away. He fiddled with his papers a moment before asking, "Dean, were you and President Merton lovers?"

"No, Mr. Blessing, we were not."

The Sergeant thought he'd better rephrase the question. "Had you been?"

Was there a hesitation before she shook her head? Was it a definite "no"? Anne proceeded calmly. "We were the subject of gossip and a great deal of speculation, officer. You must be aware of that by now."

Brandon gave the photo another skeptical peek, and waited. Unexpectedly, Anne volunteered an explanation. "If I were to guess at what was occurring, I would say that the president had scored a point of some kind with which he was pleased. Or had just told a funny story. He was a very clever raconteur. And he could be, well, playful in certain moods. However, that's just a guess."

"Yes, ma'am." Their eyes held. She was the first to look away.

In the library of the president's house, Brandon Blessing was studying the portrait of a stern woman in a pince-nez, head held high, well supported by the stays in a lace neck-choker.

"That's Louisa May Arrington, Sergeant. She was the first Dean of Women of the college."

Sergeant Blessing turned to face the woman who had just come in. She had his card in her hand. Priscilla Merton, her blond hair and fair complexion handsomely set off by a black linen dress with a broad white collar, introduced herself.

"I understand that you are the officer in charge of the investigation?"

"Yes, ma'am."

She motioned him to a chair, placed his card on an end table.

"Dean Arrington was not only as determined as she looks, but she also had a good deal of money. This was her home, and in her will she designated it to serve as the president's residence."

A woman Brandon adjudged to be the house-keeper came in with a tray.

"I thought you might like a cup of coffee."

Brandon carefully reached for a fragile white cup with a gold band, refused cream but helped himself to sugar. Mrs. Merton took a sip of her coffee. "I hope you don't mind decaffeinated; I find that people rarely notice the difference."

"It's very good." He set the cup carefully on the table before him.

Priscilla Merton put hers aside and leaned forward earnestly. "I don't have to tell you how devastated and — and baffled I am by what is going on. When Chief Walker was kind enough to come by and explain about the coroner's action, I'm afraid I didn't take it well at all."

Brandon waited expectantly.

"I'm not a hysterical woman, but I just couldn't take it all in. Chief Walker was so vague. Oh, I'm sure he told me what he could. But it's not possible that anyone would want to kill Julian. Not in this kind of community."

"Mrs. Merton, you do understand that we have evidence that points away from death from natural causes?"

"I saw that dreadful article in the *Ledger* this morning. That can't be right . . . " She looked at him. "But it is, isn't it?"

"I'm afraid so, ma'am."

Priscilla nodded, with a slender finger she traced the tapestry pattern on the arm of her chair for a moment before looking up. "How can I help you, officer?"

Brandon decided he needed to vamp before getting down to playing the melody. He spent fifteen minutes learning about life at the college, Julian Merton's contribution to it, in particular. A very large contribution, according to his widow. And one that was on the verge of being nationally significant, until the events of two days ago interfered.

"Did you notice what the president was eating at the party?"

"Oh, Julian never ate anything at cocktail parties, unless it was absolutely unavoidable."

"And what was considered unavoidable?"

"At a private party, for instance, if the hostess pressed something upon him. Even then, he tried to dispose of the canapé or whatever in an ashtray." She smiled. "Or a planter, I'm sorry to say."

"Did you notice what he was drinking?"

"Perrier, I believe, but I can't be sure."

"And when you last saw him? Right after the presentation of the gifts, I believe?"

"Yes." She seemed to be struggling to remember. "I recall Leslie Filmore proposing a toast to Ward Finlay. And then Julian. I didn't notice what was in his glass."

Brandon didn't react, but went on to lead her through the time she had spent at the reception. Other than recalling some of the people she had spoken to, Priscilla Merton seemed to have been particularly unobservant. Or, recalling Pete's comments, had she been lapping up the booze? Brandon sensed that she was growing restless. He handed her a copy of the guest list, explained what he needed and then, "Would you tell me what you did after you left the reception, Mrs. Merton?" He listened solemnly to her account of going home, seeing her daughter off on her first date, getting the phone call from Weinert, trying to reach her husband several times by phone, then walking the short distance to Wyndham.

"You didn't hurry?"

"I — I don't think so. It never occurred to me . . . But the minute I saw those paramedics, I knew. I knew even before they told me."

Her eyes glistened with tears.

Brandon let her rest for a moment, then asked, "Did you leave the reception for a while at any time?"

She thought a moment. "Yes. One of the secretaries called me to the phone."

Brandon turned back a couple of pages in his notebook; Miss Taper hadn't mentioned that.

"A call from our daughter, wanting to know whether her father was coming back to the house with me."

"When was that?"

"I'm not sure. 5:30 maybe."

"I see." Brandon made an additional entry in his book, then looked straight at Priscilla Merton. "I apologize for asking personal questions, Mrs. Merton, but would you say your marriage was a happy one?" And got the reaction he somehow expected. First indignation, then patient and stoic acceptance of the job he had to do. Brandon listened quietly and quickly reached a conclusion: She presented herself as the faithful wife; he saw her as one well-trained in the arts of PR.

"Did your husband have any financial worries, Mrs. Merton?"

"No more than anyone has — who isn't rich."

"How would you describe your financial situation?"

"Comfortable, Sergeant. Definitely not rich."

"What about insurance?"

The small smile was knowing, as though she had read behind the question. "We have a modest portfolio, Sergeant. And we own the house Julian's father lives in — in Arizona. It was purchased with royalties from a rather successful book of Julian's. Julian had a life insurance policy; not large — by today's standards. He believed there were better uses for money than investing in a large policy."

"I see." Brandon frowned, looking for his place in the script. "To return a moment to your personal life. I guess you know there was talk about the president . . . "

She finished for him, with an airy wave of the hand. "And Dean Parker-Brown. Of course. It's inevitable, wouldn't you say, whenever two handsome people of the opposite sex work together? And I've always found the academic community to be particularly prurient in its interests."

She lifted her hand from the chair arm and smoothed down the front pleat of her dress. Then, with great tolerance, "So childish, wouldn't you say?"

Brandon returned her smile with a barely perceptible lift to the corners of his mouth and pulled the photograph from its folder. "I wonder if you're familiar with this picture."

The smile faded as she took the glossy. An answer was quite a while in coming. "I don't believe I've seen it before."

"Don't you think you would know for sure? It's a pretty intimate shot, isn't it?"

Priscilla seemed once again very sure of herself. "Not at all, Sergeant, though it might seem that way to an outsider. My husband was more Latin than Anglo-Saxon in some ways."

Latin, Brandon wondered? With that Scandinavian physiognomy and light blond hair?

Priscilla went on. "He touched people. He could be very — very playful."

Where had he heard that before? Oh yes, Dean Parker-Brown. Had the dean called Mrs. Merton, he wondered? Was it possible that the wife and the mistress were in cahoots? It wouldn't have surprised him. Detective Blessing took another sip of his coffee and leaned back as though he had all the time in the world. He had long ago learned the value of silence. Few people could endure it.

Priscilla seemed hypnotized by the picture. She turned it over, then looked up brightly. "Oh well, here you have it. I thought the setting seemed familiar. This was taken at our last Trustee-Faculty Retreat. I thought I had seen all of the pictures taken by the photographer at Arrowhead."

Brandon didn't correct her.

"Maybe I have seen this one and just didn't notice. Is it important?"

Brandon shrugged. "I wondered what it was doing in your husband's office desk — among his personal things."

Priscilla sat up straighter. Her expression had turned hostile. "Well, unless you're good with a Ouija board, officer . . . " Her voice broke as she turned away, digging a Kleenex out of the pocket of her dress. "Why don't you ask Dean Parker-Brown? I'm sure she will be able to explain things satisfactorily."

"Yes, ma'am."

Priscilla sniffed into the Kleenex, her face still working. "I don't think it is very considerate of you, Sergeant Blessing, to bring this to me at such a time. Any sudden reminder of my husband . . . "

"Yes, ma'am." They sat in silence for a while. The Sergeant started to get up, then thought better of it. "Would you say the dean and the president were off someplace alone when this was taken?"

"I doubt it. They could hardly have been alone, given the nature of the Retreat."

"Why was that?"

"Everything was so scheduled. For Julian in particular. He had literally no time to himself — except when sleeping."

But with whom? Brandon allowed the question to remain unspoken.

As Mrs. Merton accompanied him to the door, Brandon noticed a very pretty teenager with a sullen face sitting on the steps of the hall staircase. Mrs. Merton ignored her, turned to open the front door. The girl got up, languidly, pulled out a black scarf from somewhere, put it over her head. Brandon, who counted six girls among his seven children, was used to the self-conscious, dramatic gesture of adolescents. Nevertheless he was somewhat shaken. The girl in the black hood just stood there, like an executioner.

Terry Logan could hear her phone ringing. She hurried down the hall, unlocked her office door, and grabbed for the phone.

"Oh. It's you again."

"Terry, did you take that dreadful picture of Julian and Anne?"

"What picture?"

"The one that prissy policeman has. He said it was found in Julian's desk."

"Oh that. I wouldn't call it 'dreadful.'"

"It was cruel. Cruel. I thought you were a friend."

"Is that what you thought last night? When you practically accused me of . . . Hello?"

Terry shrugged, dropped the phone back into its cradle. "Have it your way, toots."

She went around the desk and sat down. Glancing up toward the open door she saw Brandon Blessing standing there, waiting.

Brandon Blessing tilted his head, frowning. "What do you mean you gave the president the photo 'out of pique,' Professor Logan?"

"I mean I was fed up with their holier-than-thou attitude around here — Merton's in particular. The way my tenure case was handled — such a farce. If you've done your homework, you know about that."

Thanks to Willie Hefner, he did. More or less.

"When I got back from England about ten days ago, I was in a pretty foul mood. Depressed. Love life on the fritz. No job. And damn it, Sergeant, I'm good. A good teacher and a damned good scholar. Though I haven't hit my full stride yet. Anyway . . . Things were at an end here."

Terry broke off, gazing out the window and across the quad, where sprinklers were playing. "I was sorting through some prints — I'm having a show at Reflections — opened last Saturday."

Brandon looked blank.

"That's a bookshop and art gallery in town."

He made a note, waited for her to continue.

"So, I was going through my recent work and came across that photo of Julian and Anne I took at Arrowhead, and I got mad."

Brandon held up his pen to stop her from going on. "Just a moment, Professor Logan. Why did you take it?"

"Pretty obvious, don't you think?"

"Not to me."

"Let's just say that double lives, people who wear masks, interest me. And there are plenty of those around here. Well, they had moved off a bit from the others. I might have gotten something a bit more, shall we say explicit? But Anne pushed him away."

"So you followed them?" Brandon had a hard time imagining this tough, outspoken young woman lurking behind bushes.

"You could say that. And why the hell not? The hypocrite. Ah, Anne's OK — as OK as a dean can be. Which isn't saying a hell of a lot. But Merton, a real prick."

"When did you give him the photo?"

"Wednesday morning. I went in early, so that Beulah wouldn't stop me."

"You didn't mention that when Agent Wiggins spoke with you."

She shrugged. "Why should I have? He was only interested in whether or not I thought the president looked sick at the party."

"So you saw President Merton Wednesday morning. And?"

"And I told him off for a sanctimonious, mealy-mouth son-of-a-bitch. I don't care what kind of rationale they cooked up." She was leaning across the desk toward him, her face reflecting the anger she had felt on that day. Brandon was grateful not to have been in Julian Merton's shoes.

"I didn't get tenure because I'm a lesbian. I know it. I know what Merton and some of the others around here think, no matter how much they play the enlightened and tolerant academics. Gay is dirty. Beyond the pale. But when it comes to fornicating around with students or cheating on one's spouse — that's perfectly legitimate."

"Are you saying you know for sure that the president and Dean Parker-Brown were having an affair?"

Her laugh reduced Brandon to a naive adolescent. "Aw, come on, Sergeant."

"But have you proof?"

She shrugged. "The photo and what I saw satisfy me."

"Just what did you see?"

"Oh, the way they were acting. An intimate, private way of looking at each other."

"You couldn't be called an unprejudiced observer though, could you, Professor Logan?"

"Unprejudiced? Not on your life. If you want to know everything, officer, I hated the bastard.

Hated his pomposity. Hated his phony charm. Hated his hypocrisy. Hated everything he stood for." She gave a harsh laugh. "In a word, that is."

"You sound like the person I'm looking for, Professor Logan."

She gave him a wide grin. "Don't I just. But then if I had murdered him, you'd probably find out — and he'd have the last word." She swung a bit in her chair. "I sure felt like killing him at times. Me and others."

"What others?"

"Listen, Sergeant, the line forms to the right."

Sighing, Brandon closed his book, put his pen back in his shirt pocket. He asked Terry Logan a few questions about the reception that didn't bring him anything new and handed her a copy of the guest list to review. "A last question, Professor Logan."

"Yeah?"

"The Retreat was in April. Why did you wait until July to give him the photograph?"

"I didn't develop that roll right away — got side tracked with all the stuff to do at the end of the semester. Besides, there wasn't any special hurry. Then I got my grant and took off for England."

"Maybe you weren't sure how you wanted to use the picture. Could that be it?"

She shrugged.

"When you gave President Merton the photograph, did you ask for anything in return?"

Terry gave him a scorching look that made Brandon wonder about her classroom technique. She might be a good teacher, but he was ready to bet his Kennedy dollar that she was an intimidating one.

Terry leaned across the desk, arms folded. "Listen, Sergeant Blessing, there isn't anything that bastard could have offered me that I would accept. Not anything."

Brandon's expression didn't betray his thoughts: Oh yeah?

Brandon Blessing and Officer Wiggins sat hunched over drippy hamburgers at a corner table of the Student Union. The snack shop was almost empty except for a few students with summer jobs and a scattering of college personnel.

Pete Wiggins grabbed for some paper napkins from the holder. "When they advertise 'luscious and juicy' they aren't kidding."

Brandon didn't appear to have heard him. "How did it go for you this morning?"

"I'm about finished passing out those lists."

"Any interesting reactions?"

"People seemed pretty subdued. Some wanted to ask a lot of questions."

"Anybody say it was a loss to the college?"

"Yeah, one. A professor Zumholtz. Department of Religion."

"Maybe he believes in brotherly love. Anybody say it was about time?"

Pete started to answer in all seriousness, but caught a now recognizable movement at the corner of Blessing's mouth.

Sergeant Blessing reached for the last of his french fries, pushed the plastic basket aside and got out his report book.

"Our first assumption is that someone at this college wanted to murder President Merton. Until and if we get a strong lead to the contrary, our second assumption is that it's someone who was close to Merton: wife, VP, or a person working in Wyndham. On the alternate list: one of the trustees or a faculty member who attended the party. Whether the death was triggered by something in the wine or his bum heart may be a question for trial lawyers to play with. However, the bottle of wine and the coroner's findings could hardly be more conclusive. As to motive . . . "

Pete took a sip of his Coke. "Chief Walker and I sure got plenty of unsolicited comments. But now that murder's involved people are clamming up. 'Yes the president was difficult, but . . .' "

Brandon worried his napkin into a shredded ball. "A man in his position usually has plenty of folks mad at him for one reason or another. But it takes a heavy load of desperation and fear, or just plain common or garden variety rage to turn someone to murder."

"Unless the person is psychotic maybe?"

Brandon looked thoughtful. "Maybe. The murderer could hardly have worked out a more complicated scheme for wasting someone. It suggests someone who thinks that God Almighty should abdicate in his favor. Professor Logan volunteered there were plenty of 'double lives' at this college. Maybe she's got something."

Pete nodded, though his mental Filofax failed to yield any immediate candidates.

"Finish passing out those lists. I'm going to have a shot at the remaining vice presidents this afternoon. If my luck continues to hold, I won't get much more out of them than I have from the Dean of the Faculty and the widow."

"A goose-egg, huh? No sex angle?"

Brandon sketched an ambiguous gesture.

"It's kinda hard to think of someone like that dean having an affair with a married man. And her boss to boot."

"You're a quaint one, kid, you know that?"

"Come off it, Brandon. You know, you get a feeling about certain people. Everyone I've talked to thinks she's one fine lady. You really think that the dean and the president . . . ?"

"I don't 'really think' anything at this point. Just a feeling there may be something exceptional about their relationship."

Pete stopped chewing. "Exceptional." That was sure a new one for screwing around.

"What about Professor Logan?"

"She's in a class by herself. Outspoken. Dead certain they were lovers — without anything that could be called serious evidence. She hated the president's guts and makes no bones about it. Funny woman. Setting herself up as a possible suspect. We'll oblige." Brandon added some sugar to his coffee and stirred reflectively. "Pete, soon as you can, get on the horn to San Francisco, downtown division; ask for Lieutenant Sam Pachman. We need a rundown on this Pericles Society Outing of Merton's. And see what he can find out about Dean Parker-Brown's stay at the Carlton."

"Will do."

Sergeant Blessing fished around in Pete Wiggins' hamburger basket for the remaining pickles, then sought solace in a very large chocolate chip cookie.

Monday, July 24

A BROADBEAMED WOMAN IN STILETTO heels teetered along ahead of Brandon to the door of Victor Laszlo's office where she announced him in hushed tones. The office had a no-nonsense look about it. Victor, the picture of industry with rolled up sleeves and open collar, rose and came around his desk. Brandon did a quick summing up: vigorous, muscular man (mid-fifties?); large head made even more leonine by a shock of white hair (premature?); eyes, bright blue, in odd contradiction to the dull complexion with its faint network of broken veins. The blue eyes were twinkling a welcome as Laszlo took Sergeant Blessing's hand in a hearty crush before gesturing him to the leather couch that was part of what looked like a mini conference center. The detective added "professional greeter" to his first impressions.

"Sit down, Sergeant. How about a cup of coffee? Or some iced tea maybe?"

The secretary, who had been hovering, vanished in the wake of Brandon's negative response.

Victor sank into one of the large burgundy leather chairs and leaned back, knees apart, in the position that had earned him his nickname. "Now, how can I be of help?"

The question was promising, but Victor was less than satisfactory in reconstructing the events between 4:00 and 6:30 on the day of Merton's death. Except for his role as toastmaster, the afternoon seemed to have been largely a blur.

"What were you drinking at this gathering, Mr. Laszlo?"

Victor threw back his head and guffawed. "Seem a bit vague, do I, Sergeant?"

That was not what Brandon had been leading up to, but the jolly self-deprecation suggested a possible opportunity.

"I may have had a glass or two of wine along the way, but mostly I stuck with my standard tipple: good old Jack Daniels. Didn't drink much, actually."

Brandon wondered what would qualify as "drinking much."

"Weren't you with the president right before the toasts were proposed?"

The leonine head bobbed. "Right."

"And who else?"

"Filmore. Chairman of the Board."

"That's it?"

"Sally Cochran — our chairman of Ways and Means — was supposed to make a toast, but she decided against it."

"Where was she just then?"

He made a vague gesture. "Around. I had spoken with her earlier, of course." He leaned forward as though about to impart a confidence. "Always pay attention to the trustees: rule one of the game. But as to who might have served a drink to Julian . . ."

"Did you notice what the president was drinking?"

"To tell you the truth, I was preoccupied with some problems that have come up here at the office — afraid my mind was elsewhere much of the time."

"What kind of problems?"

"Oh, I have some discontented alumni on my tail — not happy about our admission policies. I'm not either, for that matter," he grumbled. "And we have a donor who is mad at us and another one who wants to leave Tipton some very valuable property, with a life-time annuity payment to go to his wife, then to his children. But there's a first wife who is making some claims on the property — if that gives you an idea. We're trying to work things out. The college could benefit by several million." Victor smiled, treating Brandon to a display of impressively white and handsome teeth. "That's the sort of thing that is part of my daily worry diet, Sergeant Blessing."

If Victor expected a sign of commiseration or even of understanding, he was disappointed. Brandon could have modeled for a cigar store Indian.

"Merton had just finished his third year here, right?"

"Right."

"Mr. Laszlo, how would you describe the working atmosphere in Wyndham Hall?"

Fleshy lips pursed in reflection. "I think we all get along pretty well. Little ups and downs, of course, but we're a good, solid team."

"Do you know of anyone with whom the president was having a problem?"

"Not really. Except for Beulah Taper. Julian complained about her a good deal."

"Anything specific?"

Victor shrugged. "If you ask me, she just wasn't his type somehow."

"What about at the administrative level. Anyone who might have had it in for him?"

"Beats me, Sergeant. It really does." Victor ran a hand through his handsome head of hair as though to clarify his thinking on the subject. "Oh sure, there were people who weren't members of the fan club . . . " He let it hang.

"Such as?"

"Well, faculty are always bitching about one thing or another. Professor Logan was breathing fire this spring — maybe you know about that."

Brandon admitted he did.

"Some of the old guard can get uptight about almost anything."

"Like this Weinert project I've been hearing about?"

"Right. But that proposal is just now coming out from under wraps. The kind of thing intellectuals will wrangle endlessly about. But murder? No way."

"Back to you, Mr. Laszlo. You and the president worked well together, did you?"

The impressive teeth were flashed again. "I have been crossed once or twice, sure." The tone indicated indulgence for presidential vagaries.

"You had been at the college almost twenty-five years when Merton was appointed, is that right, Mr. Laszlo?"

"Right. But not in this position. I started out in Financial Aid."

"And what did you think of him?"

Victor leaned back again, expanding his chest. "A brilliant man, brilliant."

"Aside from having been disagreed with occasionally, did you find President Merton easy to work with?"

The chuckle was almost creamy. "Have you ever known a real brain that was always easy to work with?"

"I'm not sure I've had much contact with 'real brains.' "

Victor chuckled again. "You may have been lucky."

"Would you say that you and the president saw eye to eye on business matters?"

Victor thought it over. "Not always, of course not."

"Any particular area of disagreement?"

Laszlo's smile was becoming increasingly forced. "We had some discussions about how he was handling the Weinert gift."

"Discussions or arguments?"

The smile perked up in concert with the jolly tone. "A little of both. Mostly healthy discussion."

"So what didn't you agree on?"

Victor considered that one for a moment. "I thought that he and Leslie Filmore were in too big of a hurry. In my opinion the plans for accepting and implementing the gift needed fuller discussion at the administrative level." He frowned and Brandon caught it.

"Were you being excluded from discussions, Mr. Laszlo?"

"Of course not."

Brandon nodded and wrote "V. L. ignored" in his book.

"You must understand, Sergeant, Julian's and my differences were merely procedural."

"You felt secure in your position here, did you?"

The smile flickered, then Victor brought it back, clearing his throat as he did so. "After all these years? After all the friends I've made for the college? I should hope to tell you."

And that, Brandon thought, is another lie.

"And you gotta remember, Sergeant —" Victor was back on track, the tone of complicity had returned — "I know where too many bodies are buried around here."

"For instance."

He answered with a gesture of dismissal. "All old history, long before Julian came on board."

"To return to President Merton, Mr. Laszlo . . . Were you at all close? Did he confide in you?"

"Not often. Not in me he didn't." The light tone and bland expression did not entirely conceal the resentment.

"In whom did he confide?"

Victor's large face seemed to sag, the bounce now gone from it. "I would say he was pretty much of a loner."

"What about the dean? Don't the Dean of the Faculty and the president of a college have to work closely together?"

"Ah well," Victor said. The tone of voice was suggestive; the blue eyes twinkled the remainder of the sentence.

Brandon returned to the basement to make a phone call. On his way back to the first floor he encountered Crystal Mathews. She favored him with an expanded smile.

"Hi there, Sergeant."

"Is your boss in his office?"

"You bet. Just go on in. I'm on my coffee break."

Sergeant Blessing stared at her retreating back for a moment; no girdle encircled those lush hips. He shook his head and plodded on up the stairs.

Turner Van Voorhees was busy hammering in a picture hook when Brandon showed up at his open door. If Victor's office evoked a men's club, Van Voorhees's domain suggested something from the late Twenties, though it was beyond Brandon's competence to pinpoint the prevailing style as a mix of art déco and art nouveau. The office was impeccably neat and rather sparse in its furnishings. The desk was a large table with legs that looked like twisted vines. The four straight chairs and small table echoed the motif of the desk, two chrome-trimmed suede arm chairs and the desk lamp whose base was a languidly draped woman holding an ivory hoop, added up to an unusual setting for a place of business.

"Come in, Sergeant. I've been expecting you. Please, sit down."

Turner lifted a picture onto the hook and stood back. "Well, what do you think?"

Brandon studied the black-and-white photograph of a derelict wrapped in a collection of nondescript clothing, hunkered down in a doorway surrounded by trash, eyes narrowed against a shaft of early morning light. Brandon felt certain that if he went closer he would catch the odor of unwashed flesh, of must and urine.

"Interesting," was the best he could manage. He might have said the same thing about the young man before him who hardly seemed old enough to be a vice president of anything.

"A present from my wife; today's my birthday."

"Congratulations."

Brandon tried guessing his age, but Turner solved the riddle. "Thanks. Creeping up on old number thirty-five. Just one more year to go." He stood back, studying the photograph.

"Kitty would have my hide if I didn't hang this. She's been on a Terry Logan kick. She has four or five more at home. Are you interested in photography, Sergeant?"

"Only what I have to do sometimes in the line of duty. Not what you'd call artistic."

"I guess not." Turner tilted his head as he studied the print. "I'm not sure this is either." He gave a small shudder. "Seems to me art should strive for beauty, for perfection." The serious tone vanished as he said lightly, "But at that, it's the least melancholy of the lot."

Brandon, who had more contact than he cared for with the "melancholy" of this earth, couldn't imagine anyone wanting to photograph the destitute for money. Or wanting to put them on display in an office. So he said nothing.

"Actually, it's very good technically, but one doesn't want to be made to feel guilty while dealing with the finances of a college for the intellectually and financially privileged."

The grin was boyish — definitely shy of thirty-five. Brandon couldn't peg this self-assured young man as someone conversant with guilt.

"Professor Logan goes in heavily for social content. Probably doesn't hurt to have our complacency get a jolt or two now and then." He studied the photograph once more. "Though preferably not in the work place."

Except for the filing cabinet, personal computer, and a couple of framed diplomas, the office didn't look much like a work place to Brandon. Turner moved a vine-leaf chair in order to sit opposite the Sergeant who had settled more or less into one of the sling-back jobs.

"Mr. Van Voorhees, I'm hoping you can help reconstruct the president's movements at the reception on Wednesday afternoon — and of course your own."

"I'll do my best. Shall we start with me?"

Brandon was kept busy taking notes. Here was a subject with a good memory.

"I think it was close to six when the party began to break up." Turner frowned in thought. "I know the wine was almost all gone. I poured the last of one bottle for the president and Victor shortly before the toasts — if that's a help."

"Was it red wine?"

"No. Rosé."

"You're sure?"

Turner smiled. "Absolutely. I had some myself."

"Do you know who was with President Merton shortly before the toasts were proposed?"

"I don't think I noticed. Kitty asked me to call home, sometime around five-forty I think, to see whether the children were back from a birthday party. Then I was behind the bar again for a short while — until the speeches were made."

"Where did you go to phone?"

"The office next to Victor's. His secretary's."

"You didn't notice an odd bottle around at any time? A Château d'Yquem?"

"No. And I rather think I would have, if I had seen it. It's an expensive wine. Hardly suitable for an office party. The Mertons gave us a couple of bottles at Christmas."

Brandon sat up a little straighter. "Do you still have them?"

"Mercy no. Kitty had me uncork both of them for a small dinner we gave at New Years."

"When was the last time you saw President Merton?"

"Wednesday evening. When I poked my head through our connecting washroom — over there." He gestured toward the door in the west wall. "Kitty, my wife, was with me."

"What time would that have been?"

"Mm . . . I was at the gym by 6:30. . . . So, 6:15 — 20 maybe."

Detective Blessing glanced down at his book. The time checked with Chief Walker's notes.

"Did he say anything?"

"Julian? Just body language. He was on the phone — with Mr. Weinert, an important donor."

"And what did his body language say, in your opinion?"

"Oh, Julian was just being playful."

"Playful." That was at least the third time he had heard this description of Merton. Didn't seem to jibe with the critical comments Thad and Pete had registered.

Turner continued. "He made a face — like someone does who is bored or being held captive on the phone. Then he raised his glass, in a kind of salute. And Kitty and I took off."

"You say you went to the gym?"

"Kitty went on home. I went for a brief workout."

"Which gym?"

"Pusey. Here on campus — right across the street."

"Did you see anybody?"

"Yes. Mary Walker — from the News Bureau. I had just finished my Nautilus workout. And Coach Beeson."

"And then?"

"Home."

"You went straight home?"

Turner nodded. "I got there before eight. 7:45 maybe."

"Did you drive or walk?"

"I walked. Took me less than ten minutes."

Turner waited patiently while Brandon referred to his notes once again.

"The glass President Merton waved with. Was there something in it?"

"I think so."

"Water or wine?"

"Wine, I think. But that may be an assumption."

"Did you see him take a drink?"

"No. Just the flourish with the glass."

"I see. Was the glass full?"

"Sorry, I don't think I noticed."

Both Brandon and Turner Van Voorhees seemed to be pondering something. Then Turner spoke, restrained emotion in his voice.

"It's hard to think of Julian's being gone. I keep wanting to open that door . . . It's a terrible loss for us, Sergeant."

"Any thoughts on who might have murdered him, Mr. Van Voorhees?"

Turner shook his head. "And believe me I've thought about it, Sergeant."

Brandon blinked a few times, as though signifying reception. "I understand the college books have just been audited."

"Right. I guess you'll need the name of the auditors —"

Brandon interrupted. "I've got it. Colby-Forstman."

"They'll tell you that everything is in order."

"I know. I've talked with them."

Turner gave him an approving look. "You've been busy, Sergeant. Now, how can I help you?"

"You've been here just two years, is that correct?"

"Yes. But I'm a fast learner, Sergeant."

Brandon remained noncommittal. "You and the president got along, did you?"

"Oh yes. Well, most of the time. He could be erratic, changeable. But I admired him. And I owe him a lot."

"How so?"

"He hired me, Sergeant Blessing. It's as simple as that."

"And did you feel you would stay hired?"

"Absolutely. Julian supported me all the way. And so did the Board." He grinned. "There's nothing like trustee support to make a fellow feel secure, officer."

Brandon's facial muscles didn't react. "Well, do you know of any enemies Merton might have had among those trustees you mentioned?"

Turner shook his head.

"Can you think of any action of his as president or in his private life that would give someone an itch for revenge?"

"He crossed people sometimes, sure."

"Like Professor Logan?"

There was again a hesitation. "To be frank, I've considered that. But Terry is a person who fights out in the open. She's a gutsy lady, not a sneaky one."

Brandon seemed to muse over this a moment before asking, "Could you comment on the Mertons' married life? Did they get along?"

"So far as I know. Oh, I believe there was some tension there at times . . . "

"Because of the dean, perhaps?"

Turner smiled. "I've heard the rumor, like everyone else. But I don't believe it for a moment. Look, Sergeant Blessing. We all work closely together, the vice presidents, I mean. We often travel together. Drive in to LA and back for meetings together. In the two years I've been at Tipton I've never seen a gesture or heard the slightest remark that would betray an intimate relationship between Julian and Anne."

Brandon waited, sensing that more was coming.

"Well, I think I might as well tell you this, too. Julian favored me, somewhat. I'm the only vice president he hired personally, you see. That may have been the reason. We've travelled out of town, just the two of us, on a number of occasions." Turner picked up, then put back down a bulbous crystal object on the table beside him. "I guess Julian felt he could relax with me. He rarely drank, but a time or two, at the end of a long day, well . . .

When that happened, even just a couple of drinks could hit him hard, and he wasn't always as discreet as he should be. At least with me, I mean. I've heard him talk about Anne. And in terms that didn't always flatter her administrative judgment. But never a word that would suggest there was or had been an intimate relationship."

"Was he going to fire her?"

Turner was shocked. "He would never have done that."

"Ask her to resign, then?"

"Julian was a bit miffed at Anne's reaction to a new program he was keen on."

"That would be this M.B.A. plan?"

"Oh, you know about that? Well, Anne's first reaction was negative, and Julian was disappointed. But as for asking for a resignation . . . I, I have a hard time believing that."

"Thank you, Mr. Van Voorhees. You've been very helpful."

"Look here, I hope you won't repeat what I've said — about Julian's confiding in me about the dean."

"The information we're gathering is not for publication at this time, Mr. Van Voorhees." Brandon closed his report book. "Do you know whether your wife would be at home?"

"Kitty? Why, yes, I think so."

"I'd like to talk to her."

"Of course. She could be helpful. Kitty's a most observant woman."

As he was leaving the office, Brandon lingered a moment in front of a small table cluttered with what appeared to be family pictures: a group on skis, a man and woman on horseback, presumably Turner and his wife; the same couple and two children waving from a sailboat, with tennis rackets, in karate outfits, in back-packing gear . . .

Turner came up to him. "My rogues' gallery, officer."

Thinking of his own indolent brood for whom TV watching seemed to be the main activity, Brandon was lost in admiration.

Brandon stood mopping his face in front of imposing dark green double doors with gleaming brass hardware. Chimes rang in response to his finger on the button, and a moment later he was ushered out of the hot, murky sunlight into a cool hallway. After taking his name, the maid directed him to the living room to wait. It was a large room with French doors along the back wall giving onto a garden with a pool beyond. It had, he thought, a summer-time look: The hardwood floor, devoid of rugs, was polished to a lustrous finish; all the furniture and small tables wore what he took to be summer covers of a pale green and white striped cotton. Brandon looked around for a Logan photograph or two, but the pictures on the wall were either oils or prints.

"Turner called and said you were coming by, Sergeant Blessing." Kitty extended her hand. "I'm Kitty Van Voorhees."

Brandon shook her hand, mumbling a how-do-you-do. The snapshots he had just seen didn't do her justice. Her auburn hair worn full and near shoulder length was the same shade as her husband's. Her elongated physique matched his elegance. A perfect, very lightly tanned complexion was enhanced by large hazel eyes, dark eyebrows, and a generous mouth. Kitty Van Voorhees was stunning and Brandon was not impervious. This could be a pleasant interlude in a trying day.

Kitty directed him to a chair and sat down opposite him. He'd hoped the maid would return with iced coffee or tea, but the very rich were evidently not as hospitable as ordinary folk, and he had been told that Turner's wife was very rich indeed. It showed in the fabric and cut of her white silk suit. It showed in the two pieces of jewelry she was wearing: Navajo-inspired cuff bracelets heavily encrusted with turquoise.

The maid did appear, but only to call Mrs. Van Voorhees to the phone. She was gone no more than a few minutes.

"I'm so sorry. That was my father — in New York. He's coming out for his annual visit in two weeks, but he still phones almost every day. The problem of being an only child."

She seemed more pleased than annoyed at the parental attention.

Kitty settled into her chair, crossed her long legs primly at the ankles, and smiled at him.

The interview was disappointing. Turner had called his wife observant; Brandon labelled her an air-head. She babbled on in a disconnected manner in answer to his questions, interposing editorial comments of her own on the personality of the people she was discussing, comments that were punctuated by thoughtless hyperbole. Julian was "just too brilliant," Priscilla Merton "too sweet," the dean "too marvelous," and Terry Logan "too terribly talented." Kitty's vocabulary, like her judgment, was lacking in discrimination.

"You're well acquainted with your husband's colleagues, are you?"

She pouted on a long-drawn-out "well" before going on. "Well, we see them a lot at college functions. Turner and I feel it's important for us both to attend those as much as possible."

Uh-huh, Brandon thought. OK to hobnob, but not at one's home.

Sergeant Blessing walked out into the oppressive heat with only one interesting observation to record: Kitty was certain there was red wine in the president's glass when last she saw him, an almost full glass. "When he waved with it, I thought surely it was going to slosh out. And that early nineteenth-century Kerman Laver carpet in his office is worth three hundred thousand at the very least. Gramps had one that was a tad smaller, and it was appraised at over two hundred thousand four years ago."

At last, Brandon thought, the real Kitty Van Voorhees had stood up. Kitty might be a feather head, but she knew the value of a dollar. He was willing to bet that she kept the family checkbook.

It was close to four o'clock when Brandon returned to the office in the basement and called forensics — the toxicology lab. "Fritz? Blessing here . . . Yeah, well blessings on you too and how about throwing that record away? . . . Fritz, just want to double-check something. Are we now certain that the poisoned wine is that Château stuff? . . . Couldn't possibly be another white wine? . . . OK. And thanks . . . Sure, pass me on to criminalistics . . . Hi, Brandon Blessing here. Understand someone wants to talk to me . . . Are you sure? . . . Where? . . . Please. Have the report delivered here to Wyndham Hall — at the College. And thanks."

Pete Wiggins came in as he hung up and handed him a small package. "This just came by messenger from the coroner's offfice."

Brandon slit the envelope and extracted a small black leather book, President Merton's pocket appointment book. He dropped it on the desk without opening it.

"I had a talk with the Mertons' housekeeper, Brandon. When she finally opened up it was all the way."

"Let me guess. Not the ideal happy home."

"Things were smooth the first year and a half, but since then . . . Straight downhill. Particularly this last year."

"Knock-down drag-outs?"

"No. Breakfast scenes, over small things — like who promised to do what or who said what at some party. But they didn't fight in public. Just a lot of tension. Sounds of anger from behind closed doors. Real chilly atmosphere. The kid didn't help. Buttered up to daddy and sassed mother."

"Anything about the dean? Or another woman?"

"Nope. She was evasive on that score. Wouldn't say yes or no. She did volunteer that women guests at the house made a fuss over him. Mrs. Merton, by the way, has been drinking more and more. And alone."

"Since when?"

"This past year mostly."

"I see."

After waiting a moment for a question or some further sign of life, Pete said, "By the way, Brandon, there's someone who wants to talk to you. Mary Walker. The Chief's sister."

"What's she doing here?"

"She works here. Part time, in the News Bureau."

"And the rest of the time?"

"Heck, I don't know. Except that she's an artist; has a small studio at home. She just said she needed to see you and that it was personal."

Brandon was ruminating. "Seems to me there's something I've heard about her . . . "

"That she's a paraplegic maybe."

"Automobile accident about four years ago, right? Thad Walker lost his wife."

Pete nodded. "Shall I tell her it's OK?"

"Sure. But first I've got a fresh item for you to play with. Some trace evidence. Looks like Julian Merton's body was moved."

"You're kidding."

"Nope. Colton did tell you he vacuums the president's office early every morning?"

"Yeah."

"And he vacuumed the morning of the day of the murder, right? Well, the crime lab has identified samples they took from the rug in his office — some hair, and fibers from the cloth of the suit he was wearing that day. Picked it up from just behind his desk. So, unless he was rolling around on the floor . . . "

"You've seen too many X-rated movies, Brandon."

"And you're beginning to get fresh, kid." He almost smiled. "From the record we have of his day, I think we can rule out both erotic play and gymnastics. Something else: there's a bit of metallic thread under two fingernails of his right hand."

"You think someone was with him when he died?"

Brandon nodded gloomily. "We'll make the assumption for now. He may have clung to someone when the poison hit him. After he hung up on Weinert."

"Unless the murderer hung up the phone."

"And then unhooked it?" Brandon rubbed his forehead. "I think I feel a headache coming on."

"Too much chocolate." Pete was ignored. "We've got the time people said they left the party. Better start checking on what time folks got home. And what they did in between."

"Will do. After my date with Joelle," Pete said.

"Let's see what Mary Walker wants."

"By the way, she looks upset. Folks here in Baja Wyndham say Mary was very fond of Vincent Riley." Brandon looked vague. "The guy found dead in his bathtub this morning. He lived next door to the Walkers."

A few moments later Brandon was looking into the largest and the saddest brown eyes he thought he had ever seen. The knuckles of the hands on the chair wheels showed white; the cords of what could have been a graceful neck stood out under the tension that had invaded the young woman's upper body. No breath moved the light flowered cotton of her blouse, as though all vitality was held captive by some paralyzing emotion.

"How can I help you, Ms. Walker?"

"The police are saying that Vince Riley's death was accidental. I want you to know that it wasn't, Sergeant Blessing. Someone killed him. Thad doesn't take me seriously. But I tell you I know."

"Could you explain that?"

Out of kindness Brandon listened attentively as she put forth her argument, becoming increasingly tense, eager to convince, to be understood.

"I mean, given the hour it was and what he had to do before leaving on his trip, it doesn't make sense that he would have taken any more than a quick shower."

He sighed, wishing he didn't have to look into those despairing eyes. "I know that a death like this is bewildering, but I don't understand how I can be helpful."

"It concerns you, Sergeant. I think Vince's death is connected with Julian Merton's murder."

Brandon had heard wilder ideas from those faced with the arbitrariness of death. He remained unperturbed. "The autopsy should tell us . . . "

Mary interrupted impatiently. "Thad has been saying for years that the coroner's office is overworked and understaffed. You must know yourself that there are autopsies and autopsies."

Indeed he did.

"Besides, Vince was in his fifties, a bachelor with no family but an eccentric brother in New Mexico." Her voice took on an edge of resentment. "He was no one important, like President Merton. Unless they hear from you, the coroner's office will think of it as another household accident — and handle it that way."

"What you're saying is you think that he was poisoned, like President Merton, then that someone put him into the tub to make his death look accidental?" Brandon hoped he didn't sound as incredulous as he felt.

Mary looked away. When she turned to him again, her face had softened. She even managed a shadowy smile. "I'm sure I must seem hysterical, Sergeant Blessing, but I know Vince Riley as no one else does."

Brandon wondered whether there was an implication in the remark. "Then maybe you have an idea of why anyone would want him out of the way."

She nodded solemnly. "Because he knew something. Wyndham Hall held 'mysteries,' he said."

That startled him. "What?"

"It sounds ridiculous, doesn't it? Like the title of an old-fashioned thriller: The Mysteries of

Wyndham Hall. We were in his study — Friday night, late. Vince was working at his computer, writing a report he wanted to finish before leaving on vacation. I was teasing him about recording the mysteries of Wyndham Hall. Because there are never any secrets at the Hall, don't you see? Everybody here always knows everything. But Vince was quite solemn in agreeing with me. Now I believe there was something serious and confidential in his report."

"Wouldn't he have told you if there were?"

Mary nodded. "Probably. At least, he said he would discuss it with me later. But he was in a hurry to get finished and so . . . " She looked away for a moment, apparently to steady herself before going on. "It was unusual for him to work at home. Someone should check out his computer, Sergeant." She rolled back a turn of the wheel, then stopped. "And maybe look for footprints. Of running shoes."

Pete had asked Joelle to meet him at the Student Union during her afternoon break. She had seemed miffed this morning when he passed her desk, calling out that he might at least give her the time of day when he went by. Pete hoped that the laid-back atmosphere of the Union might revive her inclination to talk freely without encouraging her interest in his unofficial person.

Joelle stuck a straw in her Coke, looking up at him as she sipped.

"Something wrong?"

She stirred her drink with the straw and smiled archly. "Hunh-uh. I just can't get over how you've changed from high school days."

"For the better or for the worse?"

"For the better. Definitely." She wiggled her eyebrows at him.

"Well, thanks." Pete wondered how to steer her in a different direction. Not feeling particularly inspired, he said, "You've certainly done well. The job at the college seems to suit you to a T." She shrugged. "Tipton is first class. And it looks to me like you have a good deal of responsibility."

Joelle brightened, glanced up at him sideways. "Well, like I always say, I am at the center of things."

He nodded understandingly. "That's why I thought you could be particularly helpful."

"Oh?" She seemed wary.

"I wonder if you would know of any problems between the president and the VPs for instance."

"I'm not sure I should discuss it."

Road block. Pete thought for a moment. "I understand. I thought maybe you would want to contribute . . . But look, I can ask someone else."

"If you mean you can ask Crystal Mathews, forget it. She'll blab anything. I'm in a much better position to have an idea of what's going on in the

Hall. But I don't want things repeated to the newspapers. Mr. Donaldson gave us a lecture this morning. He was kinda cross about something. He told us staff people to be cooperative with you guys, but not to volunteer info. We're supposed to refer you all to him for information."

"I'm not sure he can tell me what I need to know. I think you can."

The arch expression slid back into place, but she continued sipping on her drink.

"I can't make any promises for down the road, Joelle, but the information we're gathering is confidential at this stage."

She nodded. "Well, OK. What do you want to know?"

"I was wondering whether you knew of any quarrels between Mr. Merton and any administrators — or staff — in the Hall?"

"He didn't chew out the staff. I can tell you that right now. If someone had done something he didn't like, he sent Miss Taper to make the criticism. She was much easier to take, believe me."

"You didn't like him?"

"He was always pretty nice to me. I never had any problems. He was certainly, well, glamorous, I guess you'd say. But no, I didn't much like him. Particularly after the shouting match with Dean Norton."

"When was that?"

"About a month ago. I'd heard from upstairs that the president could really tell people off, but I hadn't seen it myself. And he did this in public," she exclaimed in obvious outrage.

"Oh?"

"Yeah. You know Dean Norton's office is right across from me? Well, the dean was standing at Jackie's desk — she's his secretary — when Mr. Merton came tearing down the stairs. The delivery boy from the mail room was there, and people from Admissions across the hall could hear it too. Talk about embarrassing."

"What did he say?"

"He shouted that Dean Norton was never to do that again, that he would regret it if he did, that he would not stand for it, and on and on. I mean he was insulting."

"Why was he so angry?"

"According to Jackie, Dean Norton had sent some parents upstairs and the president hadn't gotten the message they were on their way. I guess the parents were really steaming about something. Anyway, I thought Merton, I mean the president, was going to have apoplexy. Talk about red in the face."

"What did the dean say?"

"Nothing. At least nothing I could hear. He just listened, then turned and went into his office. Jackie said she thought Dean Norton would pack up his things and quit right then and there. But I wasn't so surprised. I mean Dean Norton is great — a real cool character."

"Sure sounds as if he had a hair-trigger temper. President Merton, I mean."

Joelle nodded sagely. "He was hard on Mr. Laszlo too. I never saw anything myself, and Mr. Laszlo's secretary is a tomb. But Crystal Mathews says she's really heard His Nibs tell him off." She bent the top of her plastic straw back and forth. "I'm not what you could call real keen on Mr. Laszlo, but, I mean how unprofessional can you get? Like with Dean Norton. To put someone down in public?"

Pete agreed that it was pretty unprofessional all right. "What about the Dean of the Faculty?"

"Gee, I just don't know. Just between us, Pete, I kinda think they liked each other a lot. Know what I mean? But Crystal says not any more. She says the president was off Parker-Brown like a dirty shirt. But you can't always trust Crystal. She exaggerates a lot. And I mean a bushel."

"I was wondering . . . If he was rough on people like that, didn't anyone ever talk back? You'd expect that someone might tell him off."

"I guess nobody dared. Except Mrs. M."

"Oh?"

"Sometimes when Mrs. Merton was in his office, I guess they had words."

"This comes from Crystal?"

"Mm. If you ask me, I bet she went into that connecting washroom and eavesdropped."

"Joelle, are you sure you heard the president say that Dean Norton would regret it, if he did anything like that again?"

"Scout's honor."

"Well, thanks a lot, Joelle. You've been very helpful."

Joelle put her elbows on the table, cupped her chin in her hands, and gave him her most beguiling smile. "For you, Pete, anytime."

Pete could feel the uncontrollable warmth suffusing his face. He ducked his head as he fumbled for his wallet. Autopsies and animal dissection made him queasy, taking a tough line of questioning made him uncomfortable, and he couldn't even manage to remain impassive with silly, flirtatious young women. Pete was beginning to wonder whether he was cut out to be an investigator.

"She what?"

"You heard it right, Pete. She thinks the guy was murdered. A reaction to shock is my guess. Am I right that this Riley fellow was someone pretty special as a neighbor?"

"I think so. Thad says Riley helped her a lot after the accident. Mary must be all worked up over this. Doesn't seem like her somehow."

"Why?"

"Mary is always so calm — 'serene' is how my mother describes her."

"Mm. Well, still waters and all that. Her imagination may be working overtime, but it won't hurt to keep an eye on this angle — check it out. That is, you keep an eye on it. I take it you know her."

"A little. From high school. She was two years ahead of me."

Brandon got slowly to his feet. "For the heck of it, check out what's on Riley's personal computer. And you might see whether your people or the coroner's guys found any footprints of running shoes around the place. If not, take a look yourself."

"Why running shoes?"

"Seems she noticed a runner on their street around midnight Wednesday night, and the same person the night before Riley was supposed to leave town. And at about the same time. No one she had ever seen on the street before."

"Man or woman?"

"She doesn't know. Tall, wearing a dark jogging outfit and a baseball cap. She thinks it had a red or orange stripe."

"How would she be able to tell?"

"She said the runner passed right under a street lamp."

"I still don't get the connection with Riley's death."

"It's mighty slim. The print she noticed was to the left of the walk, as you enter the back garden. Won't hurt to take a good look around."

"Will do."

Brandon fished out a few hundred calories from the sack in his pocket. "How are you doing with the staff?"

"OK, but no cigar — except Joelle Lieberman maybe." He reported on his conversation with "the nerve center of Wyndham Hall."

"Uh-huh. Interesting."

"The secretaries I talked with said he was handsome and impressive, but not friendly."

Brandon's grunt indicated the information had been registered. "Well, press on. Think it's time for a waltz around the floor with the Dean of Students. Find out why he didn't sock Merton in the kisser and where he stands on the dean-president affair. Right now, we're three for, if you count Hefner, and four against — including the wife and concerned party."

The telephone rang just then, altering the sergeant's plans.

Leslie Filmore had decided to be politic. He saw himself as majestic graciousness itself as he directed Brandon to a chair in his temporary office. Brandon thought he was hopping around like a nervous bird. At last Leslie settled, lighted an imposing cigar.

"Would you care for one?"

"I don't smoke."

"I allow myself two a day."

Brandon considered saying that was his ration too — for his packets of M&Ms. Just imagining Filmore's reaction lifted his spirits.

Leslie exhaled a wreath of smoke. "I regret that pressing business has kept me away — just when I'm needed here the most. But one can't always control such matters."

Brandon remained at his most owlish.

"I haven't made a statement yet. As I told the mayor at a small dinner party last night, I don't want to be precipitate."

Leslie paused to let the implications sink in. Brandon allowed them to sink out of sight.

"Before I do meet the press, as chairman of the Board and acting president, I thought we should have a visit."

Brandon nodded. Leslie grew impatient; he was talking to a dumb ox. He took a deep and leisurely drag on his cigar to regain his composure. "Sergeant, this crime can't have been committed by one of the college community. It's got to be some nut, like the Tylenol case a few years back. Someone with an animus against this place or higher education in general must have added that bottle of poisoned wine to the supply for the party."

Though he got the general drift, Brandon made a mental note to look up "animus."

Confronted by silence, Leslie continued. "That's a reasonable hypothesis. The room was crowded. Some psycho could have slipped in. At this stage of the investigation, which seems to be going no-where . . . " Leslie paused to let the barb sink in. "You could at least raise the possibility of some disturbed individual from outside the college."

"I could. But it would be misleading. The poison was the product of research made by one of your professors, Mr. Filmore. And kept in a freezer in the Chemistry Department, where there's only a semblance of control. So if you're right about the 'psycho' angle, it was most probably a college em-ployee." Brandon opened his report book. "If you would be good enough, Mr. Filmore, to answer a few questions, beginning with your relationship with President Merton . . . "

As the session continued, Leslie revised his opin-ion of the "dumb ox," but was no happier at having done so.

The afternoon had been all downhill.

Leslie Filmore listened for a moment to the buzz that followed Milton Weinert's abrupt disconnect. He replaced the phone in its cradle and leaned back in the desk chair. Pulling on his lower lip, he stared off in the distance. Beulah came in silently, placed the tea he had ordered on the desk, and just as silently left the room.

After a moment, Leslie picked up the cup, resisting the urge to throw it across the room. It had been some forty years since anyone had criticized Leslie Filmore to his face. Since he had been in business, no one had ever implied incompetence on his part, let alone openly criticized him as had Milton Weinert: "It's obvious to me, Filmore, that something is basically rotten at the college. You can't keep your house in order."

What rankled, too, was the knowledge that, in Weinert's place, he would have said the same thing. Damn Julian Merton anyway. What was it that Julian had kept from him? What had he done to get himself murdered? Leslie had looked forward to running the college, to demonstrating what true efficiency was. That feeling was gone now. He would no longer be riding herd on multi-million deals that would bring attention to the school — and to his acumen. He would not be known as the man who could manage an oil business and a leading liberal arts college with equal skill. Weinert's withdrawal had changed all that. His own association with Tipton could become an embarrassment. He had little interest in the dreary day-to-day running of the college. Now he would no longer be associated with building and innovation. He would be associated with failure. Leslie Filmore, since his one and only F in a junior high typing class, had never been associated with failure.

Monday, July 24

THE DEAN OF STUDENTS' OFFICE WAS IN-
viting. A light-filled room with cream- colored walls
and a fine collection of hanging plants, it seemed
less consciously planned — and less orderly —
than the other administration offices Brandon had
visited; more like a home for favorite things: a
footstool covered in Moroccan leather, some prints
from Hogarth's "The Rake's Progress" (a warning
to students ?), the imprint of a child's hand in baked
pottery with the scrawl, "For Daddy 1984" (a family man?), an Indian sand painting, and a jumbled
collection of furniture that could serve to illustrate
the expression "lived in."

The man who greeted Detective Blessing was
about forty years old and as casually put together
as his office: well-worn jeans, a tennis shirt washed
so often or so carelessly that the logo, an embroidered unicorn, had lost part of its horn, and feet
shod in Nikes with little mileage left on them.

Except for the clothes, however, there was nothing laid-back about Henry Norton physically. Tall
and wiry with small well-defined features and a

wide smile, he exuded energetic purposefulness as well as personal warmth.

Henry sat down next to Brandon on a couch covered in striped chintz. "I suppose it's foolish to ask how things are going, Sergeant."

"Not foolish, Dean. Premature."

"Is it OK to ask whether you've scratched the possibility that the murderer might be someone outside the college?"

"We haven't eliminated anything, Dean Norton. Do you see that as a possibility?"

Henry Norton drummed with his fingers on the arm of the couch a moment, then answered dispiritedly, "Not really, I'm afraid."

"And how do you figure it?"

The dean looked surprised. "You're asking me?"

Why not? Brandon thought. I'm nowhere so far; Filmore was right. But he nodded soberly. "I'm interested in your opinion."

Norton frowned, then took off. He spoke rapidly, as though he had said, or thought, all this before. "Given the time factor, it's obvious the poison had to be in the last drink the president had. It must have been given him by someone who was at Ward's party. Or whom Beulah would have seen go into the office immediately afterwards. And he must have downed about all of it there, otherwise the reaction would have set in during the reception."

Something akin to a smile crinkled the corners of Brandon's eyes. "You've really gone into the details."

"I suspect most of us have done little else since yesterday but think about those couple of hours. Wondering how, who, and why."

"Any candidates?"

"Nope. Just that the man or woman had to be familiar with Charlie Peese's research."

"Like yourself?"

"Exactly — among others. You know, then, that I once taught in the Chemistry Department?"

"So I figured from reading the catalog. For seven years, I believe. Then you were appointed Dean of Students six years ago."

"Correct." He put his left foot up on his right thigh, massaged his ankle.

"And you knew the late Professor Peese?"

"Very well. Charlie kept mum about his work as a rule, but he did discuss it with me occasionally. And I helped Mary Walker a bit with the editing of his article for *Tipton Topics*." He shook his head. "I wish now we hadn't been so explicit. It's a blueprint."

"What do you think, Dean. Did the murderer need to have much chemistry to figure it out?"

"Not much," Norton said, putting his foot back down and sitting up straighter. "If any. Once you know how many microliters it takes to kill a — oh, say a twenty-five gram mouse, in x number of minutes, your pocket calculator can do the rest for a man of Merton's weight. Of course, the imponderables remain, and they're serious ones: such as the strength of a particular batch of toxin, or to what extent gastric juices might degrade the material, for example. It would be an exceedingly risky undertaking without prior testing."

"You would need quite a lot of liquid, wouldn't you?"

Norton looked thoughtful. "I suppose. But I believe Charlie had worked up some highly enriched broths, to expedite his experiments, among other reasons. To know about those, however, someone would have had to talk with him."

"As to who that person might have been . . . Would you care to make a guess?"

"No way."

Brandon opened his report book and jotted down: "Get Peese's app't book."

"You mentioned wondering about the why of this killing, Dean Norton. Any ideas?"

"Nothing that would warrant murdering a man for. And in such a premeditated and elaborate fashion."

"Do you know whether your late president had put a spoke in anyone's wheel? Or was thinking of demoting or firing someone?"

The dean leaned back, studied the ceiling for a while.

"Some changes or shifting around were contemplated, perhaps. If implemented they could have resulted in bruised egos, but not in shattered careers."

"Did he discuss these proposed changes with you?"

"He didn't confide in me, Sergeant."

Was there anyone the late Julian Merton confided in, Brandon wondered. Or should he ask whether anyone would admit to being in his confidence?

"Well, what were some of the proposed changes you had heard about?"

Norton shifted his position a couple of times before answering. "Just talk, you understand."

It was the same talk Brandon had already heard, the rumors about Victor Laszlo and Dean Parker-Brown, and reported with a reluctance that was becoming familiar.

"What about yourself?"

Henry Norton grinned. "If Julian was thinking about replacing me, I'd be the last to know."

"Are you saying he was close-mouthed?"

"Pretty much."

"But there were exceptions?" Norton shrugged. "Can you recall any in particular?"

The dean reflected briefly. "Well, once was last spring, when the trouble over Professor Logan's case had just erupted. Several of us were at his house for some official function or other. He started in about her. Really tore her apart. That's the only incident I remember. To tell you the truth, I spent less time socially with Julian than some of my colleagues."

"Your choice or his?"

Norton grinned. "A little of each."

"When you say he 'tore her apart,' exactly what does that mean?"

"Oh, just that if Terry went ahead with her suit she'd regret it. Character slurs. That kind of thing."

"Sounds like a threat."

"An empty one. Julian could be briefly threatening when someone had crossed him. But not to the person's face."

Brandon gave him a hard look. Dean Norton smiled in return and remained relaxed.

"What do you know about the Mertons' family life?"

Norton threw up his hands. A surprisingly feminine gesture, Brandon thought.

"I won't touch that one, Sergeant Blessing."

"Discretion or ignorance, Dean?"

Norton hesitated a split-second. "Ignorance."

Brandon responded with a non-committal nod, then asked, "How did he get along with Van Voorhees and Laszlo?"

"He was very keen on Turner; less keen on Victor."

"Why?"

"Turner is old family — and very capable. Victor is also good at his job, but I believe Julian saw his style as more," he hesitated, "well, the booster club type, if you know what I mean."

Brandon thought he did, though he wasn't much of a joiner himself.

"Are you saying your president was a snob?" Henry's answer was another shrug. "And how did you and he get along?"

"All right."

"Are you old family?"

Henry doubled over, laughing. "Definitely not. An Arkie."

"Beg pardon?"

"My grandparents migrated to California from Arkansas during the dust bowl days. So I'm straight out of Bakersfield. But he didn't have to see me every day. That is to say, he pretty much left me alone."

"Any quarrels?"

"Some differences of opinion, Sergeant. Usually regarding how my office handled an irate parent or a troublesome student. Julian wasn't happy when I didn't succeed in calming someone down, and he was forced to deal with a problem himself."

"Did this happen often?"

"If it did, I think I wouldn't still be in this job, officer."

"But it did occur last month?"

"Oh." He grinned. "So that's why you were looking at me crossways when I was talking about Terry. You mean when Julian barreled down from upstairs and bawled me out?"

"Publicly, I hear."

"Yeah. *That* was an exception. Stupid behavior." The dean stretched out his legs, perfectly at ease. "What you haven't heard maybe is that I went to Julian's office the next morning and told *him* he was never to do that again. If he had a criticism it was to be discussed in private."

"How did he take that?"

Norton grinned, remembering. "He made a little joke about it, looked sheepish, but he ended up apologizing."

"Did that satisfy you?"

"Why not? I haven't the time, nor the stomach, for playing games."

Brandon took a moment to make a notation in his book.

"What about the president's rapport with faculty."

The dean grew suddenly impatient. "You're referring to the Weinert project, of course. Look, Sergeant, we've got some pretty intense faculty people around these parts, true. There are some who would just about lay down their lives for Tipton, but they wouldn't take one. No matter how much they might scream or holler about Julian's policies."

"What would they do?"

"Appeal to alumni. Petition the Board of Trustees. Rally students. That kind of thing."

Brandon considered this before going on. His next question did nothing to lessen Norton's impatience.

"Wild-eyed conjecture, in my opinion. Or vicious idle talk. Dean Parker-Brown is a woman of the highest professional standards, Sergeant Blessing. What has been suggested to you is unthinkable." The dean's expression modulated to relaxed again, but a door had closed.

Like the other administrative officers, except Victor Laszlo, Norton would not implicate a colleague. Blessing took the hint and changed the subject.

"Let's talk about that reception. Were you there for the entire time?"

"Uh-huh."

"You never left?"

"Oh yeah. I'd forgotten to tell Lucille about the party. So I went to telephone."

"Did you get hold of her?"

"Nope. Missed her."

"Where did you call from?"

"Here. My office."

"Why didn't you use one of the phones upstairs?"

A bemused expression came over Henry's face. "I honestly don't know." He grinned. "Should I think about it?"

Brandon responded to the smile with a level look. "That's OK. For now." A few more questions and Brandon closed his book; he had taken a lot of notes, he reflected, without getting any wiser.

It was almost five when Brandon Blessing left Wyndham Hall, and a hair past five-thirty when he walked down the steps of Reeves, the building that housed Fred Zumholtz's office. He was ready to pack it in; Zumholtz, so far the lone ardent supporter of the late president, had been an undammed stream going nowhere while meandering everywhere — except for dropping a couple of names that Blessing had heard before and that he thought might be worth exploring.

Brandon doggedly crossed the street to enter Fiedler Hall. A few minutes later, in room 16, he sat talking with George Macready, Chair of Classics who, he thought, didn't look too much unlike the bust in the niche above his head. Professor Macready encouraged students to note his resemblance to Cicero, a resemblance that had been more marked in former times when he had allowed a few stray locks to curl across his forehead. In the late sixties when hair was flowing over shoulders and down backs, the stray locks had been disciplined into a marine-style haircut as George's way to signal his sympathy with "our fighting men."

"Chief Walker has quoted you as saying that the president's death might be considered an exception to the rule that only the good die young." George lowered his chin to his chest and looked senatorial. Brandon continued. "You didn't care for Julian Merton?"

"I was not an admirer of his view of the presidency of Tipton College."

"And did he know that?"

"You bet your Dior booties he did. Julian had turned out to be a closet technocrat."

"I don't get it."

"We're a small liberal arts college, Sergeant. Recently, he had embarked on an idiot graduate program scheme that would have beggared the humanistic side of the ledger and corrupted Tipton's purpose as an undergraduate institution. The idea of a Business Administration program here is preposterous. I might add that I was not the only one to share those sentiments."

There was no ignoring the emotion in Macready's voice. It confirmed the one interesting thing Fred Zumholtz had said: that Macready and a certain Professor de Grancey were militantly opposed to Milton Weinert's proposal.

"We had words when I first got wind of this nonsense. But I didn't kill him, officer. There are other and safer ways to get rid of a bad college president."

"Yes sir. You say you didn't kill him. Have you any idea who did?"

"Who did? Or who could have?"

"Either one. Or both."

George shuffled a few papers around on his desk. "There are a hundred and ten full-time faculty at this college, and I'd say at least two thirds of them were disillusioned with this president. But I'm not about to impugn motives to my colleagues."

The chin came down once more; the eyes, peering over the rims of George's half-moon glasses, hardened. "That's your job."

Brandon couldn't quarrel with that so said nothing. He hoped not to receive the same response when he inquired into Merton's personal life. He was disappointed. Curmudgeony Professor Macready was no tattle-tale. At least, not with the police.

Pierre-Xavier de Grancey, head of the French Department, was another matter. Brandon had never met a Gauloise smoker before, and as Pierre exhaled a long stream of smoke he hoped he never would again.

The Frenchman confirmed much of what he already knew: that he and Macready had arrived together at Wyndham after the party had started, had stayed just long enough to speak to the honoree and to exchange a few words with trustees; they had left together. They did not speak with the president. On the question of Julian Merton's relationship with staff and faculty, Pierre became more expansive, and in a supercilious way that set Brandon's teeth on edge.

Complimentary: "There is no denying Merton's considerable gifts . . . "

Translation: I hated the guy.

Analytical: "He was, one might say, very creative in his thinking, an innovator."

Translation: He had crazy ideas.

Thoughtful: "Some of us wondered how well he understood Tipton, however. He didn't seem to be sensitive to tradition — or to be open to the ideas of his faculty."

Translation: He wouldn't listen to me.

Generous: "Perhaps he needed more time. After all, he had only served three years."

Translation: Three years too long.

Reminiscent: "He knew success at an extraordinarily early age. Something of a *wunderkind.*"

That one Brandon understood, thanks to three semesters of German at State College.

Professorial: "The theories he expounded in his major work raised quite a furor both with economists and philosophers. The impetuousness and daring of youth, don't you know."

Translation: It's bullshit.

Worldly: "As to any possible involvement with women . . . Temptation is always in the path of energetic, powerful men, don't you think? Though as to his *vie sentimentale . . . "*

"His what, professor?"

"His love life. Well, one should never listen to rumors, don't you agree? Julian had a very handsome and committed wife. Without facts, why not presume a happy marriage? No matter what gossip whispers — or literature might suggest." He smiled.

Translation: Merton was a womanizer; he was having it off with the dean.

In his report book, Brandon drew a small snake with a forked tongue.

Brandon gave it his best country hick tone. "Well, thank you, Professor dee Grancie." He was rather pleased to see Pierre-Xavier de Grancey wince.

Brandon had been working in the downstairs office about an hour when Pete Wiggins showed up. Brandon held up the late Professor Peese's desk calendar.

"This bears out the picture we've gotten of the late Charles Peese."

Pete peered over his shoulder. "I don't get it."

"Nothing to get. It's a blank, since the first of the year, except for a daily entry for twelve noon: lunch, Faculty Club."

"Looks like he didn't trust his memory," Pete said.

"Or else it was the big social event of his day. There's one other notation for a dental appointment. As his chairman reported, seems like he saw precious few people outside of his department. One of those guys to whom nothing is important except his work." Brandon laid the calendar aside. "The president's pocket engagement book didn't produce anything that could help us — just the dates for his visit to the San Francisco area." He stretched. "Well, as an old English professor of mine used to ask, 'What news on the Rialto?'"

"Huh?"

"Shakespeare. Get with it, Pete, we're in the land of the egg-heads."

Was it the reaction to a long and trying day or was Brandon showing his lighter side?

"I don't know about the Rialto, but San Francisco hasn't anything, not yet anyway. They'll call tomorrow. That society must be about as exclusive as they come; real keen on their privacy."

"Yeah. Lots of big shots to protect. What progress with the young ladies?"

"Willing to talk — up to a point. Loyal to their bosses. But Ms. Mathews made a few things crystal clear." Pete grinned expectantly.

Brandon ignored the play on words. "Is this worth my undivided attention?"

Correction, Pete thought, Brandon has no lighter side. "I think so. Crystal confirmed that there were important administrative changes in the wind."

"For instance?"

"Victor Laszlo. And the resignation of the dean. The requested resignation."

"How come she's so sure?"

"She was asked to sit in on a confidential meeting once and take notes — a meeting between Mr. Filmore, Mr. Weinert, Merton and her boss. Project planning and financial stuff, but as she was leaving she overheard something." Pete stressed the "overheard."

Brandon's eyebrows shot up. "So much for confidential. And to what does the chatty Ms. Mathews attribute these proposed changes?"

"She believes the president wanted a younger, more dynamic team."

"Any candidates?"

"Nope. Just people who were more 'with it' as she said — and," Pete looked down at his notes — "classier."

"I would have thought Dean Parker-Brown was dynamic and classy enough."

"Ms. Mathews doesn't seem to be in her cheering section. She was pretty coy on the subject of the dean and the president."

"That figures. She's Hefner's informant and bed pal, isn't she?"

Pete nodded. "I also talked with Phil Gertmenian. Very loyal to his boss. Protective, I'd say."

"How protective?"

"Huh?"

"You think there's anything going on there?"

"Best guess is no."

"What about lusting in his heart?"

Pete didn't crack a smile. "Crystal didn't mention it."

"Or maybe he doesn't lust after the ladies."

Pete scowled. Brandon shook his head. "OK, OK. I can't get used to the idea of a woman having a male secretary."

"We're almost in the twenty-first century, Brandon."

He sighed. "I know, kid. That's what I hear all the time at home. But why would a smart fellow want to take shorthand?"

"To earn a living. In Gertmenian's case, I understand he's a writer. Spends free time on that — and looking after his invalid father."

"I see. Well, any idea why the dean came home undercover via San Francisco?"

"The answer was 'why not?'"

"A smart ass is always a big help."

"But he was. A big help, that is, regarding people's movements during the party. He and Miss Taper were on the sidelines for a good half hour. Taking in the sights."

"Any suggestions as to why Merton was murdered?"

"Nope. Just about everyone is eager to dump on the guy as a bear to work for, but no one can think of who would want to kill him."

"Normal reaction for round one of an investigation. Give them a little more time, increase the pressure, and they'll loosen up." Brandon sighed wearily. "Or so I once read in a police manual."

"What did you get from Dean Norton?"

"Pretty much the same tune. He settled that business of Merton's chewing him out to his satisfaction."

"And to yours?"

"I guess. You'd think these VPs had signed a pact about their statements. Arguments and differences of opinion, but essentially upper Wyndham was one happy family."

"And the adultery angle?"

"Kid, wash your mouth out with soap!"

Brandon shook out a few M&Ms and continued looking over the guest lists Pete had collected.

"We have about a sixty percent return so far; the remainder should trickle in tomorrow."

Brandon nodded absently. "An additional name or two. Apparently no unknowns wandered in."

"Did you talk to that other trustee who was at the party — Neville Barnes?" Pete asked.

Brandon nodded.

"And?"

"The president was a wonderful man and a wonderful leader. Mr. Barnes is appalled. Mr. Barnes deplores. Mr. Barnes didn't notice anything. Mr. Barnes was not helpful."

"Sergeant Blessing?"

Brandon shifted the phone to his other ear. "Yes, ma'am?"

"This is Beulah Taper. I just realized I'd neglected to mention someone . . . "

"Yes ma'am?"

"When the president, Mr. Filmore and Mr. Laszlo were conferring — before the toasts to Ward, Mrs. Sally Cochran was with them for a while. She had been scheduled to make one of the speeches, then dropped out."

"Thank you, Miss Taper."

"I'm so sorry to have omitted her name."

"That's all right Miss Taper. Thanks."

Cochran. The trustee Laszlo had mentioned off-hand as "around" somewhere. And he had neglected to phone her. His seventeen-year-old daughter would say, as she often had, that women rarely registered as power figures, therefore as worthy of attention. Maybe Belinda had something.

Sergeant Blessing consulted the trustees' roster provided him by Miss Taper and dialed a Beverly Hills number. After he gave his name, badge, and telephone number, a soft Hispanic voice finally told him Mr. and Mrs. Cochran were fishing off Cabo San Lucas. Return date: unknown.

Brandon was on the phone when Pete Wiggins walked in. He gestured to Pete to pick up the extension.

"Professor Tidwell?"

"Mark or Claire?"

"You, sir. This is Sergeant Blessing."

"What can I do for you, Sergeant?"

"You said that anatoxin-a could cause death in two to three minutes, possibly less."

"Yes?"

"How long would it take for the triggering reaction to set in?"

"In the circumstances you're assuming?"

"Yes, sir."

"That would depend on a number of things. Whether the stomach was full or not, whether the toxic liquid went directly to the small intestine where it would be more slowly absorbed. And how long it took the intended victim to finish off the drink; whether he sipped along at it very slowly or chug-a-lugged it down."

"Let's say the president took a few sips at the party, then finished it off over a ten-minute period."

Mark paused before answering. "I really don't know, Sergeant. It could be very rapid, or take as many as ten, fifteen minutes maybe — counting from when he began drinking. But that's a guess."

"But the reaction wouldn't be instantaneous after the first sip or two?"

"I wouldn't think so, no. But once he'd absorbed the lethal dose, then it would be curtains in a hurry."

After he had hung up, Brandon turned to Pete. "You know, kid, either this killer is a big gambler with delusions of invincibility or else he got one heck of a lot of precise information out of Professor Peese." His sigh was a record-breaker. "Let's get at it."

For almost two hours Brandon and Pete worked at the table in their office, writing up and comparing notes, then moving on to sketch out, as Blessing called it, the choreography of a couple of hours of the fatal afternoon. At a little past eight, with his second and last allotted package of M & Ms a crumpled reminder, Brandon called it quits.

"That may do it. Kind of interesting: three administrators left the party for a few minutes: Norton, the dean and Van Voorhees — also Lieberman to handle phone calls."

"What about Vince Riley?"

"Yeah, but he didn't come back. And he's out of the picture anyway. So, let's see . . . Mrs. Merton was called to the phone, and a couple of people saw Laszlo go into his office for a moment." Brandon scratched his ear. "If you were the killer, would you return to your office to get the wine?"

"And parade through the halls with a package? No way. I'd have stashed it in the room just before the party. Like in that antique sideboard. Right next to where they set up the bar."

"You're OK, kid. You've got a devious mind."

Pete grinned. "Is that bad?"

Brandon took a handkerchief from his pocket and wiped his brow. "I'm heading home. Greg Tomono said he'd meet me back at the station around nine."

"He's your crackerjack computer guy?"

"Yeah. Greg's got a new data base management system he's hot to try. See you at seven tomorrow morning. Here."

"Brandon," Pete called after him. "About Vince Riley."

"Did you talk to Thad?"

"Not yet. I'll try to catch him on my way home. But there is one thing that strikes me as kinda odd. Joelle Lieberman told me someone played a practical joke on Riley right at the end of the reception."

"That so?"

"He was called away by a phone call. Some joker reporting an emergency problem in the bell tower. Poor guy climbed up almost two hundred steps for nothing."

"College pranks."

Except, Pete reminded him, summertime is not the right season.

Brandon Blessing headed his old Mustang toward the freeway, then changed his mind and pulled up outside the president's house. Getting out, he checked his watch, then started for Wyndham Hall, taking smaller steps than usual, unavoidably accentuating his normally swishy walk. A college security car came abreast and slowed down. Recognizing the sergeant, the officer waved and moved on, shaking his head in bewilderment. At the Hall, Sergeant Blessing looked at his watch again, then, reluctantly, jogged back to his car. A last check of the time, and he was on his way.

Thad and Mary sat quietly over the late supper he had prepared.

"Afraid I overcooked the noodles."

"They're fine, Thad." Her voice was listless.

"Some wine?"

"No thanks." A pause. "Thad?"

"Yes?"

"There's no need to be so — well, so gentle with me."

Thad turned to better face his sister. "And there's no need for you to be hostile, Mary." She looked away, out the window. "I hadn't intended to say anything, but the situation is becoming intolerable. You've shut me out entirely."

She looked at him then, her face expressionless. "I know. I'm sorry."

"Can we talk about it?"

"Except I don't know what to say."

"Don't you trust me any more?"

"It isn't that. My lousy disposition gets the better of me. I have so much resentment in me. Anger about losing Vince. And I take it out on you."

"As the nearest whipping boy around?"

"It looks that way, doesn't it? I don't understand, Thad. Maybe it's because you're so patient — so damned nice to me. That's a dreadful thing to say." She paused a moment before blurting out. "You're saddled with me, Thad. Now this, this new grief only complicates things more. And I can do nothing for you. For your own loss. And I feel guilty about that. Because I'm alive and Fiona's dead."

He hadn't expected that. "I thought those demons had been laid to rest."

"I thought so, too." She picked up a spoon, put it down. "Vince helped me be — more tranquil. He — he smoothed me out somehow. Thad, I was so happy with him." Her voice tightened. "For the measly few months we had together. As lovers. But all during that time, whenever we were apart, there were moments when I was overwhelmed with fear. Terror, in fact — that something dreadful would happen. That I would lose him."

"Mary . . . " All of his helplessness and affection were in the word.

"When I saw Vince . . . dead . . . The terror and the old anger came rushing back. It spilled over me, like the water running over his arm." Her voice broke. "Back to square one. Before all the dumb therapy. Before anything." There was a long silence. She managed a small smile. "Vince said I should be nicer to you."

"Vince was right." He pushed his plate aside. "You're grieving, Mary. You need to recognize that. And accept it."

She cringed at the hated word, but remained silent.

Thad turned the stem of his wine glass back and forth. "Do you really believe that everything Vince gave you is gone? That it was all for nothing?"

She looked at him, startled, her eyes clouded. At last she said softly, "I can't let that happen, can I?"

Two hours later Thad was reading in the den when his sister came in. Mary rolled her chair up to his, reached for his hand, held it a moment against her cheek.

"I'll be all right. And thank you. No more histrionics."

Her brother leaned over and gave her a hug. "Good night, Mary."

At the door she turned her chair around. "You're being very restrained, not saying anything about my visit to Brandon Blessing. You must have heard."

He grinned. "Oh I heard all right. Pete came by the office. I figured tonight wasn't the time to mention it."

"Maybe I wasn't, well, quite myself as the saying goes. But I meant what I said to him, Thad. I know Vince was murdered."

The Tidwells' spacious kitchen, with its tiles, copper pans, old trivets, and Quimper plates hung around the walls pointed to the background of one of the owners and the sympathetic Francophilia of the other. The Tidwells and Anne sat at the old refectory table, lingering over coffee and calvados.

As Mark lifted up the bottle, Anne quickly covered her glass with her hand.

"Absolutely not. Even one glass of your Normandy fire water is dangerous for me."

"Dangerous or not, you can hit me again, Mark." Claire pushed her glass toward him.

"OK. But only if you swear not to wonder for the tenth time why I didn't confide in you."

"Agreed. And I won't make any further nasty comments on your hit-or-miss experimental methods." She snorted. "The idea of just using a measly dozen mice . . . But only because if I don't shut up I'll drive Anne away."

"As a matter of fact I find your pretense at bickering quite comforting this evening."

"What do you make of the detective?" Claire asked of no one in particular.

"He has a funny walk. Reminds me of John Wayne. Remember that kind of tight-assed swing of his?"

"I mean what about his brains?"

"Seemed like an intelligent enough fellow. Dead-pan."

"I wonder whether he's going to get around to me."

Mark mumbled something that might have been "God help him."

"What's your opinion of him, Anne?"

"I would say he was feeling his way. I certainly agree with Mark as to his deadpan style."

"It's funny. Not one of us has come up with a possible suspect. Do you realize that?"

"What's funny about it?" Mark finished off his calvados and speared the last bit of Bel Paese from the marble cheese tray. "This is too serious a matter to be indiscriminately tossing out candidates for murder."

Anne didn't answer. She seemed to be brooding about something as she carefully picked up bread crumbs from the table, put them on her plate.

Claire sipped on her drink, then, "Well, I've been thinking." She looked smug. Neither her husband nor best friend paid any attention. "What makes everybody so sure that Julian was the intended victim?" Hearing no comment, Claire was encouraged to continue. "It came to me this morning, while nodding over an archaic article on variations in potty training between urban upperclass families and the urban poor."

"Enough to addle anyone's brains," Mark said in mock commiseration.

"You know how people wander around at cocktail parties, put down their glasses anywhere. Everybody's more or less distracted." Claire finished defiantly, "Well, it certainly could have happened. Julian could have picked up a glass intended for someone else."

"While the murderer stood by and watched him drink it."

"Maybe he didn't stand by. Maybe he hadn't noticed."

"Or she," Anne said. She stretched and rose to leave. "It's an interesting theory, Claire. You might try it out on the detective."

Mark disagreed. "I wouldn't, if I were you."

"And why not?"

"Because there's a hole of meteoric size in your theory. Two holes. The murderer would have to feel one hundred percent certain that the drink was going to the intended victim. And that the timing would be right. Otherwise, why go to all the trouble? Second, and for me this is the clincher: just consider the people at that party. Can you think of a single person anybody would want to eliminate? Except Julian?"

"We certainly don't know all about everyone's private life."

"I thought you did."

"Well, not about the secretaries or all those as-sistant deans and directors and what-have-yous we've got rattling around these days."

"You're slipping, wife."

"A dean of the Faculty is always fair game," Anne reminded them, returning to the earlier question.

"To take verbal potshots at deans is an academic ritual. No self-respecting faculty member would ever pass up the opportunity. But as for moving from word to action, no way. Certainly not in your case, Anne. You couldn't possibly compete. In the bastard class at TC Julian stood alone."

"That's very comforting, Mark." Then she smiled. "But a dean might easily find some candi-dates for bastardom from among her faculty."

"You're right," Mark agreed. "But you wouldn't waste a bottle of a superb French wine."

Brandon Blessing couldn't sleep. He walked down the hall, stopping automatically at each of the four bedrooms and checking seven beds on his way to the kitchen. As usual, Brandon Junior's head came up from the pillow to flop right back down with a mumbled, "Hi, Pop." In the kitchen, Brandon poured himself a glass of chocolate milk and reached for a peach. Then, abandoning all caution, he put the peach back in the bowl and made himself a pastrami sandwich. He munched gloomily, mentally reviewing his list of suspects.

Too many people in the picture. He had to get this one down to size.

He tossed off his chocolate milk and considered the pile of CVs he intended to study. But first he opened the magazine he had brought with him to a well- thumbed page 47: "The Very-Fast-Death Factor," by Charles Lunsford Peese, Roger Hughes Whitman Professor of Chemistry.

Tuesday, July 25

BRANDON LOOKED OSTENTATIOUSLY AT his watch as Pete entered the Wyndham Hall office.

"Sorry. Thad needed to see me a moment."

"So long as you were going about the Lord's work."

Pete grinned. "I doubt the Lord had much to do with it. How are you, Brandon?"

"Didn't get enough sleep. Those faculty CVs will never beat out a Louis L'Amour western, let me tell you."

"Pick up anything?"

"Lots of smarts. Lots of interests. Lots of accomplishments. Only one visible chemist in the bunch."

"Dean Norton?"

"Yeah."

"What about the staff?" Pete asked.

"Solid citizens on the face of it."

"You never know. Downtown may pick up a police or psychiatric record."

"I doubt that much will have slipped by that personnel lady. She runs a tight ship if you ask me." Brandon opened his a.m. pack of candy, peeked in, then laid it aside. He stretched long and hard. "That's enough exercise for the day. Get anything done last evening?"

"Made the rounds: Nortons, Laszlos, Van Voorhees."

"Were the wives there?"

"Yep. Norton and Laszlo left Wyndham shortly after the reception ended — by six-thirty. And went straight home."

"If they're telling the truth."

"Well, the Laszlos were expecting company for dinner; Dean Norton was scheduled to go to a night ball game with a couple of his kids."

"What about Van Voorhees?"

"Like he told you, he left Wyndham Hall with his wife around six-thirty and went across the way to the gym. Worked out and got home close to eight."

"Did you check it out?"

Pete nodded. "The head of the P. E. Department saw him working on the Nautilus equipment. A little after seven maybe."

"Did you think to ask what he was wearing?"

"You bet. What he most always wears, the coach said: shorts and a plain white T-shirt."

"Anybody else in the gym?"

"Just Mary Walker, Thad's sister. Van Voorhees volunteered that Mary saw him."

"And?"

"I phoned Mary. She recalls that he was coming out of the Nautilus room when she was leaving after her workout."

The sergeant gave in and reached for his candy. "Time?"

"Her best guess is seven-fifteen."

"Walker and Van Voorhees — and that's it?"

"According to the coach."

"Anything else?"

"Well, Norton and Laszlo are certain nobody was in their office areas by the time they left the building."

Brandon leaned forward, elbows on the table, chin in his hands. "It would be tight, but I suppose Turner Van Voorhees could have slipped back into Wyndham."

"Except that the registrar and Tom Donaldson of the News Bureau were visiting on the bench, right by the front door. They talked until almost half-past seven."

"What about the side doors?"

"Coming from the gym he'd still have had to cross the area right in front of where they were sitting — unless he made an awfully wide detour. He could have done that, of course."

"Did they see him at all?"

"Nope."

"Did they notice Mary Walker?"

"Negative."

Brandon straightened up, rubbed his eyes. "Can you smell the smog?" Pete shook his head. "Must be coming in through the vents somehow. Sure makes my eyes itch. Well, how did the folks you talked to react? Indignation? Nervous hands, shifting of eyes, or clearings of throats?"

"Hunh-uh. They weren't too keen about repeating what they had already told you, but they were friendly enough — except maybe for Mr. and Mrs. Van Voorhees."

"Yeah?"

"They were cooperative, but they kept me standing in the hallway."

"You should have introduced yourself as Peter Van Wiggins." A growling sound emerged from Brandon's throat; young Wiggins interpreted it as merriment.

Cissy Merton answered the doorbell. Except for nearly black lipstick and the assorted chains and leather belts that pretended to hold up an already skin-tight miniskirt, her attire came close to parental standards of suitability. Her T-shirt was devoid of nose-thumbing announcements, her hair was neatly combed back, nails were short and without glitter. A laconic "Hi" answered his "good-morning."

"Is your mother available?"

"Yeah. I'll get her." Cissy didn't move for a moment, then burst out, "Do you know who murdered my father?"

"Not yet. Do you?"

She pivoted on her heel. "Ask me no questions and I'll tell you no lies."

"Good morning, Sergeant Blessing." Priscilla, simply dressed in a tan cotton skirt and a white shirt, stood in the archway that connected the entrance to the living room. Careful makeup hadn't completely effaced the shadows under the eyes, the drawn expression around the mouth. Ignoring Cissy, Priscilla accepted his apology for disturbing her at such an early hour. The girl hung swinging on the newel post staring after them as they went into the living room. After a moment Brandon heard steps running up the stairs.

"My daughter is a very troubled child right now."

"Yes ma'am." Brandon took the chair she indicated. Priscilla sat down on the couch, smoothing her skirt with one hand — a gesture he recognized.

She looked at him calmly. "She thinks I killed her father."

Brandon considered that for a moment, before asking straight-faced, "Did you, Mrs. Merton?"

Priscilla's voice was steady, the tone patient. "Sergeant Blessing, leaving aside any marital considerations or the question of affection, would I give up all this?" Her gesture encompassed the room. "Would I give up security, a most agreeable

and comfortable life for one of loneliness and un-
certainty?"

"I don't know, ma'am."

She gave him a long look. "No, you wouldn't."
She paused before continuing almost briskly. "Well,
what can I do for you?"

"I just have one question, Mrs. Merton. For
now." He opened his report book. "I understand
you purchased three cases of Château d'Yquem
from The Cork and Bottle last Christmas."

"That sounds familiar, but Julian took care of
ordering our wine."

"Do you have a record of the purchase? Would
you know whether you used any — or gave any
away as gifts?"

"Possibly. I paid the bills, and of course took care
of any gifts. I'll have to check my records."

She was gone for quite a while, returning with a
notebook and a sheet of paper. She handed him
the floral-covered notebook. "Perhaps you'd like
to see the gift entries for yourself. I found the bill
for December purchases from The Cork and Bottle; it lists three cases of Château d'Yquem, along
with other items." She waved the bill at him. Brandon looked at it, then nodded, satisfied, and returned to studying the notebook. He turned over
a section headed "Guests," glanced quickly past
the list under "Family" and one with the heading
"Friends" before coming to "TC administration and
personnel."

It would seem that Château d'Yquem had been the gift of the season.

Lucille Norton grimaced as she read aloud the statement printed under Leslie Filmore's picture on an inside page of the *LA Times*. "There's also a statement from the Sheriff's office — one of those uninformative things, followed by another little entry that quotes Willie Hefner's report on the nature of the toxin: 'According to the *Altamira Ledger,* the isolation of the toxin, believed to come from a poisonous alga, was the result of research undertaken by a late member of the Tipton College faculty in Chemistry: Professor Charles Peese.'"

Henry continued drinking his coffee in silence as Lucille tossed the paper aside. "Great. You're going to have your hands full reassuring parents and students that there isn't a dangerous sociopath loose on campus."

Henry trickled honey on his English muffin, wiped his hands on a paper napkin. "The problem is, can I honestly say that?"

"Then you don't think it's one of us?"

"The two are not mutually exclusive, Lucille."

Lucille shook her head at him. "Henry, this campus may shelter some weirdos, but it stops there, if you ask me. Surely this isn't a gratuitous, totally irrational crime?"

"I'm not saying that. I think someone targeted Julian for personal reasons, and that the person is probably a deeply disturbed or psychotic personality."

Lucille grinned at him. "Well, that lets you out, sweetie. You are Mr. S. N. Square."

"S.N.?"

"Super Normal."

"How do you know what I do when the moon is full and you're snoring?"

Lucille cradled her coffee mug in both hands. "To back up a moment. Are you thinking that this 'deranged personality' won't stop with Julian's death?"

"It's crossed my mind. The idea of someone having that culture of Charlie's in his — or her —possession . . . Well, it makes me a mite nervous."

In their Baja Wyndham office, Brandon Blessing was reading to Pete Wiggins from his notes: "Two bottles each to the vice presidents, one each to the late Charles Peese and an unidentified group labeled 'Department Heads.' With twenty-four departments, that comes to . . . "

"Thirty-three bottles," Pete finished for him. "What about the remaining three?"

"According to Mrs. Merton's guest book, two were served at a dinner last spring for a former Prime Minister of Britain. The third was still in the cellar. I checked."

The phone rang just then and claimed Brandon's attention for quite a while. Pete deduced the call was from San Francisco, but the "uh-huhs", "yeahs" and cryptic remarks didn't give him much room for guessing the nature of the report.

Brandon's unhappy expression as he hung up was not encouraging. "Why didn't you pick up the extension?"

"I wasn't invited."

Brandon shook his head. "You're a real little gentleman, kid."

Pete grinned. "Thanks."

"A goose egg, so far as the Carlton is concerned. She was there three nights; a couple of local calls on her bill. No one remembers anything significant about her — whether she had visitors, overnight or otherwise, whether she herself was always there or not — zilch."

"Anything on the Pericles Society?"

"Maybe." Brandon scratched his chin. "Merton was an honorary member. The festivities for this year's Outing were scheduled for three days."

"What's that 'Outing' business anyway?"

"A kind of think-tank get-together for power brokers is the way I read it. The society owns an old mansion in the Napa Valley."

"I get it. A real rugged few days in the wine country."

Brandon growled a 'yeah.' "This year's shindig was held from the evening of the fifteenth to the evening of the eighteenth of July. Those dates include the days our man was away from Altamira."

"And Julian Merton was in attendance the entire time?"

"No comment. They won't give out information on members or guests."

"Well, I've got something," Pete said.

"Yeah?"

"The result of a visit to the Business Bureau and a look at the expenses Mr. Merton turned in for the trip; airplane ticket and car rental — a Volvo. He drove it three hundred and seventy-one miles. At a rough guess, the distance between the airport and the heart of the Napa Valley is about seventy miles."

"Which leaves two hundred and thirty miles for possible hanky panky in San Francisco between the morning of the sixteenth and the midnight flight home on the eighteenth." Brandon doodled an elaborate "H" and "P" in his notebook, then heaved decisively to his feet. "We'd better start working our way through the list again — beginning with the Dean of the Faculty. And maybe you ought to give the VP daily diaries a look-see."

On his way out he ran into Donaldson.

"I was just coming to see you, Sergeant. I thought maybe you'd want prints of these photos."

Brandon took the envelope. "Yeah?"

"Taken at the reception for Ward Finlay."

"Say, thanks a lot . . ."

"Nothing to get excited about, sorry to say. Just a few group shots of Ward and the officers. Too dense a crowd to get anything interesting."

Brandon nodded as though he hadn't expected anything more. "Would you happen to know when you took them?"

"I didn't. Mary Walker did — around quarter to six, she thinks. I've given you enlargements, so you'll pick up a few faces in the background, but that's about it." Brandon looked a question. "No one I didn't recognize," Tom said.

Brandon sighed.

Instead of going directly to Dean Parker-Brown's office, Brandon veered off to the right to stop by Beulah Taper's desk. Beulah punched the Save button on her word processor and pivoted her chair around to face him.

"Good morning, Sergeant."

"Ma'am. I wonder if I might take a look at your desk calendar."

As she reached for the leather appointment book, he stopped her. "No ma'am. Just the little one." He pointed to the calendar with chrome rings sitting by her phone.

She handed it to him without a word.

Brandon flipped through the pages for July 15 through July 19 and back again. He held it out to her, a finger indicating an entry on 17 July.

"It looks like something was erased here, Miss Taper."

She studied the page a moment. "So it does."

"Could you tell me what it was?"

She took her time, then calmly, "I really couldn't say."

Brandon held on to the calendar. "I could take it to the lab . . . But it would sure be a help if you could remember."

Beulah took the calendar from him, peered at the indicated page. "I believe it was a note to myself to call President Merton."

"At the Pericles Society?"

"Yes."

"And did you talk to him?"

"I tried once, he was not available. Then I decided it wasn't anything that couldn't wait."

"What time would that have been?"

"Where the entry was — about four in the afternoon."

"Not available or not there?"

"He didn't answer his phone, Sergeant."

"Did you have him paged?"

She looked uncomfortable. "Yes."

Brandon persisted. "Do you know of any appointments he had away from the society?"

"Only the one on the afternoon of the eighteenth in San Francisco, with Mr. Van Voorhees and the chairman of the Board's Finance Committee."

"Did anybody at the society's headquarters say when he might be back? Or anything about where you might reach him?"

"No. Just that he didn't answer his phone or the page."

"Was it usual for the president to be out of touch?"

She bristled. "You could hardly call it being out of touch, Sergeant — just because he wasn't in when I happened to phone."

Brandon was unmoved. "Why did you erase the entry, Miss Taper?"

"I really couldn't say. I know I decided I wasn't going to call again. A reflex action, I suppose."

"When Mr. Merton returned, did you say anything about trying to reach him?"

She shook her head. Familiar by now with the lady's ethics, Brandon thought he should ask the question another way.

"Did the president ask you why you hadn't gotten in touch with him?"

Beulah hesitated. "I'm not sure he was expecting me to call, Sergeant."

"What was the call about, Miss Taper?"

"A message from Mr. Laszlo, relative to the Finance meeting on the eighteenth. I told him I hadn't reached the president and he phoned the committee chairman himself."

Brandon let it go at that, almost smiled his "Thanks, Miss Taper," and headed toward the dean's office, reflecting yet once again that Beulah Taper was a lady who had had little practice in fiddling with the truth.

Phil Gertmenian's greeting was glacially correct. Yes, the dean was in. He would see whether she was free.

Once again Brandon found himself seated in one of the Hancock chairs facing the caricature of the dean as Louis XIV. He moved his chair as Anne came around her desk and took the second chair. She leaned back, relaxed.

"I just have a couple of questions, Dean."

She smiled, but said nothing. What was it about this woman that made him uncomfortable?

"You purchased a half case of Château d'Yquem around Christmas time, I believe."

"That's correct. I ordered a number of things from Harry — at The Cork and Bottle. I particularly remember the Yquem because I almost gave some to the Mertons."

"And they gave you two bottles."

"Oh. So you know about that?"

"Yes ma'am. Have you any left?"

"I think not. But I'm not sure."

"Do you keep a guest book, Dean?"

"Not with any regularity, I'm afraid."

"We'd like to check. Both the book and your wine supply. If you don't mind, I'll send Agent Wiggins along with you when you leave for home." Brandon thought she seemed amused.

"That will be fine, Sergeant. I have no objections. And now for the second question?"

He cleared his throat. "About your stopover in San Francisco . . . "

She waited for him to go on.

"Had you planned the stay before you left on your vacation?"

"Yes, I had."

"It would help if you would tell me why no one knew of your plan."

"I was on my own time, Sergeant Blessing. There was no reason to inform anyone."

"It would help me even more if you would tell me why you decided to come back early."

"I thought I had already explained that."

"Not to my satisfaction, ma'am."

"Just what is it you want to know, Sergeant?"

"Did you see anyone while you were there?"

This time her smile was almost lazy. "You mean, did I see President Merton?"

"Yes ma'am."

"No, Sergeant, I did not."

"Did you see anyone?"

"Why is that important?"

Brandon was blunt. "Because that person, or persons, might corroborate your story, Dean."

Anne Parker-Brown spread one hand on the arm of the chair, closed it again. She then looked him coolly in the eye. "Am I a suspect, Sergeant?"

He nodded. "Right now you are. Along with a few others."

"Well now, that's comforting, isn't it?" Anne rose and went back to her desk chair. "I can't provide you with any corroboration for my stay in San Francisco. I saw no one but the people at the hotel. And I did not kill Julian Merton, Sergeant Blessing; nor do I have the faintest notion who did."

Brandon took a while to mull that over. Then he asked, "You made some phone calls, didn't you?"

If she was taken aback by the question, she recovered quickly. "Yes. I telephoned a restaurant, La Tour, for a dinner reservation. On the seventeenth. They said a reservation wasn't necessary."

"And you went there?"

"No. I changed my mind. I settled for the Carlton Hotel dining room."

"And the other call?"

"To the Windsor Hotel. I considered dining there before my flight back to Altamira — but I decided not to bother."

"You didn't call back to cancel the reservation?"

"I changed my mind before I was connected with the dining room."

Brandon looked disbelieving. "When was that?"

"The next day — the eighteenth."

"You seem to have trouble making up your mind about restaurants, Dean."

"I don't enjoy solitary dining, Sergeant, if you must know. I think I should make the effort and then . . . " The sentence ended with a shrug.

"So where did you go?"

"No place. I really wasn't very hungry; I had some fruit and crackers in my room. And a candy bar, to be precise. Chocolate." She smiled at him.

Wiseacre, he thought. How had she found out? But he didn't react, except to blink a couple of times before continuing. "What did you do in the city — with all your time?"

"Walked, shopped — but just looked. I didn't buy anything. I went to the museum in Exposition Park: California Artists from Nineteen-Thirty to Nineteen-Sixty. And I slept quite a bit — to get over my jet lag. And read. Will that do it, Sergeant?" She stood up.

Brandon knew he was dismissed. He thought he had figured out why she disconcerted him. Whether or not the dean had had any romantic interest in Julian Merton when he was alive, it seemed evident that she had little interest in him dead. Or in who killed him. It was her indifference that bothered him. Genuine? Or faked?

With a hand on the doorknob, Brandon hesitated, then turned. The dean was reading a paper on her desk. She looked up.

"Yes?"

"During the time you were in your office Wednesday evening after the reception, did you see anyone? Hear anything?"

"No."

"You didn't leave your office? Like go to the ladies' room?"

"No."

"Any phone calls?"

"I had transferred my line to the outer office. If there were any calls, I didn't hear them. As I told you, I fell asleep."

"Yes ma'am."

"Anything else, Sergeant?"

Brandon shook his head and let himself out. He stopped in front of Phil Gertmenian's desk.

"I'd like a few minutes, Mr. Gertmenian."

"Could we talk here? I'd just as soon not transfer our calls to another office."

"Sure." He sat down. "What did you think of Julian Merton?"

Gertmenian hid his hands; his expression hardened. "If I said I did not admire the man, that would make it unanimous, wouldn't it?"

"Did you know he was going to fire your boss?"

"Look here, Sergeant, haven't you discussed that matter with the dean?"

"I'm asking you."

"I believe they were discussing an eventual change, yes."

"What did you think of that?"

"I certainly understood the dean's interest in returning to the classroom after seven years in the Hall."

"You would be out of a job, wouldn't you?"

He shrugged.

"Would you want to be secretary to anyone else?"

"Probably not."

"You think a lot of your boss, don't you?"

"What are you driving at, Sergeant?"

"Just answer the question."

"Yes."

Brandon seemed to drift off for a long moment. "I'd kinda like to go over again what you were doing at that reception."

Gertmenian's impatience gradually modulated to resignation. What Brandon heard corresponded with the report Pete had been given, yet he was dissatisfied. He didn't take to this young man, but he didn't know why. Unless Pete — and his daughters — were right, and he was a victim of old-fashioned prejudices. He was fishing around aimlessly and he knew it. Out of the blue he asked, "Do you know anything about French wines?"

"A little."

"What about that Château d'Yquem?"

"I'm familiar with it."

"Do you ever buy it?"

"Not for myself." His knowing smile set Brandon's teeth on edge. Phil went on, "I bought a bottle some months ago for my father; he likes a fairly sweet wine."

Brandon looked puzzled. "I thought he was an invalid."

"Pretty much so, yes. He has precious few pleasures, Sergeant, and a small glass of a very good wine before he goes to bed is one of them."

"You just bought the one bottle?"

"Right."

"Any left?"

Phil shook his head. "Dad drank it all."

To Brandon, Gertmenian's smile was both a challenge and an insult.

Shortly after the detective had left, Phil rang to say that Mrs. Merton was on the phone. Priscilla's voice seemed more relaxed, less shrill than usual as she thanked Anne for the help she and the office staff had given her during "this horrible week."

"What I want to talk to you about . . . Oh, it's so hard." She broke off; Anne could hear her take a deep breath. "The coroner's office has called. They will release Julian's body to the funeral home today. Father Merton has talked to them. He's being wonderful."

"I'm sure."

"We thought we would have the graveside service on Friday, at ten. I'd rather it were just family and close associates — since there will be the public memorial service in September. But I wanted to

check with you. Do you think that will cause bad
feelings?"

"Priscilla, the service should be the way you want
it."

"I'll bring a list over. I'll ask Beulah to handle the
invitations. Would you ask Mr. Donaldson to get
out the appropriate notice for the papers?"

"Of course." Anne waited, sensing that Priscilla
hadn't yet gotten to the real reason for the call.

"I was wondering, Anne, if you would be willing
to read Baudelaire's *'L'invitation au voyage'* at the
graveside service? It was Julian's favorite — as I
think you know."

The voice was gentle, tremulous, but the insinuation was unmistakable. Anne took a second to
regain her self-control. "Are you sure you mean
'L'invitation au voyage' and not *'Le voyage'* "?

"Oh my goodness, have I gotten the titles mixed
up? *'L'invitation . . .'* that's the love poem, isn't it?
With that sensual line about *'luxe et volupté'?*" Anne
remained silent. "Well, that would never do.
Though I adore it. And Julian recited it so beauti-
fully, didn't he?"

Anne didn't respond.

"I guess I mean *'Le voyage';* the one that ends
with something like, 'O Death, old Captain, the
time has come . . . '" Priscilla broke off, her voice
unsteady.

"Don't you think it's too long for the occasion?"

"Couldn't you just read the first and last sections? I'm asking Leslie to read a biblical passage. Something from the Psalms, I think. Anne, you *will* read the Baudelaire?"

"Very well, Priscilla."

"I know Julian would be pleased. In French, of course."

"What?"

"I thought I would read the English translation. Don't you think that would be appropriate? For each one of us to read something?" Before Anne had time to reply, Priscilla changed the subject. "By the way, Anne, if you would like to see Julian . . . "

"I think not."

"Father Merton is going to the funeral home. They've told us we may view . . . I don't know whether I can or not." Her voice choked up again. "It's so hard, Anne, to think of his having been cut apart then sewed back up . . . Like a — an object, a thing."

Anne slowly returned the phone to its cradle. She sat motionless before the mental image Priscilla had created, an image composed of recollections from the past and the ugly reality of the present. She got up, walked over to the window, looking at without really seeing the quad and the occasional passer-by.

Mary sat sketching at the northern end of the oval, her face shaded by her favorite old straw hat. Runners from the Geriatric group began coming off the track. Most of them waved; some came over to where she was sitting.

Henry Norton removed his cap, looked over her shoulder. "Mind if I take a peek?"

"Not at all. You all aren't going out across campus today?"

"Most of us not, I guess. Too hot and smoggy."

Victor Laszlo, Turner, and Phil Gertmenian crowded round.

"Something for the magazine, Mary?" Victor asked.

"I hadn't intended it to be. But maybe a short item on the Geriatric Jogging and Chowder Marching Society would be amusing."

Phil leaned in closer. "You've got a great sense of movement in your sketch. Almost . . . " He caught himself. He had almost said, "Almost as if you were a runner yourself. I mean," he finished, "one can almost feel the pumping of the legs."

Mary held the sketch pad away from her. "Can anybody of you identify these figures?"

"Easy. You don't need a face on him to see that this one is Victor." Turner pointed. "The way he carries his head down."

"Hunh-uh. Looks more like Tom Donaldson to me."

"Isn't that Henry — with that high knee action?"

"Not skinny enough."

"This has got be Turner — look at those floppy hands."

"Or Phil, maybe."

"And that's Anne, isn't it? With that strong backward kick?"

"I don't think so. That's you, isn't it, Phil?"

"Kitty Van Voorhees is my guess; her elbows are always in, tight to the body."

And so it went for another few minutes, until the style of some ten runners had been dissected and argued over.

Mary had tried putting initials under the figures as the group talked, but gave up in front of their differences of opinion. When they had drifted off, she turned the pages of her sketchbook to compare the figure she had drawn on Vince's last night on earth with the runners so tentatively identified. Only Henry and Phil were wearing baseball type caps today; neither one had a stripe. The only thing she could be sure of was why she had unthinkingly blackened the runner's hands the night she had sketched him. It had occurred to her as they argued. The runner had worn gloves.

Claire and Mark Tidwell waited in the parking lot of the Faculty Club until Mary's car had pulled away, then started walking back toward the campus.

Mark drew his wife's arm through his. "I'm glad you thought of inviting Mary to lunch. She's quite a person."

"And so lovely. Why is it that crippling always seems worse when it attacks beauty?"

"It's too hot for me to try and answer that one."

"Mark, young Pete Wiggins was in the club. He was checking on Charlie's lunch-time habits — who he ate with and so forth. We chatted a bit while I was waiting for you."

"And of course you told him your theory."

"Never mind that." Claire waved a hand, as if to chase the idea from his mind. "What worries me, Mark, is the direction the investigation might be taking."

"Oh?"

"Pete asked me a couple of questions . . . I had the distinct impression that they're suspicious of Anne."

"I'm surprised you're surprised. The gumshoes would have found out about our local gossip by now. The adulterous as well as the professional kind."

"I think it is a most disturbing development."

"I'd be mighty surprised, kiddo, if Anne were the only suspect. You might console yourself with that."

"Yes, but . . . Mark, this is something I have never mentioned to anyone — and never will."

"That will be a first."

"Ce que tu peux être emmerdant."

"Naughty, naughty."

"Just listen, will you? You see, I think there *was* something between Julian and Anne."

"Are you serious?"

"Never more so. It was right at the beginning of Julian's second year. Most of us were still enchanted by him. Anne too. Well, you remember how enthusiastic she was about working with him."

"I do indeed."

"They had been on a trip to New York. Some big alumni do. Priscilla didn't go; Cissy had the measles or something. When Anne got back, I asked her whether she had met anyone fascinating."

"As you always do."

"I know she hates it, but I'm always hoping . . . Anyway, she laughed, as she always does, then got very serious and said something about her personal life being complicated enough, thank you."

"And you didn't press her for further explanation?"

"I started to. But she changed the subject very quickly. I knew she didn't want to talk about it."

"Sounds like a pretty standard kind of answer to your question if you ask me."

"But Anne always weighs her words."

"Claire, there could be a number of explanations."

"Mm. Except I can't find one that satisfies me."

They walked on in silence for another half block, then Claire took his arm again. "Gumshoes indeed. Good grief."

Pete was writing up his notes in the basement office when Brandon ambled in.

"You look satisfied with yourself." Brandon sounded cross.

"I had a pretty good morning."

"Youthful enthusiasm." He shook his head wonderingly. "Well, share the joy." Brandon rocked back in the old-fashioned swivel desk chair that Jeff Colton had dug out from a storage area.

"First. Vincent Riley's computer isn't in his house."

"Where is it?"

"I don't know — yet. But the fact that it's missing might be significant."

"Anything interesting turn up? And what Mary Walker was so upset about . . . prints of running shoes? Lab come up with anything?"

"Well — no. To all of the above."

Brandon sighed. "Continue."

"As we know, Joelle Lieberman handled the calls that came in during the party. Almost all the office phones were put on call forward to a phone in one of the Development offices." Pete glanced up from his notes. Brandon seemed to have dozed off. "So, of course she was the one who took the call from the prankster."

Brandon opened his eyes. "And of course she couldn't identify the owner of the voice."

"No, but listen: she's pretty sure it was male."

"Pretty sure, huh? Now that's precise reporting."

"It was hoarse — muffled."

"Surprise."

"But it was deep."

Brandon made an impatient gesture. "Next."

"Well, Charlie Peese always lunched at a round table at the Faculty Club where lots of different people eat at various times. And he never invited anyone to a private lunch. A real tight-wad. I went to see the woman with whom he boarded the last ten years of his life. She said the only visitors she could recall were his daughter and Professor Mark Tidwell. Professor Tidwell took him out to dinner about once every other week. Oh, and Henry Norton called on him, occasionally. Looks like we can forget about pinpointing any nonscientists who might have spent time alone with him, to pump him about his research."

"Pete." Brandon spoke softly. "Are you for real? Did I hear you indicate you had good news?"

"Damn it, Brandon, there's more than one way of making progress. There's a certain amount of clearing out that has to be done."

"You've done that all right, kid." He tipped his chair back to forward position. "Is that it?"

"No." Pete was grumpy in his turn. "I checked out the VP appointment books, like you said. I did find something."

"Yeah?" Brandon was clearly bored.

"Turner Van Voorhees was in San Francisco from the eighteenth to early a.m. on the nineteenth."

"Right."

Pete was deflated. "You already know about that?"

"Let's get your reading on it."

"Well, he and the president met with the chairman of the Finance Committee of the Board in the bar of the Windsor Hotel. At about 4:30 on the eighteenth. That accounts for some of the mileage on the rented car and does place Merton in San Francisco."

Brandon greeted the comment with a forlorn expression.

"And there's more."

"Just can't wait."

"Have you considered the possibility that Julian Merton wasn't the intended victim?"

"It's crossed my mind."

Pete refused to give up that easily. "Mary Walker could be right. That there's a connection between Riley's death and Merton's."

Brandon shuddered. "Don't wish that on us." He zipped open a fresh sack of M & Ms. "These little buggers really give you a lift."

The call that came in from the coroner's office a few minutes later settled the matter. Pete was returning from a trip to the water fountain as Brandon hung up the phone.

"That was the medical examiner on the Riley case. The post confirms accidental death. They even checked the inside of his mouth for signs of forced ingestion. No suspicious marks on the body. Nothing to indicate anything but that he hit his head on those metal tub fixtures as he fell, was knocked unconscious, and drowned."

Pete looked crestfallen.

Brandon's eyes crinkled. "Don't be downhearted, Pete. You won one and you lost one. And we don't need a second murder investigation on our hands. This one is giving us trouble enough." He yawned, shook his head. "I didn't get enough sleep."

Pete found Mary in the News Bureau. There were deep circles under her eyes; she looked drawn, tense. She listened calmly to what he had to tell her.

"I hope that relieves your mind some, Mary."

She shook her head. "It doesn't change anything, Pete. All it says is that the murderer is smarter than everybody else."

Pete knew he shouldn't encourage her stubborn mind-set but found himself saying apologetically, "We haven't found Vince's computer yet, Mary, but I'll keep trying."

"You needn't bother, Pete. It's turned up. Max Dingam has it."

"What?"

"Vince had arranged for him to pick it up that night. So they could use it here in the office. Max must have come by Vince's right after I left."

"Oh. Then I guess that's that. Maybe that explains the footprint as well."

She shook her head. "Max wears mountain boots in the winter and sandals in the summer. I know. I asked."

For tenaciousness, Pete thought, fragile-looking Mary Walker could give lessons to a bulldog.

"But there's nothing in the computer, Pete. And Vince was writing a report when I left him."

"You're thinking someone erased it?"

"Maybe. But it's more likely he did himself — after he put the material on a diskette for backup. But as for where it might be . . . " Mary absently picked up an eraser then put it down again. "There is something else." She sounded breathless. "Max said Vince was wearing a bathrobe when he arrived. Vince told him he was about to take a shower."

Tuesday, July 25

AGENT WIGGINS CAUGHT UP WITH MAX Dingam on the Quad, where he was talking to the head gardener. Max wiped the sweat from his broad face with a bandana handkerchief and moved toward the shade of a live-oak tree. Pete gratefully followed.

"That's right, officer. Vince said he wanted to get away by two — a. m., that is. He was headed for the shower when I got there."

"I've heard that Riley had something against tub baths. That right?"

Max nodded in fond remembrance. "Vince was a regular guy, but he sure had some crazy notions. Oh, he had a sense of humor about it — what he called his brewer's yeast syn — something."

"Syndrome, maybe?"

"Yeah. Syndrome. Vince didn't mind being kidded, but he was as stubborn as a Missouri mule."

"Yeah?"

"He wouldn't swim in a pool either. Crazy. But there you are. Vince was a shower man all right."

"Was this common knowledge?"

"Sure. Like I said. We all teased him about being a health nut. But he didn't mind. I think he got a kick out of it."

"We all?"

"Oh, the guys and gals in the Hall."

Pete scribbled in his notebook, then looked up at Dingam. "About Friday night. Kind of late for picking up the computer, wasn't it? Couldn't it have waited until morning?"

Max pondered that a moment. "Oh sure. Glory, it's hot." He eased his damp shirt away from his body. "Sure it could have. But I didn't mind. Seemed simpler not to have to arrange about keys. And I generally have a couple of last-minute things to ask Vince. He was such a swell guy. This is a real bummer, you know?"

His eyes watered. Reluctantly, Pete brought him back to the matter at hand.

"How come you needed his computer?"

"Oh that. Vince kept it at the office most of the time. Our oldie began to have problems a couple of months ago."

"Oh?"

"Yeah. Crystal, Miss Mathews, was supposed to get us a new model, a Mac SE, but it hasn't come through as yet. So Vince brought his in."

"Did you pick up any floppies along with the computer?"

"Hunh-uh. Just the Mac."

"Did he say anything about what he was writing on the computer?"

"Hunh-uh."

"Was he alone?"

"Old Vince? At that hour?" Max chortled. "You bet."

"How did he act? Did he seem nervous, worried?"

"Naw. I waited while he finished up with what he had going on the PC. We talked business a couple of minutes, then I took off."

"Well, thanks, Mr. Dingam." Pete turned to go, but was stopped by the other man.

"Officer, do these questions mean that there might be something fishy about Vince's death?"

"Not at all, Mr. Dingam. Routine. Part of winding things up after an unattended death."

The other shook his head in admiration. "You guys sure do a thorough job."

Brandon no longer looked sleepy. This time Pete had his full attention. Within thirty minutes the keys to the Riley home had been retrieved from the police station and they were unlocking the front door. At that same moment, Joelle Lieberman, returning from a dental appointment, was driving down First Street. Within the next thirty minutes news of police interest in the Riley house was spreading up, down, and sideways through Wyndham Hall.

The bathroom was shadowy and cool. Leaves from bushes outside the window dappled the wall and fixtures with moving shadows. Brandon carefully placed handkerchief-covered fingers on the outer edge of the old-fashioned spoked metal handle and turned the bathtub water on and off. He went through the same routine with the shower faucet; it jiggled.

"There's our answer, Pete. The faucet activating the shower is on the blink."

"Could it have been rigged?"

"Possible. Looks to me like one of the screws just fell out — here at the base. See that? This installation is an antique; must be over fifty years old. We'll call the lab, get one of the boys to check it out. And look for the screw. Until then, might not be a bad idea for Thad to put someone back on duty here."

"Crazy."

"Huh?"

"Why would anyone want to do away with Vince Riley?"

Brandon was silent a moment, then exploded. "Who needs a reason to waste anyone these days? We live in a stinking cesspool. Or haven't you heard?" And he was heading for the front door, grumbling an "I'm off to LA. See if there's any more to be gotten out of Milton Weinert."

Pete called after him, "I'm going to look around a little longer, Brandon." He went into Vince's study and started going through the drawers of a battered Mission-style desk.

Anne handed the letters she had signed to Phil Gertmenian and glanced at her watch.

"I think that's it for the day, Phil. I've got a date with Agent Wiggins. To check out my wine supply. 'The potion with the poison.'"

Phil looked baffled.

Anne explained. "You're too young to have seen that Danny Kaye film — unless on television maybe. It had a medieval setting."

"Sure. *The Court Jester.* It was a howl."

"Remember that formula he kept repeating? So that someone wouldn't get the wrong drink? 'The potion with the poison's in the vessel with the pestle; the chalice from the palace has the brew that is true.'"

She laughed. Phil didn't.

"Never mind, Phil. Maybe I'll try it out on the detective. It would make the perfect epigraph for our local drama."

Phil was still not amused. "Sergeant Blessing gave me a little quiz on Château d'Yquem this morning."

"Oh?"

"I bought a bottle for Dad's nightcap supply a while back. I have the notion that Blessing wonders whether dear old Dad was the only one to drink it."

Anne raised her eyebrows. "He must be getting desperate."

"So what is Agent Pete's assignment?"

"The good Agent Wiggins is trying to track down how many bottles of Château d'Yquem we can account for. Those of us who had it in our cellars, that is. Though cellar is certainly pretentious for the kitchen closet that holds my supply."

"It would be easy for the murderer to fake accountability, it seems to me."

"I suppose it's the kind of thing the police have to follow through on. There's always the off-chance of carelessness. Or even sudden confession under pressure, I suppose." She rose, picked up her briefcase from the side of her desk. "See you in the morning."

"Better go through the registrar's office and out the south door."

"Oh?"

"Donaldson called to say he'd been talking to a couple of LA reporters. He thinks they're still hanging around."

"OK."

"Anne."

"Yes?"

"Do you think that maybe Victor could have done this?"

"Why pick on him?"

"Seems to me he's become increasingly tense, under that blustery, cheery exterior. He overdoes it. Then there was the way he acted at the reception. I thought he looked kind of green around the gills."

"Maybe he had indigestion. But to answer your question, I don't know. On the other hand, I do know who is in first place where Sergeant Blessing is concerned."

Her mocking expression made it clear whom she meant.

"That's impossible."

"Not at all. Take a walk in Blessing's moccasins, Phillip; think it through for a moment. It makes perfect sense."

Brandon Blessing, looking lugubrious, stepped out of the elevator and made for the phone booth in the foyer of Weinert's building. "Pete? . . . I'm through with Weinert — or maybe it's the other way around . . . Yeah. Gotta check with the coroner, then stop by the Sheriff's office; should be back on campus in a couple of hours . . . Naw, it wasn't a total loss. Weinert's washed his hands of Tipton; says that things are out of control and that intellectuals are a bunch of cracked pots and commies. So, you could say the anti-business-school faction have got what they wanted. Maybe we oughta take another look at that crew," he added half-heartedly, and hung up before Pete could comment. Brandon checked his notebook and dialed a Pacific Palisades number. The same soft Hispanic

THE FAST-DEATH FACTOR 393

voice gave the same answer. The Cochrans were still not back from Cabo San Lucas.

"I'm going to have a drink, officer. I suppose you . . .?"

"No, ma'am, thanks just the same."

Agent Wiggins and Anne were standing in her kitchen near the open door of a storage closet. As she moved off to fix herself a vodka and tonic, Pete continued studying the guest book she had provided him.

"Any luck?"

"No ma'am, not much. There's an entry for one bottle on the second of December."

Anne came over to look at the page. "Oh yes. That was a dinner for a few faculty and midyear graduates."

"One bottle doesn't seem like much for ten people."

"It was served with dessert, officer. And not everybody drinks."

Pete turned a few more pages. "The last entry is in March. Again one bottle. Is that right?"

"Possibly." She took a sip of her drink. "I don't often entertain here at the house, Agent Wiggins. Officially, that is. I rely largely upon the Faculty Club."

Pete closed the book and went back for a final check of the closet.

"What's the final count?"

"Four. You bought six, the Mertons gave you two. So there are two bottles unaccounted for."

"I see."

"Any idea when you might have served them?"

Anne looked thoughtful, then shook her head. "Not a clue. I'm curious about something."

"Ma'am?"

"I knew you were coming here this afternoon. I had ample time to make additional entries in the guest book."

"Yes ma'am, that's correct."

"Do you think I'm a woman of honor?"

Pete wondered why she was teasing him.

"We knew you had this book, Dean; you told us. And if we felt it necessary we could ask the lab to check it out. They're pretty good at figuring out the age of any writing."

"Now why didn't I think of that? By the way, Agent Wiggins, did you ever see a Danny Kaye film . . . "

Back on campus Pete was at a loss to explain why the dean had treated his visit as a joke. Brandon had an explanation.

"She's nervous, Pete. Frightened maybe. But still shrewd enough not to invent some cock-and-bull story about those two missing bottles. Ve-ry in-te-res-ting."

Pete shrugged. "I'm not so sure. Did you stop by the de Granceys'?"

Brandon nodded. "Both bottles huffily accounted for. Ditto at the Laszlos. Mrs. Laszlo was friendlier but is she ever a sad looking lady," he said parenthetically. And the Nortons still have theirs — stored in with the Hamburger Helper."

"These wine checks are a waste of time, if you ask me, Brandon. Unless they keep careful records, people don't readily remember what they drank when. And the murderer could fake it anyway." Pete was grumpy.

"I know, kid. There's only an off chance we'll stumble onto something, but it's a chance we have to take — and it builds up the pressure. A killer can never be sure of what you do or don't know. Or what your angle is. Even if you don't know yourself."

Brandon punctuated the remark with the lip twitch that passed for a smile and picked up a large manilla envelope that had been delivered by messenger. He ripped it open and laid out the results of the computer consultant's work on the table before them.

Using a database program, Greg Tomono had created a computerized time grid with symbols for the guests and graphics to represent locations in the room: table, bar, chairs, drinking fountain, entry, back stairway and offices. He had run off a program of the last hour of the reception that showed, symbolically, the location and observations of some thirty people according to thirty different interviews. Tomono had tracked the president's movement in time and place as reported by the individuals Brandon had selected as witnesses, and the movement of those guests each of the thirty recalled having seen talking with Merton or standing in his vicinity. In addition, Greg had worked out his program so it was possible to check at which points reports coincided and where they differed.

"What did I tell you, Pete. Pretty impressive, huh?"

Pretty overwhelming, Pete thought.

"Well, let's dig in."

Pete checked his watch: almost quarter to seven. "How about digging into some food first?"

"If you'll put on the coffee . . . " Brandon was opening his briefcase. Inside was a supply of sandwiches and what looked suspiciously like squashed chocolate cake.

Thad entered by the backdoor, went to his room to take off his jacket, then walked down the hall to Mary's studio.

"Hello, Big Bro. Long day."

"Mm. Have you had supper?"

"I'm not hungry. The Tidwells insisted on a rather copious lunch. Part of their cheering-Mary-up program."

"Is that to be read as a cynical comment?"

She looked up from her work. "I didn't mean it to be. They're both as dear as can be. Just obvious is all." She studied her brother a moment. "You look tired. Could I fix you something?"

"Thanks, no. I stopped off at Solly's." He sat down in the room's one easy chair. "Can we talk?"

"Sure. There's something I want to ask you about too. But you go first."

"We finally reached Vince's brother, Mary, thanks to the New Mexico Forest Service. He had packed in to a spot about twenty miles from his cabin, for some fishing. George wasn't worried; he thought Vince had just been delayed. And his cabin is never locked anyway."

"Did you speak with him?"

"Yes. The New Mexico people had told him about Vince's death."

"How did he take it?"

"Quietly, I'd say."

She nodded. "Somehow that sounds like brother George."

"He asked that the college handle things as they see fit. That is to say, he does not attend funeral services."

"I don't blame him for that."

"He did ask that his brother's ashes be delivered to him — and any books on the West that Vince might have in his home library. And family photographs."

"Is that all?"

"No. George Riley said that Vince had left you the house, Mary."

"Oh, Thad." She looked stricken.

"He never told you?"

"No."

"I gather George inherits whatever money Vince left, but the house and its contents are yours."

"Vince told him that?"

"Yes. And George has a copy of the will. The original is supposed to be in Vince's box at the bank. Al Bates drew it up, but he's vacationing at his Montana ranch. That's why you haven't heard anything."

Mary was troubled. "But George must be terribly hurt . . . "

Her brother interrupted. "You've got it wrong. George said he had no interest in owning city property. What Vince wanted is what he wants."

Mary's head was lowered. Her brother watched her in silence for a long time. When she spoke, it seemed to be more to herself. "He wanted me to be independent. Less dependent on you."

"Would you like to live there?"

She looked up at him. "I think so. Yes. But not quite yet. I would like to go over there, though. That's what I wanted to ask you. May I?"

"I think it can be arranged."

"I saw there was a policeman on duty again. Some new evidence has turned up, hasn't it?"

"It's possible." He got to his feet. "You may have been right. Vince may have intended to take a shower. But it's far from conclusive."

"Have you heard Claire Tidwell's theory?"

"No."

"She thinks that the poisoned drink was intended for someone else — not for President Merton."

"You're thinking it was meant for Vince? But why?"

"I don't know."

Thad looked worried. "Mary, don't let this murder theory become an obsession. It's so much more likely that Vince's death was an accident. If you would just accept that . . . "

She clenched her fists. Why did he have to use that word?

"Mary?"

A rather enigmatic smile answered him. Discussion closed. Mary returned to her drawing.

Thad got up to leave, went over to the table, looked over her shoulder.

"Is this for the magazine?"

"No. Just an interest in the movement of runners. I went to the track before my luncheon date. What you see here are some of the hardiest or craziest members of the 'Geriatric Jogging and Chowder Marching Society' — that group from the college. There has to be a life-threatening smog alert to stop them."

"They're mad."

"Maybe one of them is."

Her brother didn't hear. Or didn't pay any attention. He was at the door. "Want to catch the news?"

"Go ahead, Thad. I may join you later."

At 11:40, Brandon dropped his pencil and reached back to rub between his shoulder blades. Pete took a couple of aspirins. Tomono's mountain of work had labored to produce a mouse. Or rather the same mice they had been chasing in circles all along: Turner Van Voorhees, Anne Parker-Brown, Henry Norton, Victor Laszlo, and Beulah Taper were serving drinks near the president, either within an estimated thirty minutes preceding the toast to Finlay or within approximately fifteen minutes afterwards — when Merton was called to the phone. Almost everyone, including assorted professors and secretaries, had circulated in the vicinity of Julian Merton during the same period. Merton, Filmore and Laszlo had gone off to one side for a very brief confab minutes before the toasts were proposed. Norton, Turner and Joelle Lieberman recalled having served the president some wine — whether a fresh glass or a topping-up wasn't clear. Phil Gertmenian thought he had seen the president with a bottle in his hand, right before Filmore made his remarks, as had Mrs. Merton also.

"Looks like open season still, doesn't it, Brandon?"

A grunt was his reply. "We know who poured the last of the rosé — or what we were told was rosé . . . Oh, hell."

Startled by Brandon's use of the expletive, either a sign of exceptional frustration or a candy shortage, Pete remained silent. Brandon pressed the heels of his hands against his eyes a moment.

"Next question. A pop quiz for you: supposing the murderer stashed the bottle in the buffet before things were set up for the party, as we speculated, what would be the next move, kid, once the festivities were getting under way?"

"Put it underneath the bar — at the back. Or better yet, in the trash can. It would be empty at the start of the party, so put the bottle in, throw some paper or junk over it. The can was right next to the bar. Then the murderer just lifts it out when ready."

"Go to the head of the class."

Pete was startled.

"Sure," Brandon went on, "that's gotta be it. The trash can. No chance of anyone picking up the bottle by mistake — until the murderer was ready to use it."

It was Pete's turn to throw in a "but." "But suppose somebody asked for some wine, when the killer was walking around with the poisoned bottle in his hand?"

"Easy. Carry two bottles."

"'The potion with the poison's in the vessel with the pestle.'"

"Huh?"

"Nothing."

"With a bottle in each hand, the murderer could always serve untainted wine. Then the bad stuff went back into the trash as an empty." He yawned. "He or she. And it listens like a female to me. A red-headed one."

"Do you think the dean would have stuck around a whole hour afterwards, Brandon? Then wait for the custodian to find her with him? Even try to revive him?"

"You know a better way to look innocent?"

Pete shook his head in disbelief. "You would sure have to be a cold customer to do that. And have a hell of a lot of hate in your heart."

"Try this on for size, Pete: We're dealing with a secretive woman. And a proud one. She would not take kindly to rejection. Professional or personal. She was about to be booted out of the dean's chair — some reward for having done time on the presidential couch. That photograph taken at the Retreat could not be labelled 'Just Friends.' Not with those expressions on their faces. Or maybe he had changed since then, had told her that 'just friends' was all he wanted to be. If Merton was the bastard some say he was, and if he had played rough with her, well — there's motive enough."

"I don't buy it," Pete said.

Brandon ignored him. "Then, too, the way I read her, she could be boiling at what Merton was doing to the college. Not a direct motive for the murder, granted, but another deep-seated black mark against him."

He pulled on his lower lip, then leaned forward. "Here's the scenario. Dollars to doughnuts they met in San Fran — or at least talked. Something goes very wrong. She leaves San Francisco steaming. Has plenty of time for the plan to shape up during the flight back. The more she reflects on what happened, the more enraged she becomes. Possibly the time she spent with Merton alone in his office tipped her further over the edge. She knows exactly what to do: head for the Chemistry Department when no one's around. Which she does just a few hours after she returns to Altamira. Only someone was about. Faithful Ulrich."

Pete shook his head. "I have trouble with it, Brandon."

"Then she could have made a quick run home in her car to pick up the wine — or maybe she brought it to the office with her that morning." Pete still looked skeptical. "For that matter, she could have gotten the poison, arranged everything after she arrived from San Francisco at one a. m. All of the VPs have masterkeys." Pete still looked his disbelief. "That Logan's no dummy. Remember what she said about double lives around here. In my book the dean's psychological profile could be a snug fit for that category. She's a solitary type — despite all the professional bustling about. And she's been a widow for how long? Almost twenty years? At forty- three she's susceptible, vulnerable, approaching the change . . . "

Pete interrupted. "Aw, come on Brandon. Don't give me that postmenstrual hormonal imbalance routine. Women don't go off their rocker any more."

Brandon blinked. "You sound like my oldest girl. I may be out of date, kid, but there are some things about human nature that don't change."

"I sure don't see her the way you do. Not as an unbalanced lady with some kind of dark secret life."

Blessing harrumphed. "She's an impressive, attractive woman and you like her. Just the way you sympathize with Mary Walker. " He looked disgusted. "Where did you pick up this weakness for damsels in distress?"

Pete blushed in defiance. "I call it common sense."

"In a pig's eye. That's the trouble with having a local boy on a case. Nice home-town folks are never killers. You're allowing subjective impressions to interfere, kid."

"You can't just toss out all the other people who hated the guy's guts."

"Kid, I'm not. But right now I'm more interested in so-called friends."

"Then what about Filmore? Just as a for instance?"

"No opportunity, if our reconstruction is on target. Furthermore, even if he had the mix and stir
recipe, a guy like Filmore never does his own dirty
work."

Pete wasn't giving up. "What about the
president's wife? She and the president sure
wouldn't have won the couple of the year award.
Terry Logan said he treated her like shit."

Brandon was scornful. "The comment of an unprejudiced observer. And a lady who is not exactly
keen on men." He got to his feet, picked up his
rumpled jacket from a chair. "Let's go home, Pete,
and maul this over, as an old army buddy of mine
used to say."

Wednesday, July 26

THE WEDNESDAY EDITION OF THE AL-
tamira *Ledger* was stacked, tied and ready for the
pre-dawn delivery. Within the hour Altamira subscribers could retrieve it from their front porch and
consider the headline over their morning coffee.

A BLUE-PRINT FOR MURDER? One and a half
illustrated pages of the Wednesday edition pur-
ported to examine the question: "Carelessness in
the Chemistry Department?" The question mark
here as in the headline no doubt a stab at insurance
against legal action. A boxed section headed "The
Very- Fast-Death Factor," provided highlights from
Professor Peese's article on toxic waterblooms
that had appeared in the spring edition of *Tipton
Topics.* Hefner then drew a bead on Wyndham Hall,
intimating disarray in the administration of the college, hinting obliquely at conflicts over policy and
"professional and personal differences" within the
administrative hierarchy. After the blast came the
self-protective back-pedaling: " . . . all problems
that naturally follow any administrative changeover." Willie prophetically speculated on how the

crime might affect the future of the college and mused on the possible consequences of Milton Weinert's "regrettable" withdrawal of his major gift. To ascertain that all fronts were covered, Hefner concluded: "Could it be that this killing is a banal crime of passion? Was it coldly conceived by an analytical mind? A member of Altamira's respected educational community? Or was it the work of a disturbed personality acting according to a sick reasoning known only to him or herself? A sociopath who might strike again and just as erratically? So far, the Sheriff's office is saying only that the investigation is progressing. Our community can but hope." Among the photographs Willie had selected to illustrate the piece was one of the late president, his widow, and the vice president and Dean of the Faculty standing together, smiling, at the ground-breaking ceremony for the new Women's Center.

It was still dark. Seated at the breakfast table, Angel's friend quickly read through Willie Hefner's "exclusive" report, impatiently pushed the unfinished fruit juice aside. Everything had been carefully calculated, but fools kept interfering. Bungling low life fools. No reason to panic. All that was needed was for Dodie to stay in control, as Grammy always said. Grammy liked to quote "Vinegar" Joe Stillwell to Dodie about not letting the bastards grind you down.

Angel's friend went through the rest of the paper randomly, stopping at page six and a review of Terry Logan's exhibit. Two photographs were reproduced: one of transvestites in a British pub and one of a bum eye to eye with a pigeon perched near him. Underneath the photos was the attribution: "Tipton College News Bureau."

The weather bureau's announcement of an impending heat wave was fast proving to be prophetic. At 4:30 in the morning, when Terry Logan arrived at the all-weather track, the thermometer was already climbing toward 90 degrees. Terry did stretches for a few minutes, then took off. She was coming up on her tenth mile when she saw the other runner. A wide grin spread over her face. On impulse she cut across the infield. "Hi there, Dodie." A moment later she was moving easily beside the figure in running shorts and a black and orange baseball cap.

Once around the oval, Angel's friend left her to sprint to a parking area to the north of the track. Terry didn't hear the revved up motor fading fast in the distance as she continued steadily on to finish her once-a-week 20K run. Nor did she register the car coming back to a stop some fifteen minutes later.

Angel's friend, standing motionless within the dense growth of oleander bushes at the southern end of the oval, hesitated and let Terry Logan run by, hoping that she had at least one more lap to go. There was no one on the track, no one in sight. The friend once again felt the cramp in the gut followed by the looseness of the bowels that came with excitement and fear. But not panic. Panic was for the little people of this world, the losers. The sensation of fear slowly melted into the more habitual one of supreme confidence, of invulnerability. The armor of a superior mind. "Grammy's little Dodie is the smartest baby . . . " The fetish song began to fill Dodie's head.

Terry was running on the inside lane and would pass by at too great a distance. It was dangerous. But Dodie could do it. Dodie always knew what to do. She had seemed to think the discovery was a joke.

"I guessed. From something Angelo said. Look, however you want to play it is OK with me. I'm getting ready to split from this dump . . . Anything that makes fools out of those pricks in the Hall suits me just fine. Bye-bye, Dodie." Terry had laughed and speeded up to pull ahead.

She shouldn't have laughed. The scene at the gallery, the pretense that she knew nothing — all that was a put-on. Vulgar, stupid dyke. She shouldn't have laughed.

Terry had the track to herself. She'd have to tell Ellen about the encounter. What a kick. All Angel had told her was that his friend was "very important." Which did narrow the field somewhat. The rest had been guesswork. Terry was rather pleased that her remarks had been upsetting. Made her feel lighter, faster.

At six-twenty-five and breathing harder now on her last lap, the woman approached the turn at the southern end of the oval. She heard her name called and cut across toward the outside lane in response. There was a loud report, and Terry Logan lay sprawled on her back, her running shorts a splash of red against the bright blue of the track.

Minutes later Anne Parker-Brown was standing over her, then racing for the nearest phone.

Thad Walker entered the track house to face a stricken dean.

"My God, Chief Walker. What is happening to us?"

"You'd better tell me what you know, while we wait for Sergeant Blessing."

"I need a drink of water . . . "

"I'll get it for you, Dean."

Thad returned with a paper cup filled at the fountain. She drank thirstily then crushed the cup in her hand.

"I left home about six-thirty, give or take a little — I walked over. It takes me about ten minutes. At first I didn't notice anything. Then I saw — saw someone laying on the track down at the far end."

"Anybody else around?"

"Not that I was aware of."

"Did you recognize Professor Logan?"

"No. Not until I had almost reached her."

"How did you know? Her arm was thrown up over part of her face."

"It was her clothes, I think. The red shorts. Terry frequently runs — ran — very early, about six or even before. I thought she had just stumbled — was unconscious perhaps. As soon as I was beside her . . . " Anne bit her lip.

Thad waited a moment before asking, "She was dead?"

Anne nodded. "I did feel for a pulse, but when I saw the wound, I knew." She swallowed hard. "I ran back here — to the track house — to telephone." She stopped in obvious distress.

"Did you see anyone?"

Anne removed her cap. Thad felt a jolt as her hair sprang out around her face, a cloud of red and gold glinting in the early light from the clerestory windows. The picture she made seemed familiar; he had seen her like this before, but couldn't remember where, or when.

"There was no one. No one I could see."

"Did you hear anything? Any sound at all?"

She took her time before answering. "Shortly after I entered the athletic grounds from Wyndham Way, I did hear a loud sound."

"You didn't identify it as a shot?"

"I knew it had to be gun fire from someplace. But it never occurred to me that . . . " She picked at the crushed cup in her hand. "Perhaps Leslie Filmore is right."

"You mean that Tipton has been targeted by a deranged personality?"

"This is our second murder and third death, Chief Walker. The third in just over a week."

The paper cup, Thad noted, was now in shreds.

It was almost eight when Brandon Blessing parked his car in a shady spot and hurried over to join Pete Wiggins, the medical examiner, and the other officers busy in the taped-off area near Terry Logan's covered body. After a brief confab he joined Thad at the door of the track house.

"Morning, Brandon."

"Not a good one, is it? The fellows say she was shot from those bushes over there. There's a small open space inside, where the killer may have stood. The informed guess is that she was shot from the edge of the stand of oleanders — about six to eight feet away. No evidence of powder or bullet particles on the skin, so it had to be over five. Looks like the slug went through the sternum and lodged in the heart. No exit wound. And no sign of any cartridge case." Brandon released a very large sigh and jerked his head toward the track house.

"Is the dean in there?"

"Right." Thad gave him a brief résumé of their conversation.

Brandon listened, head bent, solemn. "So. Another murder. And here she is again."

"I wouldn't be in a hurry to jump to conclusions if I were you, Brandon."

"You wouldn't, huh? Well, the lab might find traces of nitrate powder on her track suit; bits of twigs or juice exuded from the oleander leaves maybe — if she's willing to let us take it." Adding glumly, "She could have slipped into the suit afterwards, of course."

"She would have to be a pretty fancy quick-change artist, wouldn't she?"

"We only have her word about the time of her arrival, Thad. She could have gotten here earlier than she said. The M. E. estimates the death within a possible forty minute range; sometime between six and six-forty. Parker-Brown may have known about Logan's running schedule."

Thad elected not to confirm Brandon's speculation.

"You're really zeroing in on the dean, aren't you? Why her? Why would she shoot this woman?"

Brandon mopped his face. "Somebody is killing people around here, Thad. If you've got a better notion, I wish to hell you'd let me know."

"I thought you never swore."

"I'm out of M&Ms."

"I got a call from your boss."

"So I understand."

"Inocencio said he couldn't spare anyone. Too heavy a case load at your shop."

"I'm glad he asked you to help out. I mean that, Thad."

"How do you want to divvy things up? Shall I concentrate on the Logan killing?"

"Yeah. For now anyway. I'll come in on it as I can." He looked past the track and the surrounding growth to the two houses that were on the far side of the street that ran past the west side of the oval; the only habitations around. "Wonder whether anyone over there saw or heard anything."

"I'll check it out."

Thad left to join the officers on the track, and Brandon, with Pete Wiggins in tow, entered the track house. They listened silently as Anne repeated what she had told the chief.

"It seems to be your misfortune, Dean, to come across dead bodies." Anne didn't respond. "Professor Logan ran here on a regular basis, did she?"

"I believe so, yes."

"And always early in the morning?"

"That's usually when I've seen her."

"On Wednesdays? Was that one of her regular days?"

"Possibly. I — I'm not sure."

"Do you own a gun, Dean Parker-Brown?"

Her head jerked up, eyes smoldering. "You're heading toward a ridiculous line of questioning, Sergeant."

"You think so? I'd still like an answer."

Pete shifted uneasily in his chair in a corner of the room.

She looked at him defiantly. "I'll simplify things for you, Sergeant. You could easily find out from my university records that I was on a rifle team when I was an undergraduate. We won three state and two regional championships during that time. I was a very good shot. That was then. I do not now own a gun of any kind."

Brandon considered that a moment before heading in a different direction. "Professor Logan was a troublemaker in your life, wasn't she?"

"Dealing with faculty angered about tenure or contract decisions is everyday fare for a Dean of Faculty, Sergeant Blessing."

"You know, Dean, I can't help thinking of another kind of trouble. That picture Professor Logan took of you and the president. Maybe that wasn't the only one. Just what did she know about you and President Merton?"

"This is becoming tedious, Sergeant. For the last time: There was nothing to know."

He nodded slowly, reflectively, then leaned forward, bringing his face closer to hers.

"Dean Parker-Brown, you're concealing something. Listen well: We're going to dig. We're going to dig until we find whatever it is you're keeping from us."

Anne returned his gaze with no show of emotion. Brandon walked over to the open door, looked out for a moment, then came back to stand in front of her. "Do you run every morning?"

"I try to get to the track at least three times a week. When, depends on my schedule. A group of us have a standing date for a noon run. Not everyone makes it, however, when it gets this hot and smoggy."

"Who belongs to the group, Dean?"

"Almost all of the administrators in Wyndham run with some regularity. A few secretaries. And a sprinkling of faculty and spouses."

Pete jumped in. "Mrs. Merton too?"

Anne nodded. "Mrs. Merton uses the track — but infrequently." She rose. "May I go now, Sergeant?"

"One moment." He studied her jogging outfit with TIPTON COLLEGE in metallic thread on the front of the sweater top. "Do you always wear that get-up at the track?"

"No."

"Pretty warm, isn't it?"

"An understatement, Sergeant. If I had known it was going to be so hot this early I would have worn something else."

Brandon seemed to consider that, blinking a couple of times. Pete thought he looked like an unhappy owl.

"You aren't wearing a cooler outfit under that one? Like shorts?"

"No, Sergeant, I am not."

"Where do you change?"

"At home. Sometimes at the gym. Why?"

"Would you object to my sending a woman officer home with you, Dean? It would be helpful if we could borrow your track suit — if you'd be willing to volunteer it."

Anne seemed suddenly amused by the studied politeness, the legal implications of the phrasing. "Not at all. And I have no objection to undressing in front of the officer — if that will put your mind at ease."

Brandon remained solemn. "It might help. And your running shoes, Dean, if you don't mind."

As she got up and turned to leave, Brandon noticed the lettering running across the back of the shirt: GERIATRIC JOGGING AND CHOWDER MARCHING SOCIETY.

Brandon called her back. "Dean, just a moment. This 'Chowder Marching Society' . . . "

"Yes?"

"Is that a club?"

"In a way. It's the group of noon regulars I mentioned to you."

"What does it mean?"

"Nothing in particular; it's supposed to be humorous."

"Do you all have the same kind of warmup suits?"

"Most of us, I believe. It was Dean Norton's idea. He and Vince Riley came up with the name and first got the group together about two years ago."

"Where do you buy your outfits?"

"Henry Norton's office ordered them for us."

"And are all the suits black?"

"So far as I know."

Brandon's tone was lugubrious. "Thank you."

He went to the door and beckoned to the policewoman from the Altamira station standing by the group near the body. He drew her to one side and gave her instructions, adding, "I want you to try and get a look in this woman's closet." The young officer drew back. Brandon was impatient. "Never mind the irregularity. I'll be responsible. Look for a blue silk suit and blouse to match — with some red and white figures on it. Check any labels. See if there's any metallic thread. Just look. That's all I'm asking. Understand?"

The young woman, still uneasy, mumbled a "Yes, sir." Brandon sighed in despair.

"What was that about, Brandon — that business with Karen Olson?"

"That her name? Just wanted her to keep her eyes open, kid."

Pete didn't believe him, but knew better than to say so. "So much for matching up one particular suit with the stuff found under Merton's finger-nails, Brandon — if twenty or so people have those embroidered outfits."

"Maybe, maybe not. The lab can get pretty re-fined at detecting minute differences in material. Right now I'm interested in their checking out the dean's sweats. The shrubbery where the killer stood could have something to tell us too, by the time the guys get through."

Pete sighed. "Don't count on it."

Brandon's head snapped suspiciously toward him. Young Wiggins looked his most wide-eyed.

Pete sauntered over to the door of the track house and watched the activity at the far end of the oval. They were putting Terry Logan into a body bag now, ready for transportation to the morgue. In a few minutes her presence at the college would be nothing more than a white chalk outline on the blue surface of the track. Pete re-called his interview with her, their quick exchange in Spanish that followed her flip comment that ap-pearances at Tipton were deceiving. "People say that life is but a dream," he had quipped, and Terry Logan had topped him with, "Only for those caught napping." As he saw it now, they were both right.

"The ground under the shrubs is stone hard." Brandon was back. "There are lots of leaves on the ground; they look disturbed, but there's small chance of getting any significant trace evidence."

"Anything snagged on branches?"

"Not that they've found so far."

"What makes you so sure, Brandon, that this isn't a freak killing? Some weirdo getting his kicks." The Sergeant was unresponsive. "Remember that case up north? The coed runner who was dragged off the track into some bushes, raped and then killed?"

"Professor Logan wasn't raped. I'll bet on that."

"But her body was close to heavy shrubbery. As you said the other day, who needs a reason to waste someone?"

"I say all kinds of things."

Pete ignored him. "And if the guy didn't show himself . . . "

Brandon had grown increasingly impatient. "Listen, kid, that woman was obviously a serious runner. And serious runners use the inside, not an outside lane. Furthermore, she was shot from the front, facing those bushes. Facing someone she knew."

"But not necessarily. Curiosity . . . "

Brandon went on, unheeding. "Someone who probably called to her."

"So, you're saying the dean switched m.o.'s to shoot Professor Logan. And for the second time hung around to be found with the body? Give me a break."

"An intelligent murderer may count on improbability, kid. And this woman is long on brains." He automatically reached in his pocket for his M & Ms, scowled as he remembered he was out.

"So is everybody around here." Brandon didn't comment. "And what did she do with the gun?"

"She had time to stash it someplace before she called in about the shooting. Or before our guys got here."

Pete went doggedly on, "OK, assume Logan did have something on the dean. And was blackmailing her. Suppose the dean and Merton were lovers and Logan threatened to tell the world. So what? Nobody thinks twice about fooling around any more. Look at what goes on in Washington."

"I'd rather not."

"A scandal creates a stink for a while, then the smell goes away. Business as usual."

Brandon's mulish expression didn't budge. "Maybe not at a private college. They depend heavily on private funding, don't they? And not everyone would face up to damaging disclosure with the happy-go-lucky attitude you've described, kid. It's my hunch this woman would not." He stretched. "Pete?"

"Sir?"

"Get the list of suit orders from Dean Norton's office; see if anyone has more than one. I've got to run over to town for a moment, pick up something at the grocery store."

Anne watched the policewoman leave with her track suit and shoes carefully and individually wrapped in plastic bags. She stood immobile for a long moment, then spoke out loud, running a hand through her hair. "Come on, Anne. Snap out of it." She moved briskly to the phone, first to call the News Bureau, then, reluctantly, Leslie Filmore.

"I knew it, Anne," Leslie said, his tone one of satisfaction. "It's exactly what I told that bumbling officer. This killing proves that we have a psycho on the loose. Maybe now the police will begin to show some sense. What did they say to you?"

"Very little." She hurried on. "What time will you be on campus, Leslie?"

There was silence for a moment at the other end of the line. "I won't be out for a while, Anne. I've got to be in London for a few days; leave this afternoon. Confidentially, Anne, I think it wiser to maintain a low profile at this time — until we know when and if a cavalry charge is going to be called for."

"I see." Did he hear the scorn in her voice? If so, she didn't care. Filmore was now uneasy about being associated with a college in this kind of trouble. "Any particular instructions?"

"You and Turner can handle things. I'll notify the Executive Committee and clue Jerry in, he should be kept informed. Call on him if the police or the media get any funny ideas. You'll have the full backing of the Board, Anne, rest assured of that."

She hung up.

The full backing of the Board? Anne wondered what would happen to that support if Blessing began to do more than saber-rattle in her direction.

Wyndham Hall was unnaturally quiet. However noisily staff and administrators entered the Hall, Joelle's stricken face and somber announcement quickly silenced them. On the second floor, secretaries drifted in to Beulah's or to Phil's office, seeking some kind of reassurance with rhetorical questions: "Is it true?" "How could anyone have done such a thing?"

By 9:30 Anne had talked to Terry Logan's parents in Eugene, Oregon, and had asked Phil to check the files on Terry's cousin and try to locate her. As her fellow administrators began to file in, no one said much beyond mumbled good mornings. People avoided looking at each other. There was tension in the air, a reluctance to start the discussion. Tom Donaldson broke the ice with a comment on the *Ledger* article, which not everyone had seen. Victor had. He was choleric.

"The trustees are going to be mad as hell. Not only about the good name of the college but about their own legal responsibilities and liabilities. Anne, you'd better sic Jerry Lazeroff onto that big mouth."

Henry put in that he questioned whether there was anything libelous.

"There's nothing false, that I can see. Willie wants to make our mystery sound as sensational as possible."

Tom Donaldson agreed. Victor still grumbled.

"Filmore's printed statement worries me even more," Henry said. "The possibility of a deranged person running loose on the campus will not be reassuring to parents. Or students."

Victor still had his mind on the *Ledger.* "Christ, you can't say Willie's article makes the College look good, Henry. Alumni and donors sure as hell will be upset."

"Console yourself, Victor. It's questionable that many alumni or any donors will even see it."

"But the city papers will pick it up."

Tom spoke up. "Victor's right about that. I'll see what I can do with the out-of-town reporters. The city boys have a less flamboyant view of serious journalism than Willie. But understand this: If I emphasize that what happened was a fluke, that the Chemistry Department does not provide self-service in poisons for whoever comes shopping, the implication will be clear."

Victor frowned. "Huh?"

"That we think someone on the inside killed Merton. Which is to say, one of us."

Anne fiddled with her pencil. "Well, isn't that precisely what we believe? We can't avoid it."

Victor opened his mouth, then shut it again. Tom continued.

"As for Hefner, any bad light he directs our way reflects somewhat onto the town. The elected officials — and merchants — of Altamira will not welcome too much bad-mouthing of the college. I think he knows better than to go too far."

"But how did he know about Weinert's backing out on his gift? Who feeds him all this stuff?" Victor asked.

Heads turned toward Turner, who looked rueful. "I'll speak to Crystal. Though please remember that what was in the paper could just as well have come from another source. Via secretaries here and in the Chemistry Department, for instance. Or from faculty members. It's not only the Hall that leaks like a sieve."

Anne nodded. "All too true, Turner. Now, I think we had best discuss what needs to be done in light of the dreadful incident this morning."

When Phil Gertmenian came in with coffee for all and took a chair at the back of the room, Tom was saying, "We can expect the media to dredge up the brouhaha caused by her tenure case last spring. Some may choose to raise the question of prejudice because of her sexual orientation."

Turner put in, "Are you going to speak to the press, Anne?"

"I'm counting on Tom to hold them at bay. If not, I shall say as little as possible. I think the only tactic is to describe our procedures on the award-ing or denial of tenure and to state that they were faithfully followed in Terry's case. Our criteria for promotion do not differ in any significant way from those of other colleges."

Tom looked thoughtful. "There is a chance that they may not dwell on that too heavily, if at all. There's no discernible connection between Terry's death and her position here. I understand she was about to accept an offer from McIlveny College."

Anne was surprised. "I hadn't heard that."

Henry Norton finished off his coffee and, fidgety as always, resettled himself in his chair. "I had. She told me Saturday — at the gallery. Anne, there are going to be heavy seas ahead. We can expect a flow of calls from alarmed parents and students worried about their safety. You're bound to get your share, and from faculty too."

"I suggest we treat it like what it is: an extraor-dinary and inexplicable random event. Outside the control of any safety program."

"I agree," Turner said, reaching over to set his coffee cup down on the edge of Anne's desk. "Were the police at all forthcoming with you, Anne? Do you think they have any leads?"

She wondered fleetingly what would happen if she told them that she was suspected. She sensed that her colleagues were sufficiently uncomfortable that for the second time in as many weeks she had been the one to discover a dead body, so said nothing but "I think the police know very little at this juncture, Turner."

"You've talked with Filmore, I suppose?"

"Mr. Filmore thinks it wise for the time being to keep a low profile, as he puts it. He's leaving for London today."

Henry Norton stuffed his hands in his pockets and snorted in disgust. Turner's face was expressionless.

Victor, who had been staring at the carpet, looked up. "Does anyone here know whether Logan had any enemies? A disgruntled student perhaps?"

Henry shook his head. "The students that have passed through my office have been generally enthusiastic. Terry was a popular teacher, which is why her tenure case was so difficult."

Victor continued, "I never really understood that." He looked questioningly at Anne.

"To simplify somewhat, Victor, the negative assessment of her collegiality and scholarship by the majority of her colleagues in Psychology was qualified variously as jealousy, sour grapes or sexism by her supporters and the women's coalition; the choice of outside evaluators was labelled a put-up job."

"In other words," Turner added, "if Terry had taken a potshot at one of us — at Anne or Julian in particular — that would make some sense. But it doesn't add up the other way around."

Except to Sergeant Blessing, Anne thought.

"What about the sex angle?" Victor queried. "I mean a dyke like Terry Logan . . . "

Five pair of eyes stared at him.

"Well, I mean —" Victor floundered, — "let's call it the way it is. Those people do lead irregular lives."

Anne broke the embarrassed silence. "We need to consider the kind of statement the college should make, and how we are going to notify faculty and students . . . "

Henry Norton interrupted. "Before we get started on that, Anne. What about funeral or memorial services?"

"We'll discuss that with Terry's parents when they arrive."

"We could have a group service," Turner said glumly.

Victor's short laugh was mirthless. "Yeah. Three for the price of one."

Seated at opposite sides of the table in their GHQ in Baja Wyndham, Brandon and Pete had squared off against each other. After another fruitless argument as to what lay behind Logan's murder, they had segued into airing their differences concerning the Merton case.

"I can't get it out of my head, Brandon, that the killer's plan went haywire. Julian Merton may have been the wrong victim."

Brandon fixed him with a cold stare. "Because your boyhood friend's mama said so."

"That's not fair, Brandon. Mrs. Tidwell had nothing to do with it. Listen. It would be crazy to try to poison the man during the party. Too great a risk of the attack coming on with everyone present; help would be available, and the victim might recover."

Brandon became avuncular. "Pete, kid, I told you. Enough people knew about the expected call from Weinert for our murderer to have gotten wind of it. The dean knew when the president would be called away from the party — when he would go to his office."

"So did Mrs. Merton. Anyway, I think your theory is biased."

"Huh?" Brandon was nonplussed and Pete defensive.

"You've got this notion that poison is a woman's weapon."

"It's not a notion. It happens that more women use poison than men. So what's biased about that?" Pete scowled. "Who just mentioned Mrs. Merton as a possible suspect?"

Pete remained silent.

Brandon made a placating gesture. "All right, as if I didn't get enough of this at home. And if Weinert didn't call in on schedule, maybe *he* or *she* had a backup plan for getting Merton into his office on some pretext or other."

Pete was unconvinced. "How could the killer be sure the president would be alone when the poison reaction kicked in? He might have tossed off that glass of wine fifteen minutes or so before he left the reception. Anyway you look at it, Merton could have had up to three minutes in which to call for help."

"The timing was tricky all right; it had to be fine tuned. But it could be done. It was done. And remember the president wasn't alone. Someone moved his body. So, his killer was there, or came in — maybe when the seizure started."

Pete was now plainly disgusted. "And just stood there? Watching the man die? Can you honestly see Dean Parker-Brown as that kind of sickie?"

Blessing let out a long breath as though in pain. "As sure as God made little green apples I can see that woman in his office — over six feet, remember — and strong enough to get him from the floor to his chair — or to help him, if he weren't yet dead." Brandon's tone of voice deepened to sepulchral. "Once under way, she was committed, couldn't turn back."

Pete continued to look skeptical.

"Somebody was with Merton when he died." Brandon was on the defensive. "So, who've we got in the building between the time Beulah Taper left and when the dean says she found him? Riley had returned, and so had Donaldson — just. They were in the basement, and they didn't see anyone; Colton was on the first floor most of that time until he went upstairs, and he didn't see anyone else around. There's only one logical conclusion."

Pete was still dissatisfied. "But the dean wasn't wearing anything with shiny thread on it."

All too true, Brandon thought. He had kept the policewoman's report to himself. She had managed a quick look in the closet when Anne had stepped into the bathroom: the labels on the silk suit she had worn to the reception were not embroidered with what he was looking for. He frowned at Pete. "So, who've we got left? Jeff Colton? Now there's a likely candidate," he said with heavy sarcasm.

"Someone might have sneaked back in the building, using a side door."

"Why?"

"Because the murderer realized he had killed the wrong person."

Brandon grunted. "So let's hear it. Who was the intended victim?"

"What about Vince Riley? When he was on that phony errand. He would have been alone when the attack hit him."

"I've played with that one, kid, I told you. The guy has an A-plus record as a supervisor; he led a model life; not a single soul gains from his death."

"But Mary Walker said Riley knew about some 'mysteries' . . . "

Brandon interrupted, impatient. "That poor girl is grasping at straws. We've investigated enough by now to know that the only no-no undercover activity going on around here was in bed — the president and the dean."

Pete let that pass, but stuck to his guns. "Maybe you're right about Riley. But aren't there other possible victims? Terry Logan maybe. When the party ploy didn't work, the killer shoots her at the track."

Brandon remained stubborn. "Who knew she would be there? She wasn't invited to that party, she just showed up." He shook his head. "Nope, it doesn't listen."

"Mrs. Merton? Maybe she came back . . . "

"Yeah. Problem is, Monday night I walked and jogged the distance between Merton's house and the Hall. Didn't you say her housekeeper last saw her at seven-ten before leaving to catch her bus? And Weinert phoned at seven-thirty-five, forty-ish. Mighty tight — even if she is a runner."

"What about during the party? There was an awful lot of milling about. People jostling each other . . . "

"But we can't place her near her husband more than once. With other people. No. She's strung up tight, I'll give you that. But if Mrs. Merton went after anybody, seems to me it would have been the dean."

"Well?"

Brandon shook his head and sighed. "Kid, I've still got the gut feeling that the redhead is the only one who could have planned it — with the know-how and enough repressed rage to see it through."

"Seems to me the scenario works just as well with someone else as the intended victim. Then the murderer comes back and finds that Merton got the drink by mistake."

"Just like that, huh? And risk being seen by those folks sitting outside? Or running into the janitor or the dean? 'Hi, everybody, I'm back.'" He frowned, momentarily lost in thought. "The business of the phony call needs explaining, I'll give you that. But it sounds like a prank to me; there are a few kids working around campus . . . All right," Brandon snapped, "give me a reason for someone killing Riley. Go on. Let's hear it."

"Maybe if we dug around . . . "

Brandon cast his eyes heavenward in despair. "That would satisfy your young friend, Mary Walker. Then all we would have to do is connect Terry Logan to Vince Riley . . . You're driving me batty. I need to talk to someone with a scientific mind." He reached for the phone and dialed LA, the crime lab.

Pete took the opportunity to go to the men's john. When he returned, Brandon was chewing on a chocolate fix and looking smug.

"Sorry to squelch your pet theory, kid, but it looks like nobody was gunning for Riley. Elmo in criminalistics said that the shower handle was a fifty-year-old fixture at least. Looks like the old screw just fell out — so the knob turned but the shaft didn't. The tech boys found the screw — it had dropped behind the tub. No fresh marks on it."

"You're saying that when he went to shower he found the thing broken and didn't have, or take the time, to fix it?"

"Exactly. He was in a hurry to leave on his vacation, wasn't he?" Pete nodded reluctantly. "Pretty conclusive, Pete. Particularly with Riley's prints on the shower handle."

"So he was running a tub, slipped when he got in and konked his head on the metal fixtures?"

"What else?"

"Having turned around, with his back to them?"

"Maybe the guy liked to face east. How do I know?"

"Why don't I like it?"

"Because Mary Walker got to you, Pete. I told you: You've got to learn to stay uninvolved."

"Do you? Always?"

"Nope." Brandon sounded positively cheery.

Mary was about to leave for work when Thad phoned with the news about Terry Logan, adding that Vince's house was no longer under surveillance, that she was free to come and go as she wished.

"Does that mean they've ruled out the possibility that Vince was murdered?"

"They've tried. Really they have."

"But what about Max Dingam's statement?"

"Blessing says the lab report has come through. It's conclusive that the shower was out of commission." Met by silence, Thad continued: "I talked to the medical examiner myself. I'm satisfied that the autopsy was thorough, Mary. And they did check for the toxin that killed Merton." Continued silence. "Mary, please accept the facts."

"They're your facts, Thad. Not mine. I don't accept them."

Crystal Mathews sailed in to the News Bureau with a big smile for the secretary, Rosalie Despina, just back from vacation.

"Hi, hon. Was it great?"

Before Rosalie could do more than nod, Crystal's expression changed to mournful. "Isn't it awful about Professor Logan? And with her show going so well too. Though I can't stand the stuff myself. Turner has hung a creepy one in his office. But I don't have to sit looking at it, thank God. Hon, maybe you can help me."

"Sure, Crystal."

"Mrs. Van V. is being a pain. She gets so damned impatient."

Rosalie made sympathetic sounds.

"She bought a bunch of photographs at the show and now she wants information on Terry — like a CV — or critical reviews, anything you might have about her and her work. If I know the Heiress, she thinks she's made an investment. Particularly now that Professor Logan is, well, you know, passed on."

Rosalie had risen and gone to a file. After a moment's search, she handed Crystal an envelope.

"You can copy what you need from here. If you can get it back to me right away. Tom will need to refer to it this morning."

"I'll be back within an hour. OK?"

Mary caught her breath as she entered the bungalow by way of the ramp at the kitchen door. This was going to be even more difficult than she had imagined. She didn't see just the sink, but Vince in a ridiculous apron washing the dishes while she dried them. She didn't see the old stove, but Vince stirring a pot and discoursing in a mock-serious manner on the infamous five vegetable recipe he had invented. And everywhere, Vince smiling at her; Vince teasing her; Vince leaning over to kiss her; Vince lifting her out of the chair to hold her to him. Vince tender with her, excited by her, loving her.

She went slowly around the room, touching the stove, the towels hanging near the sink. She looked in the refrigerator Vince had turned off and cleaned the night he was to leave. Empty, but for a bottle of vitamins. She removed it, held it against her for a moment. "Ridiculous," she said aloud and put the bottle back. Mary rolled herself into the living room, then past the mercifully closed door to the bathroom, past the second bedroom Vince used as a study, delaying the moment she both dreaded and needed. Decisively, she opened the door to the bedroom, their room, and went in to emptiness and silence. She whispered his name. For the first time since his death, deep sobs shook her upper body. Eyes blinded with tears, Mary went to the closet, reached in to take his old bathrobe from its hook and put it around her shoulders.

Returning to the study, she began a careful search for a copy of the memorandum he had been working on. Or for diskettes that might contain copies of his records, but she found nothing that related to Vince's job. There was precious little in the desk drawers: stationery supplies, his checkbook, and what appeared to be financial and personal business records. She looked, but didn't touch, quickly closing the last drawer. She felt like an indiscreet stranger. She had no right to pry, to be pawing among the intimate left-overs from his life.

Back in the bedroom, Mary took off the bathrobe, buried her face in its folds, breathed in the very faint but still identifiable odor of Old Spice. She smiled. No newfangled stuff for Vincent Michael Riley. As Mary was hanging up the robe something hit her arm, something hard in one of the pockets. Two somethings. Two diskettes. One labelled with the name of a data base program; the second diskette labelled: "1. Copy of annual report. 2. Report on items found July 14 in Room 2, Wyndham Hall (Lawrence and Penelope Croft collection — 1925). 3. Use personal code."

Wednesday, July 26

THAD WALKER SAT WAITING FOR CLAIRE Tidwell to get off the phone. She hung up and worked a dangly earring back into her left ear. "Really. You'd think McIlveny College could manage more than a 'How dreadful.' They were more upset about having to look for a last minute replacement than about what happened to Terry. Well now, where were we?"

"I was about to ask you how well you knew Terry Logan, Professor Tidwell."

"After seven years of working in the same department? Quite well — as a colleague, less well as a person. We served on a committee or two together, but we rarely saw each other off campus."

"Any particular reason for that?"

"Well, there's the age and interest gap. Different life styles as the current jargon has it. Our professional interests didn't coincide either. My field is child psychology. Terry's area was at the other end of the spectrum. She was doing work on aging — memory loss and memory retrieval in particular."

Claire picked up a pencil and threw it down. "What kind of sick individual could have done this, Chief Walker?"

"I was hoping you could tell me."

"I would like to believe that even a clinical psychologist might have trouble tying anything so brutal to someone in our little world — as weird as it is."

"Then you do believe the murderer was connected with the college?"

Claire looked startled. "I don't know why I said that. Because of Merton's death, I suppose."

"What can you tell me about Professor Logan's personal life? How did she get along with people at Tipton?"

"She was a splendid teacher; her students were highly enthusiastic. Some of her colleagues were — well, less so."

"What about yourself?"

"I would say we respected each other. But that's about it. Terry was very professional and organized. And highly opinionated. That didn't bother me; some colleagues were not as tolerant of her devotion to speaking her mind. My reading is that she overcompensated, that down deep Terry was painfully shy — and lonely."

"What about outside your department?"

"She was on good terms with the women's coalition — and the gay and lesbian organizations on campus. She participated in an active way when asked. Terry could be sharply assertive. But that was her public face. She kept pretty much to herself. In private she was a loner."

"That surprises me, Professor Tidwell. I met her at the opening of her exhibit. She struck me as quite gregarious."

"Yes, but again, that was the public face. Terry was a highly ambitious young woman. She worked extremely hard as a teacher and on her research, and she gave an inordinate amount of time to her students and to her photography as well. That doesn't leave many hours in the day for socializing."

"What about the administration? Any particular friends there?"

Professor Tidwell cocked a left eyebrow. "Hardly. Terry was very bitter that her promotion to tenure was turned down."

"Did she blame anyone in particular?"

Claire studied a side wall for a moment. "Well, yes. The colleagues who did not support her. But mostly she blamed our late president."

"Oh?"

"She was convinced that he had mounted a campaign against her, that it was his influence that defeated her."

"What about the Dean of the Faculty?"

"I thought she seemed less bitter towards Anne. At least I never heard Terry say anything against the dean specifically — just general bitching."

"Do you think you would have known if there was any specific friction between Professor Logan and a member of the administration, such as the dean?"

"Well, except for her feelings towards President Merton, I — I just don't know. I think Terry just lumped everybody in Wyndham together as 'them.' "

"You said you thought she was lonely. Then she wasn't living with anyone?"

"You mean, did she have a lover? She did have, Paula something or other, but that ended over a year ago. The woman went back east."

"What about . . . " Thad glanced at his book. "What about this Ellen Forsythe?"

Claire nodded. "Her cousin, yes. Ellen taught here part-time for a couple of years — Asian Art. She commuted from the beach some of the time, but stayed at Terry's quite often."

"Then you don't know of any recent relationships?"

Claire shook her head.

"Was she ever involved with students?"

Claire thought a moment. "There was a woman student who had a crush on her awhile back. Terry put an end to that. She had strong professional standards."

"But she didn't get tenure?"

Claire looked distressed. "That was a horrid business. Messy. No, she didn't. I supported her, but as a minority of one from the department."

"Yet you say she was a fine teacher with high standards."

"The opposition zeroed in on her scholarship, Chief Walker. They found it insufficient, derivative, and lacking in promise. The kind of partial truths that are usually trotted out when the real problem is one of personality." Claire shrugged. "They carried the day."

"I see. Do you know whether people were aware she was leaving soon for another job?"

"No, I don't. You're wondering why kill her if she were leaving town?"

Thad smiled. "Just asking, Professor Tidwell."

Claire grinned back.

"Would you know how regularly Terry ran at the track?"

"You bet. She was religious about it; ran at least three or four times a week. And once a week she did a 20 K run. On Wednesdays."

"Always on the track?"

"I — I think so. I know she preferred it."

"Was this generally known?"

"By others among the faithful perhaps. We certainly were aware of it here in the department. Terry used to say that if anyone wanted a favor, to ask her on Wednesdays, because she was always in a good mood."

"Thanks, Professor. If you think of anything else that might shed some light on this, let me know."

"Of course." Claire accepted the proffered card, hesitated, then made up her mind. "There is someone at the college Terry saw with some regularity. She might have some useful information."

"Who's that?"

"Mrs. Merton. She once told me she thought highly of Terry."

"Was it a two way street?"

"So far as I know. I'm sure Terry was aware of the irony — and that could have amused her."

"Oh? Could you explain that?"

"That Mrs. Merton was friendly when the president was so adamantly opposed to her."

Thad nodded and got to his feet. "Are any other professors in their offices this morning?"

"The three other senior faculty are away right now. A junior member of the department is in town — but he didn't really know Terry. Shall I ring him for you?"

"I'll leave it here for now, Professor Tidwell." He moved towards the door, then turned. "What about your secretary?"

"She's a summertime temporary, Chief Walker. Just started yesterday."

"I see. Well, thank you again."

Thad Walker gave the temporary a brief smile and a nod as he went through the outer office. The woman smiled in return and stared at his retreating back. This guy, she mused, could jump on her bones anytime.

Unaware of having passed muster as a sex object, Chief Walker got in his car and headed for Terry Logan's house on Dickson Street.

Arriving at the News Bureau, Mary chatted with Rosalie for a moment, then went on in to a former storage closet grandly referred to as the computer room.

She turned on the News Bureau's Macintosh, slipped in Vince's diskette. A moment later she was scrolling slowly down the text of his reports. "1. Copy of Annual report; 2. Report on items found July 13 in Room 2, Wyndham Hall (Lawrence and Penelope Croft Collection — 1925)." She stopped at item 3: "Use personal code."

"Mary," Rosalie was in the doorway, a folder in her hand, "Tom left a message for you. Would you write up the release on Terry Logan's death?" She held out the file.

"Any special instructions?"

"Tom said you'd know how to handle it."

"By which he means as delicately as possible."

"The good old Tipton tradition. But what can you say about this nightmare except that it happened? Tom said the police still don't have a clue as to who or why. It's scary."

Mary gave the command "Eject" and shut down the machine. She slipped the diskette into the bag attached to the side of her chair and returned to her own cubicle. She opened Terry Logan's file, read through it, studied the glossies Terry had dropped off before the opening of her exhibit. Then looked through them again, slowly, thoughtfully. She wasn't really sure what she was looking for.

The campanile bells were ringing twelve noon when Mary heard the tap at her door. She turned to find an ashen-faced Ellen Forsythe standing there. Mary hastily reached over to remove a pile of folders and magazines from the chair beside her desk.

"I was just upstairs — talking to the dean's secretary . . . " Ellen sank down on the chair.

"I'm so sorry, Ellen."

Ellen moved her head up and down, not speaking.

"I drove down from Santa Barbara early this morning intending to stop by and say hello to Terry." Her voice broke. She paused a moment before going on.

"I thought I'd go by the house first, and I found the police . . . Oh God." She bent over as in pain, arms wrapped around her waist, a veil of hair falling forward, hiding her face. After a moment, she straightened up, lifting her hair back over her shoulders.

"Terry and I practically grew up together . . . " She broke off, unable to finish the sentence.

"Did they tell you how it happened?" Mary asked.

"Phil Gertmenian told me. I can't believe it. Not someone as vital and young as Terry. She wasn't an easy person, I know that. But who would want to kill her?"

Mary gestured helplessly.

"It's — it's madness." Ellen wiped her eyes with the back of her hand. "The police said they wanted to talk to me. I'm to stop by the station."

"You might check at Room 4, right down the hall. They have an office set up there. Ask for my brother, he's helping with the investigation. Chief Thad Walker."

Ellen nodded dumbly.

"Is there anything I can do to help, Ellen?"

"Phil suggested I talk to you. He said you had a file on Terry."

"That's right."

"I would like to have something to remember her by, Mary. Something from her professional life, I mean. If you have an off-print of that article she published last winter . . . "

"I think so." Mary reached across her desk for the folder, located a copy of the article Ellen had asked for.

"Thanks." Ellen leaned forward, peering. "I see you've got some glossies. From the show?"

"Yes."

"Could I possibly have one?"

"Sure."

"If you have a print of the 'Fallen Angel' that would be great. Terry shot that one last week when she was at the beach with . . . " Her voice broke.

Mary started flipping through the photographs. "I know I have it. Didn't it used to be called 'Dodie's Friend'?"

"Right."

"I remember Terry's asking me if I knew a Dodie here at the college. Did she ever find out?"

"Not that I know of. She said she was 'working on it.' "

Mary shuffled through the pictures, then went through them again.

"I'm sorry, Ellen. I don't seem to have it. I'm sure it's just misplaced. When I find it I'll send it to you. In the meantime, perhaps you'd like to select one of the others."

Ellen, obviously disappointed, shook her head. "I'll wait. I'm leaving for Japan on Friday. Coast College has given me a semester's sabbatical. I can't say I feel much like going right now, when I think of the family — but everything's been arranged."

As she jotted down Ellen's Laguna address and phone number, it occurred to Mary what it was that she had been looking for earlier in the morning.

After Ellen Forsythe had left, Mary backed up to the doorway to call out, "Rosalie?"

"Yo?"

"I don't suppose you'd know whether anyone has borrowed the Logan file?"

Rosalie came around the corner. "Sure would. Crystal Mathews had it for a while this morning. To Xerox some information for Mrs. Van Voorhees. Is something missing? Shall I call Crystal?"

"No. That's OK. Thanks."

Mary finished the draft of Terry Logan's obituary for Tom's approval and returned to the computer room, once again inserting the diskette. She read quickly through the copy of Vince's annual report for Buildings and Grounds, almost overlooking the note at the end: "July 18, 1989: Copy of annual report delivered to president's office. Original inventory of Croft collection attached." She read the second section more attentively: "For the record: Report on items found July 13 in Room Two, Wyndham Hall (Lawrence and Penelope Croft Collection — 1925)."

Late afternoon of Thursday, July 13th, I came across a chest containing a collection of seventy-five Asian art objects hidden behind a pile of lumber and some large pieces of furniture in a box room (Room 2) of Wyndham Hall. I phoned Mr. Van Voorhees and he came down to look over the find. These items were not on my working inventory. A later search by Development staff and Beulah Taper failed to turn up any inventories with these items. Mr. Van Voorhees surmised that many of the pieces were over a hundred years old at least and extremely valuable: a number of what appeared to be jade and amber snuff bottles, jade vases and bowls, small ivory figures (Japanese), and various other items.

Following Mr. Van Voorhees's instructions, I put things back as I found them and locked the room. That evening, President Merton telephoned me at home, having just heard from Mr. Van Voorhees about the find. Early the next morning, the 14th, Mr. Merton and most of Wyndham Hall came to see the objects. Then Jeff Colton, Mr. Van Voorhees and I moved everything into the second floor vault. Mr. Laszlo instructed his staff to start a throrough search for any mention of the collection and the donors; Miss Taper was instructed to help with the search and to make an inventory of the collection, prior to having it appraised.

Saturday a. m., July 15, I checked with Miss Taper as to who had keys to the vault. The list is extensive: the president and Miss Taper, the four vice presidents, the Dean of Admissions, the director of the News Bureau and myself. Miss Taper pointed out that heretofore the vault had contained archival material and had rarely held anything of monetary value. Mr. Van Voorhees agreed with me that a safer place should be found for such valuable items or that another deadbolt be installed and restricted access established.

On July 18, while working in Room 2 with Jeff Colton in late afternoon, I came across an inventory of the Asian art collection, presumably the original, with the donors' name and the date of the gift on it: Lawrence and Penelope Croft — September 4, 1925. It had fallen behind the drawers of the chest that held the collection. I went to the vault that afternoon and made a cursory check of the collection against the original inventory. Since Mr. Van Voorhees and the president were both out of town, I did not report the recovery of the inventory. I attached it to my annual report for the president's review and left both with Miss Taper the evening of the 18th. I made a copy of the inventory for Mr. Van Voorhees and one for myself.

On the morning of July 19, I spoke to Mr. Van Voorhees, when he returned from San Francisco, about recovering the lost inventory. For reasons which will be clear later on, he asked that the news of finding the inventory be kept between him, the president and myself until he had the opportunity to discuss it further with the president and Mr. Laszlo.

Mary could almost hear Vince's voice as she read through his notes. This kind of meticulous log was so very typical of him. She scrolled on down to come up against "Section 3. Use Personal code."

The "reasons to be made clear later on" were missing. An oversight? Accidentally erased? Or would they be in section 3? Mary fiddled with various menu possibilities for a while, looking for a function or an icon that required a password, then gave up. She would see what she could find out upstairs.

As she headed for the elevator that had been installed in '73 to comply with the regulations concerning access for the handicapped, Mary looked in at Brandon and Pete Wiggins' office. Empty. She went on to the end of the corridor, waved to the people in Duplicating, and entered the elevator. She hated using it, but bumping herself up the stairs as she had learned to do at the rehabilitation center had its drawbacks, so she bowed her spirit of self-sufficiency to the pressures of time and the sensitivity of others.

Mary exchanged a few words with Beulah Taper before going on to Crystal's office. Waiting at the door for Crystal to get off the phone, Mary slid Terry's glossies out of their envelope. She was positive there had been four. She clearly remembered Terry's asking, "Do you know anyone around here named Dodie?"

At the suggestion that a photograph was missing, Crystal was huffy. ("Believe me, I would never want one of those for a souvenir. That stuff is gross.") As Mary began to propel herself backwards out of the office, Crystal, mollified, called after her, "Seriously, hon, I'm sure nothing slipped out of the file. But if I do run across it, I'll let you know."

"Beulah, what do you know about the Lawrence and Penelope Croft collection of Asian art objects?"

Beulah lifted the tea bag out of a cup of boiling water, let it drain for a second before dropping it into the wastebasket.

"I've never heard of it, Mary. There was the collection Vince found here in Wyndham just a few weeks ago. But we still haven't discovered the source. What was that name again. Croft?"

"Lawrence and Penelope."

"Where did you come across those names?"

Mary hesitated, reluctant for now to confide in anyone. "Didn't Vince find something with the donors' names?"

"I never heard that. We have certainly been looking for a record of the gift. I'm sure this office would have been informed."

"Maybe there's an inventory attached to the annual report he turned in."

"I'm sure I would have noticed it. But let's just take a look."

Beulah rose, automatically adjusting her suit jacket with a quick tug on either side as she rustled off. She returned seconds later with a copy of Riley's report.

"Let's see . . . The section on inventory . . . He mentions locating a collection of Asian art objects — behind some lumber and a pile of furniture in Room 2, in the basement. Used to be Professor Ho's office umpteen years ago. That was on the thirteenth of July. None of those items figured on any inventory that we could locate. Victor's people did a thorough search, and I checked out the archives myself." She paused in recollection, adding wryly, "President Merton was furious that such treasures could have been lost sight of all these years. He was positive they had a value well in excess of a quarter of a million. At least." Beulah refrained from volunteering that she had been the target for much of the Mertonian ire.

"May I see?"

"Of course." Beulah handed over the document. "I even talked to President Cyrus Tipton. But his memory has grown rather dim, I'm afraid." She took a sip of tea. "These objects must have come to the college before my time."

Mary absently agreed as she continued to glance through the report.

"It's shocking the way things can get lost around here. Mr. Van Voorhees's project for a complete inventory was years overdue." Beulah looked wistful. "And Vince was the right person to entrust with it."

Mary looked up, smiled. "Yes, he was." She handed back the folder. "You're right, there's no attachment, nor any mention of a donor. Vince didn't drop off the inventory at a later date?"

"Not that I know of. And he handed his report for the president to me personally." She checked the stamped notation on the first page: July 18, 5 p. m. "Who would have thought that . . . " She shook her head despairingly, adding, "I must get at that inventory. Recent events . . . "

"When you finish it, might I have a copy?"

"Of course. Such beautiful things. Didn't you see the collection, Mary? When the president had us all troop downstairs for a showing?"

"I wasn't in the office that morning."

"And to think of its being behind that junk for so many years. We all gave Vincent a round of applause — at the president's suggestion, I'll have you know." Beulah allowed herself a small smile.

She hadn't known. How like Vince not to mention it.

"Mary, if you think you know the name of the donors, you should tell Victor. This could be an important lead."

"I'll do that." Mary stopped at the outer door to the reception area. "Beulah, does the name 'Dodie' mean anything to you?"

Beulah pursed her lips, then shook her head. "No, never heard of it. Rather charming though. Sounds like a child's name."

Before returning Vince Riley's report to the file, Beulah reread the attached computer-generated memoranda that she hadn't removed when Crystal returned the document: "July 18. V. Riley to President Merton: Annual report, including information on Asian collection. Request meeting with concerned parties. Copy: T. Van Voorhees." "July 19. JM to TVV: Need to meet on this a.s.a.p." Everything seemed as she remembered it. But there was something. She riffled the pages of the report. What was it? She recalled her annoyance that, once again, the president, as he so often did, had circumvented her in handling documents. But that wasn't it. What was it that was squirming sluggishly someplace, deep in her memory?

Max Dingam's pugilist's face broke into a wide grin. "Hi, Mary. What can I do for you?"

"Max, do you know whether Vince had a personal code for his computer?"

Max was thoughtful. "Don't believe I ever heard him mention one. Might be something in his personal files. You want me to have a look-see?"

"If it's not too much trouble, thanks. One other thing. You have a copy of his annual report on file, haven't you, Max?"

"Sure."

"Would you see whether there's an attachment to it — the inventory of the Lawrence and Penelope Croft collection? Or it might be in a file related to his inventory work in the Hall."

Max made a note: "Lawrence and Penelope Croft. With a 'C'?"

"Yes."

"Gotcha."

"Those names don't mean anything to you?"

"They're Greek to me, Mary."

"Well, maybe . . . " She hesitated. "You're familiar with Vince's computer, aren't you?"

"Sure. We're real friendly."

"Would you see what you make of this?" She reached in the bag on the side of her chair for Vince's diskette. "I'm thinking about writing something about the Asian collection. There's an item on the diskette that requires an access code. Maybe you can find it. And it's confidential, please, Max."

"No problem. Get at it right away, Mary. It should make a good story for the magazine, right? Vince's finding that valuable stuff."

Mary Walker recognized the dean's voice in the outer office, talking with Rosalie. Then Anne was at her office door.

"May I come in?"

"Please." Mary looked around in vain for a chair with nothing piled on it. "Just put those magazines on the floor, Anne. A real mess, isn't it? But I do know where everything is, believe it or not."

"You haven't much putting space, as my mother would say." Anne placed the stack of *Tipton Topics* on the floor and sat down. "I thought we should talk about a memorial service for Vince."

The words cut like a knife. "Why doesn't Turner handle it?"

Anne was taken aback by the irritation in her voice. "We understand his brother doesn't want to be involved. I thought that you, more than anyone, would know Vince's wishes. But if you'd prefer . . ."

"I'm sorry, Anne. It's just that the idea of the need for a service makes me so angry."

"Perhaps you'd rather discuss this at a later time?"

Mary brushed the proposal aside. "No. I'm sorry to be so ungracious."

"It's all right, Mary. Shall I have Phil draw up a plan, suggesting music and speakers, for you to look over? Would that be a help in getting things started?"

"Thank you. Yes, it would."

"What about a time? Late this Saturday morning, maybe?"

Mary nodded. "And in Bosman Hall of Music, please — if possible. Vince loved that room."

"Of course. We'll put out the notices. Phil will get in touch with you first."

"I'd appreciate that. And Anne?"

Anne straightened from retrieving the magazines she had put on the floor. "Yes?"

"Anne, does the name Dodie mean anything to you?"

The dean reflected a moment. "No, I don't recognize it. Someone at Tipton?"

"Possibly."

"You might check with Henry Norton. Could be a student."

Henry Norton took a moment then asked, "Did you say Totie or Dodie?"

"Dodie — with a 'd'. Do we have a student here with that nickname?"

"Male or female?"

"I don't know."

"Hold on, and I'll ask Jackie."

In less than a minute he was back on the phone. "Doesn't ring a bell with either one of us, Mary. Can you give me any information?"

"Afraid not."

"Sorry."

"It's not important, Henry. Thanks anyway."

"If I learn anything, I'll give you a ring."

It was after one when Chief Walker, Pete Wiggins, and Detective Blessing kept a rendezvous at Solly's coffee shop. Teen Wonder had been replaced by a blond veteran of fifty-odd summers, top heavy with a bee-hive hairdo. With an eye to future fidelity and the establishment of sound tipping practice, the Veteran advised them against the day's special and approved their unanimous decision to settle for the soup and salad combo.

As soon as the ice tea and milk (for Pete) had been deposited, the three settled down to compare notes.

"All in all, pretty much of a *nada* for me," Thad said after he had repeated his conversation with Claire Tidwell. "Her neighbors had little to add. Logan was quiet but distant. Never lingered to talk on the sidewalk or over the back fence. People had more enthusiastic comments about her cousin, Ellen Forsythe: 'so sweet and feminine.' That's a quote."

"Did you see Mrs. Merton?"

"I'm coming to that."

"And?"

"She was 'shocked.' Her word."

"What about their relationship?"

"If you mean were they having an affair, a 'no' is my educated guess. They both served on a committee that dealt with women's concerns at the college. Seems to have been the only common interest. She didn't know anything about Logan's friends. Says she only saw her occasionally to discuss committee questions."

"Where did they meet?"

"At Delmonico's for morning coffee — lunch infrequently; the hostess at Delmonico's confirmed."

"Did you ask about that photo?"

Thad nodded. "Logan had never shown it to her, and she doesn't know why she took it. And finally, Mrs. Merton says she was at home this morning."

"Can she prove it?"

"She was in the kitchen making coffee around six. Couldn't sleep. Her father-in-law says he heard her go downstairs. He joined her soon afterwards."

"Logan didn't have any love life?"

"Nothing current, at least nothing's surfaced."

Brandon frowned. "So that's that. You got more?"

"I took another look around her house, the desk in particular. A few unanswered letters from what appears to be family. Checkbook in order — with quite a nice balance entered from the sale of photographs from the exhibit. No unusual credits or debits. There are her negatives to look over — and her office. I'll start on that after lunch."

"What about those two bungalows opposite the track? On Palm Road?"

"One person was awakened by a loud report, but went back to sleep. Too early for everybody. Except for a child at number 2560 — Todd Nelson, age seven."

"Yeah?"

"Todd was waiting for his 6:30 a.m. TV program to start and saw a car pull in at the edge of the paved parking area near the track; behind some shrubbery. He said it was red."

Brandon looked up expectantly from drawing rings on the table.

"Todd thought it was a Subaru."

Pete laughed. Brandon scowled. "A real unusual make."

"Still," Thad said, "it's a lead."

"How much before six-thirty was it, that Todd noticed the car?"

"'A while,' he said. Which could be two minutes or half an hour. You know kids that age."

"Did he see the driver?"

"No. He said he turned on the set and watched 'something dumb,' I'm quoting, until his program came on."

"TV," Brandon complained. "I thought I knew all the kid shows. What's on for them that early on a week day?"

"An exercise program. Not for children, but his mother said he was into fitness."

"Todd and this entire community. What gives with college towns anyway?"

Thad correctly assessed the question as rhetorical. "He heard 'a loud kaboom.' "

"When?"

"When he was doing his jumping jacks."

Brandon groaned.

"Well, at least we know his program had started."

The Veteran brought their orders, checked out the table with a practiced eye, then moved away with a pert "If you want anything, kids, just whistle."

The three took a moment to digest this proposal, then Pete spoke up. "Dean Norton's secretary found the exercise suit orders for me. He and Victor Laszlo each had two." Pete fished a list out of his pocket. "Riley, Merton . . . "

Brandon interrupted, startled. "He ran?"

"Well, he had an outfit anyway. So has she. Mrs. Merton, I mean. Also Gertmenian, Tom Donaldson, Van Voorhees, and three or four faculty members. Plus a couple of people from admissions and the registrar's office. Oh, and Mrs. Van Voorhees."

This rated a sepulchral sigh. "Why couldn't it have been an exclusive group?"

Thad crumbled some saltines into his split-pea soup. "What's this exercise suit business?"

Brandon let Pete explain, then went on to say, "Before we look at any other sweats, let's get the report from the lab on the dean's clothes."

Thad picked up his soup spoon and put it down again. A picture had formed in his mind as Brandon and Pete had talked; a memory from the night Merton had died: a beautiful woman, head bowed, sitting at a desk outside Merton's office. "I take it," Thad said, "that you're concentrating exclusively on Dean Parker-Brown?"

"Who else? If you've got any candidates for the hot seat, Thad, I'll be happy to consider them."

"Can't say that I have," he said, beginning on his soup. "Just have trouble with your idea is all."

"You and Pete. Must be all that red hair."

Thad almost spilled some soup.

Brandon explained. "The likeliest scenario is that things had sizzled then cooled off between Merton and Parker-Brown. That photo shows them looking mighty cosy in April. Then things did a flip-flop. He wanted her out of his life, personally and professionally."

"I know the rumor, but do you have proof of that, Brandon? That he would have really fired her as dean?"

"It doesn't take a genius to read between the lines. Too much protesting; too much hemming and hawing. I'm betting she'll admit it, under pressure. Professional rejection and personal humiliation." He savored the words before going on. "If Merton was half the s.o.b. most people claim, he could have put her through the wringer — and that's one proud lady."

"I don't quarrel with that."

"Whether she knew it was coming or not, Thad, I think what happened to her in San Francisco was a ten on the Richter scale — and she may have been shook up a lot more the day she got back here. She spent a long time in his office. And don't forget that visit to the Chemistry Department shortly afterwards — when everybody but the stock room manager was out of the building. And by rights, he should have been in his office working on his pumpernickel and wurst."

"Where do you put Terry Logan in your picture?"

"Logan may have figured out something connecting the dean to the murder. She sure as heck was wise to the affair. Or maybe there are more explicit pictures than the one we've seen. Logan must have had it in for her over the tenure business, wanted to make her sweat via a little blackmail."

"Money?"

"Maybe. Or plain old raging revenge."

"Creative guess work, Brandon. But that's all you've got."

Sergeant Blessing took a drink and wiped his mouth. The paper napkin fluttered outward with his weary sigh. "There's a ways to go before I can pin it down, but I think the distance is getting shorter." Brandon fished in his pocket, handed a slip of paper to Pete. "That's Lieutenant Sam Pachman's number at the San Francisco P D. — a direct line. I got an OK for the expense, so I want you to hop a plane tonight and noodle around. Sam's willing to cooperate, but he can't run all our errands for us."

"What's happened?"

Brandon took his time. He took a bite out of his sandwich, chewed carefully, "Some steward or hired hand at that place in the Napa Valley . . . "

"The Pericles Society."

"Yeah. Well he finally came through with the info that Merton did not spend the night at their mansion either the sixteenth or seventeenth of July."

"When the dean was in San Francisco?"

"You've got it, Chief — from the sixteenth to the nineteenth. The president went up on the sixteenth and took the midnight flight back on the eighteenth."

"That's no great news," Pete grumbled.

Brandon stared at him. "Well, maybe this will meet your requirements. I had another word with Miss Taper. With a little prodding, the lady was good enough to recall that she hadn't yet turned in all of Merton's expenses to the Business Bureau. Including a room at the Cortez Hotel."

Pete wasn't the only one who took this in with ambivalent feelings.

"For the sixteenth to the eighteenth," Brandon went on. "Miss Taper insisted that was regular procedure when he went up to San Francisco for the Outing."

Thad frowned into his soup.

"Says he usually shuttled back and forth between the Valley and the city for appointments and such, so he liked to have a place where he could rest or change. Get hold of some pictures of Merton and Parker-Brown, Pete, and check out the Carlton and the Cortez. If that's a goose egg, make the rounds. I don't see him or her as motel types. So go for the fancier ones first."

"OK. Where do I stay?"

Brandon looked at him unblinking. "Who said anything about sleeping?"

Mary Walker's office phone buzzed. It was Max Dingam.

"I haven't had any luck, Mary. No files on the Crofts or an inventory of that Oriental stuff. And I looked through a bunch of personal files. His 'Computer' file folder didn't have what you're looking for either."

"What about the diskette?"

"I'm coming to that. I couldn't locate anything, so I checked with Gloria. She never heard Vince mention a personal code."

"You told Gloria?"

"Don't worry, Mary. She understands your inquiry is confidential."

"I hope so."

"Gloria's a whiz, and she thinks that access to the material you want may be via a systems disk. But you'll still need a password — if it's a protected function."

"I see."

"Listen, if you'd like to take a look yourself through Vince's files, or talk to Gloria . . . "

She interrupted. "It isn't that important. Thanks, Max. And may I have the floppy back?"

"Sure. Bring it right over."

Mary hung up, feeling she had made a mistake. Knowing how the secretary's grapevine operated, the buzzing at coffee breaks, she expected little from Gloria Traynor's pledge of confidentiality.

It was Gloria herself who returned the diskette. "I hear Vince left you a secret message."

Mary tried to look uninterested. "Just a joke, I think."

"It sounds like him, that dear man. He sure thought the world and all of you, Mary. And he was having so much fun with his new PC." She was silent a moment, then said brightly, "I've got an idea for you to try."

"Oh?"

"I know Vince had a new systems disk, a relational database for the Macintosh. I helped him with it some."

"Was it called Fourth Dimension?"

"That's the baby. If you want to find a personal password, you can do what the hackers do: Create a program to look at all possible letter combinations . . . "

Mary interrupted with a wave of the hand. "I think not, Gloria."

"If you have the systems disk, I can play with it."

"Maybe later, thanks."

"One thing, Mary. You have an old 512K, right?"

"Yes. But up-graded."

"Just the same, the one in our office has more memory and could facilitate things for you. Why don't you try using Vince's SE?"

The housekeeper admitted Brandon Blessing and showed him into the small drawing room dominated by the severe portrait of Louisa May Arrington. Cissy Merton was nowhere to be seen.

Priscilla Merton, carrying a tray, entered a moment later.

"This is unquestionably lemonade weather, don't you agree, Sergeant?"

"Yes ma'am, thank you." He took the proffered glass.

"Please — sit down."

"Thank you for seeing me, Mrs. Merton."

Large gray-blue eyes opened wider. "But of course. Though I'm mystified. I can't imagine what we have left to talk about." Priscilla put a hand to her chignon, allowing an apricot voile sleeve to fall back and reveal a smooth upper arm and soft hollow. She let her arm fall suddenly. "Unless it's about Terry Logan. Have you learned anything?"

"We're working on it, ma'am."

"That unfortunate young woman. I suppose you know that Chief Walker came to see me? I simply can't understand murder. Julian . . . Now Terry . . . To be shot down by some mad or thrill-seeking person . . . Her poor parents."

Brandon gave the merest nod, his mind else-where. Priscilla waited for him to begin, then stirred impatiently. He woke up. "I think you're wrong about there not being anything left to dis-cuss, Mrs. Merton."

"Oh?"

"Everybody has things that are not easy to talk about. But in a murder investigation, privacy can't always be respected."

"What are you leading up to, Sergeant Blessing?"

"Your relationship with your husband."

"That's a very broad — and a very personal question."

"Yes ma'am. But I need an answer."

"I've already answered you."

Brandon considered this smooth and elegant woman with an unwavering stare. "Your husband was murdered, Mrs. Merton, and the question of his fidelity is a matter of concern in this case. We did not discuss that."

Priscilla seemed to grow taller in her chair. "Julian was a faithful husband."

"So far as you know."

"I know."

"Well, excuse me, ma'am, but what makes you so sure?"

"I'm sure, Sergeant. Not because of any notion that Julian was in love with me. Though I know he was. But because of his own egoism, or sense of self, if you prefer."

"Afraid I don't follow."

"My husband was a perfectionist. As hard on himself as he was on others. A man of tremendous pride and sense of dignity where his self-image was concerned. Any tawdry, hole-in-the-corner kind of affair is unthinkable."

"Well ma'am, I'm not talking tawdry."

The large blue eyes narrowed, the tone hardened. "For heaven's sakes, officer, what are you 'talking'? This is becoming tiresome."

"Then I'll be blunt, Mrs. Merton. I think your husband was having, or had had an affair with Dean Parker-Brown."

The laugh was a pitch too high. "That again. Really now. And what does Dean Parker-Brown have to say about this fantasy of yours? Or have you asked her?"

"The dean says there was nothing between them."

"But of course you don't agree. You prefer to listen to local gossip, don't you? I want to know whose."

Brandon stared at her without expression. "Did your husband phone you while he was at that Pericles Society get-together?"

"Why are you ignoring my question?" Her voice was shrill.

Brandon allowed the silence between them to grow before pursuing. "Did your husband call you from the Napa Valley?"

Priscilla glared at him before finally answering. "Yes. Every evening. Before he went to bed to be precise. He always tried to do that when he was away — to talk to Cissy — and to me."

"And he did that this last trip — on the sixteenth and seventeenth of July for instance?"

"Whatever the dates were, yes, of course."

"Where did he call from?"

"From the Pericles Society, naturally."

Brandon sighed. "The thing is, Mrs. Merton, he didn't sleep there on those two nights."

Priscilla looked away. When she at last turned her head toward him again, her eyes blazed with resentment.

"Of course he was with Anne, damn you. Damn you to hell."

Brandon was writing up his notes and popping colored M&Ms for a change of pace. Thad wandered in, tossed his suit jacket onto the back of a chair before going over to the table that had been set up with a coffee maker. He poured himself a cup.

"Hope this is the real stuff."

"It is." Brandon looked up expectantly. "Anything interesting?"

"Not yet. Logan's negatives have gone into LA. They'll check through the past twelve months' worth for starters. They're filed by months and years, however, and that's a help."

"You agree that the blackmail angle is the likeliest one to follow?"

Thad took a sip of coffee. "Wow, that's hot. I guess so. So long as we're running out the string of local possibilities." He didn't sound happy. "Though there's no record of money to back up that theory."

"She could have concealed it someplace — in cash. Maybe she hadn't been paid yet."

"Maybe."

"Or perhaps she was angling to be reinstated here at the college."

"Maybe."

Brandon scowled. "You've sure got a limited vocabulary."

Thad grinned. "I try to adapt it to the mental level of my interlocutor."

"Smart ass." Unperturbed, Brandon continued. "Then when she got the other job, Logan threatened to tell her story anyway. Parting shot. A way to damage the dean's and the president's reputations."

Thad frowned. "It's all possible, Brandon. But I don't see it matching up with what we know about those women. Logan was direct — at times embarrassingly outspoken. Not a sneak."

"And the dean? What do you really know about her?"

Thad didn't answer. Had he done so, he would have had to say she was a mystery.

"You see? You don't know. And who does? Just about everybody we talk to admires her. Like you'd admire a statue. But nobody says anything that gives you a sense of what she's really like. As a woman."

"She's a professional, Brandon. And discreet."

"Now I've heard everything. As if that protected her from snapping under enough pressure. Listen, Thad, we gotta keep our eye on what facts we have. You worked in LA long enough to know that if we get embroiled in personalities this investigation will stay right here — in the doldrums."

"I also recall that it's a mistake to try to manipulate coincidences into evidence."

Brandon maintained a stubborn expression. When Pete Wiggins wandered in, Brandon was saying, "Your so-called best people have lives that don't bear scrutiny; upright citizens secretly living out fantasies or evening up old scores. The trouble with working with small town local cops is that they want to protect the good folks of their town. You can't see the trees for the forest."

Thad burst out laughing.

Pete listened impatiently as his superiors argued back and forth: Brandon, using Priscilla Merton's admission to strengthen his theory regarding the dean's motivation; Thad, stubbornly prodding holes both in that supposition and the idea that Logan was a blackmailer.

"I'm still unconvinced that Terry Logan and the president were murdered by the same person, Brandon,"Thad said. "And Pete agrees, right?"

Pete swallowed. "Well, I did," he said unhappily.

Brandon and Thad stared in unison.

"It's that car business. The college has a fleet of new Subarus — all green. So I had a talk with Joelle. She checks the cars in and out, but the VPs have one that's always reserved for their use. And each one has a key." Pete let the import of this sink in.

"But the kid said the car was red, Pete," Thad said.

"Uh-huh. The thing is," Pete went on slowly, "Todd's mother told me he was color-blind. Red and green are two colors that color-blind people confuse."

Pete caught Brandon's look. He nodded. "I'll get on it."

Mary was proofreading the alumni notes for the next issue of *Tipton Topics* when Victor Laszlo burst through the door.

"What's this I hear, Mary, about your locating the inventory of the Asian collection?"

Mary pulled her chair back from her desk, turned to face him, reached forward to remove a stack of publications from a chair. "Sit down, Victor. I was about to call you."

"I would hope so. I understand you have the original inventory."

Damn Gloria. Damn the wildfire spread of gossip.

Victor bounced his heels up and down on the floor in his impatience.

Mary's mind rapidly checked reasons for withholding information and found only undefined apprehension. Should you bluff when you don't know the stakes of the game or who your opponent is?

"Not exactly, Victor. I don't have the actual inventory. I happen to have a diskette of Vince's — it was in his house." Let him think what he wants to about that. "It contains a copy of his annual report and mentions the existence of an inventory and the donors' name."

"Well, where is the damn thing?"

"He attached it to the annual report he gave the president."

"For Pete's sake. So it's been sitting in a file all this time."

She shook her head. "It seems to be missing. But Vince made a copy for Turner."

"Anything to do with donors is a concern of my department. Why the hell didn't Turner copy me?"

"I wouldn't know. Murders have priority over misplaced inventories, wouldn't you say?"

He put his hands on his thighs and pushed himself up, shaking his head in bewilderment. "Sometimes lately I get the feeling this place is falling apart."

Since no comment seemed called for, Mary said nothing.

"Who were the donors?"

"Lawrence and Penelope Croft. I believe the gift was made in 1925."

"Doesn't ring any bells. Thank God it's unlikely they're still alive. We'll have to find out about their heirs . . . If you've got that floppy, I'd like to have a look at it."

Mary released the tote bag from her chair. She peeked in to make sure she had hold of the right diskette and that the systems disk was still there in its folder. Suddenly she changed her mind.

"I thought I had it here. I'll get it to you first thing tomorrow."

"Thanks, Mary." At the door Victor turned and smiled, eyes twinkling. "Say, you're looking mighty cute today, you know that?"

Mary listened as his footsteps went down the hall. Then she picked up a magazine and threw it at the doorjamb. Rosalie came rushing in, stopped as Mary rolled across to retrieve the missile. Mary smiled ruefully at her. Rosalie understood.

"Old Crotch at it again, huh?"

The two women went back to work.

The grim expression on Victor Laszlo's face told Crystal Mathews that chatting time with her boss was over. As she left Turner's office, Victor went in and closed the door.

"Yes, I've got a moment," said Turner.

Victor ignored the jibe. "I need more than that. First I hear that Mary Walker has one of Vince's diskettes with a report on the inventory of the Crofts' gift, and that you've known about its discovery all along."

"Not all along, Victor. Since a week ago — the nineteenth as a matter of fact."

"Vince gave you a copy, I hear."

"That's right." Turner got up and went over to one of his files and pulled out a folder.

"Where's the original?"

"Somewhere in the president's files, I suppose. Vince told me he gave Julian the original."

"Mary Walker says it's been misplaced."

"How would she know? Well, no matter. Julian and I spoke briefly about Riley's find shortly before the festivities for Ward. Julian had it in his hand then, as I recall."

Victor choked back his resentment. Julian hadn't said a thing to him, and the matter concerned his department, not Turner's. Another sign of being shunted aside.

Turner held a document out to him. "Here's the copy Vince gave me with his accompanying memorandum — and you were copied."

"What! Let me see that."

Turner placed the papers in the outstretched hand.

Victor mumbled through the memorandum. "'July 18th, 1989. To Turner Van Voorhees from V. Riley. cc: Victor Laszlo. Attached is copy of inventory of Lawrence and Penelope Croft 1925 gift to the college. The original showed up this a.m. in Room 2 when I was moving the chest that had held the collection. It had slipped down behind the bottom drawer.' I sure as heck never got a copy of the memo or the inventory."

Turner shrugged. "That's too bad. I had intended to discuss it with you before now, but under the circumstances . . . "

Victor grudgingly accepted the excuse. "Well, OK. Anyway, we've got our mitts on the list and the names we need. We can at last start a proper search. The Crofts may have some heirs who might be interested to learn about the collection — and the college. There's a chance there's some real money there — if all that jade is an indication."

"You never know."

Victor started for the door. "Have Crystal make me a copy of the inventory and the memo, will you?"

"Of course. By the way, Victor, you say Mary has a diskette with a report on the inventory?"

"Yeah. At home. She's bringing it in tomorrow. She found it in Vince's house. After his death."

"What!"

"I heard at a Chamber of Commerce lunch this noon that Vince left her his house."

"I see. That's very nice to hear. I know he was devoted to her."

Victor nodded. "Vince had a big heart. I bet he had that in mind when he bought the house from the college this spring. He never said anything to you about it?"

"Not a word."

"I suppose you'll want a copy of whatever's on Mary's diskette?"

"Fine, Victor. Appreciate it."

As Victor went out, Turner picked up the phone, dialed Buildings and Grounds.

"Gloria, is Max in? . . . Well, would you see whether Vince has a copy of that Asian art collection inventory in his files? . . . You've already looked? . . . For whom? . . . I see . . . And you're certain it's not there? . . . Just tell Max I called about it."

Turner hung up, then went out to the reception area.

"Beulah, we seem to be missing something."

Beulah, who was doing her end-of-the-day filing, slid the drawer shut and walked back to her desk.

"What's that, Mr. Van Voorhees?"

"The original inventory of the Asian art collection. I know Julian had it."

"I don't think so, Mr. Van Voorhees."

"He had it in his hand when he spoke with me — the morning of the nineteenth."

"Well, I shall certainly look again."

"Again?"

"Mary Walker was asking about it today. She thought the inventory had been attached to the president's copy of Vince's annual report — but it's certainly not there."

"Strange. At least we have a copy. But do keep looking, will you?"

"Of course."

Beulah absently stared after Turner as he walked back to his office. It was there again, the amorphous something squirming around in her memory, refusing to surface. An attachment? A memo? What?

Pete finished talking with Joelle and headed downstairs. All the Subarus were accounted for the evening before Terry's murder. There was no way to tell whether the executive car had been taken or not. Joelle was certain it was in the lot when she arrived this morning.

"Henry Norton took it this afternoon, Brandon; he still has it."

"Did Joelle know when it was washed last?"

"Yep. Three weeks ago. It gets pretty regular use, Joelle says."

"So any souvenirs we might find could be explained away. Great." He scrabbled for some M&Ms. "I'll still have it gone over. Just as an exercise in futility."

At a few minutes to five, Pete Wiggins appeared at Mary Walker's office door.

"Come in, Pete. Sit down."

Pete took the chair vacated earlier by Victor.

"By the way, did an Ellen Forsythe come by to see you fellows?"

"Thad talked to her. I'm flying up to San Francisco this evening. Will be there a day or two. Just wanted to say hello — and good-bye."

"That's nice of you. I don't suppose this trip has any connection with Vince's death?"

He shook his head, conscious of a thumping in his chest. At least he wasn't blushing. He remembered Mary from high school days when he had adored her from afar. A pipsqueak freshman looking up at a junior class leader. How quick and graceful she had been. How admired. How lovely. And still was. There was something elfin about her that made the contrast between her upper and lower body all the harder to bear. He wanted to protect her, to make a grandiose gesture, to create a miracle.

"Pete, am I completely off base? About Vince?"

He hesitated.

"Suppose I were to tell you that I had come across something — well, perplexing?"

"Do you want to tell me about it?"

She didn't answer right away. "I'd like to. But I think I'd better not. Not just yet."

"Look, Mary, if this has anything to do with either murder, you'd best tell me."

"I will. Promise. For the moment it's just something personal."

"I see. Wish I could help you."

"Maybe you can. Or help me think something through. If you wanted to have a protected access code for your computer, what would you select?"

Pete thought a moment. "A birthday, maybe. That's what many people use for luggage locks."

"That had occurred to me."

"A street address. Telephone number. Family name. A special date. Like the year you got married."

"Or had your first affair."

Pete blushed this time; the hated, uncontrollable blush. Then grinned. "Sure. Why not?"

"Keep going. You're doing great."

Mary had never particularly noticed Pete's smile before. Warm, open, inviting trust.

Mary decided to call it quits for the day and made a stab at cleaning off her desk. She checked through her Filofax and dialed Reflections.

"Deirdre? Mary Walker."

"Mary, can you believe this about Terry?" The deep voice vibrated with emotion. "The gallery has been crowded, wouldn't you know? Lookers *and* buyers. I keep thinking what Terry would say about it. It's awful, in a way."

"Macabre curiosity. Deirdre, I have a favor to ask."

"Sure."

"Could you tell me who bought the picture entitled 'Fallen Angel'?"

"I'm dreadfully sorry, Mary, I'm not sure I should give out the information without the buyer's OK."

"Could you ask?"

"Maybe you ought to tell me why you're interested."

Mary thought fast. "It's for Terry's cousin."

"Oh, Ellen, yes. What a darling."

"I thought I had a glossy to give her, but I can't find it. She was with Terry when she took the picture, so it means a lot to Ellen. Any chance the owner would sell it?"

"I doubt it. I'll see what I can do and call you right back."

In less than fifteen minutes her telephone rang.

"Mary, the owner will not sell, but if the negative isn't available, and if Ellen would like to photograph the original, that's agreeable."

"Thanks, Deirdre. Whom should I tell Ellen to call?"

"Kitty Van Voorhees."

WEDNESDAY, JULY 26

KITTY VAN VOORHEES, WEARING THE skimpiest of bikinis in the way skimpy bikinis were meant to be worn, emerged from the house carrying a pitcher of lemonade and two glasses. Turner, dozing at the poolside table, came to with a start as she pressed the cold pitcher against his neck.

"Hey, Kitty!"

"Can't have you sluggish. With Allison and Jamie gone, this is our night. I'm fixing dinner myself."

Turner clapped weakly.

"So, I don't want to hear anything about going to the office."

"If I do, I'll make it fast."

"You work too hard, Turn."

"It's your Yankee influence."

Kitty wrinkled her nose at him. "Mabel has terrible hay fever. I said I'd manage. She got dinner started though, so take heart."

Turner poured the lemonade, handed his wife a glass.

"Before you sit down, Kitten, walk over toward the pool."

Kitty did so, pausing with her back to him.

"Now turn around and come back." He watched her critically. "I do believe those massage and drainage treatments are effective."

"God, I hope so, given her prices." She looked down at her legs, giving the thighs a little pinch here and there to check for any cellulite dimpling. "Madame Laurent says I have perfect hips and thighs."

"I applaud her judgment."

Kitty dropped a kiss on the top of his head. Turner looked up at her and smiled, admiring her radiance, her strong, perfect body.

"It will be lovely to have the place to ourselves for a couple of days, though I do miss the children."

"Me too," Kitty said automatically, "But they adore going to the Mercers at Newport. As Allison says, 'It's so-o-o neat to have cousins.'" She sat down, jiggled the plastic straw in her glass. "Turner, maybe we should get a place at the beach."

"Why? You have your parents' place at the Cape."

"But it's too far away. And Newport, or Emerald Bay, are lovely most of the year."

"Bit rich for us right now."

"Mm, I don't know about that. Daddy called this afternoon."

"Again!"

"Now, Turn."

"Kitty, I think it's marvellous that you're close to your father, but sometimes this Daddy's little girl routine is a bit much."

"You may change your mind about that."

Turner caught the arch tone. "Oh?"

"Did I tell you he's bringing his tax attorney with him?"

"You did indeed; he forewarned us a month ago. Thank God. One needs to be prepared for Willard Meecham."

"I think Willard is kind of cute — in a quaint way."

"His quaint way almost discouraged me from marrying you."

"I bet."

"True. His pursy manner when the prenuptial agreement was being drawn up really put me off."

"He's just super careful, Turn — like you."

Turner looked quizzical. "I'm not sure that's a compliment."

Kitty went blithely on. "You know what I think? I think Daddy not only wants to go over our investments with you, but that he is going to make us a very handsome gift."

"His statement or your wishful thinking?"

"Neither one. But I know when Daddy is trying not to give me hints."

"That would be a great and generous gesture, Kitten, but don't count on it. When is he coming out?"

"As scheduled. Two weeks from today."

"I hope the mess at the college is cleared up by then."

"It's so super dreadful about Terry Logan. So talented. By the way, Turn, Deirdre called. You know, from the gallery. Mary Walker wanted to know who had bought the 'Fallen Angel'."

"Oh?"

"She was inquiring for Terry's cousin. Remember that pretty blond girl we met at the opening? She may want to photograph it."

"Why?"

"Dunno. Oh, yes I do. Deirdre said something about her wanting a remembrance."

Turner nodded absently and poured himself another glass of lemonade. "Chief Walker was making the rounds in Wyndham today. Another one of his 'routine checks.' He was interested in where Upper Wyndham was between five and six-thirty this morning. You can expect a visit."

"Well, I know about you, early bird. I heard you rattling around in the kitchen."

"Not for long. As a matter of fact I went for a run. I haven't an alibi, unless the paper boy remembers seeing me go by. I'm getting chilly, darling. Let's go in and get a start on this erotic evening you have planned."

Kitty tossed her head and tried out a sexy drawl. "Now who said anything about *that?*"

Claire Tidwell was at the kitchen sink chopping onions and weeping. Mark came through the back-door and walked over to plant a kiss on her cheek.

"I keep reading handy hints about how to avoid onion tears, but I can never remember one when I need it."

"Isn't there something about a burnt match?"

"And you call yourself a chemist? Too late now," she sniffed. "I'll try a drink instead. A Manhattan."

"I thought you were an old-fashioned girl."

"Gawd, Mark. How your students ever stood it I'll never know."

"The day of my memorial service you'll realize how beloved I was."

"With your invincible genes you'll be placing pos-ies on my tomb. And you will remember to make it red poppies, cornflowers, and white daisies?"

"I've made a note, Frenchie." He busied himself at the counter that served as a bar. "Here's your drink."

"Mm, yummy. Thanks, sweetie. Any news from embattled Wyndham drift over your way this after-noon?"

Mark sat down on a kitchen stool to supervise Claire's dinner preparation.

"Nope. Are you making a meatloaf?"

"Just for you, baby." She laughed. "Remember how shocked Pierre de Grancey was when I served him and what's her name — his second wife — meatloaf? I thought he was going to denounce me to the Académie des Sciences as a traitor to France." She took a sip of her drink, then added, "Well *I* have a bit of news. Thad Walker came by my office. He's working with that Sergeant Blessing on the Logan shooting."

"Oh?"

"He was interested in her private life of course."

"Don't tell me they think she was shot by someone who knew her!"

"I'm not sure. Though I didn't like the way he asked about possible bad feelings between her and Anne."

"Just because of that tenure hoop-tie-do?"

"Needless to say, I had a thing or two to tell him on that score." Claire plopped her mixture into a loaf pan in punctuation to her statement and began to shape it. "I'm worried about Anne, Mark. After that sinister experience with Terry this morning I thought she might like to come by for a drink or dinner, but she begged off."

"Maybe I should give her a ring."

"She and Phil Gertmenian are going to get a bite someplace, catch up on office business."

"Well then. The lady hasn't become completely reclusive."

"Mark, she's been — well, different with me lately. Stressed out, I think. Still . . . "

"Still what?"

"When we had coffee together day before yesterday, with my usual delicacy I said something derogatory about Priscilla's feelings for Julian. Anne got testy. Can you believe it?"

"Sure I can. Haven't you ever heard about where angels fear to tread?"

"She said she was certain Priscilla loved Julian. Almost belligerent about it."

"What did you expect her to say, for gosh sakes?"

"It was the defensiveness, the tone . . . And the next moment, so remote, so . . . "

"Let it drop, Claire. And let's spend the evening talking about something happy for a change. Like you and me."

Claire blew him a kiss and returned to her cooking and her worrying. To a moment that kept drifting through her mind. "In one of his novels, Camus compares humans to piranhas," Anne had said. "Do you remember, Claire? People whose little teeth rip you apart spiritually and psychologically. Julian was like that. A piranha." Anne had made the statement with no show of emotion. She seemed to have forgotten that her friend was there; Claire wished she hadn't been.

Mary heard her brother's car turn in the driveway. She took the vegetables and the fried chicken out of the warming oven and had everything on the table by the time Thad came into the kitchen.

"Smells good."

"There's blueberry pie to follow. A good old mid-western meal. Thought you might need indulging this evening."

"Bless you, Sister Mary." He hung his jacket on the back of a chair, loosened his tie as he sat down. "I've been sedentary too long. Not in shape any more for the active life. May I serve you?"

"Please. Pretty hectic day?"

"Well, we're trying to put on the steam in this Logan affair. Nothing very promising, so far. The idea that Terry might have been blackmailing someone isn't holding up."

"I hadn't heard about that theory."

"She did go in for candid shots. The guys at the lab have been checking through her negatives, but haven't come up with anything scabrous — or even racy — to date."

"So you think it's a random shooting."

Thad nodded as he chewed. "I'm leaning in that direction. Brandon doesn't agree with me, how-ever."

"Oh? What's his idea?"

"I think I shouldn't discuss that just yet."

They ate in silence for a while. Mary felt the impulse to confide in her brother. She wanted to tell him about her discovery and the questions the diskettes were raising. But the possibility of hear-ing him declare yet once again that she should accept the facts decided her against it. Accep-tance. She would always strike out against that word and what it stood for in her mind: passive submission, abnegation of the will, a tolerance of the unacceptable. Instead, Mary asked, "Thad, did Ellen Forsythe get hold of you?"

"Yes. Very thoughtful of her to check in. She was helpful in clearing up questions about Terry's personal life. She was with her parents in Santa Barbara until early this morning, by the way. They confirm that she left about the time Logan was shot."

"I'm glad. I like her. She came by my office today."

"Oh?"

Thad's intonation was an invitation to explain Ellen Forsythe's visit, but Mary backed off from it, again reluctant to try his patience with what he considered an obsession. And she still had nothing but unfounded suspicion, nothing to cling to but the slim hope of discovering Vince's personal code and the even fainter possibility that the protected section three would confirm her instincts. Her rational mind told her that what she labeled "instinct" could be the despair of loss rather than a specially keen intuitive sense, but she willfully ignored it. "By the way, Thad, I got a letter today from Vince's lawyer, informing me that I inherit the house and the contents."

"Have you gone over there at all?"

"Only once. I can't quite face it. But I must go through things and send George what he asked for. I wrote him today that I would do it before the end of next month."

"Perhaps after the memorial service on Saturday . . . Ceremonial events do help a little. Or so they say." He looked away, remembering.

After a few more minutes of idle chit-chat, Mary asked, "Thad, would you mind getting your dessert and putting the dishes in the washer? I need to go to the office for a while."

With their four children fed and out of the way, Henry and Lucille Norton were enjoying a beer in the quiet of their comfortably shabby living room. A room where teenagers could have a party that left parents worry free — at least so far as the furnishings were concerned — and where dogs and little ones could roll around on the two sagging couches with impunity. Lucille Norton was looking at it this evening with a less than indulgent eye.

"Two more years, Henry, and we're going to get this place redecorated."

"I thought we had decided to wait until the whole kit and caboodle had made it through puberty."

She shook her head. "No way. Ready or not, we're going for it. And we should be able to afford it by then."

"That's debatable."

"You never had the chance to say anything to Julian about the percentage of your salary raise, did you?"

"Afraid not. I expect his answer would have been the same as last year: that the difference between my raise and that of the other vice presidents was made up for by our college house."

"Baloney."

"Since I now know what their raises were, I'm inclined to agree. You want another beer?"

"Not yet, thanks." She frowned. "I wish I were a better manager, Henry, and knew how to sew and put up fruit and do all those housewifely things."

"You do just fine. And we might fare better under a new régime at the college. If we stay."

"Please — don't even have the thought. I can't bear the idea of moving."

"OK." He drained his glass and chuckled.

"What's so funny?"

"Chief Walker. He came by the office late this afternoon. He's working on the Logan investigation, so he wanted to know where I was early this morning."

Lucille sat up, indignant. "Well of all the . . . "

"It's perfectly normal procedure, Lucille, under the circumstances. He's checked on all of us: Anne, Victor, Turner . . . Victor made a point of telling us, why God knows, that he stayed at the Metropolitan Club last night. He's gotten so paranoid, poor guy. Anyway, Walker looked a mite startled when I told him I was sleeping in a wigwam in the backyard. You can tell he's never had children."

Lucille sketched a vague smile, then looked at her husband with concern.

"I didn't think to mention it to you, Henry, but Andy came in and woke me up around six. He had had a bad dream. He said that Chief Strongbow had left the teepee."

Henry nodded. "That's right. I went for a walk. The air in the tent was a trifle ripe. Be sure Chief Stargazer has a full-scale scrub-down tonight." He fidgeted a moment and looked at his watch. "I've got to make a long distance call from the office — to Hawaii. Won't take me more than a few minutes."

"OK. Then if you're not going to take the car, I think I'll go pick up a strawberry pie at The Pie Hut."

"You've got a deal. How about if I barbecue some steaks?"

"I think my cholesterol count can stand it. But we'll skip the pie."

At her desk in Baja Wyndham, Mary took the new floppy she had retrieved from the News Bureau's stock and attached a label. With Vince Riley's disk in front of her, she carefully copied from it in block letters:

"1. Copy of annual report. 2. Report on items found on July 13 in Room 2, Wyndham Hall (Lawrence and Penelope Croft Collection — 1925)."

Mary booted up the computer and copied sections one and two onto the new floppy, carefully omitting any mention of section 3 and the reference to a personal code. Mary then slipped the diskette into an envelope addressed to Victor Laszlo and dropped it in the box for campus mail.

From the pile on her desk Mary dug out the slip with Ellen Forsythe's number. She was hesitant about disturbing Ellen. Because of one missing photograph? It could have been missing from the folder before Crystal took it. Or the glossy might have slipped out, gotten misfiled. She didn't even have a good reason for being concerned about it. A missing photograph; the change of a title . . . Something about Terry's manner in asking her about — what was it, Dodie? She was desperate, she told herself, seeing shadows everywhere.

Ellen was blow-drying her hair and failed to hear the first four rings. She switched off the dryer and made a dash for the bedroom.

"Ellen, this is Mary Walker. Am I calling you at a bad time?"

"That's OK."

"I've located the owner of the photograph you were interested in, and she says you're most welcome to make a copy if you wish."

"Well, thanks a lot, but I'm not sure I want to do that. I'll ask Terry's parents to let me look for the negative."

"Ellen, I have a favor to ask."

"Yes?"

"It's about that young man, Angelo."

"What about him?"

"Just — what do you know about him?"

At the silence from the other end of the line, Mary hurried on. "I'm sure this must seem like idle curiosity, Ellen. I'm sorry I can't explain what I expect from the information; I don't really know myself at this point — except that it's important to me."

Ellen didn't hesitate. "I'll tell you whatever I know, Mary, but it's precious little. According to the papers here his name was Albert O'Hana. The Angelo was probably an attempt to glamorize his identity. He moved into a house on our block about six months ago. A quiet type by all accounts. At least I rarely caught a glimpse of him. The landlady went to his house for some reason or other about ten days ago and found him dead. Of an apparent overdose the police said. He was a user."

"Didn't I hear you tell Terry at the gallery that the police were interested in the case again?"

"Yes, that's right. There was a brief flurry. All of us on the street were interviewed. But nothing came of the investigation as I understand. Our mutual landlady lives next door to me, and accord-

ing to Emma Worth, Angelo's parents showed up
— from Michigan. Maybe they spurred some further official interest."

"But nothing?"

"The Laguna newspaper reported he had a juve-
nile record — petty theft I believe — and a drug
bust. There was the question of how he lived and
how he could afford all the electronic and video
equipment they found. There was some expensive
jewelry also. Emma Worth said his rent was paid
well in advance, though he didn't have a job. Apparently he wasn't looking for one; stayed close to
home — again according to the landlady. All a bit
odd, but I believe the police decided he must have
been dealing."

"Didn't he have any friends?"

"Not that we heard. That is kinda funny, come
to think of it. He must have had one at some time
or other. That Dodie person."

"Ellen, did Terry ever tell you why she was curious about this Dodie?"

"Because the kid said he knew someone at
Tipton, I suppose." She laughed. "It's a cinch
Angel was never a student."

"Male or female friend?"

"I guess he didn't say."

"Did you mention this to the police?"

"Why no. I never saw anybody around his place
— rarely caught a glimpse of him. Terry had become pretty perceptive about her 'marginals,' you

know. She had Angelo pegged as an AC/DC hustler, and probably a congenital liar to boot, so who knows what to make of it."

"I see. Well, thanks a lot, Ellen."

There was a silence at Ellen's end, then she asked, "Mary, I know your brother is Chief of Police. Have your questions anything to do with Terry's death?"

"I don't know. Possibly not. We've had three deaths connected with the college in one week, Ellen. One that the police insist is an accident."

"But you don't think so?"

"No. It's — it's someone who was close to me. There are things that add up all wrong. At least I think so. But no one agrees with me. And they may be right."

"I see. Look, I'm leaving for Japan in a couple of days, but I'll manage a little chat with Emma Worth before I go. If she has any interesting information, I'll give you a call."

Mary spent an hour on an editing job for the next issue of *Topics* then left the News Bureau and let herself into the offices of Buildings and Grounds across the hall. She turned on Vince's Mac SE, removed the systems disk from her bag, inserted it, and called up the view function, clicking on the "View By Name." There it was: "Croft inventory — section 3." At the next click the anticipated request came on the screen: "Enter password."

Mary opened a notebook, placed it beside the Mac, and began the tedious task of going through the list she had prepared: first, various combinations of Vince's name, of his address, of his birthday; then she did the same with her name, and with George's; she tried various configurations of his old home town, Mangum, Oklahoma. Recalling her facetious suggestion to Pete Wiggins, she typed in the date they had first slept together and berated Vince's shade when the screen flashed "No application can be found for this document." She tried to think of special things he had liked: Falcons, lions, and irises; the Canyon de Chelly and the gardens of Capability Brown. Favorite movie stars: Gary Cooper and Ingrid Bergman; favorite author, Mark Twain . . . Nothing was working.

Leaving Wyndham Hall and heading for the parking lot, Angel's friend noticed both Mary's car and the light streaming out from an office of Buildings and Grounds. Protected by the heavy shrubbery, the friend looked in at the window. What was she doing at Riley's computer, the repugnant freak? Angel's friend stood watching, not moving. "Grammy's little Dodie is the smartest baby . . . " The song that haunted Dodie's mind began its relentless melody. Humming softly, absentmindedly, Angel's friend moved away.

Lieutenant Inocencio Mendez of the Los Angeles County Sheriff's office was irate. "Damn it, Brandon, you gotta put the mark on someone at that college and soon."

Brandon said nothing.

"That place has got some powerful trustees and they aren't singing halleluja about the kind of media attention they're getting. I'm getting calls from the Mayor of LA, a gaggle of politicians and one U. S. Senator. Not to mention my boss and the DA's office."

"For cripes' sake, the murder investigation is only three days old. And we started with a cold trail, one bottle of toxic wine and one smudged fingerprint."

Lieutenant Mendez shook his head at the proffered sack of candy.

"This case is like boxing with a featherbed, Lieutenant. You think you're making a mark, and it vanishes on you. The tech guys did a full sweep of the relevant areas in the Science Building and the Administration Building . . . And what was the yield? Lint from Merton's suit on the carpet and some bits of metallic thread. And as for that college crowd . . . Real glib. Smooth talkers. You think they've told you something, then you realize it's mostly air."

Lieutenant Mendez nodded sympathetically. "I know the kinds of people you're dealing with are as slippery as a greased pig. But you're a good investigator, Brandon. Stop futzing around."

Brandon gave forth a gargantuan sigh. "The stars haven't been with me on this one, Lieutenant — or else that Saint Anthony who's such a pal of yours isn't doing his stuff."

"Let me have it straight, Brandon. Haven't you got anything? Just how far away are you?"

"Maybe not too far. If I can find one tiny piece to fit into the puzzle. I should know tomorrow whether I have it or not."

"In that case I'll say a prayer. I don't want to bother Saint Anthony for nothing."

Anne closed the book she was reading and was reaching for the switch on her bedside light when the doorbell rang. 11:30. She considered ignoring the summons, but when the chimes sounded again and insistently, she slipped on a robe and hurried to the door. It was Priscilla.

"I know it's late, Anne. I apologize. I just had to see you."

Anne led the way into the study, turned on a lamp.

"Might I have a drink, please?"

"Of course. What would you like?"

"A small vodka on the rocks would be fine."

Anne was back a moment later with the drink. It wasn't until she was handing it to Priscilla and looked into her eyes that Anne realized she was drunk.

"I shouldn't have come."

"It's quite all right, Priscilla. How can I help?"

"Is it all set for people in the Hall to have tomorrow afternoon off?"

Anne had already confirmed with her earlier, but she did so again without comment.

Priscilla sipped at her drink. "I'm worried about the service. Do you know that Leslie Filmore won't be able to make it? That's what the son of a bitch's secretary said." Her voice went into a snooty register. "'Mr. Filmore is so sorry. He's been detained in London.' We're an embarrassment to the s. o. b. is more like it."

The proverbial perceptivity of the drunk, Anne thought.

"I'm sure that one of the vice chairmen will do a fine job."

"No. Julian's father. Into the breach. And then you and I will read — with feeling of course, won't we, Anne?"

"Do you honestly think it's a good idea? For me to read the poem in French?"

"Lousy idea, actually. But symbolic."

"I don't see how."

"Oh don't you. Don't tell me he never recited Baudelaire to you?" She laughed at the expression on Anne's face. "Look, Anne. Cards on the table at last. I know about you and Julian."

"You couldn't. There's nothing to know."

"Bullshit."

Anne almost jumped at Priscilla's unexpected use of the vulgar word. The mid- Atlantic accent had suddenly disappeared.

"Julian never told me. He didn't have to. He implied. The master of the innuendo. In yo' endo, in my endo." The burst of laughter was raucous. "That's our Julian."

Anne held herself in. Never argue with a drunk. "Let's discuss this some other time, Priscilla. We both need sleep."

"Oh no. It's now or never. I saw it all before, you know. When we were at Staunton. And with a Dean of Students at Ludlow when he was president. Poor old dried-up virgin almost committed suicide."

"Priscilla, I don't want to hear this. And you shouldn't be telling me . . . "

"Yes I should. And yes you should. Julian had superb technique. Su-perb. He would pick his victim, some lonely woman, get her gaga about him. Turn on the charm. The deep looks. The little confidences. Then the dependency bit. He needed her. Intellectually of course. Mental masturbation. Julian specialized in the meeting of true minds routine. And you want to know why?"

"I'd rather not . . . "

Priscilla ignored her. "That's how he got his kicks. Mental masturbation. Julian was not really so hot for the other kind, if truth were told. He just looked like the great lover. But no woman he seduced mentally ever had to be afraid of physical rape, let me tell you." She laughed. A harsh laugh. "Though maybe you turned him on. Did you, Anne?"

Anne said nothing. She thought of the old fairy tale: The girl punished for her viper tongue whose mouth spewed forth toads and snakes. Anne wanted to shut Priscilla up, but she couldn't. The small drunken woman sitting curled up on the couch had her hypnotized.

"His line with a woman was that she was the only one he could count on. The only one who understood. He'd go cold. Then he'd come on again. Keep her off balance. The specially patented Merton power play. Believe me I know all about it. I fell for it often enough myself. What a sap."

Priscilla laughed again, then lowered her head. Was she crying? Had she passed out? Anne stirred, started toward her. Priscilla's head jerked up and, surprisingly, the eyes focused steadily on her.

"Whether Julian fucked you or not, I know he had you wanting it. I know he made you suffer. If you killed him, Anne . . . "

Toads and snakes. "Priscilla, that's enough."

"If you killed him, congratulations. You did the world a favor."

Anne rose. "I think I should drive you home."

"No. I walked over and I can walk back. Like a homing pigeon." She chuckled. "I'm a pigeon all right. But so are you, Anne. So are you."

She got to her feet, put down her glass and headed somewhat uncertainly in the direction of the door. "I just wanted you to know." She touched the back of her head; the carefully done chignon was still in place.

Priscilla had reached the door to the study when Anne called to her. She turned.

"My turn, Priscilla. Did you kill Julian?"

A strained peal of laughter was her answer. A moment later Anne heard the front door open and close.

How long she sat there Anne didn't know. She recalled what she had said about Priscilla to Claire Tidwell only two days ago. She couldn't have been more wrong. She had been wrong from the beginning.

Thad Walker shut off the ignition and doused his headlights. He got out and walked the block from where he had parked his car to Wyndham Hall, avoiding the pools of light cast by the street lamps. He moved in close to the bushes at the south side door, stood listening, looking. Lights burned in the main floor foyer, and in the stairwell, but the rest of the Hall seemed to be in darkness. Thad took a ring of keys from his pocket, let himself in, and went silently and quickly up the steps to the first floor, to room 201. He turned on his flashlight, selected a lockpick, then tried another. Seconds later he stood before the open closet in Dean Parker-Brown's office, his light focused on a jacket brightly embroidered with shiny thread.

THURSDAY, JULY 27

MARY WALKER AWAKENED TO THE whoosh of automatic sprinklers turning on next door at Vince's house; her house now. She wondered whether she would be able to think of it that way, so long as disquiet tugged insistently at her mind; the unfounded conviction that someone had deliberately and brutally killed Vince Riley. Friend? Stranger? A night runner in a dark suit and striped baseball cap?

Mary pulled herself to a sitting position. She could still detect the marks on the ceiling from the installation of the bar and swinging metal arm on which she had once relied. She remembered perfectly the moment she had decided to do away with them, the moment she had decided to become a "well person," in the vocabulary of the rehab center. It wasn't the dedicated and skillful therapists who had finally convinced her she could become self-sufficient, nor the discussions with her fellow "gimps," as they called each other in gallant self-mockery. The change had occurred when Vince had been sitting for her. She was working on the expression in his eyes, studying him, when suddenly she knew that she loved him. They had looked at each other a long moment, not speaking. Then Vince had smiled, walked over to lift her and hold her to him. Two weeks later she had asked him to take down the pulleys and bars. Vince . . . Everything good in her life was connected to him. Everything good in her life had died with him.

Mary looked over at her chair and leg braces beside the bed, started to get up, then lay back against the pillows. Arguments and questions churned through her mind as they had been doing for nine days, while she waited for a flash of intuition, for an answer to come popping to the surface, a tip-of-the-tongue phenomenon. She stared up again at the traces on the ceiling, wake-up reminders of her old dependencies, and felt courage drain out of her. She had been foolish to allow her pride to interfere; foolish to fear rejection and think she could go it alone. She needed help. But not her brother's. What Thad considered an unhealthy fixation distressed him, and any token indulgence on his part would irritate her. Her boss, Tom Donaldson? A good friend, but not for this particular confidence. Besides, Tom had his hands full these days coping both with the media as well as the News Bureau's regular business. Phil Gertmenian? She had already imposed on him. Phil had stopped by last night to discuss the memorial service for Vince; sensitive to her distress, he had volunteered to take care of everything. Beulah? So many people had been fond of Vince, but she couldn't conceive of confiding in any of them. She needed someone who would listen, but not merely to humor her; someone who was not too close a friend, yet someone she could trust. A young man's smile, the shadowy figure of an earnest teen-age boy who blushed on the rare occasions when she spoke to him during their high school days, a boy who seemed always to be there in the background — waiting . . . A smile, a figure . . . The two floated together into her memory to fuse into the image of Pete Wiggins.

"Elmo? Thad Walker here . . . Yes, it has been a long time. Look, Elmo, I have a favor . . . " He laughed. "Only slightly irregular. I'm working on the Logan shooting . . . That's the one. But my question relates to the first Altamira killing . . . Right, the college president. I'm sending in some bits of thread I'd like you to look at and compare with what was removed from under Julian Merton's fingernails . . . I know it's not my case, but . . . No, I'd rather you didn't mention this to Blessing right now. Or to anyone . . . Come on, Elmo, you know me better than that. We're not into the competition game. I want to be sure about something before discussing it with him . . . You know when I expect your report . . . Right, like yester-day . . ."

Thad Walker hung up the phone, picked up the small plastic envelope containing minute bits of thread, tapped it against his thumb. He was remembering the photograph Brandon had showed him, recalling a woman's brilliant, embracing smile. It occurred to him that he had never seen Anne smile. Possibly he never would.

Brandon Blessing returned to Altamira disgruntled from the early morning drive into LA. Terry Logan's body had been removed from the stack-up confronting the medical examiners, but the post mortem hadn't yet been completed. The technical boys had little to report: no casing, no slug; not surprising, since there was no exit wound. No discernible fresh tire tracks near the area; no significant telltale traces of any kind to be found under the bushes. The killer had left no souvenirs except for the freshly broken twigs of oleander around the spot where he — or she — had presumably hid at the moment of shooting. The distance to the hardened ground from the broken off or crushed parts of the bushes indicated the estimated height of the murderer as between six feet and and six-three. Dean Parker-Brown was six-one. But her running suit and shoes showed no bits of twigs, or residue from flowers or leaves, no traces of nitrate powder and, so the policewoman had reported, the Dean had worn nothing but light underwear under the suit. And the sourest note of all: the thread on her running gear did not match with what had been found on Julian Merton's body. Lieutenant Inocencio Mendez's Saint Anthony had not come through.

To bring Brandon's gloom ratio up to ninety-nine percent of possible, the Sheriff's discontent at the lack of progress was growing louder and meaner, the media were having a field day, the Mayor of Altamira had begun to chime in with her dissatisfaction, and his dutiful third attempt to locate Sally Cochran, the Chairman of Ways and Means, had been unsuccessful. The Señora and her husband remained incommunicado on their boat off Cabo San Lucas. Date of return, according to the soft Hispanic voice, remained an uncertain "sometime soon." He'd give it one more day, then get in touch with the Mexican authorities.

At a little past noon, the call came from forensics giving a summary of the autopsy performed on Terry Logan, adding nothing he didn't know or suspect. The slug, from a .32, had entered from the front, passing through the sternum to lodge in the heart muscle. There were no signs of physical aggression; she had not been raped. Written report to follow. Brandon let the phone drop into its cradle. The outer edge of the oleander plantings was about seven feet from that part of the track where Terry fell. Who had called out to her? Gotten her to turn? To leave the inside lane? Maybe it wasn't anybody she knew. Maybe he was completely off base about the dean. Brandon reached automatically for his candy pack, then pushed it aside. Only good news from San Francisco could brighten his state of mind. In the meantime, there was one more chore to be done. In the interest of tidiness. And to quiet the small but nagging doubt Thad Walker had planted in his mind. Brandon rose dutifully to his feet.

Priscilla Merton exploded.

"Absolutely not! You have no right . . . " She turned to go down the entrance hall toward a phone. "I'm going to call my lawyer."

"One moment, please, Mrs. Merton. I have only a few questions — and you may certainly be present."

"The child has been profoundly disturbed by what has happened. I can't allow her to be upset any further."

"It's up to you, Mrs. Merton, whether I get a court order or not. You have quoted your daughter to me. I think it's important that I hear what she has to say herself."

Priscilla's inimical expression slowly collapsed into one of resignation.

"I'll bring Cissy to you, Sergeant."

The sullen fifteen-year-old who faced him in the Mertons' study was not the toughest-looking specimen of adolescent rebellion he had encountered, but she would do. Brandon took in the stony-eyed expression, the lack of makeup, the hair, cropped since the last time he had seen her to near-penitentiary length, the blue jeans, bare feet, tank top with a monster painted on the front — and the bitten nails.

Priscilla put a hand on Cissy's shoulder, only to have it shaken off. Silently she walked over to sit in a window seat behind her daughter.

"One of the last times we met, Cissy, you asked me whether I knew who had killed your father. I'm sorry to say I don't. Not yet. But we will do everything possible to find the person. I want you to believe that."

Cissy gave him a bored look.

"I'd like you to tell me what you remember of the evening your father died. Beginning perhaps with when your mother came home from the reception at Wyndham Hall."

Priscilla Merton stirred in the background, but said nothing.

"What do you want to know?"

"You were going to a party, I believe."

"Yeah."

"And your mother came home before you left?"

She flicked a quick glance at her mother before answering. "Sure."

"What time was that?"

Cissy nibbled at a hang nail before answering. "A little after six, I guess."

"And what time did your date come by for you?"

"Six-thirty."

"You're certain of that?"

Cissy rolled her eyes in exasperation. "Mike Talbot is always on time. He's got this dopey mother who is always preaching about punctuality being the privilege of kings."

She darted a look Brandon's way to see what his reaction would be.

Sergeant Blessing remained expressionless.

"You're fifteen, aren't you, Cissy?"

"Yes."

"I believe I heard this was a first date?"

She shrugged. "Big deal."

"Was it a good party?"

Again a shrug. Then she added languidly, "Randy Tung brought some booze and Jennifer Mokrej got drunk and barfed all over the living room rug. Gross."

Brandon ignored the opening to explore a teenage party scene. "Was there anyone here at the house before you left for the party?"

"Lucinda. She's our housekeeper."

"And your mother was with you until you left?"

"Yes."

"What did you talk about?" Cissy shrugged. "You don't get along with your mother?"

Brandon was aware of movement on the window seat, but again Priscilla remained silent.

Cissy averted her eyes and muttered something.

"I didn't hear you, Cissy. What did you say?"

She raised her voice, "I said, sometimes I don't."

"What time did you get home from your party?"

"Eleven."

"And you learned about your father then?"

She nodded.

"Who told you?"

A jerk of the head toward the window seat. "Her."

"Your mother was here alone?"

"No. Mrs. Lowenthal was with her. Doctor Lowenthal had given her something, but she came downstairs when she heard me come in."

"You were together for a while, then?"

"No. She was kinda dopey from the medicine. Kept saying how we needed each other. Then Mrs. Lowenthal went back upstairs with her."

"Why have you said your mother killed your father?"

"Because."

"That's not an answer. Because why?"

The look of sophisticated disdain crumbled. It was a child who broke into tears. Brandon could barely make out the words distorted by sobbing: "I want my Daddy . . . "

He went over to the window seat. Priscilla looked up at him.

"I trust you're satisfied, Sergeant."

He thanked her for her cooperation.

Cissy stood at the hall window watching as Brandon Blessing went down the walk to his car. She then sauntered back into the living room where Priscilla still sat in the window seat.

"That policeman sure asked dumb questions."

Priscilla didn't seem to hear.

"How did you like my act?"

The VPs had assembled in Anne's office for a brief meeting, brought together for a change by college matters. The murder investigations hadn't been mentioned once. They were now on their feet, the men getting ready to leave, when Victor caught everyone's attention.

"I think you all know that Turner and I now have copies of the Croft inventory." He had decided to be gentlemanly and say nothing about Turner's sitting on the information. "Anybody else want one?"

"I think I should have a copy,"Anne said. "And Mr. Filmore."

Victor drew his brows together in puzzlement. "Doesn't he have the original that Riley unearthed? The one that went to the president?"

"That I don't know," Anne said.

"I do," Turner put in. "It's been misplaced; at least Beulah hasn't located it yet. Good thing Riley was farsighted enough to make copies."

Henry Norton scratched an elbow, nodding. "Vince never made assumptions or left anything to chance. That was his one piece of advice to me when I came over to Wyndham. The best advice I received."

They began to move off once again, when Anne stopped them this time. "Any luck, Victor, on tracking down the Crofts?"

"Not yet. We've got a new lead to run down; the controller's office is working on it. Looks like the college disposed of some of the pieces. There's a 'sold' stamped by five items in the inventory: an imperial jade necklace among other things. Damn it. I phoned an art appraiser we've worked with; he said if we had it to sell now, that single piece could go for about a million bucks."

"Can't we find a record of the sale?" Turner asked.

"The business offices, like most offices around this place, have been moved several times since 1925. Four to be exact — two before the computer age. You know what happens to records that get switched around."

"Mm. I want to go back to something you said, Victor. Why would Tipton have sold part of the collection?" Anne queried. "Seems unusual."

"Not so very," Henry opined. "If the pieces were sold during the Depression."

Victor agreed. "I'll see that you get a copy of the inventory, Anne. You want one of Vince's report too?"

"I have his annual report."

"No, I'm talking about the one on the diskette Mary Walker had. It reads like something Vince wrote for his own files — a kind of log about finding the collection. You want a copy?"

"Why not?" Anne said.

"You've got yours, Turner. Henry?"

Norton raised his right hand to signal halt. "No thanks, Victor. I've got more than enough useless paper on file as it is."

After her colleagues had filed out, Anne sat for a long moment with her hand on the phone. Then she punched in the number.

"Priscilla? This is Anne."

"Yes?"

"I'm confirming that I'll be at the Garden Grove Cemetery at ten tomorrow morning. But under the circumstances I can't possibly read the Baudelaire."

"Under the circumstances I don't expect you to."

At twelve-thirty, Thad Walker and Brandon met at Solly's to be cheerily greeted by the Veteran, who now considered them her property. Placed at her table and docilely accepting her recommendations for lunch, the two officers dispiritedly exchanged notes.

Brandon reported on his talk with Cissy Merton, stubbornly refraining from mentioning that he had left the president's house less certain about Priscilla Merton than when he had arrived. He had not found Cissy Merton's outburst reassuring. The entire interview had left him with an itch he couldn't get at to scratch.

Thad reported that his investigation hadn't flushed any enemies, personal or professional, and the blackmail theory was fading fast. The Wednesday morning activities of the main players at Wyndham Hall had been checked out. Victor Laszlo had indeed breakfasted at the LA Metropolitan Club after having spent the night there. "Too soused to drive home," was Thad's judgment. Phil Gertmenian had been helping his invalid father with his morning toilet. A neighbor had seen Henry Norton go by at "some time around six maybe," they had waved to each other. The Dean of Students' house was about an eighth of a mile from the track. Henry himself explained that he had walked around for fifteen-twenty minutes, then gone back to the house. Lucille Norton had confirmed. Kitty Van Voorhees heard her husband rattling around downstairs about six; the noise had awakened her. And a *Ledger* paperboy "was pretty sure" he had seen someone answering Van Voorhees's description running west on Sixth Street 'around 6:40,' about a mile from the track. Turner himself said he left the house close to quarter after six, ran about five miles: south on Ridgeway, his street; then west on sixth to Mountain View, then back by the same route.

"So where does that leave us?" Brandon wondered.

"Stuck," Thad said. "You think we should collect all those jogging outfits and run them through the lab?"

Brandon shook his head. "Useless. If there's one out there we shouldn't see, it will have gone through heavy-duty laundering by now — or conveniently disappeared. Besides, it wouldn't help us with Merton's murder, either. Turns out the metallic embroidery thread is American made; the lab reported that the thread under Merton's fingernails was manufactured in Japan." He gave his forehead a hard rub, as though to stimulate thought.

Thad considered telling Brandon what he had done, then reconsidered. Perhaps there would be no need to tell him anything.

"Maybe we should take a harder look at what people were wearing at that reception."

"Good idea," Thad said hurriedly. "I'll take on the gun check — run names through registration. I've already got men on a visual search of likely places around town, such as dumpsters. Garbage pickup isn't until Friday, which may be a help. And we'll check out the R.O.T.C. arms room."

Brandon's eyebrows shot up.

"The college's R.O.T.C. program keeps guns in a room at the gym." Thad smiled at the look of horror on Sergeant Blessing's face.

"You can't be serious."

"But I am."

"Cripes. These people are living in the last century where security is concerned."

"Everything is carefully locked up, of course."

Brandon grunted. "I've heard from Mark Tidwell about how safe lock-ups are around here." He stirred up the thick layer of sugar in his tea and drained the glass. "We'll give it a last go, Thad, but I'm beginning to think you may be right: It's looking more and more like a sniper type killing. Unless —" and he almost brightened — "unless Pete unearths something in San Francisco that would justify a judge giving us a search warrant."

"For Parker-Brown's house, you mean."

"Yep. That's what I mean. Does that look like chocolate pie, there in the case?"

Brandon was chatting with Joelle Lieberman at four in the afternoon and taking the opportunity to quiz her on what people wore at the reception when the call came. He hurried back down to the basement office.

"Brandon?"

"Yeah, Pete."

"This was duck soup."

Brandon pulled the chair up closer to the table and leaned expectantly into the phone.

"I've got something kind of interesting about those two nights Julian Merton wasn't at the Pericles Society . . ."

"I'm listening."

"He checked into the Cortez Hotel late on the sixteenth and checked out the evening of the eighteenth — about eleven. Both times alone. He took a midnight flight back to Altamira."

"That's fine, kid, but that doesn't mean he wasn't checked in someplace else as well."

"No, except that he had room service all three evenings: two meals and one late coffee and pie — also two early breakfasts. Service for one. And the hotel people know him."

"How do we know two people didn't partake?"

"Right. But the staff is certain he was alone."

The phone crackled with Brandon's sigh.

"Nobody at Merton's hotel, the Cortez, recognized Dean Parker-Brown's picture. She's pretty hard to overlook."

Brandon was not impressed by the Wiggins reasoning. "Haven't you ever heard of hanky-panky in the afternoon?"

"Sure. I saw a movie about it once."

Brandon grunted. "Well then, keep looking. Maybe they met away from their respective hotels."

"I think I can save the taxpayers some money."

"Yeah?"

"Looks like Merton was involved in activities at the Pericles Society during the daytime. Both days. That's what accounts for the extra mileage on the rented car. Two and a half round trips."

Brandon threw down his pencil and reached for his candy. "I like it. Keep going."

"He did have that one afternoon business meeting with the chairman of the Finance Committee and Van Voorhees on the eighteenth, around four, remember? They were in the bar at the Windsor until about seven. Then had dinner in the hotel dining room. Other than that, I don't know what he was doing in the city. But I know he called her from his room at the Society's club house."

"What!"

"You heard me. He phoned her hotel from Napa Valley twice: the afternoon of the sixteenth at four and on the seventeenth, at ten a. m."

"Yeah? How did you get access to the phone company's records?"

"Lieutenant Pachman. He got me a subpoena. I lucked out, Brandon: found a supervisor who worked fast. She said I looked like her son."

"You look like every mother's son, kid."

"Thanks. I guess. The first call lasted almost thirty minutes; the second, about three." There was silence at Brandon's end. "Lieutenant Pachman is working with the San Francisco phone company. He'll get back to us tomorrow about any local calls between their rooms at the Cortez and the Carlton.

"OK. Tell Sam he has my undying gratitude. Next?"

"I showed the folks at the Carlton pictures of the dean and of the president. A desk clerk and a couple of maids remembered her. Because of her height — and all that red hair. Her bill checks out with what she told you; two local calls. No dining room charges. She could have paid cash. One waiter thinks he remembers her. But nobody recalled having seen him. OK to come home?"

Brandon murmured an affirmative, sighed, and put down the phone. Moments later he was trudging up the stairs to the second floor.

Anne came around her desk and gestured the detective toward an armchair at the west end of the office, near the windows. She took the one opposite him.

"I hope I'm not going to be hearing the same refrain, Sergeant."

Brandon seemed to be considering the scuffed toes of his shoes. "Well, yes and no."

"Does that mean you have good news and bad news?"

"I'll be straight with you, Dean. Except for the fact that Professor Logan was shot by someone about your height, I have nothing to connect you with her death."

"I can't say I'm surprised."

"At the present time, that is."

"You are a diehard, Sergeant."

"Yes ma'am. And you're a stubborn lady. You haven't been straight with me, Dean."

"How so?"

"I've got two murders on my hands, Dean Parker-Brown. And murders aren't civilized. I figure you people don't like to think about things that aren't civilized — unless they're things that have happened in books maybe." He stopped abruptly.

Anne's gaze was steady, almost sympathetic. "I'm not going to argue the point, Sergeant."

"What is it you're hiding about San Francisco?"

"But I've told you . . . "

"Don't give me that again. You finessed me. You talked to Merton on the phone. At least twice. And I want to know why and about what."

"It's a personal matter. It only concerns me, Sergeant."

Brandon stared at her, unblinking, during a long silence.

"I'm going to insist, Dean. Do I have to say at this point that it's in your interest to be up front with me?"

Anne looked out the window, trying to steady herself. The idea of discussing her most private feelings with this deadpan, pouty-mouthed policeman was repugnant. It flashed through her mind that it would be less embarrassing than if Thad Walker were opposite her at this moment. She didn't stop to wonder why.

"Very well." Anne leaned her head back against the chair for a second, then met Brandon's unwavering gaze with her own. He felt a slight jolt at the unexpected look of sorrow in her eyes.

"Julian Merton was never my lover, Sergeant. That is a categorical statement. He was, however, a very seductive man, with a talent for creating a sense of shared understanding. Quick at making someone, someone like myself, feel needed — and privileged at sharing a — a quite special relationship."

"Why do you say 'someone like yourself,' Dean?"

Anne sketched a half smile. "I don't wish to dwell on it, Sergeant, but I believe anyone who lives alone experiences moments of loneliness."

"Yes ma'am. But what do you mean by a 'special relationship'?"

"There was, at least for a while, a strong rapport between us. The attraction between people with shared intellectual and personal perspectives."

"That means no sex?"

She hesitated, looking uncomfortable. "It is possible, Sergeant, to have scruples, however old-fashioned about sleeping with a married man — or with one's employer.

"Yeah?"

"Let's just say that I began to see President Merton in a new light." She folded and unfolded her hands, twisting the wedding ring on her left hand. "I was not comfortable with what I saw."

"I'd appreciate knowing what that was."

Anne took a deep breath, like a novice diver about to go off the high board. "An opportunist. A user of people." She hesitated, then plunged on. "A cold, even ruthless individual."

"Maybe he had grown cold toward you."

She stiffened. "Don't cling to the idea of the rejected woman, Sergeant. I wasn't. I suppose," she said, in a detached tone of voice, "I suppose one might say I was toyed with."

"Huh?"

"I mean he became increasingly capricious."

"How do you mean."

"I'd rather leave it at that."

"I'd rather you didn't, Dean Parker-Brown. In your own interest."

She looked hard at him, then mimed a gesture of surrender. "Julian Merton would treat me as a special confidante, as someone essential to his life and to his work. Both as dean and as a friend. The next moment he could be not only distant, but inimical. Even rude. That is what I meant by capricious. I made the decision to go about my job and stop being affected by his mercurial moods — or by his appeals for attention."

Brandon made a quick mental note of "mercurial" and waited for her to continue.

"Unfortunately, my attitude seemed to be a challenge to the president. I see no reason to go into details of the various stratagems he used. Before

I left on vacation, for Nepal, President Merton asked me to meet him in San Francisco. He felt it was imperative that we get things straightened out — on an 'even keel' was the way he put it — before the start of the academic year. He said many things — some I mistrusted as self-serving or as false honesty. Others I believed to be sincere. The argument about a fresh start, clearing the air, was persuasive. I agreed we'd meet in San Francisco, when he planned to be there for the Pericles Outing."

"So, where and when did you get together?"

"We didn't."

"Why not?"

"Because of the first phone call. Things he said. I'm quite sure he had been drinking — which was exceptional in itself. I realized it would be a mistake for us to meet."

"It took you quite a while to decide to say 'no', didn't it?"

She frowned. "I don't understand."

"You and President Merton talked for a good half hour."

Anne didn't react. The two studied each other for a long moment, then Brandon asked, "What did he have in mind? Did he want you to go to bed with him?" She turned away momentarily at his bluntness. "So, that means he did."

She withheld assent or dissent, going on to say, "When things didn't go his way, he suggested that the meeting in San Francisco had been my idea and it was a bad one. It was clear to me that nothing had changed. That he was playing the same old games."

"What old games, Dean?"

The answer came reluctantly. "Julian Merton needed to manipulate people, to dominate them. Any indifference, in this case my indifference — or independence — was intolerable."

"You insist that you didn't see him?"

"Unequivocally."

"And the second call?"

"It began as a bad replay of the first. I hung up."

"How many times did he call you?"

"Twice — from the Pericles Society. At least he said that's where he was."

"He didn't call you from San Francisco? From the Cortez for instance?"

"If he did, I wasn't in."

"And that was it?"

"Yes."

"You're certain. No further contact?"

"That's correct."

Brandon reflected on what she had said for quite a while. Anne, too, seemed lost in thought. Then she stood up. "Sergeant, I should like to make it clear that I consider this matter to be closed."

He seemed to be thinking it over but made no direct reply. He got slowly to his feet. "Thank you, Dean Parker-Brown." And quietly left her office.

In the basement he stopped by the News Bureau and borrowed a dictionary. He looked up "mercurial," and then the word Filmore had thrown at him a few days ago: "animus." The former, he thought, would fit nearly all the people in this case. The latter aptly described the way he felt right now about Tipton College. The dean had cleared up a number of things, but she had not exonerated herself. He felt better; he was back on track.

Wheeling out of the mail room, Mary was hailed by Max Dingam. As they talked, she caught a glimpse of Jeff Colton out of the corner of her eye; he seemed to be waiting for her. She finished the conversation with Max, thanked him for the folder he handed her, and called to Jeff.

"Were you looking for me?"

"Yes ma'am." He seemed ill at ease.

"Is there something I can do?"

"I know how much Vince thought of you, Miss Walker, and I was wondering . . . I would sure like to have something to remember him by."

"Of course, Jeff. Vince would be pleased you wanted something of his. Is there anything in particular you would like?"

"Yes, ma'am, there is. Those three little monkeys on his desk . . . Would that be OK? Vince said they had taught him all he knew."

Mary laughed. "You're right. Of course you may have them. Stop by my office some time this afternoon."

Rosalie greeted her with a "Turner Van Voorhees is on line two" when she rolled through the door.

"Yes, Turner?"

"Mary, Max Dingam tells me you're looking for an inventory of the Croft collection. I'll be glad to have a copy made for you."

She interrupted. "Thanks, Turner, but Max just gave me one; he found a copy."

"You're ahead of me. So Max found the original?"

"No, a Xerox. It was filed under 'Laszlo' — with Laszlo's copy and the copy of some memorandum or other directed to Victor."

"I see. Well, that clears up one mystery. I understand you're planning a piece on the collection for the magazine?"

"Thinking about it, yes."

"Victor will be pleased. Good-bye, Mary."

Mary hung up and made a note to retrieve the monkeys from Vince's office. They were the traditional threesome sold in Chinatowns everywhere: Hear no Evil, See No Evil, Speak No Evil. At a little after four Jeff came by to get his remembrance. She detained him as he was leaving.

"Jeff, you were with Vince when those Asian things were moved to the vault, weren't you?"

"Yes ma'am, that's right."

"Did Vince discuss the collection with you at all? Say anything about it?"

Jeff thought a moment. "He explained to me about those little bottles — for snuff, you know? I got a kick out of that. My granny used to dip snuff. And he said the stuff was probably worth a lot of money."

"And that was all he said."

"Yes ma'am." He thought a moment. "He did ask me something. But it was some days later, I think."

"What was that?"

"He asked me if I remembered having seen something — a dish of some kind, I think it was. With peaches carved on it."

"Did he say why he was interested in it?"

"No ma'am. He sure didn't."

Mary retrieved a key from its place in the file drawer and took the elevator to the second floor. Beulah accompanied her to the vault to clear a passage for her chair. Photographs and maps had been removed from two large bureau drawers to make room for temporary storage of the Croft collection.

Mary opened the top drawer, removed the protective cloth.

"It's a shame to see those beautiful things jumbled up like that," Beulah remarked.

Mary nodded. "I know next to nothing about jade, but this certainly looks like an extraordinary gift.

I wonder why some of the pieces weren't on display?"

"Perhaps they were at one time. Now that we know the name of the donors, Development is working on it. And the museum curator too. The collection may have been housed there in earlier days. I've got to get back to work. Let me know if you need any help."

"Thanks, Beulah."

Mary removed the photocopied inventory from her bag, carefully moved pieces around in the top drawer, small pieces, such as Chinese snuff bottles, jade buckles, and a few Japanese items, mostly eighteenth-century ivory *netsukes*. No sign of a jade bowl like the one listed on the inventory, the one Jeff had mentioned. It was, however, in the second drawer, wrapped in a silk cloth. It was indeed a lovely thing, a small piece of a translucent pale green, about eight inches in diameter, and carved with bats, vines, and peaches. Peaches, Mary recalled from a course in Chinese history with Professor Ho, were a symbol of longevity. Finding the bowl had not brought this good fortune to Vince Riley.

At five Thad Walker strode into Brandon's basement office in Wyndham and put a large packet on the table.

"Present for you."

Sergeant Blessing gave his colleague a woebegone look. "Thanks — just in time." He ripped the package open and dipped in for a handful.

"Well, what news on the Rialto?"

"Dead end, Brandon. Or so it seems. I met Terry's parents. Pretty wonderful people."

"I hear they want the body sent home to Oregon as soon as possible."

"Right. Dean Parker-Brown had lunch with them. She told me they stipulated no services be held here at Tipton."

"Mad at the college?"

"I don't know. I gather they think it more appropriate to hold the services in her home town."

"Any idea of who might have killed their daughter?"

Thad shook his head. "None. Before her fight for tenure last spring, Ms. Logan seemed satisfied with her life here. If she had any enemies, she never said anything to her parents."

"You'll be glad to hear they told reporters that putting a face and a name on the person who killed their daughter would do nothing to help them in their grief. Mr. Logan remarked that he knew the police were doing their best."

"Good for Mr. Logan. He's right on the button."

"What's this burst of optimism?"

"That may be going too far. Let's say I've had some encouragement. A call from Pete Wiggins." Brandon reported on the telephone conversation and his follow-up interview with Dean Parker-Brown.

"Interesting, but no cigar. I don't understand your reading, Brandon. Seems to me that what she told you would tend to let her off the hook."

He shook his head. "What the woman laid out for me was an emotional blueprint for murder. She hated the guy."

Thad Walker did not look pleased. "You're reaching for it, Brandon. And I think you know it."

Brandon frowned. "She's hiding something, Thad. Something about San Francisco. I can feel it in my gut."

At a little past five Crystal Mathews and Willie Hefner were sitting in a dark corner of the Grapevine bar. Willie was brooding over a phone call from Jerry Lazeroff speaking for the trustees of the college. A. Jerrold Lazeroff, Esquire, had suggested that henceforth the *Ledger* exercise discretion and the highest standards of journalism in its coverage of the events at Tipton College. The possible legal consequences of irresponsible and harmful journalism had been expressed concisely and in silken tones, but the warning was as clear as the intimation of power and influence behind it.

Crystal, who had merrily recounted "my day" over the first martini, had drifted into a sullen mood during the consumption of the second.

"I hope you've got it straight, Willie. I'm not going to lose my job because of the nasty twist you give to whatever I tell you. Turner is a doll, but when you've been chewed out, boy, you know it."

As her complaint lengthened, Willie stopped listening, his mind on tomorrow's special issue on the progress of what had become the "Tipton College Murders." The original headline for the story on Terry Logan had been discarded after Lazeroff's phone call. "Prominent Member of Gay Community Shot" had been replaced with "Psychology Prof Shot at Track." But he had had an inspiration; an idea that consoled him for the loss in shock effect. It was subtle, but the college readers would get the point, as would the people who counted in town, while he could claim innocence of any ulterior motive. An idea that would well illustrate the old saw about one picture being worth a thousand words. In this case it would be four pictures.

In the Wyndham Hall parking lot, Brandon Blessing hailed Beulah Taper as she was about to get into her car.

"Sorry to bother you, Miss Taper, but if I might have a moment."

"Of course. But I suggest we get out of the sun." She led the way to a bench under a magnolia tree near the entrance to the Hall.

"I have a couple of things to ask you about what people were wearing at Mr. Finlay's reception."

"I thought we'd already discussed that, Sergeant."

"That's right. Just want to be sure I've got it all straight. And please be as detailed as possible."

"Very well. Where shall I begin?"

"With the vice presidents and their assistants."

Brandon listened to descriptions with which he was familiar; for a moment his attention wandered, then he came to with a start.

"Excuse me. Let me have that again."

"I said, Turner Van Voorhees was wearing a navy blue blazer with a crest on the pocket. His preparatory school emblem."

Brandon rang the bell by the handsome tall double doors of the Van Voorhees residence. It was Turner who answered.

"May I come in for a minute, Mr. Van Voorhees?"

Turner gestured agreement. "This is not a very convenient time for a call, Sergeant."

"I suppose not."

"Well?"

"I understand you have a blazer with a crest on the pocket."

Turner was visibly startled.

"Why, yes."

"Might I see it?"

"Now look here, Sergeant, I'm not sure you have the right . . . "

Brandon interrupted. "No sir. Not without a warrant. But in a case like this it pays us to be tidy. And it saves time. There are always unexplained problems that can be cleared away by people volunteering cooperation."

"Tidy, eh? Very well." He laughed. "I volunteer. This way."

He led the way upstairs to the master bedroom suite and a large walk-in closet, where everything was arranged in impeccable order. Brandon thought of the crowded jumble of clothes in the closet he shared with his wife and sighed.

Turner went to a section where some ten jackets hung together, took out a light weight navy blue blazer and handed it to Brandon. The sergeant studied the crest carefully, felt it, bent to examine the threads more carefully, then handed it back.

"Is this what you wore at the reception for Mr. Finlay?"

"That's right. But I answered that question earlier, Sergeant."

"Yessir. But nothing was said about this emblem on the pocket."

Turner shrugged. "Any reason I should have? Don't believe I described the lining either, or the label."

He was obviously annoyed. Brandon, just as obviously, paid no attention.

"Have you others? With your school crest?"

"I have one, winter weight. I suppose you would like to see that as well?"

Turner unzipped a moth-proof garment bag, extricated a blue worsted blazer. Brandon examined it in the same manner. He took his notebook from a pocket, made a quick sketch of the emblem, then handed back the jacket, pointing to the crest.

"I guess that's a Latin inscription."

"Right." Turner smiled. "It means 'Fortune favors the bold.'"

"Do you believe that, Mr. Van Voorhees?"

"Only up to a point, Sergeant."

"Well, thank you. These emblems are ordered from the school, aren't they?"

"Yes. Pittfield Academy. But mine are from the days when I was a student there. And that's some seventeen years ago."

"Have you any others?"

"Patches? No. If you would like to go through the bureau drawers . . . "

"That won't be necessary. Uh, that Pittfield Academy. Is it back East?"

"That's right," Turner said patiently. "Hanover, Vermont."

"Thanks. Sorry to inconvenience you, Mr. Van Voorhees."

As he was letting the officer out, Turner said, "I hope this clears up one of those little problems you were talking about, Sergeant."

"So do I, Mr. Van Voorhees." Brandon did not sound confident.

At nine p. m. Angelo's friend had just backed the car out of the reserved slot when a light shone out from the offices of Buildings and Grounds. The friend drove slowly around the parking lot and on into the area that was to the south of Wyndham. There were only two cars to be seen: Jeff Colton's old pick-up and Mary Walker's Acura.

The friend drove out of the lot and parked in a shadowy spot near Bosman Hall of Music. From here it was easy to cut across Thorndyke quadrangle and go along behind the plantings bordering the western side of Wyndham. Angelo's friend had a clear view into much of the space occupied by Buildings and Grounds.

Mary Walker was working at Vincent Riley's computer. Angel's friend could see the screen, but the displayed text wasn't legible. Mary typed a number of letters at a time, then paused and cleared. After each try she checked something off on the pad beside her. Evidently discouraged, she flipped the notebook shut, ejected a disk and turned off the machine. Both diskette and notebook were slipped into the bag attached to the side of her chair.

Disgusting cripple. At it again, was she? Maybe the diskette she had sent upstairs wasn't Riley's original. Was that it? Or was there another one? One that wasn't compatible with the News

Bureau's computer? Something she couldn't get at? Something she shouldn't get at. Meddling freak. Dangerous freak. The fetish tune sounded through Dodie's head like a merry-go-round calliope. Dodie would know what to do. Dodie always did.

Mary stopped at the door of Vince's office and switched on the light for a moment. His desk was still just as he had left it: his old Seth Thomas clock, a pen set, a forty-year-old photo of his family taken on the farm in Mangum. Only the three little monkey figures were now missing.

Heading for home Angelo's friend passed Mary's car going the other way. She gave a short honk of recognition. The friend honked and waved back. Quite merrily — and smiled at the pun.

Friday, 28 July

Brandon blessing rose at six to place a call to Hanover, Vermont.

The uppity secretary to the headmaster of Pittfield Academy reluctantly agreed to put him through to the manager of the school store. The latter was somewhat more cooperative, but equally nasal.

"I'm quite positive. Sergeant. Pittfield's patches are embroidered with cotton or silk thread. Always have been. We would *never* use a shiny metallic product."

Brandon thanked her and hung up. A question had been answered, and he had received a freebie from the Eastern seaboard: a lesson in good taste. He was not particularly grateful.

Lieutenant Sam Pachman, San Francisco P. D., read the note his partner had left him. The records at the phone company showed a call placed from the Carlton, the Dean's hotel, to the La Tour restaurant on July 16th at 4 p.m. and a call to the Windsor Hotel on July 18th at 9:45 p.m. As soon as he had his eye opener under his belt, he'd pass the info along to Brandon Blessing.

At 7:30 Pete had just made a pot of coffee when he heard the sound of rubber tired wheels coming down the hall. He hurried over to the door.

"Hi, Mary."

"Pete, hello."

"You're at work awfully early."

"With this heat I'd rather be up and at it. Besides, all Wyndham has the afternoon off. Good day for getting a lot done, with everyone gone."

"I heard something about that. Mrs. Merton's request?"

"Yes." She smiled up at him. Once again he felt a yearning to serve her in some way. And realized once again that he wasn't blushing.

"What's the matter?"

"Huh?"

"You're staring."

"Oh, sorry. Guess I'm a bit groggy. Just got back from San Francisco and haven't had much sleep."

"Fruitful trip?"

"Hope so."

She nodded absently. "Pete, could I talk to you a minute?"

"Sure. Would you like a cup of coffee?"

She shook her head and propelled her chair into the room. Pete sat down near her, at the big table.

"I'm listening."

She fidgeted with the wheels of her chair a moment. "Pete, am I a fool to think that Vince was murdered?"

That was blunt enough. Pete knew Thad's thoughts on the matter: that it wasn't a kindness to his sister to encourage her illusions, yet he couldn't bring himself to cut her off.

"I'm more puzzled than anything, Mary. As to why you seem so convinced, I mean. There hasn't been anything to go on, has there? Except your intuition." He smiled. "And a footprint."

"It does seem ridiculous, doesn't it?"

Pete made a hasty and embarrassed retreat. "No, I didn't mean that. Just that, by itself, it's not very significant. Why do you believe it was made by the runner you saw?"

"I suppose because it seemed like such an unusual hour."

"Aren't there other joggers who regularly use your street?"

She nodded. "Several. But I've never seen anyone running that late. I suppose I'm grasping at straws. I sketched a number of the college regulars the other day at the track . . . I thought I might pin down something that would match with the drawing I did that night. But it was a flop." The words were spoken on a drawn-out sigh. Then she leaned forward slightly, intense, hands tightly clasped in her lap.

"Still, there are so many odd bits and tag ends. I can't get them out of my head, Pete, but I can't fit them together either."

"Well, if you want to try me, Mary . . . Tell me about the odd bits — and we'll give it a whirl."

"Before you start whirling, laddy, we need to talk. Excuse me, Ms. Walker."

Brandon strode into the room, mopping his brow. Pete accompanied Mary into the hall.

"I'll stop by as soon as I can, OK?"

Mary thanked him and turned her chair toward the north end of the hall. Pete stood there a moment, impatient with his own helplessness as he watched her push herself forward.

"Pete?"

"Yes sir."

"Shoot."

Brandon was installed at the table, open notebook in front of him. He listened attentively as Pete reviewed again and in detail his San Francisco investigation. "Good work, kid." He smiled. It was fleeting and Pete almost missed it, but it was unmistakably a regular, common, or garden variety smile.

"Thanks, Brandon. Still, not quite what you had hoped for, is it?"

"Oh, I don't know." Brandon removed half the day's ration from his pocket, placed the bag on the table.

"Whether they had sex someplace may or may not be important. The thing is, they had planned to meet and they talked on the phone. It all fits in." Brandon recounted his interview with the dean. "A real sad story — complete with gypsy violins. Still, I gotta admit she was convincing."

"But you don't think she was telling you the truth?"

Brandon rubbed his left cheek. "Partial truth. She confirmed what I've believed all along: that Merton had given her a rough time. But she was too smooth, like she had rehearsed her story — delivery, gestures, the works. Still and all, it's pretty clear to me that something was eating her up. The only way a woman like that could live with herself —" he sighed — "would be to eliminate the source of the pain — and the rage."

Pete was silent a moment. "But what about that thread under Merton's fingernails?"

Brandon shook his head. "That's still a blurred part of the picture. She may have been wearing or carrying something that we haven't turned up yet." He flipped over some pages in his notebook while recounting his visit to the Van Voorhees home and showed Pete the sketch of Turner's school emblem, a shield surrounded by a banner with a Latin text, *Audaces fortuna juvat,* and the words "Pittfield Academy."

"What does the inscription mean?"

"He said it meant something like 'Fortune favors the bold.'"

"Do you think that explains why I'm not rich?"

"Search me, kid. Maybe it explains why he is." He studied the drawing again. "Van Voorhees was wearing a jacket with this emblem at the reception. A connection between this patch and Merton's body could have changed a lot of things. But . . . " There was a snort that Pete interpreted as Brandonian disdain, "for your info, metallic thread is too vulgar for the preppies at Pittfield."

"You know, Brandon, we can't rule out that someone other than the killer came in when Merton was dying."

Brandon wasn't listening. "Maybe we'll find something in the dean's office or her closet at home."

"So you're going to ask for a search warrant?"

"I'm going to do more than that, kid. I have an appointment with the D. A. this afternoon. Frank Murphy's hot to trot, and I think we've got enough to bring her in."

Thad Walker phoned in a few minutes later. Gun registration had nothing of record for anyone at the college, except a Colt .38 registered to Jeff Colton and a Winchester .22 registered to Vince Riley. Nothing as yet from the R.O.T.C. arms room in Pusey gym.

"We'll keep looking, Brandon."

A long sigh drifted through the receiver.

Brandon Blessing and Pete Wiggins observed the late morning graveside scene from a distance: the Victor Laszlos, the Henry Nortons and the Van Voorheeses stood at one end of the open grave. Anne Parker-Brown and Beulah Taper with Dr. and Mrs. Lowenthal were on one side with trustees Jerry Lazeroff and Neville Barnes; Julian's father, his wife and daughter on the other. Priscilla, in a navy blue dress and wide brimmed hat moved from her father-in-law's side to stand near the grave marker. She opened a book and began to read.

Brandon nodded to Pete and moved off toward his car. He was going back to his office for a meeting with Lieutenant Inocencio Mendez, then on into LA.

"Don't expect me before five."

Brandon was unlocking his car when Thad Walker pulled up and got out.

"Hi, Thad. What gives?"

"I had a call a short while ago from the lab, from Elmo."

"Yeah? And?" Spit it out, Brandon thought. Why did Thad look worried?

"They've identified some bits of thread and lint on the president's jacket."

Brandon almost smiled. "Let me guess. From one of the dean's exercise suits, right?"

Thad shook his head. "From a jacket she keeps in her office closet. An embroidered jacket," he added.

"Oh." Brandon studied the Chief a long moment. "I don't want to know how the lab got the sample, do I?"

"Nope."

"Does any of that stuff match up with what was under his fingernails?"

"No."

"Where did they find the thread and lint?"

"From the underside of the right sleeve — between the cuff and the elbow."

Brandon chewed on that a moment. "So he could have had his arm around her or she could have been hauling him over to his desk chair."

Thad's face flushed with anger. "He could also have picked up the thread from her office or almost anywhere else in the building. This doesn't nail down your case, Brandon."

"Maybe not. But put it together with everything else and it may be just the little nail I need — along with another one delivered this a.m. by good old Sam Pachman."

"Oh?"

"A few hours before her flight back from San Francisco, the dean phoned the Windsor Hotel. For a dinner reservation, she said. Then changed her mind."

"And?"

"We had quite a chat about phone calls. Kinda interesting she neglected to mention she called the hotel around 9:45. The dining room doesn't take reservations that late. But Merton had dinner there after his meeting; he could have been paged. And remember, his own hotel was practically next door, and he didn't check out until going on eleven. Enough time for cozies — or a fight."

Thad had nothing to say.

Brandon got in his car, stuck his head out the window. "A question, Thad. About your conversation with Elmo. Did you consider not telling me?"

"I considered it."

Brandon nodded. "That figures." He ruminated a moment more. "You know, you were pretty sneaky, Thad."

"So were you with officer Karen Olson."

The two looked at each other a moment, then Brandon said curtly, "OK, we're even," and was on his way.

Thad watched the retreating car, then walked over onto the cemetery grounds. He stood observing the group at Julian Merton's open grave. Even from this distance Anne was readily identifiable by the glory of her hair. It seemed to Thad that its uncontrolled mass was as vibrant, as free and defiant as he imagined Anne's spirit to be. He knew as clearly as though Brandon had spelled it out what would now happen to her. She would be taken to the Pasadena holding facility where she could be held for custodial interrogation for seventy-two hours. The DA would request a preliminary hearing to determine that a murder had been committed and that it could be connected to her. She would be charged with a capital offense — no bail. Guilty or innocent she would be put through the drawn-out, frightening procedure that had broken tougher spirits than hers. And he would be partially responsible. Along with that bitter realization was the equally bitter awareness that he could not have done otherwise.

Cissy buried her shorn head in her grandfather's sleeve as her mother was reading. The others looked down at the ground or off into the distance; except for Anne, who kept her eyes on Priscilla.

"O Death, old Captain, the time has come! Let us weigh anchor! We are weary of this land, O Death! Let us set sail! . . . "

As she finished, Julian's father patted his granddaughter's hand and moved to the head of the grave.

"I shall read from the Psalms."

His resonant voice reached to where Pete Wiggins was standing.

"God is our refuge and strength, a very present help in trouble. Therefore will not we fear, though the earth be removed, and though the mountains be carried into the midst of the sea."

Pete's attention wandered as the familiar words drifted his way. He was suddenly startled out of his day dreaming:

"O my God, I trust in thee: let me not be ashamed, let not mine enemies triumph over me."

So far, Pete thought, it was Merton zero with the enemy scoring. Unless Brandon was right. Studying Anne Parker-Brown, her posture that spoke of composure and quiet strength, he had difficulty picturing her as Brandon did, as a woman whose reason had been consumed by rage; a woman capable of a brutal and criminal act. A good police officer, he tried to remind himself, should have no difficulty separating the impressive facade from the possibility of a demon-ridden soul.

At the conclusion of her grandfather's reading, Cissy picked up some flowers from a basket and passed among the assembled company. Wordlessly, everyone went forward in turn to drop a white rose on the casket. Mr. Merton put an arm around his daughter-in-law and, followed by Cissy, led the small gathering away from the grave and toward the parking area.

"Not much of a send-off, would you say?"

It was Willie Hefner who had come up unnoticed to stand beside Pete.

"What are you doing here?"

"Just looking. I saw your boss leave a moment ago. Headed for LA?"

"Didn't he tell you where he was going?"

"Aw come on, Pete. The Sheriff's office feeds us pap, folks at the college are specialists in 'no comment,' and you guys act as if you were guarding state secrets. Give me a break."

"Would if I could, Willie."

"Yeah? You know what I think? I think you and Blessing are no closer to figuring this thing out than you were four days ago. You've been outfoxed. The Tipton killer gets Logan right under your nose and you guys just keep chasing your tails."

"But you've got it figured, right, Willie? That Logan and the president were killed by the same person?"

"That's right. Either it's a psycho on the loose or it's someone in a panic. Either way, the citizens of Altamira aren't sleeping very easy these days."

"Yeah? How so?"

"Waiting for the killer to hit again."

"Thanks for the analysis, Willie." Pete started to move off.

"Hey, wait a minute. Got a present for you."

He handed him a folded copy of the *Ledger.* "You oughta look at it, in case you haven't."

"Haven't had time. Why the special delivery?"

"Just trying to be helpful, Pete."

Pete nodded curtly and walked away, the unopened copy of the paper stuck in his coat pocket.

The small group that had attended the graveside services got out of their various cars and entered the president's house. There were the usual embraces, tear-filled eyes and murmured words of sympathy as people spoke to Priscilla, Julian's father and Cissy. Priscilla steered people toward the table where Beulah Taper was serving coffee and tea. A subdued Cissy passed a tray of petit fours.

Anne Parker-Brown refused the latter and, carrying her cup of coffee, sat down beside Lucille Norton on one of the sofas that flanked the fireplace.

"It's been ages since I've seen you, Anne. So much has been happening since you got back from your trip. So many dreadful things." Anne nodded. "I think that even my unflappable Henry is beginning to feel the strain."

"Small wonder. We're all feeling unsettled."

Lucille took a sip of coffee, then said, reflectively, "Didn't the service seem, well, minimal, Anne?"

"Priscilla wanted something very simple. There will be a memorial service in the fall."

"Mm. Without esoteric poetry readings, I hope. At least I couldn't understand the reason for that Captain Death thing. Depressing."

Anne didn't comment.

"I don't know how she got through it without breaking down."

"I'm sure it took a lot of — of determination."

"Well, I don't pretend to know much about literature, but the readings from the Psalms seemed more appropriate to me. I thought the quote about not letting the enemies triumph was a real cry from a father's heart." Lucille finished her cake and carefully wiped her fingers on the small linen napkin. "I just don't understand why the police aren't pinning this thing down. Have you heard anything at all?"

Anne was about to answer when she became aware that someone was staring at her. Turning slightly, she saw Cissy standing behind her — a bit off to the side — and encountered her steady gaze. The teenager came closer.

"It's weird, isn't it, Dean Parker-Brown? I mean the person who killed my father is probably right in this room."

Lucille Norton was shocked. "Oh, Cissy, that can't be."

Cissy responded with a bitter little smile and moved away.

Lucille leaned toward Anne to whisper, "That's one peculiar child. I don't envy Priscilla having to see her through adolescence."

Kitty and Turner Van Voorhees were momentarily standing off to themselves.

"How soon can we politely leave, Turner?"

"What's your hurry?"

"It's so grim. And everything I can think of to say is so banal."

"But you did speak to Priscilla?"

"Of course. And to Mr. Merton and Cissy. And the token trustees." She looked around the room.

"This is really quite a handsome house. How much longer will Priscilla be allowed to live here?"

"That has not been discussed. Until a new president takes over, perhaps." He gave his wife a hard look. "Don't tell me you're still harboring that foolish notion?"

Kitty smiled. "You need me to have ambition for you, Turner. You've always underestimated your own talent. Daddy thinks so, too." She lightly touched his cheek and dutifully moved away to be sociable, whispering as she left. "I'm even going to be nice to that dreary wife of Victor's."

Victor Laszlo had joined Dr. Lowenthal. The latter automatically noticed the tremor in Victor's hand as he lifted his cup to his lips and took in the circles under the eyes, the unhealthy skin tone. Well, Victor wasn't his patient. But he did allow himself a "You're looking tired, Victor."

Victor stood up straighter, eyes bright, suddenly his old hearty self. "Not a bit of it, doc. I've never felt better."

As soon as he could, Henry Norton sought out his wife who was now part of a group talking with Priscilla and her father-in-law. He drew her aside. "Say your good-byes, Lucille. We're getting out of here."

Lucille looked askance at him, startled by the tension in his voice and expression.

"Henry, what's the matter? We can't just hurry off . . . "

"We've been polite enough." He lowered his voice, speaking through his teeth. "I'm not up to it this morning. I can't take the social routine, all the sham . . . "

Lucille patted his arm and moved off to obey. There were still moments when her mild-mannered forty-two-year-old Henry regressed to the days of his protest-marked youth.

It was while she was pouring a second cup of coffee for Ruth Lowenthal that it came to her. Beulah had just complimented the doctor's wife on a baroque necklace of gold and jade colored beads when she suddenly saw the memorandum Vince had attached to his report. Not the memo that was there now, but another one. Something about the collection. She could see the words: "Missing jade." And something else. She almost had it. Monday, when she pulled the file and looked at it, the memo would come back to her in its entirety, she was sure of it.

Tom Donaldson opened the News Bureau's copy of the *Ledger* and let loose with an expletive loud enough to cause Rosalie Despina to make a mistake in her typing and bring Mary to the door of his office.

"Here, take a look at this, you two." He held the paper up so both women could see the top half of the front page. The headline read "PSYCHOLOGY PROF SHOT AT TRACK".

Rosalie squinted at the lead. "'Professor Terry Logan, assistant professor of Psychology at Tipton College, was shot by an unknown assailant as she was running on the college track early Wednesday morning.' What's wrong with that?"

"Get this." Tom turned the paper over. Below the center fold and covering the width of the paper was a framed series of four concentric circles; centered in each of the four was the picture of a Tipton vice president. The heading in 24 point type read: "ADMINISTRATIVE LINEUP AT TIPTON COLLEGE." Then, in smaller typeface: "Administration worried as investigators continue looking for Tipton killer." Just below the photos was an empty "target,"with a question mark where the bulls-eye would ordinarily be. Underneath were the words: "Which face belongs here?"

Rosalie frowned. "I don't get it."

Mary leaned closer. "Sure. Look. A matter of association. First, he uses the term 'lineup.'"

Rosalie nodded. "Yeah, like in police."

"Right. Then he centered the photographs on the circles, as if they're bulls-eyes — just like the empty one with the question mark: 'Which face belongs here?' It suggests it's one of the above."

Tom nodded. "Right. Not 'what face,' but 'which face.'"

Rosalie pursed her lips. "If you all say so. But it's still an 'in' joke if you ask me."

Tom folded the paper noisily. "Snide. But not too 'in' for our crowd and informed Altamira."

Mary said slowly, "Unfortunately, Willie may be asking the right question. What do you think, Tom?"

"Don't ask me. But so far as this office is concerned, we'll be just as wide-eyed as Willie. We don't get it, got it?"

The two women laughingly agreed and went back to work.

Joelle Lieberman was getting ready to leave for lunch and the afternoon when her phone rang. "Wyndham Hall . . . No ma'am, this is the administration building. Who are you looking for . . . ? Sergeant Blessing? He has an office here, yes. I'll transfer you. Who shall I say is calling . . . ? Oh yes, Mrs. Cochran, just one moment."

Pete Wiggins was at the door of the News Bureau when one part of his mind registered a phone ringing from someplace down the hall. He ignored it and went on in to knock at Mary's open door.

"Pete, come on in. Just move that stuff off the chair."

"I bet you say that to all your visitors."

"You're so right." She laughed, and he felt the all-gone sensation in the midriff with which he was becoming increasingly familiar. Pete cleared his throat and hoped he looked official.

"I have some time now, Mary, if you'd like to talk over what's bothering you."

"Indeed I would. I don't know whether I can be very orderly about it . . . "

"That's all right."

She rolled back a bit from her desk and turned toward him, tense, hands clutched together in her lap.

"First, I think the poisoned wine at the party was intended for Vince. And I think that's why he got the anonymous call that sent him to the campanile."

"I remember." Indeed he did. As he remembered his arguments about it with Brandon. "Go on."

"I think he was sent off to climb the bell tower so that there wouldn't be help available — when the poison took effect. It would look as though he had died of a heart attack — either someplace on campus or while climbing all those steps."

He went so far as to encourage her with a nod. "Then it's your idea the killer went to his house two days later and rigged the bathtub drowning."

"Exactly. Everyone around here was familiar with Vince's ideas on diet and hygiene. It wouldn't have been difficult to rig the broken faucet, would it? A very old one at that. Put his fingerprints on it?"

"No, that could be done."

She frowned. "I can't puzzle out how the killer could have knocked him out. Without leaving any marks on his body. Vince would have struggled . . . " She broke off, biting her lip.

"You haven't been watching the right TV shows, Mary. All it takes is pressure on the carotid arteries. That wouldn't leave a bruise necessarily."

"I see."

"However, the murderer would first have to take him by surprise, then be strong enough to carry him to the bathtub." And strong enough to position and bang an unconscious man's head hard against the spokes of a metal faucet before drowning him. Pete saw from Mary's expression that it was unnecessary to add that specific detail.

"But if it were someone he knew . . . It could have been a man or a very strong woman, couldn't it? Vince couldn't have weighed more than one hundred twenty pounds soaking wet."

Mary had such an expectant, almost triumphant expression on her face that Pete was reluctant to ask the next question.

"One troublesome point, Mary: If Vince were the intended victim, and since he lived alone, why not do the job at his house in the first place?"

"I've thought about that. Maybe the murderer felt the reception would be safer. After all, if he was counting on Vince's dying alone — out on the grounds some place — and on nothing showing up in the autopsy . . . Then when that plan failed, he had to go to the house."

"Could be. Next question: Can you tell me why anyone would want to kill him?" He realized he was sounding exactly like Brandon Blessing. Mary Walker was setting forth many of the same arguments he himself had made. Now they seemed extravagant. Because they didn't have a snowball's chance in hell? Or because he too had decided they just didn't add up? "According to our investigation, it seems impossible that he had seen anything, or knew anything about Merton's death. And as I hear it," Pete went on to say, "Vince Riley was a great favorite around here. Compared to your president, he sounds like a candidate for sainthood."

Mary smiled at the idea of a saintly Vincent Riley, then grew serious again. "But if Vince had uncovered something about someone . . . "

"And you still think that someone was the runner you saw?"

"That I saw twice, remember. It was the same person, Pete. I'm positive. He or she came jogging by very late, after midnight, on the night President Merton was killed, and late on Friday night — before Vince was to leave on holiday."

"That's stretching it, Mary."

"But I've never seen that runner before or since. And there was the print of the shoe by the walk . . . "

Pete was heartsick. She was so frantically looking for something and someone to match her mental fantasy. "You're positive it was the same person both nights?"

She nodded. "Because of the cap. The runner wore it each time. It was either black or a very dark color, with a reddish or orange stripe across the crown. Oh, and glasses," she added. "I never got a look at the face, but one night I could see the person was wearing dark glasses. That doesn't make sense. And gloves. In the summertime?"

Pete admitted that was unusual, but could think of nothing to add.

Mary took some sheets of paper from her desk, handed them to him.

"Take a look at this. These are printouts of a diskette I found in Vince's house. Don't bother reading the annual report. Just look at section two." Agent Wiggins read through the indicated passage, then looked up, baffled. "There's a third section; it was protected."

"Oh. That's the one you talked to me about."

"Yes. I haven't been able to find the code. See, where he says that something 'will be explained later on'?"

She reached over to point toward the sentence in question. "'Later on,' meaning in section three maybe. Something related to the collection that was bothering Vince. A missing item — or items . . . "

She related her conversation with Jeff and her subsequent search.

"But if you found the bowl . . . "

"Perhaps there's another item missing. We can't find the original inventory. And that's another thing that seems peculiar."

"Have you talked with anyone at the college about this, Mary?"

"No. But, as usual, the word did get around. I thought maybe that people in his office might know about the inventory and his personal code. Why, Pete?"

"No particular reason. Just wondered whether anyone had information that could help you." Or that would endanger you. The thought caught him by surprise; he dismissed it. He was confusing his feeling for Mary with common sense; he mustn't let himself be dragged too far into her melodramatic fantasy.

She shook her head energetically in answer to his question. "The history of the collection and how it came to Tipton is still an unknown. But Vince had the wind up about something. Otherwise why put that third section under protected access?" Mary didn't wait for him to answer. "Pete, if I could just check what's in the vault against the inventory we have . . . Maybe that would settle the question. Would you help me?"

Ten minutes later Mary was unlocking the door to the president's suite with her pass key. The reception area was empty, silent. All the doors leading to other offices were closed. Pete found the atmosphere oppressive.

As though reading his mind, Mary said, "Empty offices always seem eerie, don't they? As though they're waiting for something to happen."

A few minutes later they were in the vault. Air conditioning was missing from this small room, little more than a large closet. Pete opened the barred window and cleared space on top of a bureau so that the items could be laid out for identification. Mary started reading from her copy of the 1925 inventory:

"Jade rock, Sung dynasty; carved, mountain and pine trees; a Lohan on back. $300-$400.

"Jade buckle, Han dynasty. $50-$100.

"Jade bowl, bats and peaches on outside, wedding symbol inside, Ch'ien Lung period. $300-$500."

She stopped, head cocked toward the open door.

"What's the matter?"

"I thought I heard something."

Pete went to the door of the vault, looked out.

"All serene."

Minutes later, Pete stopped her.

"Wait a minute. How many did you say there were of those little buggers?"

"*Netsukes,* Pete. Ten."

"That's not Chinese, is it?"

"No. Japanese."

"I count nine. One is missing."

She sighed. "That seems to be the only thing."

"Are they valuable?"

"Well, they're late eighteenth-century, and ivory." She glanced again at the paper in her hand. "The 1925 estimate runs between ten to a hundred dollars each."

"So figure what in today's art market? Enough to tempt a thief?" He picked one up, a two-inch baboon beside a small rock with a miniature bush growing from it. "Easy to lose or misplace one of these. They're so tiny." Pete turned the intricately carved piece over in his fingers, then laid it back in the drawer.

"Well, that's that." She sounded discouraged. "Nothing here that merits being under protected access that I can see."

One part of Agent Wiggins' mind told him a stopping point had been reached; he shouldn't play along any further. Instead he said, "Let's have a look," and reached for her Xerox copy of the inventory. He flipped through several pages, stopped.

"What's this?"

Mary looked to where he was pointing. "Just what it says: 'Sold.' "

" 'Shoki Imari pear-shaped bottle vase; late nineteenth century. $50.' Again, doesn't seem like heavy stuff."

"Except I heard that the president estimated a value of at least a quarter of a million for the collection. If he was right . . . " She was suddenly tense. "Add up the 1925 figures, Pete. Just the ones not marked 'sold'."

"OK." He took the calculator from his pocket and tapped in all of the amounts. "Using the outside figures, the whole kit and caboodle — seventy-five pieces, right? — comes to eleven thousand six hundred. So that means, using Merton's guess-work, an overall increase of . . . " He figured it in. "An increase of over two hundred and thirty thousand dollars. Good grief. And listen to this: 'Imperial jade necklace, twenty-four inches, and two jade and twenty-four-karat gold bracelets, late nineteenth century, three thousand six hundred dollars'. Isn't imperial jade something special? *That* could be a very, very big ticket item."

"But those things don't count, Pete; they've been sold."

"Any way to check it out?"

"We can't. Development hasn't been able so far to locate anything on the Crofts or their heirs. Or a sale."

"I could get the lab to examine the ink . . . On second thought, I guess not. This is a Xerox. You say the original is missing?"

"Vince wrote that it was attached to his annual report — the one he turned in to the president. But we can't find it."

"Curious."

"I thought so. But Beulah says it wasn't attached when Vince handed in his report. She has a photographic memory for whatever passes over her desk."

"I see."

"Vince could have changed his mind. But as to where he put the original — who knows."

He looked down at her, wishing he could think of something other than, "I'm sorry, Mary."

She shook her head impatiently. "I'm not beaten yet."

"You said some people were aware of your interest in all this."

"Not explicitly."

"What reactions have you had?"

"Attempts to be helpful — that's all. People have assumed I'm working on an article about the collection."

"I see. Well, that's the important thing, seems to me — for you to find that access code."

"I will. Somehow. Even if I have to go what Gloria Traynor calls the hacker's route. But there's one more thing I find unsettling."

Mary told him then about the photograph of "Dodie's Friend" and her conversation with Ellen Forsythe.

"Don't you see, Pete? If someone from Tipton were mixed up with a beach hustler, and Terry found out who the person was . . . "

"That might explain why Terry got shot, but how does it connect with Vince's death?"

She bit her lip. "I don't know. Unless it's tied in to this collection somehow."

Against his better judgment Pete said, "I could give the Laguna police a ring, Mary."

"Would you, Pete?" She reached for his hand. He put a hand over hers for a moment before she disengaged herself, going on excitedly, "That beach boy was getting money from someplace. Blackmail, maybe."

"Or dealing," he reminded her.

She looked at him, then, her eyes gone flat. "You think this is all pretty fanciful, don't you? Unrealistic."

"Well . . . The thing is, Mary, nothing of serious value is missing." He looked at his watch. "Now, about some lunch?"

Without thinking, Mary heard herself saying, "I'd like that."

As Pete went to close the window a sound drifted up. Someone was approaching Wyndham whistling an old Southern tune that Mary hadn't heard in ages. She was disappointed, yet she felt something akin to relief for the first time in days. She smiled up at Pete and joined in with the happy songster for a couple of bars: "Mammy's little baby loves shortnin', shortnin', mammy's little baby loves shortnin' bread."

Joelle's eyes widened at the sight of Pete and Mary entering the Student Union. She studiously observed them from her table. Having recently read an article on body language, Joelle made her own interpretation of what Pete's expression was saying: the way he was leaning toward Mary, the way his hands fiddled nervously with the table-ware.

"Well I'll be." Joelle drained off her shake, then made for their table.

"Business or pleasure?" she asked jauntily.

Pete's expression modulated to that of Agent Wiggins. Mary's smile was patient.

"Won't you sit down, Joelle?"

Mollified, Joelle said, "Thanks, but I've got an appointment at the hairdresser's. I've got a message for you, Pete. Or rather for your boss."

"Yeah?"

"One of our trustees called. Mrs. Cochran."

"When was this?"

"Oh, about an hour ago."

Pete groaned, exasperated.

"Now listen, I tried having the call transferred to the basement, to your office, but there wasn't any answer. I can't be expected to chase around after you guys."

"No, of course not. Excuse me, Mary. I've got to find a phone."

Brandon Blessing sat cooling his heels in the reception area of District Attorney Frank Murphy's office. From time to time the receptionist caught his eye, giving him an encouraging smile. She looked his way now, saying, "I'm sure it won't be much longer, Sergeant."

He nodded absently, frowning not at pretty Ms. Feinman, but at his own thoughts. The Sheriff, as did the coroner, thought the argument was plausible but the evidence soft. Nevertheless Inocencio had encouraged him to try his theory out on the D. A. "Frank has gotten indictments issued on less, Brandon." Now he had something that might add up to "more."

Brandon profited from the wait by reviewing his hypothetical case, worrying over the loopholes, trying to tighten up his argument. And he'd tackle Anne Parker-Brown hard with the new information: the unexplained phone call and the lint from her jacket. He was saving both of those for what he was beginning to think of as the final interview. He imagined her telling what had really happened in San Francisco. He imagined her collapsing, describing how she rushed to support Merton as he staggered, helped him to the chair, then watched as he . . . Thus absorbed, Brandon didn't hear Ms. Feinman the first time she called his name.

"Sergeant Blessing?"

"Oh — yes, ma'am."

"Telephone. An Agent Wiggins."

Moments later he was asking for an outside line.

At the sound of Sally Cochran's drill sergeant voice Brandon came to attention. He had barely described the information he was seeking when she interrupted.

"Of course, officer. I can tell you exactly what was going on at that moment. It was almost six. More than time to wind things up, in my opinion. So I said I wouldn't propose a toast to Ward. Three was plenty — and Victor Laszlo can be long-winded. The men decided on the order: first Leslie Filmore, then Julian, then Victor. Julian said something like 'Charge your glasses, gentlemen' — he was so witty and urbane."

Brandon didn't make the connection but offered an obedient, "Yes, ma'am."

"Then he looked around for his glass. And someone handed him a drink."

"You're sure?"

The silence was chilly, the response indignant. "Of course I'm sure," she said. "I had just picked up a bottle of wine intending to serve Mr. Merton myself."

"Do you recall who that someone was?"

"I most certainly do. That little man."

"What little man, Mrs. Cochran?"

"You know, what's his name, Buildings and Grounds."

Brandon walked slowly over to the couch and picked up his jacket. Ms. Feinman looked up as he headed for the door.

"Sergeant, I'm sure he'll be with you any minute."

Brandon wigwagged a no with his hand. "Just tell the D. A. that we've got to shift gears. Tell him," he added mournfully, "tell him I'll be in touch."

In his office at the Altamira police station Pete was waiting for Brandon's return and writing up a report on his visit with Mary Walker, a report that had taken on new significance since Brandon had phoned from Los Angeles a short time ago.

"Kid, you had a good hunch." A long sigh vibrated through the line. "S.O.B's don't always get their just desserts and the meek don't always inherit the earth." The meek, Pete soon learned, meant Vincent Riley.

"Plan to work late. We've got a lot to sort out. I'll meet you at the station in an hour."

Turner Van Voorhees was alone in Wyndham Hall at three o'clock when Beulah Taper's phone rang. He ignored it for the first five rings, then got up impatiently and hurried into the reception area.

"Hello."

"I'm trying to reach Mary Walker." It was a woman's voice.

"The offices are closed for the afternoon, sorry."

He was about to hang up when the voice said insistently, "Excuse me, but if you'll just take a message. Tell her Ellen Forsythe phoned."

Turner wrote down the name, repeating it as he did so, "Ellen Forsythe." Then he remembered.

"Oh, Ms. Forsythe, Turner Van Voorhees here. Aren't you the person interested in one of Terry Logan's photographs my wife purchased?"

"Why, yes."

"Look, you're most welcome to have it copied. Or we could have it done for you, if you wish."

"Thanks a lot. Perhaps later, if you don't mind. I'm leaving in about an hour for the airport. That's why I'm eager to get in touch with Mary."

"Have you tried her home?"

"Yes. There's no answer."

"I'll be happy to do what I can do, if it's important."

"Well . . . "

"Or if there's something I can tell her for you — in case you don't reach her."

The voice at the other end of the line hesitated. "If you'd just tell her that it's about Albert O'Hana's landlady, Mr. Van Voorhees."

"I think I've got that."

"I realize it sounds odd, but Mary will understand."

"Quite all right." He laughed. "We're used to taking odd messages around here. Now if you'd give me your phone number . . . "

Turner walked back to his office and stood at one of his windows looking out in the direction of Pusey gym. Mary Walker's car was in the parking lot. He dialed the gym's main extension.

"I believe Mary Walker is working out in the gym. Please tell her right away that there's an urgent message for her — at Wyndham, in the president's office."

Mary took the elevator up to the second floor. The double doors to the president's suite of offices were open. Turner came out of his office as she rolled forward.

"Sorry to interrupt your workout, Mary, but an Ellen Forsythe phoned you. She said it was important. Something about a landlady. Here's the number where you can reach her — but call immediately. She's one step away from leaving for the airport."

"Thanks, Turner."

Turner smiled and went back to his office, closing the door behind him. Mary hesitated, then went to Beulah's desk and dialed Ellen's number.

"Oh, good, Mary. You got my message about Emma Worth — my landlady?"

"Yes. I understand it's important."

"I don't know about that, but maybe you'll make some sense out of it — did seem a bit strange. I saw Emma by chance this morning and started her talking about Angelo. She said she was cleaning out his kitchen cupboards the other day, getting ready to do some painting, and she came across a charm he had put in a coffee cup."

"A charm?"

"That's what she called it. She showed it to me. It's not exactly a charm. It's a Japanese *netsuke*, Mary. Two exquisitely carved ivory rabbits."

"Are you sure?"

Ellen laughed. "Why do you think I have a sabbatical in Japan?"

"Sorry. I forgot Asian art is your specialty."

"That's OK. I'm not exactly a world-class figure. But it's a cinch art of any kind wasn't a specialty of Albert O'Hand's." She paused. "Is this helpful?"

"I — I think so. Thanks a lot, Ellen. Oh, and bon voyage."

She was sitting motionless beside Beulah's desk when Turner came out of his office and hurried toward the stairs.

"Have a good weekend, Mary."

Mary took the elevator down to the basement. Once again she took her copy of the Croft inventory from her files and the key to the vault from the locked drawer where it was kept in Tom's office, then rode the elevator back to the second floor. Her hands shook as she fumbled a moment with the lock to the vault and as she opened the drawer where the *netsukes* were stored. She began identifying them, checking them against the inventory: One frog; a cat with three kittens; a monkey; one caricature figure of a western ship's captain; two rabbits . . . She looked again, carefully. There was no such carving in the drawer. She counted them again: nine. Checked the inventory again: ten. Mary's heart began to pound. She didn't hear the sound of the elevator; someone had called it back to the basement.

She was still sitting before the open drawer when Turner poked his head in the door. She jumped.

"Sorry to startle you, Mary — just forgot something." He was back a few minutes later. "If you're going to work in here, Mary, let me open the window; it's stifling."

"No, thanks. I'm leaving."

"Then we'll leave together. I'll help lock up." He noticed she was staring at his gloved hands and smiled, waving them at her. "These are what I forgot. I'm on my way to practice with my new putter." He took a putting stance, imitated the act of gently tapping a ball, absentmindedly whistling as he did so. An old-timey Southern tune.

In his office at the police station Pete turned his swivel chair to look out the window toward the parking lot. He checked his watch. What was keeping Brandon? Freeway traffic jam, no doubt. He had finished writing up his report. He had reread a number of earlier notes. He was restless. Mary Walker's theory still struck him as extravagant, but he couldn't stop thinking about it. Or about her. Pete reached for some distraction, the newspaper he had dropped on his desk earlier. He shook his head as he looked at Willie's "shooting gallery" photographs, glanced at his latest on the murders at the college and put the paper aside. He went over in his mind what Mary had told him. Perhaps some of it did make sense. Anyway, he had promised her . . . Pete reached for the phone and called the Laguna P. D.

"We've closed the file. Just couldn't find anything. Place was clean, except for the kid's prints. We found some marijuana and a stash of coke. He was a user; the autopsy showed that. But there was nothing else to connect O'Hana with the drug scene — and we've got some fairly reliable pipelines. Still, we figure he must have been dealing somehow. That was the best explanation for where the money for all the audio-visual equipment came from — and the jewelry. The kid paid cash. And a lot. He must have laid out a good ten thousand bucks."

Pete tried suggesting that O'Hana might have had a friend.

"Right. If he had, they met someplace else. That was a dead end for us. The landlady saw someone leaving his house a couple of times, but that's all. She said she didn't see a car. All she noticed was that the person was tall, had on what looked like sweats, and wore a baseball cap."

All of a sudden this call was no longer routine.

"Could she describe it?"

The Laguna officer laughed. "Yeah, as a matter of fact. Ms. Worth's originally from Baltimore; she wondered whether the guy was an Oriole fan."

"How come?"

"You know, that black and orange bird. The cap was black with a bright orange stripe."

Pete said his thanks and hung up the phone, his eyes fastened, unseeing, on the newspaper in front of him. Suddenly he stiffened, reached for the *Ledger* again, studied it a moment, then fumbled in a desk drawer for his magnifying glass.

He put it down slowly. Where were the photos Tom Donaldson had given them? Were they here or at Wyndham? He had almost given up when he remembered: Brandon had said to put them in the dead file. A moment later he had the photograph he almost feared to look at — an enlargement of five people at a party, vividly clear, incontrovertible. Seconds later Pete was sprinting for his car. His fear was unreasonable, he told himself, but what had she said? "All Wyndham has the afternoon off. Good day to get a lot done, with everybody gone."

Turner locked the double doors to the presidential suite and with an "Allow me, Mary," began to propel her chair down the hall toward the elevator. Mary hated to be pushed, but she didn't say anything, hardly hearing Turner's pleasant voice, or listening to his chatter about his golf game and funny comments on the golfer's mentality as he moved her slowly, deliberately down the hall. Something was wrong. Something about the gloves . . . She tried to put things together, but her mind wouldn't function. Orderly thought was swept away by the tumult in her head.

When they reached the elevator, he turned her chair around so that she could back in, as she always did, then stepped around her to press the button.

"Mm. Something seems to be stuck. Just a jiffy . . . "

She craned her head around, looking up. Turner was fiddling at the emergency doorlock with a key. At last he pushed the elevator doors apart.

"There we are."

As he bent toward her, she instinctively grabbed both wheels, her head momentarily thrown back. Hanging above her in the shell of the elevator cage were dangling ropes and cables.

Turner smiled. "As you said to your helpful friend, bon voyage, Mary." The smile vanished. Turner's eyes narrowed, his voice was a hoarse, rushing whisper.

"You meddling freak. How dare you interfere?"

He tore the bag from the side of her chair. He was panting now. Bearing down on her hands. Preventing her from reaching the brake. Mary was pushing herself forward, all of her strength locked into her hands, clutching, clutching . . . She could feel the wheels beginning to slip, screeching against the linoleum floor. Suddenly his arms went around her shoulders. He pulled her toward him. She felt his fingers on either side of her neck as he whispered, "We'll do this the easy way. In memory of Vince."

She didn't hear the feet pounding down the hall, nor hear Pete Wiggins' shout, "Mary!"

FRIDAY, JULY 28

An ANGRY CRYSTAL WREATHED IN A vapor of Scotch jerked open her apartment door.

"You're over three hours late, Willie. That dumb girl at the paper wouldn't put me through . . . " She broke off, as Willie Hefner brushed by her, closing the door behind him.

"Been tied up with Altamira's finest. And had to make an important change in tomorrow's front page. How about a fat kiss for a local hero?"

She pushed him away as he began to dig into her mouth. "What the hell are you talking about?"

"You haven't had the TV or radio on?"

"Why?"

"Guess where your hi-falutin boss is right now?"

Crystal scowled at him. "Stop acting cute."

"Turner Van Voorhees the fourth will definitely not be coming in to work for Tipton College tomorrow — or ever again."

Crystal lurched after him as Willie moved toward the living room.

"My God! There's been an accident . . . "

"He's in Pasadena. In the pokey — for questioning. No bail."

She sank down onto the couch, reached for her package of cigarettes.

"What are you talking about?"

"About a guy who killed three — maybe four — people. And was about to add to the list — if Pete Wiggins hadn't interfered. Thanks to yours truly."

"You're making this up . . . " She looked as though she might burst into tears. Willie became solicitous.

"Hey, don't cry, babe. Let me get you a drink."

He came back with a double Scotch for her and a triple for himself.

"The guy's arrogant, unflappable. Going to be damn hard for the prosecution — and for his lawyer, too, I bet."

"He admitted murdering the president and Terry Logan?"

"Naw, of course not. But he did. And add Vince Riley to the list."

Crystal's jaw went slack, her unlighted cigarette forgotten.

"Right now he just smiles and clams up. He may go for a not guilty to the Merton, Logan and Riley murders, but Pete Wiggins caught him red-handed trying to send Mary Walker down the elevator shaft in Wyndham this afternoon. That oughta give him and his hot-shot lawyer a few migraines."

"Willie," Crystal shrieked, "you're making this up!"

"No way."

"But Turner thought the president was the greatest. He couldn't have . . . "

"Looks like it was a mistake, kiddo."

"I don't believe it. I just don't believe it."

"The way it listens, your boss was having it on with a gay cutey in Laguna. The kid was found dead maybe ten, twelve days ago. Overdose, the police thought. Nobody worth bothering about. But the kid could have been blackmailing Van Voorhees and maybe the man tried some of that Chemistry Department special on him."

Crystal kept staring at him with a dazed expression, her drink tipping perilously in her hand. She jerked up as a little sloshed over and took a sip.

Willie pulled at his, then continued. "Looks like he ripped off some jade from the collection that turned up at the college. The cops think Riley found out about it. Or Turner thought he had. So he tried to slip his special cocktail to the guy at the party, then send him out on a phoney errand to die on campus somewhere. So it'd look like a heart attack. Only Merton got the mickey."

"Hold up. How do you know all this?"

"Pete Wiggins mostly — and that swishy-assed Brandon Blessing. That's the way they've doped it out so far." A sulky expression passed over his face. "They sure owed me some of their time on this one."

"You said that. Why do they owe you?"

"Some thread was found under Merton's fingernails — like he might have clawed at someone. And Turner was wearing a blazer with a crest at the party. Only Blessing discovered his school crest wasn't embroidered with metallic thread."

"I could have told them that." Crystal sounded indignant. "I've taken it to the cleaner's for him often enough."

"Could you also have told them that he was sporting another emblem at the party? One embroidered with what the police were looking for?"

"What?"

"How about one of those ritzy Swiss summer camps? Camp du Lac?"

"Oh my God. Yes."

"The picture I used for today's edition shows him wearing a blazer with that patch. That's what old Pete cottoned on to. That's why they owe me one, and why I've got the inside track on this." Willie leaned back in self-satisfaction and downed his drink.

"Hip hip hooray," Crystal said with a singular lack of enthusiasm. "What did Pete cotton on to?"

"That there was another patch to consider, dummy. That's what made him nervous about Mary."

"Why her?"

"Because she had been talking to him about Vince Riley. She was dead certain he had been murdered. And it looks like she was dead right. And almost dead. Anyway, old Pete . . . "

Crystal frowned her impatience. "Why do you keep calling him 'old Pete' ? He's just a kid."

"He's so damn earnest. Anyway, old Pete spent some time listening to Mary this afternoon. Just to be friendly, I guess. They checked out the Asian collection and only found one little ivory doodad missing — not worth much. But seems like the ivory doodad had turned up in the house lover boy was living in — in Laguna."

"Huh?"

"The Chief's little sister has been a busy cup of tea. She was in touch with Terry Logan's cousin. She lives in Laguna." Willie jiggled the ice in his empty glass, went to help himself to a repeat, and brought the bottle over to put on the coffee table between them. "Not only does this Ellen Forsythe live in Laguna, but on the same street as lover boy. Angelo somebody. A *nom de fuck*. Real name is Albert O'Hana."

Crystal was shaking her head. "I can't believe it. Not Turner. And he has such a gorgeous wife."

"What's that got to do with someone wanting a different brand of ass?"

"Terry knew about that? She found out?"

"Apparently. Turner was alone in Wyndham this afternoon and took a call for Mary. From this Ellen babe. He knew Mary was at the gym, so he phoned with a message for her to come to the president's suite pronto."

"Is this what Mary says?"

"Yeah, according to Pete. Turner relays the message, and Mary phones right away from the handiest desk."

"Beulah's?"

"I guess. Wiggins and Blessing figure Van Voorhees stepped next door to the president's office, picked up the phone and listened in. So when he next saw Mary and was all smiles, he knew that Angelo's landlady had found an ivory doodad in one of the kitchen drawers. A traceable item."

"God." Crystal poured herself another belt.

"Guess what Mary did the moment she hung up?"

Crystal shook her head.

"Checked out that stuff in the vault again. And, sure enough, the description of the missing ivory doodad corresponded to the one found by the landlady."

"And Turner was there? She told him about it?"

"Hunh-huh. I doubt she had it all figured out. He must have, though. He knew she must be aware of gaps in the inventory. He starts to get panicky, she's getting too close to identifying the guy who had frolicked at the beach. So your Turner, the perfect gentleman, offered to escort her to the elevator. Only, when the doors opened, surprise, no elevator."

"Oh Jesus, Willie." She began to cry.

"Come on, babe. It's OK. Pete got there in time. Your boss had her unconscious, but she's OK now."

Crystal kept on crying and shaking her head. Willie came over to sit on the couch beside her, put an arm around her.

"Hey, it's OK."

"It's not; it's awful," Crystal hiccoughed. "Just awful. And I'm going to be out of a job."

Thad Walker had taken his sister home and made the necessary arrangements to protect her from reporters. She had, however, disobeyed his orders to rest, and Dr. Lowenthal's tranquilizer had been flushed down the toilet. Mary was in her studio, a charcoal drawing on the table in front of her. She studied it, trying to see beyond the quickly sketched lines the form and features of Vince's murderer. She reached for a felt-tipped pen and viciously drew an X across the running figure, ripped the sheet from the pad. As she tore it into pieces, she looked up, alert. Someone was opening the front door.

"Who is it?"

"Mary? It's me. Pete Wiggins."

"I'm in here."

"Where's that?"

"Just down the hall a bit and to your right." She rolled away from her work table, turned to face the door. Pete was standing there, looking apologetic.

"Sorry. I hope I didn't startle you. I didn't want to ring the bell in case you were asleep. I understood someone was here with you."

"That's all right, Pete."

He looked around him as though searching for an opening. All he could come up with was, "So this is where you work."

She smiled and gestured him to a chair. "I'm glad you stopped by." She moved her chair closer to him. "Very glad. Pete, how can I thank you?"

"It was luck, Mary. Pure luck." He recalled his impatience when Willie had handed him a copy of the *Ledger* at the cemetery. And the irritation with Willie that had kept him from reading it right away. He still shuddered at the thought that he might not have opened the paper, might not have noticed the photograph.

Mary seemed about to say something more, but, embarrassed, he cut in quickly, "I wanted to check on how you were feeling. Thad said Rosalie Despina was staying with you."

"I told her to go on. But not a word to my brother. I didn't want to wreck her evening. And I'm OK."

He looked at her questioningly.

"Really, Pete."

"You're supposed to be resting, you know."

"That's impossible."

"You're sure you're all right?"

"Very sure."

He sat down, wondering at the fragile quiet that seemed to surround her. He was reluctant to break it, but finally said, "Looks like you called it, Mary."

She looked at him now. "Out of desperation. Because Vince meant so much to me. But deep down, much of the time, I felt that I was imagining it all — reaching for a solution to settle things in my own mind. It wasn't until he was wheeling me toward the elevator . . . " Her voice caught in her throat. Pete was about to say something, but she went on. "Something about his gloves. I've been thinking about it. Thad used to play golf, when Fiona was alive. Do golfers wear two gloves? And with fingers?"

"I don't know, Mary." He went on quickly, to turn her thought away from that moment, wanting to find something reassuring to say. "By the way, I have the diskettes that were in your bag. We'll put someone to work on getting access to that privileged section. If what you showed me is a model of Vince's thoroughness, the third part could tell us why he suspected something was out of kilter; maybe why Turner had to kill him."

She didn't respond, withdrawn again. Then, reflectively, "He knew that house, Pete. When Vince proposed to buy it, Turner and he were over there often, going over everything . . . "

Pete nodded. The silence lengthened. He was about to take his leave when Mary looked directly at him, smiled. "I really am glad to see you, Pete. I need to know what's happening. Where is he?"

"You want to talk about it?"

"Yes. Please."

He settled back down. "Well, Van Voorhees has been taken to the holding facility in Pasadena — for questioning."

"He's not out on bail then?"

"No way. He'll be charged with a capital offense. He refuses to admit having anything to do with the killings, of course. But we'll get him, Mary. The Laguna and San Francisco police will work with us. Dollars to doughnuts he stole a number of those jade pieces, intending to sell them to a fence — if that kid was blackmailing him. And he could have done just that, possibly in San Francisco — Chinatown, maybe — when he was up there on the eighteenth."

"But he didn't sell everything?"

"Nope. We're guessing that when he got the idea that Vince was on to something he put things back — like that bowl you told me about. Then he stamped 'sold' by the missing items on the original inventory — the things he had sold — and ran off Xerox copies. That way the ink couldn't be dated."

"The tangled web."

"Mm?"

"Nothing. Go on."

"Well, Van Voorhees must have written up some office memos in Vince's name and destroyed others. Probably when he learned you had Vince's diskettes and were beginning to scout around. He needed to cover his tracks. That's when he could have put that bowl back. Among other things."

"Except for the *netsuke*. There wasn't a 'sold' by that one."

Pete nodded. "Maybe his boyfriend snitched it somehow — or Turner gave it to him — didn't think it was worth bothering about at the time. Or he wasn't aware it was missing. Brandon thinks his arrogance could have made him careless."

"But why would he have to steal, Pete? I thought Turner had pots of money."

"Not enough maybe to keep — or pay off — Angelo. Maybe he was in deep someplace else. Believe me, the D. A. is going to take a very hard look at the college books. And at his wife's portfolio. She's the one with the heavy dough. We understand he handled the investment side of their affairs."

"I see. What about Laguna?"

"Somebody is bound to have seen Turner with O'Hana. We'll circulate pictures. They probably used motels for most of their meetings. Those will be combed. At the beach, around here, and all points in between if necessary. And rental car agencies."

"I'm sure he took every precaution."

"He's shrewd all right. Convinced that he's got the leading edge on brains. That could be his weakness."

Suddenly she burst out. "How could he have, Pete? How could he? Four people . . . He'll never break down and confess. I know it."

"Possibly not. But if the thread we found on Merton matches up with his jacket emblem — that could be a strong piece of evidence. And we've got a few other things going for us."

"Yes?" She still sounded doubtful.

"Beulah Taper says Vince's memo attached to his report to the president isn't the original. She now recalls an earlier one. Thinks it mentioned the need to call a meeting, to discuss some missing jade."

Mary sighed. "Bit late in the day. And I doubt that it will surface, don't you?"

Pete nodded his agreement. "Probably shredded — along with the donors' inventory. What Beulah remembers may not be worth much in court as evidence, but it could strengthen the prosecution's reconstruction of events."

Mary leaned back in her chair. She seemed to have grown listless all of a sudden, almost disinterested, but he went on. "The next item is even more interesting. The Van Voorheeses's housekeeper confirmed that Turner's grandmother called him Dodie."

"I see."

"He'll try to claim that's a coincidence, of course."

"And the *netsuke?* Coincidence too, I suppose."

"I imagine his lawyer will give it a go. But too many coincidences don't sit well with most juries."

"But can they prove that he poisoned that wine? Or drowned Vince?"

He tried not to look skeptical, as he said, "There has to be some reason for his trying to kill you, Mary. That's another part of the charge. Attempted murder."

She nodded, a far-away look in her eyes.

Pete didn't tell her that Turner insisted he was trying to hold her from propelling her chair into the shaft, that in her hysterical fear she had misunderstood his remarks and fainted. Nor did he tell her that, as extravagant as it seemed, the kind of super lawyer his family would no doubt retain might turn the extravagant into the feasible. Or transform coldly sane acts into the manifestations of a disturbed mind. He didn't tell her that there was nothing more in life he wanted than to be the one to keep this from happening.

Claire and Mark Tidwell were in Anne Parker-Brown's living room, drinks untouched on the coffee table. The excitement generated by the news of Van Voorhees's arrest, the feelings of relief, of excitement that welcomed an end to doubt and suspicion, had given way to depression. Anne had expressed what each was thinking:

"A bitter note for the beginning of the school year in five weeks."

"Exactly." Mark made a tent of his fingers, rested it on his nose. "It will be some time before the college will recover from this drama."

Claire resettled herself impatiently in her chair. "This is no time to be defeatist — or mournful. Surely we're tough enough as an institution and as individuals . . . "

The telephone interrupted her.

"I wonder whether I should unplug it," Anne said as she rose to go into the study.

"Anne. Leslie here."

"Are you back, Leslie?"

"No. I'm phoning from London. Beulah Taper just called. Shattering, Anne. Absolutely shattering. Though frankly, there have been times I've wondered about Turner . . . But that's neither here nor there right now."

"What do you want, Leslie?"

"I'm taking a plane in two hours and will come straight out to the campus tomorrow. I wanted to reassure you that help was on its way and you weren't going to have to go it alone."

"Leslie?"

"Yes?"

"I just have one suggestion, 'fella.' In the words of a well-known French author, go soak your head."

Anne had a very wide smile on her face as she strode back into the living room and reached for her glass.

In his cell, Turner Van Voorhees lay on his back on the cot, hands clasped behind his head. He stared at the unrelenting light from the single bulb, then turned to curl up on his side. Turner closed his eyes, but there was no escaping the fugitive visions that haunted his mind. Faces formed, swirled into distortions and disappeared, only to reappear again in grotesque shapes. Mouths curled down in disgust, grinned, then melted away. Undulating figures and hands swam across his mental screen. Eyes came in and out of focus. Vincent Riley's eyes as he reported on the missing pieces of jade; eyes that went blank at Turner's improvised explanation. And Angel . . . Angel's eyes grew larger and larger, staring at him. Then one lid closed slowly in an obscene wink before the eye melted slowly away.

He saw Riley again, standing near the gym, telling him about the wild-goose chase. Turner felt the sweat pearl under his arms as he saw Merton staggering from his desk, reaching for him . . . Too late . . . Grammy . . . His body felt the form of her comforting lap as she sang and rocked him, telling him over and over that he was the best baby, the smartest baby, crooning to him that she would make everything all right.

Turner closed his eyes even tighter, but behind his eyelids there was still the figure of Vince, the feel of him, limp in his arms. He had gone over everything thoroughly with senile Charlie Peese — so flattered by his interest. Every move so carefully rehearsed, so carefully timed . . . Mary Walker. A cripple. A freak.

He shuddered, shook his head as though to clear it and drew himself into a tighter knot. Think. Get it together. Work out the strategy. He wouldn't break. The fools could see that. They wouldn't be able to place him at Vince's. Dodie let his mind linger on the moment, experiencing again the excitement and the terror. The muscles in his arms still held the memory of Riley's body when he had carried him to the bathroom. How light he was. Yet how heavy when . . . But it was Riley's fault for being suspicious, for poking around about a few pieces of jade . . .

They wouldn't find any of the poison, long since poured down a toilet; nor the gun Daddy had given his little girl. Kitty hadn't looked at it in years. It could have been lost or stolen . . . It now lay deep in a hole in Baker Canyon, in the hills to the north of Altamira. He opened his eyes for a moment then closed them again. Any trace of his presence in the Subaru couldn't be dated; he drove it too regularly for that. And Kitty hadn't heard him come back into the house for the gun to kill Terry, the bitch dyke.

Kitty. His idiot wife. The look of horror on her face changing into disgust . . . The children hurried from the room . . . Dodie's one mistake. He should have eliminated her as he had first planned. The insurance would have replaced the investment money he had lost; Daddy would never have known. And he would be home free. Free . . .

He would be. They had no proof . . . No proof that he had intended to kill the hysterical freak. Her word against Dodie's. Invincible Dodie. No proof. No proof that the missing pieces hadn't been sold. It was all so long ago. No proof. The words repeated over and over in his head. Grammy's little Dodie . . . When he had strangled Lucy Minton's puppy, Grammy knew he hadn't meant it, Grammy made everything all right. As if it had never happened. Grammy's little Dodie is the smartest . . .

The original inventory was long gone. He had seen to that. As soon as the freak began her meddling. Dodie should have killed her earlier. He kept ticking off the carefully planned steps he had taken, testing them for any weaknesses. Satisfying himself that there were none. There was no hard evidence in police hands; nothing that would stand up in court. As for what he had sold . . . He'd like to see the policeman who could get anything out of Henry Wu, even if they found him.

Turner began to rock his shoulders rhythmically, in very small movements. It's all right. All right. Riley hadn't talked to anyone else about his suspicions. But to his computer maybe? Those diskettes the freak had been playing around with . . . But Riley knew nothing for certain. The Irish were prizewinners for human stupidity. There was no way stupidity could best him. Inferior minds. Inferior imaginations. Weak people with no intellectual power. He kept on smiling, relentlessly ticking off arguments, expecting the surge of assurance to take over, for the song to fill his head. The fetish song that made everything work, that meant Dodie was in control. Dodie *excelsior!*

Grammy's face swam fuzzily before his eyes; her mouth opened and shut, but no sound came. There was nothing but the opening and closing of flaccid lips. Nothing but the harsh clattering noises echoing down the passage outside his prison cell.

Epilogue

SATURDAY, JULY 29

"We are here to celebrate the life of Vincent Michael Riley . . . "

The dean's strong contralto voice opened the memorial service in Bosman Hall of Music. Mary hardly listened, any more than she did to the carefully crafted eulogy by Frazer Minton, chairman of the trustee committee on Buildings and Grounds, or to the clumsy but heartfelt remarks of Max Dingam. The man they praised with admiration and humor was the public, the professional Vincent Riley; the meticulous worker, the health nut, the "sweetheart." She had learned what no one suspected: that he was a man of passion and laughter. Passion for loving, passion for life and laughter at its absurdities. That had been his gift to her.

"That was sure a beautiful ceremony, Ms. Walker." It was Jeff Colton, who had waited for others to finish talking with her on the sidewalk outside of Bosman Hall.

"I'm glad you were there, Jeff."

She began to move forward; Jeff walked beside her.

"And I want to thank you again for letting me have those little monkeys."

"You're more than welcome."

"Vince had funny names for them. Flubbers — or something like that."

"Really, Jeff? I didn't know Vince had a special name . . . "

Mary braked to a sudden stop. No. Not Flubbers . . . She sat there, immobile. Something was scratching at her memory. She didn't hear Jeff Colton say good-bye or notice his departure. What was it? A story? One of the stories Vince had told her . . . was that it? Soon after the accident? When she thought of nothing but her anger and despair. Something about his childhood . . . the farm in Oklahoma. About his father. About a nickname he hated. Not Flubber. Flub. That was it.

"Jeff, I think . . ." She looked up, surprised to see him gone. Yes, Flutter, Fluster, and Flub; a father's judgment of three little boys and their ineffectiveness with the daily chores. And Vince had had the dubious and detested honor of being the lazy, the dreadful Flub.

Mary propelled herself forward, smiling. The hated name would be something to cherish, to slip into place among other carefully guarded memories. Her darling Flub . . . and his ironic, whimsical sense of humor. She knew now as surely as if Vince had told her what word would unlock section 3. She would tell Pete Wiggins. It didn't really matter to her anyore. Nothing that happened now would heal her wounded heart.

"Mary! Wait up!"

She looked back over her shoulder. A moment later Pete was beside her chair.

"May I walk you to your car?"

She looked up at him, smiling. Pete had the feeling that she was seeing him for the first time. The feeling was far from disagreeable.

"Thank you, officer. I'd like that very much."

Priscilla Merton lingered outside the entrance of Bosman Hall. People gave her courteous recognition and went on by; only a very few stopped for a brief exchange of amenities. How different it had been just a few weeks ago when she had been the president's wife, someone to recognize and to be seen by. Professors Macready and de Grancey, busily talking, walked by her without even a glance. The words "special meeting on Monday" drifted after them as they hurried out. Already business as usual. Resentment raced through her like a flash fire. Priscilla forced herself to walk slowly in the direction of her house, concentrating on the thought of her cool, darkened bedroom and the only solace she could depend on.

Brandon Blessing watched from the steps of Bosman as Dean Parker-Brown moved briskly across the quadrangle toward Wyndham Hall, her academic gown billowing out behind her. He considered following her — considered saying something about the phone call to the Windsor Hotel. Just to let her know. The dean had lied. She hadn't called the Windsor for a restaurant reservation. Not at nine forty-five at night. Had she and Merton arranged to meet there before his flight back to Altamira? Had they done so? If so, what had happened? Brandon didn't like loose ends. And he didn't like being made a fool of. He caught sight of Thad Walker cutting across the quad to intercept her. Brandon sighed, reached for his M&Ms and turned away.

THE END

ACKNOWLEDGEMENTS

I OWE A VERY LARGE DEBT INDEED TO numerous friends and colleagues at Pomona College, Claremont, California, for their helpful interest during the writing of this book. In particular, I wish to express my appreciation to Howard T. Young, Professor of Spanish, and Ray Frazer, Emeritus Professor of English, for their critical reading of the manuscript. Wayne Steinmetz, Professor of Chemistry, and Yost U. Amrein, Emeritus Professor of Biology, patiently served as advisors on scientific matters, and Donald M. Pattison, Director of Public Affairs, facilitated the preparation and production of this *divertissement* in innumerable ways.

Mary Fellows, Manager, Spinal Cord Injury Services, St. Jude's Hospital & Rehabilitation Center, Fullerton, California, was consulted on the physiological and psychological problems confronting paraplegics and their treatment. Captain Russell L. Brown of the Claremont Police Department and Michael D. Byck, Esq., Dallas, provided invaluable information on investigative procedures and legal matters. Andrew D. Nelson, Santa Barbara, kindly filled in gaps in my understanding of computer systems as did LeRoy K. Burket, Paris, and I.M. Chait, Los Angeles, in my knowledge of Asian art. Ansis Muiznieks, M.D., Claremont, David Nimmons, New York, Dr. Michael Prendeville and Jean Trabant, Paris, were generous in responding to a variety of questions.

Finally, I am most gratefully indebted to Catharine Carver, Paris, for the gift, from start to finish, of her vast editorial experience and talent.

The occurrence of any errors, oversights, or omissions is my sole responsibility.

THE GLENDOWER CONSPIRACY
by Lloyd Biggle, Jr.

ISBN 0-933031-25-4

Written by Lloyd Biggle, Jr., one of America's great storytellers, this memoir of Sherlock Holmes from the papers of his assistant Edward Porter Jones will satisfy the most exacting Sherlock Holmes fans and convert new readers to the fold of Conan Doyle's masterful creation.

A plea for help from two Welshmen sends Holmes and his assistant, a former Baker Street Irregular, on a journey to the remote mountains of Wales. Called in to solve the mysterious deaths of Glyn Huws and Lady Eleanor Tromblay, the famous sleuth and young Edward Porter Jones uncover a conspiracy that reaches from the Y Llew Du pub in London to the Welsh town of Pentrederwydd and the imposing Tromblay Hall.